# An Orphan's Sorrow

Cathy Sharp is happily married and lives with her husband in a small Cambridgeshire village. They like visiting Spain together and enjoy the benefits of sunshine and pleasant walks, while at home they love their garden and visiting the Norfolk seaside.

Cathy loves writing because it gives pleasure to others, she finds writing an extension of herself and it gives her great satisfaction. Cathy says, 'There is nothing like seeing your book in print, because so much loving care has been given to bringing that book into being.'

# CATHY SHARP
# An Orphan's Sorrow

HarperCollins*Publishers*

HarperCollins*Publishers*
The News Building,
1 London Bridge Street,
London SE1 9GF

A Paperback Original 2020
1

www.harpercollins.co.uk

A catalogue record for this book
is available from the British Library

ISBN: 978-0-00-838764-8

Set in Sabon LT Std 11/14pt by
Palimpsest Book Production Limited, Falkirk, Stirlingshire

Printed and bound in Great Britain by CPI Group (UK) Ltd,
Croydon CR0 4YY

MIX
Paper from
responsible sources
FSC® C007454

# PROLOGUE

## 1937

'Mummy, please don't hurt me!' the child whimpered as her mother caught hold of her arm, strong fingers digging into her flesh as she dragged her along the landing to the top of the dimly lit stairs. 'I didn't mean to wet the bed.'

'Filthy child!' Her mother's grip tightened on her arm. 'I just can't cope with this, Cassie. With your father gone and me ill it's time to end it for both of us . . .'

'Mummy, you're frightening me!' Cassie cried. 'P-please don't talk like this . . .'

'We'll go in the river together,' her mother said, eyes wild with despair. 'It's the best for us, Cassie. Your father left us and we've no money to pay rent on even these poor rooms. I can't feed you – or myself . . .'

They had reached the top of the steep stairs. Cassie clutched at her mother as she started to drag her down them, bumping her against the bannisters so that she stumbled to her knees on the worn carpeting, banging her elbows and head against the knobbly bannisters.

1

She cried out and screamed to her mother to let her go.

'I don't want to die, Mummy!' Cassie wept desperately, pushing at her mother as hard as she could, struggling to break free of the punishing grip. She was terrified of the woman she'd always loved, hardly recognising her in the wild-eyed creature who was tormenting her with threats of death. She jerked one last time, trying to evade the iron grip – and then it happened. Her mother screamed, her body hanging in the balance for one terrible moment before she tumbled backwards down the stairs, dragging Cassie with her. Cassie screamed loudly as her head struck the wooden bannister and then everything went black and she sank into an unconsciousness . . .

Gradually, through the mists and the pain, over time that she was unaware of passing, the girl heard women talking, women with harsh voices and rough hands that seemed almost to punish as they tended her ills. Her mind whirled with distress as she struggled to remember what had happened. But her head hurt and she couldn't remember properly, everything was muddled in her mind.

'Her poor mother broke her neck,' a woman said in a loud voice on the day the mists cleared for the first time. 'The police say the neighbours heard shouting and screaming – they think the girl might have pushed her mother.'

'Cassie pushed her mother down the stairs?' a second female voice said. 'Well, I never. I would never have thought it – she looks like such a sweet little girl, so fragile and pretty with that pale hair and those lovely blue eyes . . .'

'Well, you never know these things,' the first voice sighed. 'Children can be evil little devils you know.'

'What will they do with her?'

'I think they'll put her away somewhere. I mean, she obviously isn't right in the head since the fall, is she? No doubt she'll be shut up in an institution where she can't do any harm – or maybe they'll send her to Australia like they do all the unwanted kids these days.'

Tears slipped down Cassie's cheeks. She remembered her name now and her mother shouting at her before she fell . . . Was it her fault? Cassie didn't know. All she understood was that no one wanted her, no one loved her and that she was going to be sent away to somewhere she'd never heard of . . . it terrified her.

The voices were moving away now. Shivering, Cassie slipped out of bed and pulled on the clothes she found folded on a chair beside her. She walked through the long room where other children lay in beds, few of them moving, their eyes just staring. One of the children started screaming and some ladies that Cassie thought might be nurses gathered around her bed, trying to calm her. No one noticed Cassie as she walked out of the room, down the stairs and out of the front door into the street . . .

# CHAPTER 1

Sister Jean Norton shivered in the cool night air, pulling up her coat collar and looking about the street down which she needed to walk every evening after her work was done. It was a wretched place of dirty terraces with broken window frames, paint peeling from them, and gutters choked with filth; and she wished that she did not have to negotiate its length to reach her comfortable little cottage, but the only other way was a mile longer and she was tired after a heavy day's work at the Lady Rosalie Infirmary in the dockland area of London's East End, known affectionately to the locals as the Rosie.

In her mid-thirties, dark-haired with grey eyes that were often too serious, she was slim to the point of being thin, and dedicated. Jean loved her work at the Rosie despite the pain and despair she witnessed far too often within its shaded wards. With her record of exemplary nursing, she could, if she wished, apply for a job at a major hospital and expect to be offered it, but she had gone to the Rosie when her life was a living hell and Matron had shown her kindness, respect and given Jean her trust. Even when she was sick of the stink of unwashed bodies, urine and festering ulcers, she would never think of leaving her post.

'Whatcha, missus!' the cheeky voice brought Jean out of her reverie as she entered Pail Street, an even dirtier place than the one she'd just left and darker, with only one street light, the others all having been broken by louts throwing stones at the glass. She looked at the dirt-streaked face of the young urchin. By his size, he looked no more than eleven but she knew that he was two years older. She frowned; it was already dark and he should be at home, safe with his mother.

'Jamie Martin,' she said, her voice scolding and harsh, even though she did not dislike the lad. 'What are you doing out at this hour? Your mother will be worrying.'

'No, she ain't, she's stone cold dead,' Jamie said. 'Me pa came 'ome drunk and I think 'e 'it 'er on the 'ead and she fell down, dead as a doornail.' The words sounded brutal except for the underlying hint of fear in his voice and for a moment she wondered if he was lying.

'Jamie! May God forgive you,' she said and then, as she looked closer, saw he had been crying. 'Are you telling me the truth, boy?'

He nodded at her, looking a picture of abject misery. 'I swear it's true, missus. I wouldn't lie to you – not you, missus, 'cos you was kind to me and Arch when Ma was bad afore and yer 'elped Arch . . .'

'When did this happen?' Jean asked, feeling shocked and bewildered. The boy's tone was as cocky and defiant as always but his face showed his fear and misery.

'Last night,' Jamie said and rubbed at his eyes. 'I heard the old bugger shoutin' at 'er but I didn't know she were dead until this mornin' when I come down and found her on the kitchen floor. She's white and cold, her face all battered – and Pa's gone. He's took his army coat what 'e had in the war and cleared orf. Took his pipe and the money from Ma's jar on the shelf, too.'

'Goodness me!' Jean was shocked to the core. 'What did you do, child? Have you told anyone else – the doctor?'

'Nah, he wouldn't come near,' Jamie said. 'Pa threw 'im out last time Ma was sick. Pa called 'im bad names and wouldn't pay 'im and 'e swore it was the last time he'd set foot in our 'ouse. Marth next door is out and there ain't no one else what would care; they 'ate me dad.'

Jean nodded, knowing that Ted Martin was what the locals termed a bad lot. Even in these hard times most of the men in the street struggled to find enough work to feed their families and remain honest, but Ted Martin was known for being all kinds of a rogue and even the hardened working men of Pail Street steered clear of him. She realised that Jamie must have hung about the street all day waiting for someone to come he dare approach.

'Will you take me to her?' Jean asked, looking at the young boy anxiously.

'I bin 'anging around waitin' fer yer,' Jamie said and sniffed, wiping his dripping nose on his threadbare sleeve. He shuffled his feet, looking both guilty and miserable. 'I remembered you 'elped Arch when 'e was in trouble wiv the constable and I thought . . .'

'Yes, of course I'll help,' Jean said instantly, though

she feared it must already be too late. If Lizzie Martin had lain all night and all day on a cold floor in weather like this, she wouldn't stand much chance even if she'd still lived after her husband battered her. Jean took Jamie's hand and held on to it and he ran with her down the street.

'If Arch 'ad been 'ere 'e would've known what ter do . . .' Jamie was anxious, clearly feeling that he ought to have done something sooner.

'Where is your brother, Jamie?'

'Went orf ter look fer work down south last month,' Jamie told her. 'Said 'e'd come back fer me when 'e was settled – said it weren't no life fer any of us wiv Pa the way he is – said if Ma had any sense she'd leave 'im . . .'

Jean nodded. Archie was Lizzie Martin's eldest son but still only seventeen. When he'd left school to work on the docks at fifteen, he'd been forced to help his father in a robbery where he worked. The police had suspected an inside job and Archie had been questioned. He'd given Jean's name as a witness to prove he wasn't on the docks at the time the police said and she had spoken for him, because it was true. Afterwards, when they were alone, she'd made the lad tell her the truth and he'd promised her he hadn't been involved in the robbery.

'Pa made me tell him what time the watchman came on and other things,' he said looking ashamed. 'He said I had ter be there and help him get inside the warehouse where the stuff was stashed – tins of bully beef, fruit and stuff like that. He hit me so I had to say I would, but then I ran orf and went to the church hall – and that's where yer saw me. I never done nothin' bad . . .'

Ted Martin had been arrested, charged and convicted with stealing a crate of tinned food. He'd been sent to prison for eighteen months and when he came out, he was even more surly and brutal than when he went in if that were possible. He'd beaten his wife and his elder son and Jamie would have got it too if he hadn't been staying with his nan down the road. She'd been ill then and died a few weeks later, of the shame, Lizzie Martin told her friends.

It hadn't taken Archie long to decide to move away, Jean thought. His father had been back from prison only four months. Jean wondered why she hadn't known, but she was on day duty for the moment and it was late when she walked home and she hardly ever said more than good evening to anyone.

They had reached Jamie's kitchen door. She pushed it open and went in. There was no electric light here, just oil lamps and candles. She groped her way in the almost pitch-black darkness to the table and felt around, but even as she tutted in frustration, a match was struck and a candle flame flared. Jamie knew where his ma kept the candle. He lit a second and Jean saw Lizzie Martin lying on the floor.

It was immediately obvious that she was dead. Her face was a bloody mess and there was a pool of congealed blood under her head where her husband had hit her, time and again. The iron poker used to strike her was lying on the floor by her side. Either Ted Martin had been too drunk or too panicked to try and hide what he'd done and he'd just cleared off with whatever he could lay his hands on.

Jean knelt beside the dead woman, touching her face

and closing the terrible staring eyes. She felt tears sting her own as she thought of the wretched life Lizzie Martin had endured for years. Why hadn't she taken her children and left the drunk who beat her and made all their lives miserable?

It was too late now. Jean looked up at the fearful face of the young lad.

'I'm sorry, Jamie, she *is* dead. We can't help her but we have to get the police and the doctor – it is a formality and I'll see to it. Can you go next door to Marth for a few minutes while I sort this out? She'll be back by now. You can come home with me after I've sorted this out and I'll look after you until we find Arch or someone to take you in.'

'Yeah, all right,' Jamie said and gave her a frightened stare. His bottom lip was trembling; tears filled his eyes, then trickled down his cheek, and she knew he'd been hoping Lizzie Martin wasn't really dead and that, as a nurse, Jean could make his mother wake up. Now he knew for certain she was dead and there was no bringing her back and he'd realised he had no one. 'I'll be wiv Marth next door. She'll have me fer a bit . . .'

Marth Gilbert was a hard-working widow who had given birth to three sons, all of whom were now married with children of their own. She went out scrubbing floors early in the mornings and then went off to help one of her daughters-in-law until the children were in bed. Jean knew the boy would be all right with her until she had this situation under control.

Jean ran down to the telephone box on the corner of Shilling Street, which for once hadn't been damaged, and rang the police. They told her to wait and they would send a constable round. She rang the doctor next and his wife said he was out but she'd tell him when he got in. Jean told her it was too late for him to do anything in any event and put the phone down. She was angry that no one had been near Lizzie all day, though they must have heard the shouting and screaming the night before – and nor had anyone offered to take Jamie in, even though he must have been loitering outside on this bitter February day. Where was the neighbourly spirit London's East End was famous for? In this street it didn't seem to exist, but perhaps times were so hard the folk of the lane had no sympathy to spare for others. Her anger cooled as she returned to the end-of-terrace house more slowly. Most of the women in the lane worked when they could, even if their men had jobs, which many of them didn't, because there still wasn't much work going for labourers. Probably the truth was that no one liked the Martin family. Lizzie had had a sharp tongue on her at times, the children had been neglected when their mother was ill and Jamie was cheeky. He hadn't asked his neighbours for help because the only one kind enough to take him in was Marth.

Marth came scurrying in as soon as Jean got back to the narrow little house, with its parlour, kitchen, lean-to scullery and outside toilet. Upstairs were two bedrooms and a landing. Marth entered through the scullery and went quickly to Lizzie's prostrate form. She gave a little cry of shock and looked at Jean in dismay.

'No wonder he didn't know what ter do! Now what's to happen to that poor lad?' she asked. 'Lizzie wasn't the best ma to her kids but the boy loved her. I'd 'ave 'im if I were sure Ted Martin had gorn fer good.'

'I doubt he will come back now,' Jean said. 'After this, they will hang him. If you could manage Jamie, Marth, he might be better off here, at least for a while – or I could take him home with me . . .' Jean frowned as her mind sought for a better solution.

Lady Rosalie and Matron had combined to help orphaned or abused children find foster parents in the recent past, but she knew there were always more children needing homes than suitable carers to take them in. In Jamie's case it might be that the authorities would decide to put him in an orphanage outside London – and she couldn't see that suiting the boy. No, he would be better off in the streets he knew and perhaps his brother would come home and look after him.

'If he goes ter school I'd be home when he gets back,' Marth said and nodded. 'I'm used to boys, Sister Norton. I reckon he would be more trouble ter you, lass.'

'Well . . . perhaps we can get some money to help you,' Jean said uncertainly, because she knew it must be a struggle for Marth to manage on what she earned, but the older woman shook her head.

'If yer go to them bloody Children's Welfare lot they'll take him in the orphanage and like as not he'll be shifted orf ter Australia or the ends of the earth. Nah, Jamie will be better wiv me and nought said. My boys will see we don't go short. My Eddie is workin' fer a builder now, and Ernie is on the ships – and Pete, well, he's thinkin' about the army. His wife wants 'im ter stay 'ere but he's got the itch. Got married too soon, that boy did – told 'im ter be careful but he wouldn't listen and ended up 'avin' ter wed that little cat. She got 'er claws in 'im, all right – told 'im she was havin' his kid and then lost the poor little mite after she'd got my boy tight . . .'

Jean nodded, only half listening to Marth's tale of woe. She'd heard all this when Marth had come into the infirmary with a festering toe. Jean had tended it for her but Marth wouldn't stay in as a patient and so Jean had called on her at home every couple of days for a fortnight until it was better. Jean had visited several of the women in this street over the years she'd worked for the Rosie, but none of them were particularly friendly and she understood why Jamie had waited for her to come home. It was truly a horrible place to live. Jean didn't like the smell or the atmosphere of the place, but she was a nurse – and when people came to her asking for help, she could not refuse. Her manner was stern and she seldom laughed, other than when with a special friend, but she knew her duty to those in need.

'Well, if you're sure,' she said when Marth had finished her complaining. 'You know where I am if you need me.'

'Aye, lass, I know,' Marth said and grinned. 'Folk round 'ere reckon as you're a real sourpuss but I tell 'em they're wrong. I know you've a good heart on yer, Jean Norton, even if yer try ter hide it.'

Something in Marth's tone made Jean smile despite herself. 'You are a good woman, Marth Gilbert. You've had as hard a life as any round here and yet you always help your neighbours and I've never seen you lose your temper.'

'Oh, I used ter do that when me boys were young,'

Marth chortled. 'I've mellowed in me old age, love. Once they've took Lizzie away you get orf 'ome and leave the young 'un to me.'

'All right – if it's what you want.' Jean couldn't help feeling relieved. The responsibility for a young boy was a lot to take on in her position but she would have done it for a while. 'Perhaps Archie will come back for him as he promised.'

'Aye, providing he hasn't gone orf ter Spain ter fight that foolish civil war. There's four young lads gone from round 'ere this past week. My Ernie said they was fed up wiv bein' told there's no work – and they think it's romantic.'

'Until they lose a leg or an eye,' Jean said grimly.

Although a child then, she vividly remembered the injuries the terrible war with Germany had inflicted on her own family – her father and two uncles killed and Josh . . . Her mind veered away from the memory of the school friend she'd known who had volunteered when only sixteen and been returned with no legs, a ruined face and blind in one eye. Josh had seen clearly with his one eye and he'd seen the horror she couldn't hide. She thought it was the reason he'd crawled to his bedroom window and somehow managed to fall through it when his parents slept.

At fourteen years, Jean had been an idealistic child who admired the tall strong lad who, being a neighbour, she talked to nearly every day. He'd volunteered and been taken into the army, even though he was too young, but of course Josh had been a sportsman and looked older. Perhaps it was the realisation that he would never play cricket or football again that had made him take his life, but Jean was sure it was her fault and she'd never forgiven herself. She sometimes thought it was the reason she'd taken up nursing rather than following her hope of being a singer on the stage. It had been a childish dream and children of that terrible war grew up too quickly. The reality of grey-faced men who had been gassed or badly injured had made her dedicate her life to nursing and she sometimes thought that she was trying to heal Josh every time she treated the sick and dying. He'd never been her lover – someone else had broken her heart – but when she was lonely and the doubts crept up on her, it was always Josh's eyes, accusing her, that she saw in her mind.

Marth departed to get Jamie some supper and Jean covered Lizzie with a coat. It wasn't long before the police constable arrived and soon after the doctor, who grumbled about being called until he saw Lizzie lying there dead. Jean waited until the undertaker arrived to take Lizzie's body away and then she went home.

Letting herself into her kitchen, she realised the range was almost out and hurried to bank it up. She needed a cup of tea and her supper and then she might be able to get this chill out of her limbs. It was far from the first time she'd seen a dead body but it had been unpleasant to find Lizzie like that and the police had warned her to be careful; Ted Martin was a vindictive man and might resent her for reporting what his son had said he'd done. Jamie couldn't bring himself to tell the police but Jean had had no hesitation. Shivering, she scurried about the kitchen preparing her supper of scrambled eggs and mushrooms with toast.

The house seemed empty and lonely and she wished

her friend would visit but knew he would not – they met now and then but always in a public place for coffee or a drink, because it was safer. Both of them wanted more but it wouldn't do because George Bent was married and even though his wife had banished him to the spare room, Jean wasn't an adulteress and she didn't want to be the one who destroyed another woman's home.

'I'd have left her years back if it wasn't for the kids,' George had told her more than once. 'She wouldn't care – but the children would be upset and I can't do it, Jean. I wish I could but . . .'

Jean had put a finger to his lips. 'No, you mustn't think like that,' she'd said. 'We can only be friends, George. I won't be responsible for tearing your home apart.'

'I know – and I can't bring myself to do it either, because I did love her once. But I do love you, Jean. I think about you all the time . . .'

'Not when you're in court pleading a client's case, I hope,' she said, teasing him, because he was an excellent lawyer and often took cases on others might believe hopeless. 'I think a lot of you, George but . . .' She'd shaken her head.

It was strange how easy she felt with George. They'd met when he had been visiting a friend's son at the hospital – for a few weeks he'd been a regular visitor and they'd struck up their unusual friendship. She ought to be tense or upset because of their situation, but she never was – just grateful for the few minutes they snatched to be together. He was the man she might have married if he'd been free, though she'd vowed she never would marry again. but there were times now that she felt lonely and reason told her it would be better to marry for friendship rather than go into old age alone.

Sighing, Jean made a pot of tea and picked up her evening paper. The headlines were about a missing heiress. Apparently, she'd just walked out of her house and no one had seen her for days; it was an interesting story, but Jean's mind wouldn't concentrate on the news. Morbid thoughts would get her nowhere. She'd made her bed years ago and, for the most part, she was content. Besides, George had some tickets for a concert at the weekend. His wife was going to visit her elderly grandmother in Southend and taking the children so they would have a chance to meet.

# CHAPTER 2

Cassie entered the house though the open door that led to the kitchen of the large house and the table had been set for tea with bread, butter and a pot of honey. Glancing uneasily over her shoulder and expecting someone to come at any moment, she moved slowly towards the table and the food, her hand reaching towards the bread. It felt a little dry but was still fresh enough to eat, especially when you were as hungry as Cassie. Up to now she had been taking food from market stalls when the owners weren't looking, and occasionally from the back alleys when housewives had left their back doors open with the pantry in plain view while they gossiped on their front doorsteps. Her mother had told her it was wrong to steal, but it wasn't stealing if you were hungry she thought.

She broke off a piece of bread and spread it with butter and honey and bit into it, relishing the sweet taste. Yes, the bread was a bit stale but she'd eaten worse, even when she was at home with . . . Her mind shied away from thoughts of home. She'd managed to shut her memories off while she was wandering the streets alone.

Looking about her, Cassie saw a bottle of orange squash on the draining board and a tall green drinking glass. She poured herself a generous measure and topped it up with water from the tap, gulping it down. Every so often she glanced over her shoulder, still expecting to be caught and punished and she was ready to flee out of the still-open door, but as the minutes ticked by on the wall clock and she heard no sounds, her sense of fear receded. It was safe and warm here and they wouldn't look for her this far away from that awful place . . .

Cassie had walked and walked for days, hiding whenever anyone noticed her, but few people bothered to give her a second glance. She wandered around the large kitchen, touching things, marvelling at the space and how nice it was – even better than when they'd had a daddy to look after them. Since then life had been harder and harder.

Once again she blocked the memories, memories of a mother becoming ill, pale and thin and permanently shrill, of hands that had once been soft and loving which now slapped and pinched, of the loving smile which had gone, of the despair and grief that remained.

In the pantry, Cassie found the shelves were filled with tins of fruit and there were more bottles of squash. She found a bottle of milk too, but when she opened it, it was sour and smelled horrid, so she poured it down the sink.

Not liking the smell that remained, she went out into the hall and slowly mounted the stairs. They were covered in carpet and her feet didn't make any noise. After the noise and dirt of the streets, Cassie liked the quiet of this house near the river. At the top of the stairs were five doors, all but one closed. Drawn to the open door, she peeped in, half expecting that now someone would shout at her, but the room was furnished with lovely things, even though no one was there. Entering, Cassie looked about her. Everything was so pretty – cream and pink and lots of frothy lace and a fine material you could see through on the bed and the dressing table.

Approaching the dressing table, she saw that its glass top was littered with pretty bottles with silver-coloured tops. There were hair brushes and ribbons, combs and bottles with stuff in that smelled nice when she held them to her nose – and then she saw the box. It was black with flowers painted on it and when she opened the lid, she discovered a mirror that reflected all the sparkling things inside.

Cassie laughed with delight as she took rings and necklaces from the box and draped them on herself. They were all so pretty and they caught the light from the window – and there were lovely clothes on the bed and in the open wardrobe. Just hanging there, pretty pastels and deep shades in jewel colours that made her want to touch. Drawn irresistibly to one pretty dress in a shining silver material, Cassie stroked it and held it against herself.

She'd always loved to play dressing up with her mother's things but there had never been anything as beautiful as these dresses and scarves. Laughing as she started to pull all the dresses from the wardrobe and hold them to her, Cassie forgot to be afraid. No one was here. Perhaps no one lived here and she could stay here forever . . .

It was much warmer in the house than outside and tiredness began to steal over her. Clutching a furry teddy bear she found lying on the bed, she curled up in the big armchair and closed her eyes. She could stay here until someone came to claim the house – but perhaps no one would come and she could stay forever . . .

'Mary, my dear, how are you?' Lady Rosalie kissed her cheek and looked approvingly at the Matron of the Rosie Infirmary, of which, as well as various other good causes, she was a patron. Her main interest in life since her husband's death some years previously was under-privileged children and she was now chairwoman of a board that dealt with providing foster homes for abused and orphaned children. 'Forgive me for not coming to see you these past weeks, Mary, but I have been snowed under with work – and my son was home from his boarding school for a time – the poor darling had the measles and they sent him home to recover.'

Mary Thurston smiled and nodded. She understood how busy her friend was and that her only son was very dear to her, the more since she was unlikely to marry again and have the large family she would have liked. Perhaps it was because she'd been thwarted in that that she took such an avid interest in children who needed help. Whatever, it was an interest they shared and Mary was always pleased to see her and to hear what had been happening.

'Have you interviewed that couple you were thinking of placing on your list as foster carers?' she asked. 'The ones who own a little grocer's shop?'

Lady Rosalie nodded, but looked thoughtful. 'Yes, I

have. I think they will do – but one has to be so careful. We do not need a repeat of what happened to that young lad you asked me to help last year!'

'You mean Charlie?' Mary smiled as Lady Rosalie nodded. The young lad had been placed with a husband and wife who proved unsuitable and treated him as an unpaid servant, but he'd got away from them and proved his own resourcefulness by living on the streets for some time. 'Thankfully, Charlie and Maisie are safe with their aunt now, though I think he may be staying with Mrs Cartwright at the moment . . .' Gwen Cartwright had taken Charlie and his sister in until his aunt could fetch them the previous Christmas and Charlie wanted to stay with her when he left school and took up an apprenticeship as a carpenter.

'Yes – Gwen is an excellent woman,' Lady Rosalie said with a look of satisfaction. 'She is now at the top of my list and I shall not hesitate when the right child comes along. I know how fond she and Nurse Sarah are of Charlie and his sister.'

'Yes, they are,' Mary agreed. 'Would you take a glass of sherry, Rosalie – or would you prefer a cup of tea?'

'Tea, if it's no trouble,' Lady Rosalie said and sighed. 'I am still adding suitable families to my list – if you hear of any . . .'

'Yes, of course I'll let you know.' Mary looked thoughtful. 'Is it still your criteria that it must be a couple in business or full-time work – you're not interested in single-parent arrangements?'

'Perhaps, in certain circumstances, like Gwen's where she has an excellent daughter, but in most cases the foster mother needs to be at home to look after her children – and the father needs to be in permanent work.'

'Well, I suppose that is sensible – but it means quite a few good-hearted women who might take on a child in need would be disqualified.'

Lady Rosalie agreed and that made Mary think hard. She'd known of several cases in the East End where hard-working women had taken in the child of a friend or neighbour who had died. They hadn't asked for money or support and no one's permission had been sought, but the authorities wouldn't sanction their adoption or foster care if it came to their attention, yet it often worked perfectly well.

'I must go – I have other calls to make,' Lady Rosalie said after they'd drunk two cups of tea and chatted for half an hour or so. 'I shall come again soon – and do not hesitate to ask if you have children who need a foster home.' She got up and then turned, looking upset as she thought of something. 'They still haven't found the little girl whose mother fell down the stairs and broke her neck. Cassie was in a temporary holding centre for sick, problem children and ran away some weeks after Christmas. I keep thinking she might turn up here.'

'Unfortunately, she hasn't been brought in to us.' Mary looked concerned. 'The nights have been so cold I dread to think how she's managing alone on the streets.'

'If only she'd been brought to us instead of that awful place . . .' Lady Rosalie sighed. 'I'm not surprised she ran away from there; it has a bad name. Well, you know where I am if you hear anything.'

'I shall let you know as always,' Mary promised and got up to kiss her cheek and press hands before her visitor left. They'd bonded when Lady Rosalie's husband was dying of his terrible illness and had remained friends. It was a good arrangement, because Lady Rosalie often gave money to the infirmary when it was needed, even though they were officially funded by the council – but that was never enough to run the place as she liked.

Sighing, Mary got up to do her rounds of the wards. London's East End had so many sick and needy and her wards were often overflowing, some of the beds occupied by men and women who had nowhere else to go. A smile came to her lips. Sometimes she thought it was a pity she couldn't find foster homes for the elderly and sick as well as the children!

# CHAPTER 3

Nurse Sarah kissed her mother's cheek and reminded her that Charlie would be arriving some time that day. It wasn't likely that Mrs Cartwright would forget something she'd been looking forward to and Sarah knew she'd been cooking all the previous day in preparation. They both liked the youth who presently lived with his aunt but was coming for a few days to stay with his self-adopted mother. Charlie liked Sarah's 'Mum', as he called her, and he'd been writing her long letters about when he would get to live with her and start his apprenticeship as a carpenter on the docks. He'd got almost a year longer at school, but it had closed for a week for half term and so he was travelling up to London on the train by himself. His aunt had given him the money for his ticket and she'd written herself to make sure Sarah's mother was happy to have him.

'As if I'd forget,' Sarah's mother said and smiled. 'I've got his room ready and I'll be baking his favourite cakes this morning.'

'What about me?' Sarah asked, teasing her. 'What about my favourites?'

'Get on with you!' Her mother gave her a little shove. 'That man of yours will be waiting and if you linger any longer, you'll hardly see him before it's time for your shift.'

'Steve will walk me from the bus stop if he can,' Sarah said. 'He tries to sneak a few minutes from his regular beat but we're going to the flicks tonight anyway – so you'll have Charlie all to yourself.'

She laughed as her mother shooed her out of the door. There was an atmosphere of fun and laughter in their home these days. Sarah had put the uncertainty and distress of the past year from her mind. Her old, unhappy, relationship was forgotten and she'd settled down to being courted by Steve – Constable Jones as she'd first known him. He'd come into her life when Charlie had been staying in the children's room at the Infirmary, his mother dying after a brutal attack. They'd found the boy and his sister in some derelict houses after the children had run away rather than be sent to an orphanage. Sarah's mother had taken the children in for a few days and then their aunt had come for them – but Charlie wanted to live and work in London after he left school and he'd asked if he could live with Sarah's mother when he left school. Mrs Cartwright had been only too pleased to agree.

Sarah couldn't help feeling pleased too. She wasn't ready to marry yet, but she thought perhaps it might happen later that year. Steve was giving her time, because he knew she'd been let down by her former fiancé and didn't want to rush her. However, she knew that she'd fallen deeply in love with him and it was only a matter of time before he proposed. Steve was likely to be offered

28

a police house somewhere in the area when he married and they would be near enough to visit her mother often, most days in fact. Yet a police officer could be moved anywhere and Sarah hated the idea of her mother being completely alone. She'd been strong when her husband died and had never tried to tie her daughter down, but Sarah loved her and worried about her. If Charlie lived with her, as he'd asked, it would mean she had someone to fuss over and Sarah knew that was what her mother needed.

Walking in to her work at the Lady Rosalie Infirmary, Sarah was thoughtful. Her mother was a very youthful 44-year-old and there was really no reason why she shouldn't marry again, for companionship if not for love, but neither of them had spoken about the possibility. Mrs Cartwright had talked of taking in a lodger and about her friends – but never of another husband.

Sarah sighed and put the problem to the far recesses of her mind. Mum wouldn't want her to worry, but she couldn't help it now and then.

Steve was waiting for her when she reached the end of Button Street. He smiled as she went to him, hands outstretched, kissing her lips softly, his fingertips lingered on her cheek. Sarah smiled into his eyes.

'Miss me?' she asked and saw the laughter spark, because they spent most evenings together when they could and at the moment, they both worked days.

'You know I did,' he said and his eyes told her that he loved her. 'I looked in the paper earlier and there's a Laurel and Hardy film showing and an Alfred Hitchcock – which do you fancy?'

'Oh, I think the thriller,' Sarah said and looked up

at him. 'Unless you get enough of that in your work?'

'I don't mind a good thriller,' Steve said. 'Most of them aren't like life anyway – they make it seem romantic instead of sordid and the murder I was called to last night was as sordid as they come.'

'Oh, what happened?'

'I may as well tell you, because one of your nurses was involved – Sister Norton. She was the one who found the poor woman. She'd been murdered by her husband and left on the floor all night and day. Her young son was too frightened to come to us – most of them are – and his neighbour was out all day. No one else in the street will have anything to do with the family. Apparently the boy, Jamie, trusts Sister Norton so he waited all that time for her to come home, out on the street in the bitter cold, because he dared not stay in the house.'

'How terrible,' Sarah said, shocked. 'Poor Sister Norton to find that – and that child . . . How old is he?'

'Thirteen, Sister Norton said, but he looks younger; he's small for his age. You'd think he would come to us or ask the doctor to visit but his father went to prison nearly two years back and his elder brother was questioned at the time. The doctor is already owed money and might not have gone if he'd asked. Jamie must have been scared to death; probably afraid he'd be blamed.'

'He couldn't have done it?'

'No, his story checked out. The neighbour heard shouting at eleven that night but she was in bed so when it went quiet, she just drifted back to sleep. She was out at five in the morning to do her work and then at her daughter-in-law's all day – the daughter-in-law has three small children and can't cope alone so Mrs Gilbert helps her until they're safely in bed. When she got back home, Sister Norton was there.'

Sarah nodded. The story he'd just told her was not uncommon. Violence was prevalent in some of the poorer areas of the East End. Men beat their wives when they returned home drunk and many of them came for treatment at the Infirmary, but this woman wasn't the first to be murdered by a drunken lout, whether her husband or lover.

'So where is the boy now?' Sarah asked.

'Staying with the neighbour for the moment. Sister Norton offered to take him in for a while but Mrs Gilbert said he'd be all right with her until his brother came back for him.'

'Yes, I suppose that would be best. Sister Norton doesn't have time to look after a young boy – I'm surprised she offered.'

'I was too,' Steve admitted. 'She seemed different – more approachable – last night. Maybe she isn't the ogress she seems, love.'

Sarah laughed. 'No, she isn't that bad, just stern, always correcting the nurses under her and making us do things again. She has high standards.'

'Yes, I think that must be it,' he agreed. 'I know she's grumbled at you because of me a few times – but I suppose she wants her ward run just so.'

'Yes,' she agreed thoughtfully. 'I like that she offered to take the child in, though. It makes her seem more human, don't you think?'

'Oh, she's human,' he said and grinned as they stopped outside the infirmary. 'It's funny how little we know about folk we work with, isn't it? I didn't know my sergeant's little boy is a cripple until yesterday. He was born like it, poor little devil. They've just had a daughter and she's fine – I think it was the emotion and relief that made him talk about it.'

'Oh yes, I knew about Sergeant Bartlett's son,' Sarah said. 'We had him in the clinic a few months back and he was quite poorly for a while. Your sergeant came in to thank us for looking after him and sending him home well – very emotional he was – and he bought us a box of Fry's chocolates.'

'Well, I never,' Steve said and sighed as the church clock struck the hour. 'I'd better go and so had you, love. See you this evening!'

'Don't forget Charlie will be there tonight.'

'I shan't.' Steve smiled and walked off.

Sarah entered the infirmary and saw Kathy Saunders talking to her friend Bert Rush. They worked together on the cleaning staff and were supposed to be attending to the floors and stairs. Everyone knew that Bert was sweet on Kathy but until recently Kathy's mother had refused to let her go courting. The girl was still only seventeen and Bert was nearly twice her age, but Kathy's mother thought the world of him because he'd saved the girl from a brutal assault and she allowed her to go out with him. Sarah wasn't sure how the age differ-ence would work out if their relationship became serious, but she knew Kathy was happier now.

Going quickly up to the children's ward, which was where she normally worked, she saw that Sister Norton was already there and making her first round of the day. The night nurse was just leaving and she shot Sarah a look that told her to be careful.

'And where have you been, nurse?' Sister Norton asked as she went to join her on her round. Her eyes went to the clock but she saw that it was just one minute past the hour and contented herself with a frown.

'Sorry, Sister,' Sarah said. 'Is there anything you particularly want me to do?'

'Yes, I need this child given a bed bath please – and then you start the breakfasts, please.'

Sarah nodded. She bent over the little boy in question and caught the sour smell of his diarrhoea and her throat gagged, because it was unusually strong. He'd been having bouts of it ever since he'd been admitted and, so far, the medicines they'd given him hadn't stopped it.

Sarah smiled at him reassuringly and went off to fetch a bowl of warm water and cloths to wash him. When she pulled back the covers, she understood the smell. He had rolled in it all night by the looks of things and it was all over the sheets and his nightclothes.

Setting to work with a will, Sarah stripped away his dirty pyjamas and the soiled sheets and then washed him clean and dried him on soft towels. He was a little sore on his bottom so she applied a soothing cream, dressed him in clean pyjamas and sat him in a chair while she got the bed tidy. He looked at her shyly as she told him he could get back in bed when he liked.

'I'm sorry, Nurse Sarah. I didn't mean to do it . . .'

'I know that, Ned,' she told him gently. 'You've got

a nasty bug in your tummy and it's not your fault. When the doctor gets it sorted, you'll be all right to go home again.'

Tears welled in his eyes. 'Ma says I'm dirty and she thinks I do it on purpose, 'cos it 'appens so much. I don't think she wants me 'ome.'

'Of course, she does,' Sarah said and smiled down at him. Now that he was clean and fresh, he looked beautiful and she couldn't imagine any mother not loving him – and yet she knew it happened. Women with too many children, too little money and too much to do might turn from a child that habitually messed its bed night after night. Anger and tiredness made people say things they didn't mean and Sarah wouldn't condemn a woman she didn't know. 'I'm sure she loves you, Ned.'

'Nah, she don't; she thinks I'm a nuisance,' he said. 'Mark is her favourite and Jinny. She never wanted me 'cos I ain't me dad's, that's what she says, but I don't know what she means. Do you know what she means, nurse?'

Sarah shook her head. It was clear to her what the boy's mother meant but she couldn't tell him. She felt pity in her heart for the youngster. Unwanted and unloved, he struggled with an illness that recurred frequently and because of it felt he was a nuisance to everyone.

'You're not a nuisance to me, Ned,' Sarah said. 'Just call me if you feel you need the toilet quick – but don't worry if you make a mess.'

Ned clearly hadn't told the night nurse that he was soiled. If she'd bothered to check she would have known but Nora was new to the infirmary and Sarah thought her a little careless in her work. However, she would reserve judgement until she knew more.

After she'd cleared away the dirty linen and water, Sarah returned to the ward. Mabel had brought the breakfast trolley up from the kitchen. She was new too, and had replaced Ruby in the kitchens as a helper. Thankfully, the cook hadn't left them and the food served up was still hot and edible. Not like home-cooked food, but reasonable, and most of the kids ate it up as soon as they felt well enough. It was probably better than they got at home.

Sarah took the food round; she liked this job because it helped her to see whether the children were recovering from the sickness that brought them to the ward. Once they started to sit up and look for food you knew they were well on their way to going home.

Ned only wanted a piece of toast and marmalade. Sarah had told him he just had a tummy upset to comfort him but she wasn't sure what Ned's problem was, because the doctors hadn't been able to make up their minds.

'Wouldn't you like an egg or a piece of bacon?' she asked and he shook his head, looking wan. Sarah frowned; she didn't think he was getting better at all. She made up her mind to talk to Sister Norton about it.

Sister was still checking pulses and temperatures. Sarah finished her job and saw Sister heading for her office at the end of the ward. She hesitated in the doorway and Sister Norton looked up, clearly irritated.

'What is it, nurse?'

'It's about Ned Rutter,' Sarah said. 'Do you think he's any better, Sister? I think he seems worse . . .'

'Yes, he is – and I'm glad you noticed,' Sister Norton said. 'I'm worried about him. We thought it was just a stomach infection when he came in with constant bowel movements – but now I think it must be something more. I believe the doctor should do more investigations.'

'Yes. I wondered . . . do you think he has some sort of trouble with his gut or his bowels? I mean, he can't eat much and what he does eat goes through him too quickly. If it's not an infection . . .'

'Are you thinking of a growth of some sort?' Sister Norton looked her in the eyes and Sarah flinched.

'I do hope not – at his age! It isn't fair!'

'Life is seldom fair, nurse,' Sister Norton said. 'We'll keep a close eye on him, you and I, Nurse Sarah. I want you to tell me whatever you notice, even if it seems unimportant.'

'Yes, Sister, of course.'

'Good – and well done for telling me.'

Sarah nodded but made no answer. She seldom got a well done from Sister Norton, though Sister Ruth Linton, one of the senior staff was always praising her.

As she worked through the morning, Sarah's thoughts remained with the young boy. He called her once urgently and she was just in time to save him from another accident. He was close to tears and she saw that he was very upset because he felt he was naughty to cause her so much extra work and no matter how often she told him she didn't mind, he still looked unhappy. At lunchtime he once again refused most of the food, eating only a small piece of the treacle tart that had been sent up for the children.

Sarah sat on his bed and asked him if he was in pain. He shook his head, looking at her in silent misery – and then, suddenly it came out. Sometimes he had violent bouts of pain but he could go for days with nothing. However, the more he ate the more mess he made and his mother told him he was a filthy little pig and she would put him out in the yard where he belonged if he went on making a mess.

Sarah saw the tears in his eyes and felt enraged. How could any woman speak to her young son that way? It was beyond understanding, because it was so cruel. She wanted to go round and tell the woman what she thought of her but knew that she dared not. Feeling the way she did, she would be sure to lose her temper and might find herself in serious trouble – might even lose her job. However, she could not hold it inside and so she told Sister Norton a little later that afternoon.

'Thank you,' Sister said and nodded. 'He won't talk to me – but now I see what is troubling the poor child. Yes, I agree, this is mindless cruelty and needs to be stopped. I shall visit the mother and speak to her.'

'Is that wise?' Sarah dared to ask. 'Might it not rebound on him if we tell her what he said?'

'Do you imagine me a fool?' Sister's brows arched. 'I shall not go blundering in, but merely talk to her about the boy – discover where her true feelings lie. I believe this child has something seriously wrong. It is not an illness I have come across – most of these cases are infections or some kind of gastric problem – however, I think I do recall something . . .' She shook her head as Sarah's eyes questioned. 'It was in a medical journal I read a few years back. I shall speak to Dr Mitchell about the boy's condition.'

Dr Mitchell was new to the infirmary. He worked for a large hospital in London but he knew Lady Rosalie personally and gave some of his time to the infirmary free of charge, because she had asked him if he would.

'Thank you,' Sarah said. 'I can't bear to think of what that little boy must suffer at home.'

'You must leave it to me,' Sister Norton said. 'Continue to report everything to me and we shall see what we can do for Ned before he leaves us.'

Sarah felt better as she went off to finish her work. She'd always thought Sister Norton uncaring because she was sharp and strict, but now she thought she might just have been wrong. Steve said you never knew people you met or worked with until you got under their skin and perhaps something or someone had done just that to Sister Norton and the softer side was showing a little.

# CHAPTER 4

Nurse Jenny looked around the market stalls. She wanted a birthday present for one of her colleagues and had seen some pretty scarves a week or so earlier. Spying the stall she needed, Jenny stopped to look at the selection and bought a pretty pink and blue scarf and then a green one. She would give the green one to her sister Lily as a little treat. Lily was also a nurse and she liked green a lot. Jenny sometimes felt she neglected her, because she went out far more than Lily did with her friend Chris – boyfriend really, though they had never been lovers. Chris was too often away and Jenny got a bit fed up with staying home when he wasn't in London, though he was fun to go out with when he was home and generous.

Having bought the scarves, Jenny became aware that she was being watched intently as she approached a stall selling freshly-baked cakes and fruit pies and flans. Her eyes moved over the milling crowd and then she saw the little girl – a dirty little waif with big blue eyes staring at her. Something tugged at Jenny's heart and she turned to the stallholder, buying cakes for herself and Lily and then a bag with two iced buns in. The little girl was still staring at her in that intent way.

'Are you hungry?' Jenny asked, advancing towards the child. The girl took two steps back, but her eyes were fastened on the brown paper bag in Jenny's hand. Deciding that to try and advance on her would only scare her, Jenny held the bag out. 'These are for you – if you would like them?'

For a moment the child stared at her as if wondering whether to trust her and then she suddenly darted forward and snatched the bag, running off immediately as though she feared Jenny would grab her if she didn't.

'Come back, I shan't hurt you!' Jenny called but the child had disappeared into the crowd.

'Pinched yer cakes, did she?' a woman asked, shaking her head. 'Them street kids are a bloomin' nuisance.'

'No, I wanted her to have them. I think she was hungry,' Jenny said. 'I ought to have done more to help her . . .'

'Yer can't help them urchins,' the woman retorted with a sniff of disgust. 'They're all thieves and rogues; the coppers should shut the lot of 'em up in institutions if yer ask me!'

Jenny's throat caught with emotion and she felt the sting of tears; she shook her head and moved away. She felt sad that a child of that age should be living on the streets, relying on the charity of strangers to feed her, yet she couldn't do much to help the child. Neither she nor Lily had time to care for a little girl and the only other thing was to hand her over to the police who might possibly stick her in an institution. The lucky ones came to the Rosie or were placed with foster parents, but many more went to orphanages, often out of London and away from all they knew – the rest lived on the streets or with parents who cared nothing for them . . .

'I felt so upset,' Jenny told her sister when she got in later. 'I gave her the sticky buns because she looked so hungry – but she needed love and a good home, Lily.'

'Yes, I know, love,' her sister told her sympathetically. 'But she is only one of many, Jenny. She probably has a home but her parents can't afford to feed her properly.'

'Perhaps,' Jenny sighed. The child had touched her heart and yet she knew that Lily was probably right. If the little girl was living on the streets the police would have picked her up and taken her somewhere. She must have a home to go to – even if it was unsuitable.

'Did you see this?' Lily offered Jenny the evening paper that she'd bought from the shop on the corner where they lived. 'That heiress is still missing. The police are looking for her but they say she probably went off with someone she liked.'

'Why are they making so much of it in the paper?' Jenny asked, hardly bothering to glance at the article. She was more interested in the child with the big hungry eyes.

'Oh, they say she is a little bit fey . . . or not quite right in the head,' Lily said. 'She had someone to look after her but the woman was called to a sick relative and says she only left Miss Gillows alone for two days before the police were alerted.'

'Oh, I see.' Jenny frowned. 'How old is she?'

'About twenty-two.' Lily smiled. 'No, she isn't your

41

little urchin! I wonder if she's been murdered? She might have been robbed – apparently, she liked jewellery.'

'Or she got fed up and went off for a while,' Jenny said and sighed, looking round the kitchen. 'Oh, I do miss Gran!'

'Yes, me too,' Lily agreed. 'I thought she would always be here but that flu . . .' She blinked hard and wiped her face with the back of her hand.

'I know.' Jenny went to put her arms around her. 'I bought you a little present – it might cheer you up a bit.'

Lily sniffed harder. 'You're a good sister, Jenny. I hope you know I love and appreciate you?'

'Of course, I do,' Jenny said. 'Are there any letters for me?'

'No.' Lily smiled. 'I would tell you if Chris had written, Jenny – but I'm sure he's busy. He'll write as soon as he can, I know.'

Jenny shrugged. 'It doesn't matter. What shall we have for tea?'

'I thought I'd make some tinned salmon sandwiches.'

'Lovely,' Jenny agreed. 'I bought a nice cake for afters so we can indulge ourselves.'

She went to take off her coat and wash her hands while her sister made their tea and as she did so, Lily wondered why Chris hadn't written for a few weeks. It was foolish of her but she sometimes thought she looked forward to his letters more than her sister – and that was stupid. He was Jenny's boyfriend and could never be anything more to her. She bit her lip as she buttered bread and spread the salmon, mashed with vinegar and pepper, onto the bread, then cut the sandwiches neatly into triangles.

Jenny had been concerned about the little urchin she'd seen in the market but there were so many of them. Frowning, she wondered for a moment if it was the child, Cassie, the police had been searching for with no success. Her mother had fallen down the stairs at her lodging house, taking the girl with her. While the girl had been knocked unconscious for a time, the mother had fallen badly and broken her neck. When the neighbours found them, the child had been taken to a place of safety and cared for – but it hadn't been very safe after all, because she had run away when she came to her senses.

Lily couldn't understand how the people who were supposed to care for her had been so careless. She'd been in a ward with other sick and disturbed children and she'd just walked out – something that just wouldn't have happened at the Rosie. Such a pity she hadn't been brought to them but they had lived in a different area of London.

Shaking her head, Lily's mind returned to Chris's letters; he would write again soon, she was certain, because he loved Jenny.

Lily sighed, looking up with a smile as her sister entered the kitchen. Jenny was so lucky . . . but Lily loved her and she didn't begrudge her her happiness.

'Shall we go out somewhere this weekend?' Jenny asked. 'I've got Sunday off and so have you.'

'Yes, let's do that,' Lily agreed. 'We haven't had a day out for ages.'

# CHAPTER 5

Jean caught Dr Mitchell before he left after visiting the chronically sick ward. He was walking hastily towards the entrance when she touched his arm and turned to her with a frown, as if he felt annoyed that she had delayed him.

'A moment of your time, doctor?'

He hesitated, then, 'Is it important?'

'Yes, I believe a child's life is at risk . . .'

'In that case my time is yours,' he said. 'Is there a pub where I could get a beer and a sandwich? I haven't had lunch and we could talk as I eat – I'm back on duty at my hospital this evening.'

'Yes, of course. I'm sorry to have delayed you – perhaps another time . . .?'

'No, if it was important enough to ask, it deserves a reply,' Matthew Mitchell replied. 'Are *you* hungry? A ham sandwich and a beer would just fill the bill for me.'

'And me,' she agreed, feeling she would enjoy eating a meal in company with someone for a change. 'Yes, I'd be delighted to treat you, doctor – after all, I'm the one taking your time.'

'I never say no to an attractive woman,' he quipped and they left the infirmary, crossing the road. Jean led him down a narrow lane to a pub she'd had a drink in with George a few times. He nodded approvingly. 'This is clean and the food looks freshly made . . .'

They found a table and Dr Mitchell insisted on ordering at the bar. Jean was content to let him. She never drank or ate at a pub by herself and it was more comfortable that way, but she would insist on repaying him their bill.

Dr Mitchell returned with a tray with their sandwiches of crusty bread and butter, ham and mustard, and two glasses of pale ale. Jean sipped her drink tentatively and found it wasn't bad. She smiled because she'd never tried it before, normally sticking to lemonade or, very occasionally, a port and lemon.

'Thank you,' she said and took a sandwich. He was already on his second and if he hadn't told her she would have guessed that he'd missed lunch, not unusual, she suspected, for such a busy man.

'Now,' he said and took a swallow of beer, 'tell me please.'

Jean launched into an account of all that Nurse Sarah had told her. 'I wondered if it might be a nervous complaint?' she offered apprehensively, because doctors didn't like nurses giving their own diagnoses. 'I read something similar once in a medical journal but it was a long time ago and I can't recall it accurately – but this child doesn't have an infection causing his diarrhoea I'm certain of it.'

'Ah . . .' Dr Mitchell nodded and devoured another sandwich, looking thoughtful as he chewed. 'Yes, I see.

Well, you did right to ask me, Sister Norton, because I do know of the condition, though it is not generally diagnosed. It is difficult to be sure and a lot of people questioned the original thesis by Doctors Crohn, Ginzburg and Oppenheimer in 1932 – it's usually known as Crohn's Disease, by the way.'

'I don't know if that's the paper I read,' Sister Norton acknowledged. It had been published after her training and she knew that she might not have read all the articles in the medical journal she still took each month. It was difficult to keep up with new discoveries, especially when you were a hard-working nurse and lived alone.

'You're not the only one,' Matthew Mitchell smiled at her and Jean found she was smiling back. 'Some doctors are not completely convinced by their findings but I think they were probably right to publish. I'll look in on the boy tomorrow. Unfortunately, if it is Crohn's as I suspect, there is no known cure and we're not sure how to treat it – but it is a physical condition and in certain cases might be critical.'

'That's what I feared,' Jean replied and watched him wolf down the last sandwich. He certainly was hungry! She offered him the one left on her plate but he shook his head.

'No, I'm full now – and I must go. Thank you for bringing this interesting case to my attention, Sister Norton. I shall see you tomorrow.'

She took some money from her purse and offered it to him. 'For the meal . . .'

'Not necessary,' he said and gave her another blinding smile. 'It was a pleasure, Sister Norton. We must do it again sometime when I'm not in a hurry.'

She watched as he disappeared out of the door, pausing to salute her before he disappeared. For a moment Jean stared after him, feeling a little as if a whirlwind had caught her up.

Jean decided to visit Marth on her way home. Jamie was at the kitchen table demolishing a thick slice of bread and dripping and by his expression it would seem that he enjoyed the fatty treat. He looked better and brighter than when she'd last seen him and she felt relieved that she'd done the right thing. Her immediate reaction had been to take him in until a proper home could be arranged, which meant either his brother's return or an orphanage, but Jamie looked at home with Marth and actually managed a grin.

'I just came to see you were all right,' she told him, surprised to feel a tug on her heartstrings as she looked at his face, which was still slightly grubby, though cleaner than the previous day. 'Not giving Marth too much trouble, I hope?'

'Nah, 'course not,' Jamie said and looked at her. 'I'm a good boy, ain't I, Marth?'

'Well, I wouldn't say you're good but you ain't bad,' Marth said and her plump body shook with mirth. 'Yer ain't no trouble to me, lad. Yer can go and play wiv your mates for an hour or so if yer want.'

'Thanks, Marth!' Jamie scrambled down from the table and grabbed his worn jacket before shooting out the back door before she could change her mind.

'You should let him help with the work,' Jean suggested. 'Might do him good, you never know.'

'Aye, well, 'e fetched in the coal this mornin',' Marth

said, 'and 'e ran to the corner shop for a loaf for me.'
She hesitated, then: 'Will yer take a bite to eat or a cup
of tea, Sister Norton?'

Jean was about to refuse when she realised she had
nothing much to do at home that evening. 'I wouldn't
mind a cup of tea,' she said and sat down at the table.
'I had a sandwich and a glass of beer with a friend –
well, I drank half of the beer. I've never tried it before
but I could do with a nice cup of tea.'

'Sit you there and I'll brew a fresh pot,' Marth said,
smiling and nodding. 'I made a seed cake when I got
home. It's still warm, if you could fancy a slice – I'm
havin' one meself.'

'Then I shall too,' Jean said. 'Do you know if Lizzie
heard from Archie at all? Did he find a job down south?'

'Not that she ever told me, but she didn't talk most
days – it was that wretch she wed. Told her to keep
her mouth shut or he'd fill it for her with his fist.'

Jean nodded, letting the older woman talk, her gossip
spreading to others in the street. It was as well to know
what was going on, because when the women turned
up with black eyes and broken arms at the Infirmary
it helped to know if it was truly an accident or the
result of a brutal beating.

The tea was drunk, the cake eaten and only then,
reluctantly, Jean took her leave. She didn't know why,
but she was feeling down in the dumps. It had suddenly
come home to her that she had no life outside her work,
except for her occasional outings with George. Work
had always been enough for her before but suddenly
she felt that her life was empty – not meaningless,
because her job was important, but sad. Yes, she decided,

she felt sad, and she'd made up her mind long ago that she wouldn't let herself look back or regret. Then she'd met George and their friendship had filled a space in her life. For a while that had been enough but now . . .? A sigh escaped her. She wasn't sure what was wrong with her tonight, but it wouldn't do. She must pull herself together, go home and have an early night to make sure she was ready for work the next day.

Jamie ventured to the end of the lane, looking for another boy to play football or rounders with, but there was no one about on his street. Their mothers probably had them doing jobs before they went to bed, just like Ma used to with him. The thought of his mother lying on the ground, staring up at him with dead eyes and blood all round her head, made tears start to his eyes and he cuffed them away angrily. He'd shut the horror of it out of his mind but sometimes it crept back . . . He wasn't going to cry though. Boys didn't cry! His father had taught him that long ago.

'Yah, cry baby, cry!' Voices chanted at him from the shadows making him jump. He hadn't seen them standing there and for a moment he was scared but then he saw them emerge from the shadows, two boys from his school, both of them older and bigger than Jamie. He knew that they seldom attended school and came from Bull Lane, which was some streets away and an even worse area than this one. Jamie also knew that they had a reputation as bullies, but they were on his street and he was too proud to run.

'I'm not crying,' he muttered and scowled at them. 'I ain't afraid of you Red Brothers, neither.' They ran with a gang of street children who called themselves Brothers of the Red. It was a name that held no meaning for Jamie but he was aware that many children were terrified of the Brothers, associating the word red with blood, as they were meant to.

'If yer ain't afraid, prove it,' the taller of the two challenged, taking a menacing step nearer Jamie. His name was Leo Ruffard and both boys were in the class above him, or should have been if they ever bothered to turn up; the second lad's name was Mick Rimmer, but they called themselves brothers.

'All right, put 'em up then!' Jamie said defiantly and lifted his fists before him, ready to punch. He'd had enough fights at school over his father after Pa was sent to prison to learn that most boys backed down if he showed them a boxing stance. He might be small for his age but he wasn't a coward and he was ready to have a go. Not that he knew how to box properly, but Arch could and he'd shown him a few sharp moves.

'If your assailant is bigger than you, hit below the belt,' Arch had told him. 'It ain't proper rules and it ain't fair, but if he's a bully he deserves it.'

Jamie waited for the Red Brothers to come at him, thinking they would take him together, but the elder one – Leo, he thought – suddenly brought out a knife with a long blade. Jamie's blood froze. He knew he couldn't get near enough to land a low blow with someone who carried a knife. His eyes moved from side to side as he thought of his chances of escape, which were probably nil. Realising they would chase him down before he could get home, Jamie retained his stance.

'Only bloody cowards use a knife,' he said lifting his

head with reckless defiance. 'If you weren't scared, you'd face me like a man!'

Leo stopped and the younger boy took his cue from him, hesitating and looking to his senior for guidance. Jamie was scared but determined not to back down. No point in running when they'd get him anyway. He was still waiting for them to pounce when Leo suddenly laughed and a second later his shadow laughed too. The knife went back into Leo's pocket. Jamie waited uncertainly.

'What yer doin' out then?' Leo asked. 'We're goin' ter 'ave a bit of fun – want ter come?'

'Yeah, why not?' Jamie breathed a sigh of relief, hardly believing that he was being asked to go along with them and not lying beaten and bloody on the ground. 'Where yer goin'?'

'If yer want ter run wiv us, yer shut yer mouth,' Leo said. 'If yer ain't a coward yer might be allowed to join the Button Street Brothers.'

Jamie took a deep breath. Arch had warned him never to get involved with the gangs of street children but his brother wasn't around to protect him anymore and he knew if he walked away now they would gang up on him another day and that day he would be beaten or stabbed.

'I ain't no coward,' Jamie said, which was true enough. His mother and brother had warned him about getting into trouble with the law but his father had sneered at them. He was a thief and a murderer and Jamie didn't want to be like him, but he had to live in these streets for now and the best way was to go along with the bullies but try not to do anything his ma wouldn't have liked. 'I don't care what I do,' he lied – a lie he knew even then that he would regret.

'Yer livin' wiv yer neighbour now yer pa's done fer the old woman?' Leo asked and Jamie nodded. He hated that Leo had called his mother that, but what could he do?

'Yeah, until Arch comes back.'

'Yer brother's gorn,' Leo sneered. 'He won't come back fer yer – and that old bugger Marth won't want yer long. Yer better orf wiv us – reckon we're yer brothers. We're all brothers, see. Ain't got no one wot cares, just like yer – and so we look after ourselves.' He grinned at the other Red Brother. Jamie couldn't recall hearing his name and didn't think he'd ever seen him at school.

'What do I call yer?' he asked.

The boy looked at Leo, who nodded and then said, 'I'm Mick Rimmer but yer call me Brother. We don't use names . . . ain't that right, Brother?' His eyes were on Leo as usual, waiting for approval.

'Yeah.' Leo's eyes glittered in the light of streetlamps. He stopped and pointed across the street at the little corner shop there. 'That's where we're goin' – we fancy some sweets, cakes and fags, don't we, Brother?' He looked at Rimmer and winked.

'But they're closed . . .' Jamie began but the words stuck in his throat, because he knew just what they were planning. 'How are you goin' ter get in?'

'Through a window at the back,' Leo replied. 'Guy who owns it lives over the top but the silly old fool is nearly deaf and he won't hear if we're careful. By the time he gets down to the shop, we'll have grabbed what we want and scarpered.' His eyes narrowed and Jamie could see him fingering the knife in his pocket. 'Are yer in?'

Jamie took a deep breath. He knew Mr Forrest at the corner shop well and liked him. He hated the idea of stealing from the old man, but he had no choice.

'Yeah,' he said in a voice as strong as he could make it. 'I'm in.'

'Good, because yer goin' in after the stuff,' Leo told him with an evil grin. 'The window ain't big enough fer either of us and all the others 'ave iron bars over 'em.'

Now Jamie understood why he'd been given a chance. If he hadn't been the right size to get through the window, they would just have beaten him. He half wished he'd let them get on with it, but it would make them really angry if he said no now and that knife in Leo's pocket could kill.

'All right,' he agreed hiding his reluctance beneath a show of bravado. 'Tell me what yer want and I'll bring it.'

'Yer a right un'.' Leo grinned again, a proper one this time. 'I thought yer would be like yer bloody brother, but yer all right. Now listen, I've got a little torch so yer can see what we want and everything is in the storeroom. Yer don't need to go through the front. Just grab as much as yer can and pass it out ter us and then get out as quick as yer can.'

Jamie's heart was racing as they led him round to the back of Mr Forrest's corner shop and pointed out the tiny window. It was just big enough for a boy of his size to squeeze. He felt his legs shaking and his mouth felt dry as he watched Leo prise the catch open.

It was surprising how easy it was for the experienced thief to open what looked like a locked window. Jamie wondered if they'd somehow managed to fix it from inside earlier, perhaps distracting the shopkeeper while one of them slipped into his store room and moved the catch.

There was even an empty wooden crate left nearby for him to stand on, raising him up enough to wriggle through the narrow bit head-first. He slithered down to the floor, landing with a little thump. His nerves jangling, Jamie listened for sounds from upstairs but there was none. He switched on the torch and started to explore the shelves, quickly discovering boxes of chocolate bars, full sweet jars and several stacks of cigarettes, both Players and Woodbines. Knowing the Players were expensive, Jamie ignored them and swept up the Woodbines. He bundled them through the window and rushed back for the chocolate, grabbing handfuls out of the boxes and returning to throw them out to the others. He passed two big jars of sweets out and some packets of biscuits, but as he went back for more, he knocked a box off the shelf and the noise frightened him. He rushed back to the window because he thought he heard a sound from above.

'He's heard us!' Jamie said and moved a chair so that he could scramble up on it and dive head-first through the window. He'd expected Leo to catch him before he hit the ground, but the Red Brothers had scarpered and Jamie landed in a heap on the gravel outside, scraping his knees and cheek. A light had come on upstairs and, as Jamie got to his feet and ran, someone looked out of the window and yelled.

'Come back 'ere you dirty little thief! I'll teach you to rob my granda!' A boot followed the yell but Jamie was already swallowed up by the darkness of the street.

He ran and ran through the streets he knew so well, wondering if the Red Brothers would come after him, but he heard and saw nothing. At the first hint of danger they'd cut and run, leaving him to sink or swim alone. He knew then that he wasn't one of them, even though he'd done what they wanted and got nothing out of it himself, not even one chocolate bar. He'd just given it all to Leo and he'd been left in the lurch.

For a moment Jamie had the strangest feeling that he was being watched. He glanced over his shoulder but couldn't see anyone. If those bullies came after him again, he would fight, even if they thrashed him. They were rotten cowards and he hated them now for what they'd made him do.

Jamie's mouth set in a grim line. He felt sick at what he'd done and he was glad that Mr Forrest's grandson had been home from the army and heard him. He wished he hadn't given those pigs as much as he had. It was the last time they would make him do a robbery for them! Jamie would take a beating, but he wouldn't go out unprepared in future. He would fetch one of Ma's sharp knives from her kitchen drawer and give those bullies as good as he got. Jamie remembered how quickly they'd given in when challenged and he thought that, like most bullies, they were cowards at heart, just the way Arch always said they were. If his brother had still been here, they would never have dared threaten him.

His mind made up, Jamie went home to Marth's

warm kitchen. He wished he'd been braver for the start and felt sorry for Mr Forrest, who didn't deserve to be robbed. Ma would be ashamed of him and Arch would give him a hiding for it. Tears stung his eyes but he brushed them away angrily. It was no good wishing that Arch was here to help him fight the Red Brothers. He was on his own and the only one he could rely on was himself.

Watching from the shadows, the little girl shivered, pulling the warm shawl about her shoulders. She'd found it at the place she was now calling her house and loved the feel of its softness about her neck and face. She'd wandered a long way today, searching for something, though she wasn't sure what she was looking for. The mists in her head were thicker some days and she couldn't remember anything, not even her name.

Those horrible boys were bullies. The smaller boy should have run away from them but they'd frightened him, as they frightened her – except that she could run fast and they never caught her, even though they'd tried to hurt her once. She'd scratched one of the boys on the face then and kicked his shins, and when he yelled and let go, she'd run off as fast as she could and hidden. She was good at hiding.

It was a pity the small boy hadn't seen her when she'd tried to call him from her hiding place, but he'd been too frightened to see anything except the bullies who were threatening him. She thought it was a shame, because she might have taken him to her house so that they could play. Jamie looked lost and lonely, just like her. A little smile lit her thin, dirty face as she remembered the name the bullies had called him and then, just for a minute, she remembered her own name.

She was Cassie and – and her mother had wanted to drown her in the river. For a moment she recalled the desperate struggle on the stairs and then her mother's scream as she tumbled backwards down them, dragging Cassie with her. Just for one blinding second it was all so clear to her – and then the voices saying she was evil and would be locked away in an institution.

Cassie felt the sting of urine on her legs as she wet herself. Tears rushed to her eyes and she started to run. She had to get back to her house, because only there could she be safe from the people who wanted to lock her up. As she ran, panting in terror, the past became muddled again and she remembered a woman sitting by the firelight singing a song she'd loved and a man who smelled of tobacco and some sort of drink on his breath – but, in another instant, it was lost and all she could think of was the need to return to her house, the beautiful house that someone had so clearly left for her to find safety in . . .

# CHAPTER 6

Steve was waiting for Sarah when she got off her bus as usual the next morning; she didn't always bother with the bus but it was drizzling with rain and she'd decided not to walk. She went to greet Steve with a smile but saw that he was looking stern and didn't smile as easily as he normally did when they met. Touching his hand, she looked up at him, searching for clues. Had she done something to upset him?

'What's wrong, Steve? Are you upset about something?'

'Well, yes, I am as a matter of fact,' he said. 'It was a robbery last night at the corner of Bull Street, the little grocer's there.'

'I know that shop well,' Sarah said. 'Sister Norton lives not far away – and Mum has a friend who does a lot of her shopping there because she says old Mr Forrest is so lovely to her . . .' She saw the grim look in his eyes and hers widened. 'What happened?'

'Forrest's grandson was there and heard them, fortunately. He scared them off before they could take more than some sweets and a few packets of Woodbines, but

Mr Forrest was upset and then taken ill in the night, and they've rushed him to hospital. They say it is his heart and it's touch and go whether he survives.'

'Oh no! I bought Mum some chocolate there last year for Mothering Sunday and he was really friendly.' Sarah understood why Steve was so upset. He must have been called to the shop in the early hours.

'I know him well,' Steve told her grimly. 'I like him, Sarah – a lot. He's the sort you'd want as a grandfather. Often gives the kids an extra sweet but nothing untoward about him. He's not a groper, just loves kids. If I catch the little buggers who did it, I'll give them the fright of their lives!'

'You must be angry but you can only arrest them.' She looked at Steve uncertainly, because she'd never seen him this angry before.

'I know, but I can threaten them with hanging if the old man dies!' he said and she knew it was anger talking. Steve was upset because he'd known the victim of what was really a petty crime. 'His grandson was in tears, Sarah. We were at school together. He's a grown man, in the army and home on leave, and yet he was crying. He saw the lad scarper – just one and not very big – but he'd have to be small to get in the window. They've got bars over all the others. However, I looked around outside and I'm sure there was more than one lad. It looks as if they put the little one through the window and then ran and left him to get out as best he could. He probably cut himself on the gravel when he landed . . .'

'Have you any idea who did it?'

'I've got an idea.' Steve frowned. 'They call them-

60

selves The Brothers of the Red or some such fanciful thing and it's not a big gang. We think about four or five altogether, but we know they're active in the area. Most of them are thirteen or fourteen and they play truant from school all the time. We send school officers round to their homes but the officers tell us they're afraid to go near some of the houses unless we go with them – the fathers are all known criminals, the mothers often drunk or on the game. The leader of the gang lives with his grandmother, because his parents are dead, and I doubt she can do anything with him.' He shook his head. 'It isn't surprising they grow up the way they do, but we have to prove they're guilty and so far, they've not left any clues – however, this time they made a mistake. There are fingerprints all over, a child's prints, so we know it must be the young devil who got in that window – the trouble is, he was probably a first timer and it might be hard to find him.'

'I'm sorry your friend's grandfather was hurt,' Sarah said as she heard the clock strike. 'Oh, I have to go or I'll be late. Shall I see you this evening? Mum thought you might like to talk to Charlie?'

'Yes, I should,' Steve agreed and smiled. 'Now there's a young lad I like. He could have turned bad but he didn't – and I respect him for his choice to make something of his life.'

'You can tell me about it tonight,' Sarah said and kissed his cheek. She turned and ran into the infirmary. Sister Norton was going to be angry because it was already two minutes past the hour.

However, when she arrived on the ward, slightly

breathless, Sister Norton wasn't in; Sister Rose Harwell was there instead. She smiled as Sarah came up to her and nodded.

'I'm glad to see you nicely on time,' she said. 'We've got a busy morning ahead. I'm afraid we've had two new patients come in overnight – but one has gone into the chronically sick ward. Dr Mitchell came in early this morning and had Ned transferred. He wants us to give the child more time and he knows we can't keep a watch over certain patients the way they do in the critical ward.'

The chronically sick ward was small and housed only a few patients at a time, allowing the nurses to sit with their patients for hours if need be.

'Sister Norton and I were keeping a strict eye on him,' Sarah said feeling a bit distressed that their patient had been moved.

'Yes, but it seems that he was in terrible pain last night and the night nurse had to summon Sister Linton because she couldn't cope.'

'I see.' Sarah nodded, understanding now. It was the first bout of violent pain Ned had endured since entering the infirmary and the doctors were clearly concerned if they'd moved him to a ward reserved for patients who might not recover. 'I shall visit him in my break, Sister – if that is permitted?'

'Of course, it is, nurse,' Sister Rose said. She looked at Sarah gravely but with kindness. 'But you really can't allow yourself to get fond of patients, Sarah. We none of us can. Either they get better and go home – often to families who don't look after them – or sometimes they die. It can hurt either way.'

62

'I know,' Sarah took the mild rebuke as it was meant, to help rather than scold. 'But I was just getting to know him, gain his confidence.'

'Yes, I know. Dr Mitchell wants to speak to you later. He says that Sister Norton alerted him to Ned's condition, because of you. He probably wants to say well done.'

Sarah smiled and thanked her and they got on with the work of the day. She didn't ask why Sister Norton wasn't in and it wasn't until they had a tea break later that Kathy told her what she'd heard.

'Sister Norton was up all night. She was called out to an elderly man who was having a heart attack after his shop was robbed and went with him to the London. She waited until she was told he was stabilised for the moment and then went home. She rang Matron this morning and told her she wouldn't be in today.'

'Yes, I heard that Mr Forrest at the corner shop had had a heart attack,' Sarah said. 'I suppose they knew Jean lived nearby and asked her to come, rather than the doctor.' It wasn't uncommon in the lanes and narrow, dirty streets of the East End, for nurses who lived near to be called out rather than the doctor. Doctors charged more to visit and many people just couldn't afford it while others didn't see why they should pay them when the nurse would tell you just as much for free. Sister Norton would have gone immediately, without a thought, and wouldn't have asked for a penny.

Kathy had come up with the meal trolley that morning and had obviously overheard part of their conversation. She brought it up when Sarah went to fetch breakfast for one of the children, asking for more information.

'I wouldn't have thought she would bother to sit there all night for him,' Kathy said looking surprised when Sarah told her why Sister Norton wasn't at work. 'She always seems so stern.'

'Yes, but perhaps she isn't always like that?' Sarah suggested and smiled at her, deciding to change the subject. 'How are you, Kathy?'

'Good!' Kathy blushed and looked uncertain. 'You'll never guess – Bert asked me to marry him.'

'And what did you say?'

'Well, I'll have to ask my mother,' Kathy said and laughed. 'But I told him I would, if she says it's all right.'

'You're very young to marry – only seventeen,' Sarah said gently.

'But I'll be eighteen this year. Besides, I like Bert. He makes me laugh and he keeps me safe – that's what Mum says you need in a husband.'

Sarah nodded but made no further comment. It seemed that Kathy's mother, having made up her mind she liked Bert, had decided to push the girl into a safe marriage. That might not be a bad thing, but Kathy might wake up one day in the future and decide that she wanted to see a bit more life than her much older husband was up for . . . Still, that was not Sarah's business, it was Kathy's; and only she knew whether it was what she truly wanted of life.

When Sarah returned to the ward after popping in to see Ned, who was under sedation and didn't know she was there, she discovered Dr Mitchell talking to Sister Rose. He turned, looked at her and smiled in welcome.

'Good morning, Nurse Sarah,' he said. 'I wanted to have a word with you about my patient. Tell me, what was it that led you to tell Sister Norton that you were certain Ned's problem was not an infection?'

'I just sensed it was more,' she said. 'I know the signs of infection were there and we all thought it must be a nasty tummy upset when he first came in – but I talked to him and it seems he gets days of violent pain followed by days when he feels nothing, but this constant diarrhoea is causing trouble with his mother.'

'Ah yes, she wouldn't understand that her son has a condition that will, unfortunately, affect him for most of his life. It has a name, Crohn's disease, but few doctors know of it and even fewer can diagnose it.'

'What exactly is it?' Sarah asked.

'If we knew for sure, perhaps we could find a cure . . .' He sighed, his brow creasing. 'It is probably a bit of twisted gut or something of the kind, but, whatever, it causes inflammation and therefore pain. There are various symptoms: fever, pain, and the diarrhoea, of course. What little we know is that a liquid or soft diet is best for sufferers, though some do not respond – and if it comes to the worst we might have to operate and take out the inflamed section.'

'Wouldn't that be dangerous?' Sarah felt sharp concern for the young boy who had never known a loving home.

'Yes, it could be. We're not really sure yet, because

the condition has only been identified in the last few years and not enough is known yet, but if we do nothing and the diet does not work, he could die.'

Sarah felt tears prick her eyes but blinked them away. She was a nurse. She was a professional. She could not allow herself to be emotional over a patient.

'You do well to care, because he has no one else,' Dr Mitchell said, seeing what she tried to hide. 'I visited his mother this morning. Apparently, Sister Norton had been there first and was given a flea in her ear. I was almost thrown out and threatened with a carving knife! She told me she didn't care what we did to "The little brat" – her own words – but she didn't want him back soiling his bed every night.'

'How disgusting she must be!' Sarah cried forgetting her position in her anger.

'She most certainly is.' Dr Mitchell grinned broadly. 'I got out of there pretty quickly, let me tell you – and I'll be talking to people I know. Ned will not go back to that hellhole. Once he can leave us, he will go to an orphanage or an adoption centre.'

'Or a foster home?' Sarah said and blushed as he looked at her intently. 'My mother would take him in for a while, I know she would.'

'That I can't promise,' he said. 'Once I report the case it will be out of my hands – but in the meantime, I should like you to spend as much time with him as you can spare, nurse. He seems to have taken to you.'

'And then?'

'And then we'll see what Matron and Lady Rosalie say,' he suggested and winked at her as he turned to leave the ward. Sarah smiled. Dr Mitchell wasn't like most of the others, who looked down on the nurses like gods from afar. She liked him – and if she and Ned got on as well as they always had, she thought Dr Mitchell and Lady Rosalie might just see the wisdom in letting her take the child home with her, at least for a while – and now she'd best return to the ward before Matron had her guts for garters!

Jean had been very distressed to be called out the previous evening to Mr Forrest. He was such a gentle, kindly man and she often shopped with him. She could buy things more cheaply on the market sometimes, but his stock was always fresh and reliable and it was a pleasure to stop and talk to him. He allowed his customers to taste tiny slivers of whatever cheese or ham he currently had for sale and his time was yours for as long as you wished. She'd arranged for him to be taken into hospital and gone with him herself, because his grandson was busy with the police. The constable who'd turned up after a frantic phone call had been Constable Steve Jones and Jean knew he was courting Nurse Sarah Cartwright. He had a nice manner with him and she'd liked the way he'd calmed Phil Forrest down – the army sergeant had been incandescent with fury, and in clear distress over his grandfather but together they'd sorted it out and she'd been glad to help.

Sitting at the hospital waiting for news she could take back to his grandson, Jean hadn't been aware of tiredness. She was used to night duty and it wasn't as if she was on her feet. One of the young nurses had brought her a cup of tea and then a doctor had come to tell her that Mr Forrest was settled for the night and over the worst.

The doctor spoke confidently. 'He should make a full recovery, providing he doesn't have another attack immediately. You know yourself, Sister Norton, we can never be certain these things are over for at least a couple of days. If he had another attack as severe as the last it would probably kill him, but we shall keep him here and watch over him and I have every hope he will come through.'

'He is in the best place,' Jean said. 'Do you think his attack was caused by the break-in – or is it likely that it could have happened anytime?'

'We shall do further investigation while he is here,' the doctor said, 'but at his age he may well have had symptoms he's not bothered to report to his doctor.'

Jean had left the hospital then and taken a taxi home. She'd made tea and toast for herself, feeling tired all of a sudden and deciding she would go to bed as soon as she'd rung the infirmary and let them know she wouldn't be in that day. She could have gone in a bit later, but she would probably be tired and a tired nurse was not an efficient nurse. Far better someone else should take her place for a day.

Sister Ruth Linton had been very understanding. Her superior, Matron might not be best pleased at having to rearrange her staff but would do it.

Jean had taken another cup of tea to bed and slept until after two o'clock, when she got up and bathed and dressed in a skirt and jumper, deciding to walk round to Forrest's corner shop and see if Sergeant Forrest had any further news of his grandfather's condition.

She thought the shop might be closed but it was open as usual and the tall, rugged young man stood behind the counter. He smiled at her as she went in.

'Good afternoon, Sister Norton,' he said. 'I'm glad you came in. I wanted to thank you for all you did last night. I was afraid to leave the shop in case the bastards came back to finish the job – excuse my language, ma'am – but I was so angry over it. Grandfather doesn't make a fortune out of this place, he never has, just a few pounds to keep him going.'

'I doubt if a small shop ever earns much,' Jean said sympathetically. 'Some of the kids here don't know right from wrong. Their fathers are probably out of work and their mothers can't control them – but it still doesn't excuse what they did.'

'I know how bad things have been,' Phil Forrest agreed. 'My parents had their hard times, same as others, and that's why Dad wouldn't let me work on the docks. He told me the army was the place for me and he was right. I'd hate to live round here again – but I think the world of Grandfather and I visit as often as I'm able.'

'You haven't heard anything more?'

'No. I'll go to the hospital when I finish up here, but I didn't want him to lose more than he already has so I opened up as usual. I've had a lot of folk in and they all say how sorry they are and they hope he'll be back soon, but I'm not sure he can ever return to what he was.'

'There's no way he can afford to employ a full-time assistant?'

Phil shook his head. 'The shop doesn't earn enough,

Sister Norton. I think he may have to sell up and go to live with my parents. My mother will happily take him in but she's got two children still at school and Dad to look after, so she couldn't manage the shop as well.'

Jean nodded her understanding and made sympathetic noises. She knew there was no comfort to be given in such a case. Mr Forrest was old and if he could no longer run his shop, he would need to sell it and move in with his daughter-in-law and son. The alternative did not bear thinking of for an independent man.

She bought a few things and walked back home just as the schools were emptying. As she entered Pail Street, she saw Jamie Martin walking towards Marth's house, looking furtively over his shoulder. Moving quickly to catch up with him, she tapped him on the shoulder and he jumped in fear, his eyes wild as he looked at her.

'Is something wrong, Jamie?' she asked and he shook his head but she saw a bruise on his cheek. 'Are you afraid of someone – one of the boys from your school, perhaps?'

Jamie hesitated and then nodded looking at her and now she saw a different expression, which she suspected, might be shame. 'Yeah,' he said at last. 'It's a gang, Sister Norton. They gave me a bit of a 'iding last night – they're bullies and all the kids are scared of them. Arch ain't, but he ain't 'ere.'

'I see . . .' She pursed her lips. 'Isn't there anyone you could talk to about it – your teacher or a policeman perhaps?'

Now Jamie looked really frightened. Instead of answering her, he took to his heels and sprinted the few

70

yards to Marth's house, disappearing around the corner and no doubt into her kitchen.

Jean frowned, considering what to do for the best. Should she follow him into Marth's kitchen and insist on the whole story or leave him to make up his own mind how to deal with the bullies? She sighed and walked past, knowing that she couldn't interfere unless he asked. Jamie was staying with Marth, his unofficial foster mother, who had promised to contact his brother as soon as they had word of his whereabouts. Jean had no authority and no right to make him tell her his story if he didn't wish to.

She was still thoughtful as she approached her cottage and saw, to her surprise, that she had a visitor waiting. George seldom came to her home, because they'd decided at the outset it wasn't sensible. To meet for a drink or a coffee was one thing but to be alone together in her home was quite another and would undoubtedly cause gossip.

'Jean!' George came to meet her as she approached and she saw that he looked bothered – annoyed and worried. 'I'm glad to have found you. Matron told me you were at home so I came but there was no answer.'

'I went to the shop,' she said. 'Come in, George, I wasn't expecting to see you before the concert next week.'

'I know – but . . .' He glanced round, as if wondering who was watching or listening. 'I'll tell you inside.'

Jean unlocked her back door and they went into her neat kitchen. It smelled slightly of her toast from earlier and she frowned, opening a window to let some air in. Then she turned to look at him expectantly.

71

'George, you wanted to tell me something?'

'It's Lilian . . .' He paused and took a deep breath. Lilian was his wife and Jean prepared for the worst, because when he spoke of her it was usually to cancel an arrangement or complain of her tantrums. 'She wants to go and live with her sister in Bournemouth. The kids are at boarding school and Lilian is miserable. She says she's had enough of me and wants me to give her a divorce – she says she knows I'm having an affair and it is up to me to make it easy for her.'

Jean pulled out a chair and sat down, her breath suddenly gone. She felt shaken. Divorce was such a shocking thing and she didn't actually know anyone who'd been through one. It was usually the product of scandal and the other woman in the case inevitably lost her reputation. Everyone was always on the side of the wife. If Jean was named, she would be known as a scarlet woman!

'We aren't having an affair,' she said, 'so how can she know anything? We've had a drink together and been to a concert a couple of times as friends – but nothing more!'

'Of course not,' George said nodding in agreement. 'I might wish it was more, but we've been sensible. I told her it was nonsense but she says she's had a private detective follow me and he has photographs of us together and unless I agree she will go to your employers and make a fuss – and she would, Jean. I'm so sorry, my dear. I thought I had been careful but she smelled your perfume on a handkerchief and . . .' He shrugged apologetically. 'I don't even know how it got there.'

Jean frowned as she wracked her brain for the memory and then nodded. 'You took a piece of grit from my eye and wiped a tear from my cheek – it was when the men were working on the road and some dust blew into my eye.'

'Yes, of course.' He shook his head in wonder. 'Such a tiny thing . . .'

'I never wear perfume at work,' Jean said with a frown. 'She couldn't have smelled it – perhaps my soap . . .' She looked at him, seeing the flush in his cheeks and guessed that her wife had accused him more in hope than knowledge and he'd given himself away. George had made it clear he wanted an affair on several occasions. Jean had resisted, mainly because of past hurts, but also because she hadn't wanted to be the cause of a divorce.

'I thought I should warn you,' George said and looked uncomfortable under her accusing stare. 'You won't be named, of course. I can arrange something – pay a prostitute and get someone to take pictures. If it means I'm finally free we could—'

'Don't, George!' Jean said, sounding sharper than she intended. 'We are friends – and I shan't deny I've been tempted to let it be more – but that doesn't mean I want to get married!'

'Oh . . .' He looked crestfallen and disappointed and Jean wondered why she'd said it. Only a few days ago she thought she would have been pleased that he would soon be free of the wife he'd long disliked. 'I thought . . . you know how I think of you, Jean.'

'Yes, and I am very fond of you,' she replied and sighed. 'I didn't mean to be sharp, George. You caught

73

me at a bad time and – and I'm upset that I might be accused of being an adulteress.'

'Yes, of course. You look tired . . .' He looked at her, belatedly seeing the signs of strain. 'What's wrong, old girl?'

Jean ignored the form of address, though it irritated her. 'I was up all night with a patient and he is very ill – he may die and he is someone I rather like. Most of the locals do. We all visit his shop at least once a week, because we don't want him to give up – though perhaps he should have done after his wife died.'

Jean found herself telling George all about the break-in. He shook his head sadly and then nodded. 'It happens all too often when the shopkeepers get too old,' he said. 'I'm always being asked to defend little blighters who've been stealing sweets and cigarettes from elderly men and women who eke a living from these tiny corner shops. I get paid a few quid for getting the kids off with a caution or a fine when they ought to send the rogues off somewhere and teach them a lesson – a spell in the army would be as good as anything, if they were old enough.'

'Sergeant Forrest thinks it was schoolchildren.'

'That's the trouble,' George shook his head. 'If the police find them and go to the parents, they'll lie through their teeth for them, and even if there's irrefutable proof, some busybody will come along and say they should be given a rap on the knuckles and let off. Nowhere to send the blighters that's the problem. What few remand institutions for underage offenders exist, are filled to bursting.'

In his capacity as a solicitor for criminals, George

74

was well aware of the situation and Jean did not doubt his word. They'd met when she'd sought a solicitor on behalf of one of her neighbours, who was being threatened with eviction by her landlord because she owed two weeks' rent. A collection amongst friends and neighbours had paid the arrears but still the landlord had wanted Millie Jenkins out of her cottage. However, George had soon put the domineering landlord in his place and Jean had invited him for a drink to thank him for his help. They'd liked each other from the start and George had been honest about the state of his sterile marriage. Jean had told him who and what she was, but her secrets had never been discussed – with George or anyone. The hurts she'd suffered when she was a young nurse, straight out of training and full of belief, remained buried deep inside and that was the way she intended them to stay. No one needed to know that Jean had been deceived, betrayed and discarded but it wasn't going to happen again.

'Well, I'd better go,' George said and looked reluctant. 'If I stay it may be added to the list Lilian is preparing to use against me.'

'This divorce . . .' Jean looked at him anxiously. 'Are you sure my name won't be used?'

'I'll do my utmost to stop it,' he promised and came towards her. He reached out for her and then bent his head to kiss her. Jean felt the tickle of the little moustache he'd grown. She smiled and let him kiss her. She was quite fond of him, though it wasn't the blinding, all-consuming love that she'd once known and lost. George smiled down at her and then lifted her chin. 'I haven't been able to court you as I should – but when this horrid business is over, I'll show you how I really feel.'

'Let's wait and see how you feel once you're free,' she suggested and smiled at him. 'I am very fond of you, George, but I don't think we should meet until it is over.'

'No,' he agreed reluctantly. 'I took a risk today but I changed buses three times and I don't think I was followed. It means abandoning our trip to the concert but I'll let you know when it is over.'

'Thank you.' Jean went to the door with him, waved and then returned to her kitchen. For some reason she was close to tears. She'd enjoyed meeting George sometimes, but would she really want him here in her home every day and all night? She wasn't sure it would suit her to play the part of a dutiful wife. Her job was important to her and she didn't imagine she could have a successful marriage and carry on working full time at the infirmary.

Sighing, she went to the dresser drawer and took out a paper pattern. She had some material to make a dress that she'd bought more than a month earlier and put away. That evening she would cut out the pieces of one of her favourite styles. She'd used it many times before and knew it suited her tall, slightly thin frame. The neckline was modest and she normally added collars, either of lace or white linen, double stitched to make it stiffer. With long sleeves, a fitted bodice and a semi-straight skirt that ended just above the ankles it made her look elegant but respectable. A woman in her position needed to be careful and dress modestly. Anything too frivolous and the women of the lanes around her would start to speculate. She could imagine what a few of her neighbours would be thinking of George's visit as it was – and smiled as she realised that they would be counting the minutes and wondering if he'd been there long enough to have committed an indecent act with her . . .

# CHAPTER 7

'Why don't you go out and play wiv yer friends fer a bit?' Marth asked, looking at Jamie oddly.

Jamie shuffled his feet. He knew he was in the way until bedtime. Marth had given him a home but she didn't want him around all the time. She had jobs to do in the evening and preferred to be alone to get on with them.

'All right,' he said and got up, shooting out of the back door.

The lane was in semi-darkness, because only one of the streetlamps was still working, even though the council had repaired one a week earlier. Some youths had thrown bricks at the other one and it would be months before the council returned to repair the glass yet again. He loitered in the area that was lit, kicking at a stone, hands in pockets, lost and not knowing what to do for the hour or so Marth wanted him gone. If he wandered out of his lane the Brothers Red might be waiting to get him and there was no way he was going to let them make him a habitual thief. He'd done it once and was ashamed, especially because one of the

79

kids he was friendly with at school had that morning been in tears because Mr Forrest was ill.

'What 'appened to 'im?' Jamie asked his heart racing.

'Some rotten so-and-sos robbed 'is shop and it made 'im proper bad,' the other lad told him. 'Ma was upset and she told me how good 'e was to us when Dad lost his job and 'ad no money. We owed him no end when Dad started work again and we're still payin' back at two bob a week but he never grumbles or makes her feel small.'

His friend's tears made Jamie wretched. He wished he could go back and change what had happened but he couldn't and it made him want to be sick. If the other lads at school knew what he'd done they wouldn't want to know him.

'What yer hangin' about here for, Jamie?' a friendly voice asked and Jamie started, looking at the lad who had spoken. He was older, about Arch's age and he'd been a friend of Jamie's brother.

'Ain't got nowhere to go,' Jamie said. 'Where are yer orf to, Rich?'

'I'm goin' ter the boxing club,' Rich Austin said and grinned. 'Why don't yer come wiv me? Arch was a good bloke in a fight – you look as if yer might be the same.'

'Can I really come wiv yer?' Jamie lit up with eagerness and grinned when Rich nodded carelessly.

'I reckon yer can tag along,' Rich said in the lordly manner of a youth five years older than his acolyte. 'It is a club fer young'uns as well as blokes of my age. The bloke what started it says it keeps us orf the streets makin' trouble.' Rich grinned. 'He's a bloody copper but 'e's all right – and his mate is a professional boxer. They're both pretty good wiv their fists and they give us lessons in how to defend ourselves – even a little'un like you could learn to disarm a bloke wiv a knife.'

Jamie's ears pricked up at that. The landlord had locked up their house but he'd got in and found a small sharp knife in his mother's kitchen – although he was scared to use it, because he knew the consequences of wounding someone badly. It would be great if he could learn how to deal with bullies like the Brothers Red without using a weapon.

'I'd like to learn,' he told Rich. 'I'd rather 'ave somethin' ter do nights.'

'The club is open every night,' Rich said. 'They don't charge nothin' to get in – but if yer want drinks or food it costs a tanner.'

'Ain't got a tanner but I ain't 'ungry.'

'You will be when you've gone a couple of rounds wiv Steve or the Blond Bomber!'

Jamie goggled at him in surprise. 'What sort of name is that?'

'It's Mad Mick's professional name what he used for his fights. I've seen posters of 'im when he was winnin' – but he ain't fightin' no more. Got a bad beating orf some American bloke and they took his licence away, said his brains was fried. He says some odd things but he's all right – a good mate in a scrap.' Rich grinned at him. 'You ain't got Arch's physique yet but I reckon yer will shape up in a few years, Jamie. Especially if yer stick wiv me.'

Jamie sent him a look of admiration, feeling something close to hero worship. He hadn't thought Rich

81

had noticed him when he came to the house with Arch, though he'd once spun him a sixpence for some sweets. Jamie had thought he wanted to get rid of him so they could go off on their own, but if he was willing to let Jamie tag along, it would solve his problems for a while.

Steve Jones looked about him, feeling a small surge of pride mixed with triumph. When he and Mick Roberts had talked about starting this place for the street kids, no one had really thought it would work. The church had several youth clubs in the East End but the kids who attended were usually from good homes, where the fathers kept their sons from loitering on the streets and causing mischief but Steve had known that they needed somewhere for the other kids to come, those whose families didn't care what they did and willingly accepted any money they managed to steal. Mick still had money from when he was successful and they'd put fifty pounds in each and hired a hall. When it worked out well, Steve had gone to his sergeant and the station had run a raffle to raise funds. Someone had let them have a hall cheap, because it was for the underprivileged kids, and now the club was going from strength to strength.

The club was filled to capacity that evening. It wasn't always as full as this but tonight there would be three eagerly awaited boxing matches. Each of the pairs would fight three rounds and whoever was scored the highest was the winner. The boys taking part were seventeen-year-olds, fourteen- to fifteen-year-olds and twelve- to thirteen-year-olds. The top class might include a boy of sixteen if he was strong enough and so on down the line. Ages were just a guide and it mainly depended on how skilled they became in the ring. Some of the lads would never be good enough to fight three rounds, but most had learned some of the skills and how to fight back when attacked by bullies, managing more than Steve had ever expected.

That evening, some boys were being taught wrestling and judo moves, learning how to defend if an opponent came in from the rear with a knife. It was all a way of teaching the lads that there was another way to be brave. They didn't have to swank around with a knife and pretend to be big; they could be quiet but determined and learn how to put the bullies in their place.

Steve had found some friends of his wanted to help. Some had special skills, which they taught the kids, and some just helped with funds to keep the club open. He was the only serving police officer, but Jeff Hunter had been in the force for thirty years before his stomach pain from an ulcer had got too much and he'd retired on a small pension. Jeff was much better now and perfectly fit providing he ate sensibly and didn't fret too much. After years of specialising he had a way of talking to the kids and spent every evening showing them how even an old man could put someone like Steve on his back with the right moves.

'It isn't strength and it isn't size,' he told the lads who chuckled when, after a tussle, he'd put the young police officer down. 'Any of you could do it if you take the time to learn. I'm not half as fit as Steve here, but you saw me put him down fair and square.'

'But don't use it against us, because we're your friends,' Steve quipped. 'Keep it for the bullies who deserve it – and remember that most of us are trained to do what Jeff just did. The bullies who threaten you with a knife are not. They seek to intimidate and frighten and the knife scares everyone – including me. A knife in the guts kills in a very unpleasant way and if someone uses it, they deserve to hang when their victim dies, as he usually will.'

Steve's gaze was drawn to a young lad he hadn't seen before. The youth was drinking in every word, clearly mesmerised by the idea of being able to defend himself. Steve didn't know why, but he was certain the lad had been threatened, and recently.

'Hello,' he said and smiled at him. 'You're new – what's your name?'

'Jamie Martin, sir,' the lad said and looked frightened to death.

'I brought him, sir,' Rich Austin informed him. 'He's living with a neighbour but he's got no one at home now so I thought he might enjoy the club.'

'Then welcome, Jamie,' Steve said. 'You're just the size we need to demonstrate the theory. Rich, come and be the aggressor and I'll show Jamie what to do to stand up for himself.'

'Yeah, glad to, Steve,' Rich acquiesced and swaggered up, clearly delighted to have been chosen for the demonstration.

'Come to me, Jamie,' Steve said. 'Stand just here in front of your friend like this . . .' Steve showed him how to plant his feet apart so that he was square and sturdy and then how to put his hands out in front of him in the defensive mode. 'First of all, we have to warn the opponent. We just say something like . . . "Stop!

84

Come near me and I'll put you down." Once the warning is given, it's self-defence. *You* are not the aggressor; *he* is – and that is important in law. Understand?'

'Yes, sir,' Jamie said. He looked interested rather than frightened now.

'Now, Rich, come at us as if you were going to stab Jamie with a knife . . .' Rich moved forward in a slow, aggressive movement. 'Right, that's good, hold it like that. Now, Jamie, you move towards Rich and you grab his arm like this and you give a quick twist like this . . .' Steve placed his hands on Rich, held and threw him to the ground.

It was a demonstration and Rich hadn't resisted so his fall was easy and he wasn't hurt. He got up at once and took the same stance again. This time Steve showed Jamie how to place his hands on Rich's arms and hold firmly and then showed him how to flick his body so that the movement put Rich off-balance. It took Jamie several attempts but after a while, he actually managed to overbalance Rich who obligingly went down.

'Of course, Rich wasn't trying to resist,' Steve explained to the watching lads, 'but it is the trick or the skill that will put down a real opponent. You've watched a complete novice learn to *almost* do it – and now you can all pair up with someone about your own size and have a go.

'Sidney Greene, come and partner Jamie. You're about the same size, though Jamie is slightly smaller. You two will practise together until you can put each other down easily and then we'll give you harder targets.' He smiled at Rich. 'Thank you for helping. I know you've got a boxing match to go to.'

Rich nodded at Jamie. 'Wait for me after the club closes and we'll walk home together.'

Steve saw the lad grin and nod but he was already concentrating on getting to grips with his new partner and Sidney was resisting, as would happen in real life. Jamie was very determined and Steve sensed a deep purpose in the lad. He wondered what had given Jamie this determination to stand up to bullies. The nape of his neck was tingling and he sensed that he needed to encourage this boy to become a part of the club, to trust him. If that trust could be established, Jamie would come to him and tell him in the end, but asking would be a waste of time. The only way with youngsters was to let them decide when they were ready.

He was well aware that Rich Austin lived near Forrest's shop. And it was his training as a copper that suggested to him that this new young lad knew something about the robbery, knew the youths who had done it and yet . . . Studying Jamie, seeing his determination, made Steve think harder. The lad was just the right size to go through that window. Not that anyone would do it again. Forrest's family had had an iron bar fixed inside so that it would be impossible in future . . .

Jamie lay in bed that evening, his body aching as if he'd been beaten. He was so tired – and yet he was also exhilarated. He'd managed to put Sidney down three times while Sidney had only got him down once. It was a tiny triumph and he knew that he would have to get better and stronger before he could tackle Leo. The Brothers of the Red never went anywhere alone and Jamie would be in danger if he had to tackle two at a

86

time. He'd watched Rich knock down his opponent in the boxing and he'd cheered, excited by the glamour and newness of the club. Rich had told him he'd done well. Of course, he couldn't have thrown Rich if he'd been fighting back, but his brother's friend had told him that if he kept working hard, in time he would easily be able to throw down anyone but a skilled opponent, who would fight back.

'It takes years to get a black belt if yer do the sport properly,' he'd told Jamie, 'but yer can learn enough to protect yerself quite quickly if yer listen and watch and learn.'

Jamie felt a warm glow as he recalled Rich's praise for his efforts and Steve's too. The policeman had had a word with him afterwards and told him he hoped he would come as often as he could.

Jamie knew Steve went three nights a week, as did Rich, but Jamie wanted to go every night. It might mean walking home alone and that could be trouble for him, but Jamie felt more confident now. Even with just one night's training, he was more confident. He'd been shown how to grip a wrist and turn it so that a knife would drop harmlessly away. Perhaps he wasn't strong enough yet to do it – but he would be. He would practise all the moves whenever he could and next time Leo tried to bully him, Jamie would be ready – as long as it wasn't just yet.

Cassie followed the boy and his companion home. They had no idea she was watching them, following in the shadows. She belonged to the shadows now, it was where she felt safe and she'd discovered lots of hiding places – places from where she could watch children playing. She went to the school most days and watched when they played games in the playground and ate sweets or the sandwiches their mothers had packed for them. Dimly, through that ever-present mist, Cassie remembered that she'd once gone to a school. It wasn't the one she watched the children playing at – but somewhere else a long way off. She didn't know where, but she'd lived there with Daddy and Mummy, before they quarrelled and Daddy left them.

Cassie's memories of that time were of being warm and never hungry – and of a man who smelled of cigars and brandy and a mother who smelled of perfume. Her mother had always indulged the big boisterous man who had liked to sit by the fire and drink the golden liquid her mother said was brandy and smoke the strong-smelling things that Cassie knew were cigars. She didn't mind the smell because Daddy gave her toys and sweets and biscuits with icing on the top.

A frown touched her forehead. Mummy had sold all Cassie's toys and pretty dresses after Daddy went away. She'd gradually sold everything they had until they had nothing much left and they'd had to sneak away in the night because Mummy was afraid of the rent man. Cassie didn't know why – he'd smiled at Cassie and patted her on the head but she'd heard him arguing with her mother so perhaps that was why?

'Mummy . . .' she whispered. Where had her mummy gone? Cassie tried to remember but it was one of those times when she couldn't remember what had happened before she came to her house.

'Where are you off to alone, my pretty . . . ?'

As the large man, smelling of the strong drink she associated with her father but mixed with another unpleasant odour, loomed up in front of her and reached out his hand, Cassie screamed, backing away. He leered at her and she felt fear rush through her as she turned and fled into the shadows. It wasn't the first time a man had frightened her, grabbing hold of her and saying things that made her squirm and feel scared, but Cassie wasn't going to let anyone grab her. If she did, she would be sent to Australia, wherever that was.

As always in her fear, she ran and ran until she got back to her house by the river. It was strangely empty, unlike all the other houses. It was also grander than the other ones surrounding it. Its silence and warmth comforted her, surrounding her with its safety, but sometimes her loneliness drove her to look for other children. She was hungry but she'd eaten all the food that had been left in the house, except for some tins of meat that she didn't like the look of and wasn't sure how to open. She needed money to buy more food and there was none in the house – or none that she'd discovered. Perhaps she could sell some of the things she'd found lying around . . . Her mother had sold all their things to the man people called Uncle, who had a shop with three brass balls outside as his sign. All Cassie had to do was to find a shop like that and then she could sell a few small things that she didn't want and buy food . . .

# CHAPTER 8

Nurse Jenny Brown came off duty to find that her friend, Chris Moore, was waiting for her. When she'd first met him, Jenny had fallen hard for his good looks and charming manners, but then discovered that he was a member of the fascist politician Oswald Mosley's Blackshirts. She'd fallen out with him because, like her sister Lily, she thought Mosley's thugs were mindless brutes and it wasn't until she'd broken her heart over him that Chris told her the truth. He'd infiltrated the movement to report on the thugs to the Government. His cover had been blown during a riot, when he'd shown his true colours. Because he feared being murdered by men he'd betrayed, Chris had been instructed to join the army. He was no good to his employers dead and under the guise of an army captain he was continuing his work as a spy for the British Government abroad.

Jenny knew no more than that, because she seldom saw Chris these days and when she did, he was close-mouthed concerning his work.

'I've told you all I can, Jenny,' he'd said when she'd

questioned him once. 'You must believe that I'm not the mindless bully you thought me and you should know that I love you – but for the rest you have to believe me and trust me.'

'I do trust you,' Jenny had told him. 'But it is hard when you're away all the time and I never see you.' He didn't write long letters either. She'd get a note to say he'd be home on a certain day and that was it. He always signed it with love and kisses but it wasn't much and she was young enough to want more. Lily told her that she wouldn't find a better man and it infuriated Jenny when Lily said that, because her sister had thought him wicked and condemned him when they believed he was one of Mosley's fascists.

'Jenny,' he said now as she emerged into the cool air of early March 1937 and moved towards her, taking her arm and kissing her cheek. 'You look beautiful. You got my note? I'm home for ten days now and I hope to take you to the theatre and to dinner – to make up for all the time we spend apart.'

'It's lovely to see you, Chris,' Jenny said and smiled. While he was away, she sometimes thought it would be better to break it off with him and leave herself free to find someone else, yet when he was here her heart beat faster and she longed to be held in his arms and kissed. 'Lily is making a special dinner this evening. She'll share it with us and then go into work. She's on from nine until eight in the morning and then she has tomorrow off.'

'Your sister is a wonderful cook,' Chris said. 'And kind to go to so much trouble. We must take her somewhere nice and spoil her one day, Jenny.'

'What about Sunday?' Jenny said. 'We're both off then and we could go for a drive into the country and have lunch or something.'

'Good idea! I have ten days furlough so I can do pretty much as I like until I have to report back.'

'Is it safe for you to be back in London?' Jenny asked as Chris held open the door of his little sports car. It was a different car, she noticed, not new but not the one he'd driven when he was a member of Mosley's Blackshirts.

'I suppose there's a possibility that I might be noticed,' Chris admitted with a frown. 'However, the way things are going, our unpleasant fascist friends may all find themselves in a safe place before too long.'

'What do you mean?' Jenny asked, puzzled. The fascist group had been quieter recently, but they certainly hadn't gone away.

'I'm not at liberty to say anything yet,' Chris said, 'but things are moving in a certain direction, Jenny. We've got an idea what Hitler is after but as yet he hasn't crossed the line.'

Jenny stared at him, shivers running down her spine. Perhaps because she was aware that Chris was not just a soldier and was working in military intelligence, she was more aware of Hitler than others in Britain who just thought of him as a foreign dictator showing his muscles in Europe. Chris didn't tell her much because he couldn't, but she'd discussed the situation with Lily and they both thought that the British Government believed Germany was gearing up for another war. After the last one, that was a shocking and fearful thought. A lot of people spoke out against the idea, saying that

Hitler could be trusted when he talked of peace and wanting to be England's friend, but Lily was scathing about anyone who dared to say it in her hearing.

'He is dangerous – a poisonous snake,' she'd told Jenny. 'The Germans can't forgive what happened in the last war. They were humiliated when they lost so Hitler wants revenge and he'll try for it when he's ready, mark my words.' She'd said it in front of Chris once and he hadn't disagreed though he hadn't voiced an opinion.

'Don't let's talk about horrid things,' Jenny said now. 'I just want to enjoy having you home, Chris. I've got a few days due to me and Sister says I can start them on Saturday.'

'That is wonderful, Jenny. We might drive down to the country and stay with my aunt for a few days. I know she would love to meet you and I'd like you to see where I grew up.'

Jenny's heart started to race. She looked at him and felt a lift of excitement. 'I should love that,' she said. 'It will be wonderful having you to myself for a while.'

'Yes, we'll have time to really get to know each other,' Chris said and smiled, though his eyes were safely on the road as he negotiated the busy traffic. 'I didn't know if you would get time off but now, I can ring Aunt Susan and let her know.'

Sarah met Kathy as they were both leaving for the evening. It was easy to see that Kathy was bubbling over with her news and Sarah knew instinctively what it would be. As the girl lifted her left hand, she saw the small diamond-and-sapphire three-stone ring and smiled.

'I see congratulations are in order, Kathy.'

'Yes. Mum is delighted,' Kathy said and looked as if she'd lit up inside.

'I can see you're happy,' Sarah said. 'So, when is the wedding to be?'

'At the end of August. I'll be eighteen then and Mum says it's a good age to get married. Matron says we can both take two weeks off then and it will give us time for the wedding *and* a honeymoon – and then Bert is going to move in with us.'

So, Kathy wasn't even to have her own home. She would begin her married life at home, under her mother's eye. No wonder Mrs Saunders was happy about the wedding. She was getting exactly what she wanted – gaining a man about the house rather than losing a daughter.

Sarah wasn't sure why that should make her feel uneasy for the young girl. She herself wouldn't mind living with her mother, but Sarah's mother was very different from Mrs Saunders. She'd told Sarah that if she and Steve got married they should find their own home and not to worry over her; she was perfectly happy looking after her young visitor and was looking forward to the time when Charlie Howes moved in as a permanent lodger.

After saying goodbye to Kathy, Sarah decided to get off her bus earlier than usual and walk home past Forrest's corner shop. She wasn't sure why she'd been thinking about the old man, except that she knew Steve was worried about him and she and her mother had been thinking of ways they might help the elderly man.

She got off three stops early and walked back to the shop, hesitating before going inside. A young man was behind the counter and she recognised him as Mr Forrest's grandson.

'Good evening,' she said and smiled. 'I wanted to ask how Mr Forrest is, Sergeant.'

'He's a little better thank you,' he replied and nodded to her. 'You're Nurse Cartwright – Steve's young lady.'

'Yes, I am.' Sarah offered her hand and he took it, his grip firm and strong. 'My mother asked me to tell you that she wouldn't mind taking care of the shop for a few hours each day when you have to go back to work. She couldn't do the whole day, but if four hours in the morning or the afternoon would help, she doesn't mind which.'

His face lit up. 'That's very kind of Mrs Cartwright,' he said. 'We've had several offers of help and I think we could share the task out between three or four of you. Sister Jean Norton says she's willing to come in on a Saturday morning . . .' He shook his head. 'I'm amazed at the way people have come forward to help Grandfather. I've got another couple of days and then it's back to my unit. My mother is going to organise the rota so I'll tell her to pop round and have a word with your mother, Nurse Sarah.'

'I'll tell her to expect Mrs Forrest,' Sarah agreed. 'I suppose you don't know who did this?'

'It's a good thing I don't,' Sergeant Forrest growled. 'I might have broken the little blighter's neck.' He gave a rueful chuckle, then, 'With all the kindness my family has been shown, the anger has gone. Grandfather lost a few pounds but I've replaced the stock out of my savings and he'll never know the difference.'

'I'm glad Mr Forrest has such good friends and a

loving family,' Sarah said. 'Well, I'd better get home – nice to have met you, sergeant.'

'Same here, nurse,' he replied and winked. 'Tell Steve from me, he's a lucky chap.'

Sarah shook her head and laughed. She walked quickly home. You would think it was still winter even though they were supposed to be heading for spring, but March winds could be bitter. She passed a gang of four lads as she reached the end of the street; the elder of the four was smoking, though he wasn't much more than fourteen or fifteen at most. Sarah wondered where he got the money. She frowned, sensing that their eyes followed her as she walked up the street and she tightened her hand on the strap of the bag she wore across her shoulder.

The sudden tug told her she'd been wise to be aware and she held on to her bag, whirling round to look at the boy who had tried to snatch it. He was the smallest of the four and as Sarah glared at him, he took to his heels and ran off down the street. The other members of the gang stared at her, but then a burly man crossed the street towards them and they suddenly walked off in the opposite direction.

'Did one of those lads try to steal your bag?' the man asked, glaring at Sarah as if she'd done something unforgivable.

'One of them tried,' she replied. 'He ran off when he discovered I was up to his tricks.'

'The little buggers need a good thrashing,' the man said. 'I know their fathers – worthless trash the lot of 'em. I'd avoid this area in the evenings if I were you, miss.' He looked her up and down. 'I can see yer a nurse – from the Rosie, I'd say. Yer looked after my Betty when she was bad. I wouldn't see yer done down.'

'Thank you,' Sarah said. 'I just wanted to speak to Sergeant Forrest.'

'Aye, that was a bad business. I reckon it was that lot . . .' He jerked his head in the direction the gang had taken. 'Call theirselves some fanciful name and think they're up for anythin'. They should put them in the army cadets and sort the little buggers out!'

He nodded to her and walked off. Sarah smiled to herself. She knew that Steve blamed a gang of youths for the break-in at Forrest's and for various other petty crimes in the area, but knowing in your guts and proving it was a different matter. Having seen the lads in question, Sarah thought Steve was right to suspect them. They would have had her bag if she hadn't been aware of them staring at her.

'Make sure you tell Steve about the attempt to take your bag,' Sarah's mother said when she told her. 'I'll be careful not to carry anything they can grab when I'm down that way. It's a disgrace that folk can't walk the street in safety.'

'Yes, I think most of the residents are of the same opinion,' Sarah said. 'Anyway, Mrs Forrest will visit and arrange your hours, Mum. It will give you something to do when Charlie goes home next week.'

'Bless him, I shall miss him,' Mrs Cartwright said and smiled. 'Not that he's been under my feet much. He goes down to the shipyard first thing and I don't see him until nearly four when he's back askin' if there's any jobs I need doin'. He's a lovely lad, Sarah.'

'Yes, I'm fond of Charlie too,' Sarah agreed. Charlie had grown a couple of inches since living with his aunt and eating better meals. She sighed. 'I wish poor Ned had as good prospects.'

'Is the lad gettin' no better?' her mother said with a look of sympathy. 'Poor little lad, it's a rotten shame . . .'

Sarah sat down at the kitchen table, sipping the hot sweet tea her mother had poured for them both. 'Dr Mitchell says he hopes the diet will control the condition but I don't think it has changed much yet.'

'Poor little lad,' Mrs Cartwright said. 'Why should a child have to suffer that way, Sarah? He's had no life at all.'

'Working on the children's ward, I think that lots of times,' Sarah said. 'It's hard enough seeing an adult suffer pain and sickness, but children?' She shook her head and her mother touched her hand in sympathy.

'I couldn't do your job, Sarah love. I should break my heart over the poor little mites.'

'He can't go home even if the diet works,' Sarah told her mother, 'so – so I said we would have him until something permanent is arranged, if that's all right with you?'

'Of course, we will!' Mrs Cartwright smiled at her. 'You never have to ask you know that – and Lady Rosalie has me on her list.'

'Yes, I do know, that, Mum. I'm so lucky . . .'

'We both are, love.'

They held hands over the table, smiling in content at their mutual affection.

'Is Steve coming this evening?' Mrs Cartwright asked

as she released her daughter's hand and got up to see to their meal.

'No, I think he's at that club tonight,' Sarah said. 'I don't mind having a night in with you and Charlie. I've got an Ethel M. Dell novel I want to read so I'll wash my hair and read while it dries by the fire.'

Mrs Cartwright nodded. Charlie had come in from the back yard. He was carrying a bucket of coal and wood, which he placed beside the kitchen range.

'Watcha, Sarah,' he said cheerfully. 'Is there anythin' more, Mum?'

He'd fallen into the habit of calling Mrs Cartwright Mum and she liked it, just as she enjoyed having the lad around the house. Sarah had wondered once what her mother would do when she married, but she knew now that Mum would find a life for herself and be busy and happy.

'Have you enjoyed your stay, Charlie?' she asked and he grinned.

'Yeah, not 'alf,' he said. 'Mum says I can come back fer Easter – if you don't mind, Sarah?'

'I shall be pleased to see you anytime,' Sarah replied. 'And if Maisie wants to come with you, she can.'

'Yeah, I know . . .' Charlie shifted a bit in his seat. 'Maisie likes bein' with our auntie. She makes a fuss of her and she's doin' ballet dancin' now.' The look of disgust in his eyes told them what he thought of such pastimes.

Sarah laughed and her mother smiled and ruffled his hair as she passed him a plate of scrambled egg on toast with grilled tomatoes. Charlie thanked her and wolfed his supper down. Sarah ate hers at a slower rate but with the same enjoyment. Her mother's eggs were light and fluffy and the tomatoes were cooked to soft perfection.

'That was lovely, Mum,' she said. 'The kitchen sent up scrambled eggs for the children's lunch today but it didn't look or taste, like this.'

'It would spoil in the warming dish,' Mrs Cartwright said in her practical tone. 'It's much easier to cook for us three than all your patients, Sarah. I'm sure they try their best.'

She took her purse from her bag and opened it, taking out a picture cut from a newspaper to show her mother. 'Have you seen one of these, Mum?' She showed her the image of a shiny new coin with twelve sides and King George VI's head on the reverse. 'It is the new threepenny bit for when the new king is crowned.'

'No, I hadn't seen one,' Mrs Cartwright said looking at it with interest. 'They aren't about yet, are they?'

'Not yet, but they will be once the King is officially crowned.'

The previous December the King of England had given up the throne to marry an American divorcee, Wallis Simpson, and rocked the stability of the nation and the monarchy. His brother, the shy Prince Albert, was to be crowned in place of Edward, who was now thought by most to have let the nation down. Prince Albert would become King George VI of England and King Edward VIII was now an exile in France.

'I'm looking forward to the coronation in May,' Mrs Cartwright said. 'I shall go down the Mall and see as much as I can. I want to see the new queen and those lovely little girls of hers – Princess Elizabeth and Princess Margaret Rose.'

'I bet it feels strange to them, having to leave their home and go to live in the palace,' Sarah said. 'We don't talk about it much any of us – I think it shocked us all so much when King Edward abdicated and we didn't know what to think.'

'Well, I reckon we'll be better off with a family man as king,' Mrs Cartwright said. 'The last one was a playboy, if you ask me – he shouldn't have been mixing with the likes of her.'

Sarah laughed. Like most of the women of Britain Mrs Cartwright blamed Wallis Simpson for the abdication. She was, in many a woman's mind, a scarlet woman and the downfall of a king, though perhaps that was unfair because no one could control falling in love. Sarah was more inclined to be sympathetic towards the couple. If the ex-king had fallen deeply in love with a woman his people and government thought was unsuitable, he had only two choices: give her up or abdicate. He'd chosen to give up his throne for love and Sarah thought there was something sad about the whole thing.

'You'll get a day off for the coronation, Charlie,' Sarah said deciding to concentrate on the positive aspects. 'Ask your aunt to bring you and Maisie up to London to see it all.'

Charlie considered the idea and then shook his head. 'I reckon there'll be stuff goin' on where we live. The schools are doin' things and there's a party with food and a souvenir for all the kids.'

Sarah nodded and smiled. The coronation would be a celebration all over the country. The new king and queen were winning hearts, and the princesses were a delight to everyone. A picture of them was sure to sell newspapers as the people came to know their new monarch.

'We should celebrate too,' Sarah said and smiled at her mother. 'I'll ask around if there's going to be a street party here.'

'I know the answer to that,' her mother said. 'We're havin' a street party the Sunday after so we can go up the Mall on the day.'

'That won't be quite the same,' Sarah protested.

'No,' Sarah's mother agreed, 'but that's what I've been told.'

'That doesn't stop us havin' our own special party,' Sarah said. 'I'll ask Steve and we'll go somewhere special that night!'

# CHAPTER 9

Cassie watched as she saw the boy bend to lay a single tulip on one of the graves in the churchyard. She'd followed him here, laughing to herself as he looked over his shoulder once or twice as if he sensed her following – but he never managed to spot her. All at once her smile faded because suddenly Jamie looked so sad. Even as she thought about talking to him, he dashed a tear from his cheek.

Cassie had wanted to speak to him for weeks now but she was afraid he would try to grab her or hit her like those bullies did – and yet he was so sad that she thought perhaps she might risk it. Just as she started to move forward, a woman walked up to him. She was carrying a small bunch of flowers and she placed them on the grave next to the wooden cross that marked it.

'I thought I'd bring yer mum a few flowers, lad,' she said and touched his arm in sympathy. 'Yer don't mind, do yer?'

'No . . .' Jamie brushed his face swiping away the tears. 'No one ever give her flowers when she were alive. Why did she 'ave ter die, Marth?'

'I dare say it were an accident,' Marth said. 'Yer father was always a violent man, lad, but he were fond of her once – it were that damned war that changed 'im. They sent a lot of our lads back with damaged bodies but some of them were damaged in their minds and they couldn't settle – yer ma used ter get on ter 'im at times and maybe that's why 'e hit 'er so 'ard.'

Jamie nodded. Marth had her arm about his shoulders as she led him away and, as Cassie watched, her cheeks were wet with tears. So, Jamie had lost his mother too. She crept out from behind the large gravestone after they'd left and went to look at the writing on the simple wooden cross. *Lizzie Martin – Gone too soon.* That was all it said, apart from some numbers.

Cassie swallowed hard. Jamie's mother was buried here and he came to put a flower on her grave. Cassie didn't know where *her* mummy was buried – but she could bring a flower for Jamie's mother sometimes. She could take one from the garden of her house . . .

A smile touched her lips. Her stomach rumbled and she smiled, feeling the sixpence in her pocket. She would buy some of the biscuits she liked with the money she had left over from selling that hand mirror with the shiny brown back. The man who'd bought it said it was tortoiseshell. Cassie hadn't liked it much, she preferred the lovely silver one she played with every day.

Yes, she would buy some of her favourite biscuits and then she would pick some flowers for Jamie's mum . . .

Jamie glanced at the man selling newspapers from a stand at the bottom of Button Street. He was calling out the headlines, inviting people to buy his papers. It was now the end of April 1937 and most papers were filled with little else but the coming coronation on 12 May. Even the newspaper headlines that the missing heiress had been found dead, her body caught in reed beds in the river, were hardly noticed by those who scanned the columns for pictures of the royal family. At Jamie's school they'd done various projects in honour of the occasion and made their own decorations. The children would get the day itself off and some of the teachers had arranged to take their class down the Mall to get a better view of the parade, the king and his family. Every street was sporting different coloured flags as the excitement mounted.

Though much of the news passed Jamie by, because Marth had told him, he was aware that in Spain the streets of Guernica had been a wall of flame when Hitler sent his bombers to aid Franco. Death had rained down on a crowded market square and people who only read of it later shuddered at the newsreel horror of war from the air. In France, the liner *Normandie* had won the Blue Ribbon, taking it from the *Queen Mary* for the fastest eastbound crossing. In America a new Rodgers and Hart musical, *Babes in Arms*, had opened on 14 April, and in Britain the splendid aircraft carrier, *Ark Royal*, had launched the day before, on the thirteenth. Marth read her paper religiously and was a mine of information. And all the while the women of the East End streets gossiped outside their terraced houses and talked of little else but the King's coronation and how lovely the little princesses would look in their robes.

Jamie continued to go to school every weekday and to the boxing club every night. Marth no longer asked him what he wanted to do or where he was going. She knew that he was learning to defend himself against bullies and she told her friends that he looked stronger and fitter for all the exercise he was getting.

'Little mite he was when he first came to me,' she said. 'He ain't much bigger now, but he eats like a horse and he looks the picture of health.' Marth was rather proud that the boy seemed to be thriving in her care and put some of it down to her own good cooking – far better than he'd got in his own home!

The main difference in Jamie was actually his confidence. It was there in his stride and the way he held himself. He knew that he could throw most of the lads at the club in his group and that only the biggest and strongest of them could put him down. Steve had told him that if he continued to work as hard as he'd been doing, he would be put forward for the local championships by the summer.

'You could go a long way in the sport,' he'd told Jamie. 'You don't look as if you could put a man on his back but I wouldn't mind betting you will soon – if you can't already. Everyone is amazed at how fast you've picked it up, lad.' He'd looked at him with pride and admiration.

Jamie always felt guilty when the police constable praised him and talked of putting him forward for the under-eighteen championships if he continued to improve. What would Steve say if he knew what Jamie had done at Mr Forrest's shop? He wouldn't like him if he guessed he was a thief.

Jamie knew that Mr Forrest had now recovered and returned to his corner shop. While he was in hospital a team of local volunteers had continued to open the doors to customers and his daughter had managed to oversee it, despite being so busy herself. Jamie wished he could do something too. What he'd done was too awful to be forgiven, he understood that, but if there was a way of making up for what he'd stolen he would do it. Had he been given any of the pinched goods he would have returned them, but he'd never been offered anything, and it seemed as if the gang were staying clear of him. He walked back from the club several nights a week on his own, but they hadn't approached him.

His confidence had gained each night he got home safely and so, when he saw three of the gang loitering at the end of his street that night, he didn't hesitate or run away as he might have five weeks earlier. The jeers and laughter started as he got closer.

''Ere he comes,' Leo said loudly. 'Cocky little bugger now, ain't he?'

Jamie ignored him. Steve had taught them not to get involved in an argument. 'If anyone tries to hinder you, just ask them to stand aside and let you walk on. If they threaten you, say they should walk away – but when they come at you, don't be afraid to use the self-defence tactics you've been taught,' Steve had instructed the boys at the club.

'I'd like to go past,' Jamie said as he saw the way they'd spread across the path in a deliberately menacing manner. 'Please stand aside . . .'

'Bloody 'ell! Listen to the little toad,' Leo sneered.

'Just 'cos he goes to that bloody copper's club 'e thinks he's a gent.'

Jamie ignored him and decided to walk out into the road to avoid the confrontation. Leo lurched towards him and the flash of silver in his hand warned of a knife. Instinct took over and Jamie reached for the bully's wrist, gave it a swift and powerful jerk and he had the satisfaction of seeing the weapon go skittering across the road in front of him. Jamie kicked it into the drain and it slithered between the bars and fell into the water with a little plop.

'You little bugger!' Leo swore furiously, seeming dazed and uncertain what had happened to him. One of his companions made a lunge at Jamie and because he was leaning out and therefore off balance, it made it easy for Jamie to take hold of his arm and put him on his back with a thump.

The third member of the gang stared at Jamie but made no move towards him, his mouth open in astonishment. 'How did you do that?'

'I advise you to leave and don't make me do the same to you,' Jamie said.

Jamie walked on by but as he did, Leo seemed to come out of his daze and yelled, 'Get the bugger!'

Two of them came at him at once and Jamie knew it was more than he could handle. The element of surprise had been with him for a start, but now they were wary and closed in from both sides, the third member lingering in the rear, nervous yet ready to do whatever Leo wanted once Jamie was down. As they closed on him, Jamie grabbed Leo's jacket and tried to throw him, but his companion struck him from behind and he went down on his knees. He saw another knife flash before his eyes and prepared for the worst, then he heard a shout from behind him and suddenly Leo was on his back, the second hooligan was bent double, while the third was racing away as fast as his legs would take him.

Jamie straightened up and looked at his saviour. He grinned with delight when he saw the face of his elder brother. 'Arch! Oh, Arch, it's good to 'ave yer back!'

'Not a minute too soon by the looks of it.' Arch glared at Leo, who was struggling to his feet. 'You watch what yer doin', lowlife. Attack my brother again and I'll break your neck!'

'The little bastard attacked us – kicked my knife down the drain,' Leo muttered. 'You watch yer back, Arch – I'll get yer both fer this, see if I don't!'

The second boy was now on his feet and the two gang members slouched off, throwing resentful looks at the brothers. Arch touched his brother's arm, looking at him in concern.

'Why did yer get mixed up with that lot?'

'You weren't 'ere,' Jamie said. 'They picked on me – made me do stuff I didn't want ter do, so I learned how to defend myself. I disarmed Leo and put that other one down but then they came at me together.'

'What kind of stuff?' Arch said frowning. 'I came home soon as I heard what Pa did – and I'm back for good, now, Jamie. They won't touch yer again, 'cos they know I'd make them pay.'

'Yeah, well I'm gettin' stronger; soon I'll be able to take two of 'em together,' Jamie said. 'You didn't see what I did to them.'

'Been down the club, 'ave yer?' Arch grinned at him. 'Did Rich take yer? He told me about Ma when I sent him a card wiv me address. So, I came back – I had a job down there but by the time I paid me lodgings I weren't much better off. I'll get a job here, now I've got a good reference.'

'What 'ave yer been doin', Arch?'

'Travelling all over. I was on the coast fer a while and then, 'cos I'd turned eighteen, I got a better job as a doorman fer a nightclub in Birmingham,' Arch said. 'It was all right. The boss offered me more money to stay but I told 'im I had ter come 'ome fer me family, so he give me a reference for a friend of his. I've just come back from seein' Mr Morris and he's give me a job. It's only a pound a week chuckin' out the rowdies, but we can find a couple of rooms some-where for that.'

'Marth would let us stay. You could pay her some rent – she's had me fer nothing.'

Arch nodded. 'I went to thank her and she told me where yer were. I thought I'd walk yer 'ome – and that's what I will do when I ain't working, Jamie. I don't start until ten at night. Yer home by nine, ain't yer?'

Jamie nodded. 'Yeah, Marth wants me in before that, because she has to get up early – and I get two hours training every night.'

'Rich told me yer doin' well.' He grinned and tousled his brother's hair. 'We'll make a fighter of yer yet – but stay clear of that gang. Yer don't want anythin' to do with that sort.'

Jamie nodded, swallowing hard and feeling sick. If Rich knew what he'd done he would be ashamed. He would give Jamie a good slapping and he deserved it. A part of him longed to confess but he was too scared.

It was when Jamie got home from school the next afternoon that his brother told him his news. Arch was pleased as punch and Marth was congratulating him on being clever.

'You're the sort what gets on,' she told him. 'I'm not surprised you've got two good jobs.'

'I thought you were goin' ter be a doorman?'

'I am – from ten o'clock at night,' Arch said. 'But I've been to see Mr Forrest. Ma always said he was a lovely bloke and she was right. I'm goin' ter look after his shop and help him keep things right, do the stuff he can't manage. His grandson is back with the army now and Mr Forrest opens ten until five now, but he's finding it a bit too much so he said if I could go in for a few hours he'd pay me six shillings. I told him I'd go from eleven until four every day, which means he only has to be in the shop for two hours. I go to bed from six until ten in the mornin' and I can walk you home before I go to work at night.'

'You won't 'ave much time fer yerself, Arch.'

'I'm not bothered about that fer the moment,' Arch said and grinned. 'I can save money, Jamie, and that means we'll be able to 'ave our own 'ome again one day. I've sorted through Ma's stuff – most of what was any good is in Marth's shed as you know. The landlord wouldn't let me take over the house, even though I offered to pay what Ma owed at a shillin' a week. He says I'm too young and we're all right wiv Marth for the moment.'

113

Jamie nodded his agreement. He'd known the landlord was angry because he was owed rent and when he'd threatened to take all Ma's furniture, Marth had cleared the best and let him take the rest for his rent, but he'd complained that it was short by six shillings. If it wasn't for the kindness of their neighbour, both brothers would be out on the street with nowhere to live.

Now Arch was back, Jamie knew his life would improve. His one regret was what he'd done to Mr Forrest and he wished he could help him out. He was glad Arch had a job with the grocer and thought that, if he got the chance, he would pay back what he'd taken. He'd heard on the street that the value of the stolen goods had been almost five pounds. It was a huge sum to a boy who had never had more than a penny in pocket money, but one day he would start to earn a wage and he would remember the debt and pay it.

At the club that night, Steve told the boys that they were going to have a special contest to celebrate the coronation of George VI. There would be bouts between the members of his club and some other clubs from various parts of London. He told them that the best candidates would be chosen from each group and that the prize for the winner was a silver cup and ten shillings.

A silver cup and ten shillings! It seemed a lot of money to Jamie. He knew that it wasn't enough to pay back what he'd stolen, but it would be a start – of course, to win that money he would need to overcome all-comers and it wasn't likely he could.

'I've asked Steve to put me forward in my age group,' Arch told him as they walked home one night. 'I'm out of practice a bit but you can 'elp me get back into it, can't yer?'

'Yeah, 'course I will,' Jamie said. He knew that if he volunteered to help Arch win he wouldn't get picked for the contest, because you needed to be single-minded to win. So, when Steve asked if he'd like to be put forward, he said that he was helping his brother to train. Steve nodded and smiled.

'Well, that's noble of you, Jamie. I think you might have won your own group but you can't do both. Never mind, we still have the regional championships later in the year. It will give you longer to train and become stronger and better – and perhaps you were a little young for your first competition.'

Jamie kept smiling despite his disappointment. He was thrilled to have his brother home and thought it worth the sacrifice to help Arch win his group. They practised at the club when Arch had time and in Marth's garden, also in their bedroom until she complained about the noise upsetting the neighbours.

By the time 11 May arrived, Arch was back to his old strengths and Jamie knew there was no one at the club to beat him. There might be someone from away who was bigger or stronger, but Jamie was secretly sure that his brother could put anyone down in a fair fight.

Of the Brothers of the Red they had seen nothing. As far as Jamie was concerned, they seemed to have disappeared and he knew that they were afraid to meet Arch and him together. It was much easier to bully all those boys who were terrified of them and stay away from lads who fought back.

'I'll get yer breakfast in the mornin',' Marth told

them that evening, 'but then yer on yer own for the rest of the day. I'm off up the Mall first thing and I'm not comin' back until I've seen all the royal family.'

Marth was leaving very early with other women from the area on a special bus hired to take them as close to the Mall as they could get; after that they would be on their own and have to fight for a place in the crowds waiting to watch the procession and see the family pass by.

Marth had made thick cheese sandwiches for them the night before and wrapped them in greaseproof paper and a damp teacloth to keep them fresh. Arch made a pot of tea and they munched the doorsteps of bread, packed with cheese and pickle they added themselves.

'I'll be at Mr Forrest's shop until four,' Arch said. 'When I get back, we'll 'ave a pie and chips from the shop and go to the venue together. I've got the night off from me other job so I can take part in the contest.'

'Did Mr Morris mind you havin' a night off?' Jamie asked.

'Nah, he was pleased. He said if I win a cup, he'll display it in the club – and he says he'll pay me an extra five bob a week. He says if I'm a champion at the sport it will give his club a bit of class!' Arch laughed. 'It will be great if I win the judo and Rich wins the boxing, won't it?'

'Yes, it will.' Jamie grinned, excited by the thought of the two people he cared about doing well that evening.

Luckily, there was no school as such that day. Some of the kids were being taken up to the Mall to watch the procession and join in the fun. Jamie hadn't been asked on the trip, because he hadn't brought in the two

116

shillings needed to pay for his fare and a meal. Instead, he was invited to the games and free meal provided at his school.

The sky was a bit dull and overcast but the games went without a hitch and Jamie won a packet of sweets in the races for coming in first. He was third in the high jump and fourth in the long jump, and he enjoyed his morning and the sandwiches and sausage rolls set out in the assembly hall. He had a drink of orange squash and a piece of jam sponge and was given a little badge with a picture of the king on it to take home.

It was all over by three and Jamie set out for home. He had a feeling that he was being watched, but each time he glanced back the street was empty and he told himself to stop being a coward and think about that evening.

Arch got home at four thirty. He'd brought the promised treat, which they ate with a cup of tea and then washed up their cups and plates so it was tidy when Marth came home.

'We don't want her throwin' us out,' Arch said with a wink. 'I ain't ready to get our own place yet – but perhaps after tonight I might be.'

Jamie nodded. If Arch won ten shillings and got a rise at work, he could afford to rent a house similar to Marth's and Jamie knew that his brother was set on having his own home again. Marth was good to them, but it wasn't the same as having their own place.

The venue that night was packed out with those who had come to watch and those who would take part. Jamie was allowed to go backstage to the dressing rooms with his brother and watch him get ready. Afterwards, Steve sent him to sit with some of the other lads who were watching the contests and not taking part in the fights.

Jamie cheered the members of his club as they took part in their individual contests. Contestants from several clubs had come to enter the lists and the lads Jamie knew had mixed success. The first under-fifteen bout was won by a lad that he'd never seen before. Jamie watched intently. He thought he might have beaten him, but Sidney didn't even score one fall and looked shamed when he slunk off behind the curtains.

The next bout was won by a boy Jamie had fought with several times at the club. The third bout was Arch against a tall, strong youth Jamie had never seen before – and the first fall went to him almost immediately. Arch had been caught by a foot behind him, almost as if he hadn't been ready. Jamie's heart sank, even as he roared at his brother to get up and win. It would be awful if Arch was beaten.

He need not have worried because Arch took the next two falls easily and grinned as he walked off with his prize. Jamie cheered like mad as Arch was presented with ten shilling and a silver cup. A little later, the brothers watched together as Rich won his boxing match. They cheered and cheered as he was presented with a special belt to show he was the winner.

'He'll have to give the belt back next year,' Arch told his brother as they joined Rich afterwards, 'but we can keep the cup.'

'Well, young Jamie,' Rich said cheerfully as they walked home together later, 'it was a good day for us

– just a pity you didn't get a chance to show what *you* can do.'

'Steve says he'll give me a chance later in the year,' Jamie told him and grinned. 'And I helped Arch practise.'

'I wondered how he got so good!' Rich said and gave Arch a playful punch in the side. He was smiling broadly as he added, 'I'll bet even His Majesty hasn't enjoyed himself more than us today.'

Jamie was smiling at their jokes when he sensed that someone was behind them. He gave a warning shout just as five black shapes came at them out of the darkness. It was five against three but Arch and Rich fought back viciously and two of the attackers went down immediately. Jamie was fighting one of them and, to his delight, he managed to get the knife he was being threatened with and throw it as far as he could. He followed that move with one he'd seen that evening, putting his foot behind his opponent and kicking his leg out from under him. It brought the lad crashing down and he gave a yelp of pain and cried out that he gave in.

'Don't hurt me no more!'

'Clear orf then,' Jamie said. 'Attack us again and I'll break yer neck!'

The lad scrambled to his feet and went limping off as fast as he could hobble away. Three others were lying on the ground and only Leo was still standing. Even as Jamie was about to speak, Leo sprang at Rich and drove a knife into his side. Arch went for him immediately and Jamie grabbed for his wrist, twisting it and forcing the knife to drop from Leo's hand and into the gutter. Jamie kicked it into the drain so that no one could grab it again, and then saw that Leo had broken free and was running away as fast as he could. Arch had dropped his silver cup during the fight and one of the other thugs had snatched it up and run off with it. Neither of the Martin brothers gave it a thought because Rich was bent over double, holding his side to try and staunch the blood that was pouring out of the deep gash.

Arch took his jacket off and pressed it to the wound. He put his arm round his friend, glancing across at Jamie. 'We 'ave ter get him to the Rosie, Jamie. Help me get him as far as we can 'e needs 'elp . . .'

Afterwards, Jamie could never recall much of that nightmare journey to the Lady Rosalie Infirmary. He knew they had almost reached the end of the street when a police constable came and took charge. Within minutes, men were there carrying Rich into the Rosie and the Martin brothers followed. Nurses rushed to assist Rich and eventually one came to them and looked them over.

'It's a good thing you brought him straight here,' Nurse Jenny Brown told them approvingly. 'That was good thinking, lads. Don't you worry, we'll look after your friend – and you.'

Bruises were tended and a small cut on Arch's hand, but otherwise they were unharmed. When they'd been given hot sweet tea for the shock, the police constable asked them what had happened.

Arch told the police how they'd been happy, celebrating their wins at the club together and walking home, when they were attacked from behind.

'Did you get a good look at them?' the constable asked.

'Yes, I know who they are,' Arch said. 'They attacked my brother a week or two back and they made threats – there were five of them tonight. One is Leo Ruffard but they call themselves the Brothers of the Red.'

'Are you certain of their identities?'

'Yes.' Jamie added his voice to his brother's. 'It's true, sir. I don't know all their names – but Leo Ruffard is the leader and he's the one that stabbed Rich. Someone else took the silver cup.'

'The cup doesn't matter – it is only silver plate,' Arch said, looking upset. 'It's Rich that matters. If – if he dies it's murder.'

'Yes, it certainly is,' the officer said. 'Thank you for giving us such clear information, sir – and your brother for backing it up. It's what we need to get a conviction.'

'Yes,' Arch said and looked angry. 'I wouldn't normally snitch on anyone – but Rich is my best friend and I won't let the devil that knifed him get away with it.'

'We'll pick them up immediately – and the ringleader will go to prison for a long while; I give you my word.'

Cassie shadowed the brothers from a distance. She was more wary now that Jamie's brother was with him because she didn't trust grown-ups because they wanted to shut her away and Jamie looked miserable again. Cassie would have liked to speak to him and tell him she understood what it was like to be alone and miserable, but she didn't dare to go near him when his brother was there.

She scratched her head. It itched so much and she felt the tangles where her hair had matted and got greasy and dirty. She ought to wash it but the only water in her house was cold and she didn't like the feel of cold water on her skin and head. Sometimes, she tried to brush the tangles out, but it hurt and there was no one to do it for her.

'Mummy . . .' she whispered turning away, back into the shadows. 'Mummy . . . where are you? Why don't you come for me . . . ?'

# CHAPTER 10

'It's a damned shame, that's what it is,' Bert Rush said to Kathy that morning as they sat talking over their coffee. 'I saw that young lad win his boxing match fair and square last night and now the poor young devil is fighting for his life.'

Kathy nodded, her eyes filled with sympathetic tears. She'd heard Matron talking about it to the doctor who had stitched the wound and knew that it was a matter of prayers and fingers crossed. The young lad had been stabbed deep in his side and it had damaged some internal organs; he would be lucky to live and it was likely that his boxing career was over before it had started.

'The men who do that sort of thing want hanging,' Kathy said vehemently. 'In fact, I should like to see them birched and then hung.'

Bert gave her an amused glance, because it wasn't often that Kathy was roused to anger like that. She was a placid girl, pleasant to know and never argumentative. 'Trouble is, they're only young lads,' he told her and reached for a ginger biscuit. 'They think it's big to carry a knife and then something like this happens and some-one's life is ruined.'

'I know that nice policeman Sarah is courting was in tears over it,' Kathy said. 'When you see it in the films, or read about it, you don't think it's real – but when people you know are affected . . .' She shook her head. 'Sarah was so upset. She was begging Steve to be careful, because he and some other officers are going to arrest the thug today and Jenny said she would like to thrash the devils that did it.'

'If they can find him,' Bert said. 'If he's got wind of the seriousness of what he's done and realises the conse-quences, he'll have scarpered. The lads they attacked could only name one of the gang – the others were just his followers, doin' what he told them.'

Kathy shook her head and then looked at the clock on the wall. We'd best get back to work, Bert. Are we still goin' to the pictures tonight?'

''Course we are, love. It's *Snow White and the Seven Dwarfs* and I know you really want to see it.'

'Oh yes, I do!' Kathy said and smiled. 'We'd better get on – first we've got all the walls to wash with disinfectant today.'

Kathy was happy as she worked that morning. She loved going out with Bert because he looked after her, bought her sweets, drinks of orange or occasionally a port and lemon, and made sure she was comfortable. He also gave her little presents, just a book or some magazines, flowers, chocolates, once a bottle of Evening in Paris perfume and another time a pretty scarf. She thought she was lucky to have a boyfriend like Bert, because he was nice-looking and he smelled freshly of soap whenever he took her anywhere. He might not have the looks of Errol Flynn or one of the other film stars she loved to watch, but he had a solid, dependable look. Her mother had told her she would go a long way before she found another man as kind and generous and so Kathy had been happy to say she would wed him. It was exciting to get married, and although she would be just eighteen, she was more than ready for what she thought of as an adventure.

They were going to move in with Kathy's mother for a while. Bert only rented and they thought it would save money living together.

'We might as well make yer mum happy,' Bert had said when asked if he'd be willing. 'One day we might get our own little house, Kathy, but just for a while I don't mind livin' with yer mum.'

Kathy didn't mind either, though a part of her wished Bert had insisted that they have their own house. Yet it didn't really matter because Kathy was going to keep on working so that they could save for the future and if Mum continued to do some of the housework and the cooking it would be easier on her for a start . . .

Jean Norton watched the nurse changing the dressing on the young lad's leg and nodded her approval. She knew that Nurse Sarah Cartwright had been upset that morning by the news her young man had given her. Jean had heard gossip on the bus as she came into work, but hadn't realised that Nurse Sarah would know the young lads involved. She felt involved herself, because she'd had the chance to take Jamie Martin in and had let it slip away. Perhaps, if he'd come to her, he wouldn't have been involved in that horrid fight that had led to his friend's near-fatal wounding.

'Are you all right to carry on, nurse?' she asked Sarah as she wheeled the dressings-trolley towards her. 'If you feel you need to sit quietly for a while, I can probably manage.'

Sarah gave her a startled look. 'Have I done something wrong, Sister?'

'No, of course not. But I understand you received news that upset you this morning.'

Sarah looked at her, hesitated, then, 'I don't know the lads involved, Sister – but Steve does. He helps to run the club they attend and he was very upset about the stabbing. It has ruined the injured lad's prospects of becoming a professional boxer. Apparently, with his injuries he would never get a licence.'

'Yes, it is very sad,' Jean said. 'I know all of the ones who were attacked, particularly the youngest Martin boy. His mother was murdered some weeks ago. The elder boy had left home and their neighbour thinks Lizzie Martin must have been struck by her husband, because she heard them arguing. We believe the police are still looking for him . . .'

'Yes, I heard about the murder – how dreadful!'

'It was awful and Jamie was very upset, as you might imagine.'

'The injury to his friend will upset him all the more then,' Sarah said. 'It is a very unfortunate business, Sister.'

'Yes,' Jean agreed. 'I shall visit the lady the boys are living with this evening and see if I can be of help but

I very much doubt there is anything I can do, other than offer sympathy and update them on Rich's progress.'

'What can anyone do in a case like this?' Sarah asked and shook her head. 'If a little money would help, we could have a collection but I'm not sure what good it would do.'

'It might help the family of the injured boy,' Jean said and smiled at her. 'Yes, they will notice the loss of his pay and they will have costs perhaps. I think it is a good idea. I will put ten shillings in to start it off. See me before I leave and I'll give it to you.'

Sarah was surprised but pleased. Sister Norton really did have a heart after all! It was nice to know that she was human and not a machine, as she'd so often seemed. Nurse Jenny had already asked what she could do, so Sarah knew she and her sister, Nurse Lily Brown, would also contribute to the fund. They were both on nights that week but she would speak to them before she went home. It was the least they could do for those young lads.

'I'll put ten shillings in – and ten for Lily,' Jenny said when Sarah spoke to her that evening. 'It's her night off but I know she'll want to do something.' She took a couple of shillings from her purse and gave it to Sarah. 'Have you asked Matron for a donation?'

'No – do you think I should?' Sarah asked doubtfully.

'Yes – go and ask now,' Jenny urged. 'Lady Rosalie is with her and she might contribute as well.'

Sarah thanked her for the advice, hesitating for a moment, because it seemed an imposition to approach matron – and yet a few extra shillings would help the injured lad and his family. She walked along the corridor to Matron's room and knocked and was told to enter. Matron and Lady Rosalie were having a cup of tea together and Matron gave Sarah a frosty stare.

'Yes, Nurse Cartwright?'

'I'm sorry to interrupt you, Matron – but I'm collecting for the young lad who was stabbed and brought in – and for his family . . .'

'Oh yes, a terrible thing,' Lady Rosalie said. 'I'm so glad you came while I was here, nurse.' She opened her expensive leather handbag and took out two one-pound notes. 'Please put this in your fund.'

'That is extremely generous of you, Rosalie,' Matron said and offered Sarah a pound note. 'I'm afraid I can't offer you as much . . .'

'Most people put a shilling, maybe two, in,' Sarah assured her with a smile. 'It is so generous of you both – and should help the family while Rich is recovering from his injury.'

'I am glad to have been of help,' Lady Rosalie said and smiled at her. 'We've just been discussing Ned's case, Nurse Cartwright, and I was telling Matron that I think your mother will be an excellent carer for him when he is well enough to leave. I can't give you permission just like that, of course. Although his mother disowned him, she might change her mind – so I am applying to have Ned made a ward of court and then we can give him into your mother's care once he's well.'

'Oh, thank you!' Sarah looked at her happily. 'Mum will be so pleased.'

'It is subject to Ned being made a ward of court,

naturally – but the courts seldom turn us down if the case is properly prepared.'

'You do such wonderful work, ma'am,' Sarah said. 'We see so many children who need help and I'm always cheered by the knowledge that you can provide them with new homes.'

'Only the lucky few,' Lady Rosalie said sadly. 'We can help the ones that come to our notice but I fear there are many who just disappear into the streets and we don't even know of them – until the police bring them in or they're found dead on a piece of waste ground.'

Sarah nodded, close to tears. 'Thank you for your donation. At least we can help *this* family.'

She left then before the tears fell. She now had eight pounds in her fund, which was a small fortune and would help Rich's family through the hard time of his convalescence – but as for the children of the streets . . . Sarah sighed. She knew there were so many of them who could expect no help at all.

As the door closed behind Sarah, she heard Lady Rosalie say, 'I told you about that child whose mother fell down the stairs and died, didn't I? The one they were going to send to an orphanage but she ran off and no one has seen anything of her since. I often wonder if she is still alive.'

'A young child alone on London's streets – she probably died of the cold, because it was just after Christmas she ran away, wasn't it? Her body may never be found or identified.'

'Yes, poor little thing,' Lady Rosalie said and sighed. 'Just one of the hundreds – no, thousands – who slip through the net every year . . .'

Sarah felt the tears slide down her cheeks. So many little children, abandoned or abused by desperate parents who could not afford to keep them. Times were hard and it was always the little ones who suffered the most . . .

## CHAPTER 11

'Do yer think he'll die, Arch?' Jamie looked at his brother in distress. It was Friday night and they'd heard nothing much about their friend since taking him to the infirmary. 'Will he be all right – able ter box again?'

'I don't know!' Arch spoke sharply, far more so than he had ever done to his brother before and Jamie flinched, because his guilty conscience told him that he deserved it. He deserved that Arch should go off again and desert him – and he would if he knew that it was all Jamie's fault that Rich was lying in a hospital bed. 'For goodness sake, Jamie, can't yer see I'm worried ter death over me mate. Go away and stop botherin' me.'

Jamie stared at him, tears of misery welling up inside him. Arch was right to blame him, because it *was* his fault. If he hadn't gone with Leo and his gang to steal from Mr Forrest that night, they would have given him a hiding and then forgotten him. The fact that he'd learned how to stand up to them and beat them had angered them and so they'd attacked him and Arch and Rich and done it with knives to punish Jamie. He'd brought the attack on them and so it was his fault if Rich's life was ruined – or if he died.

Tears spilled over as Jamie ran from the house and into the lane. Marth called to him about having his tea but he didn't listen. The misery was mounting inside him and he felt as if he wanted to die of guilt and grief. If only he could go back to that first night and not do what the gang had asked him to do; better that he should be the one to be knifed than Rich. It was his wicked secret and it was eating at him, making him feel wretched. He'd thought he would be able to make it up to old Mr Forrest one day. He would earn some money and pay him back every penny he'd stolen for the gang – but how could he make up to Rich for what he'd done to him?

The tears were running down Jamie's face and he was sobbing as he ran. The May evenings were light and it was warm. He forgot about his fear of the gang as he ran towards his school. It was closed now for the weekend but Jamie didn't know where else to go. Arch didn't want him around – and if he knew what Jamie had done, he would hate him. Pa had cleared off and Marth only tolerated them because she was a kind woman. No one truly wanted or loved him since his mother was killed . . .

There, Jamie's thoughts came to an abrupt end. He'd shut the sight of his mother lying there dead out of his mind, but now it came flooding back. He recalled lying in bed, listening to his father yelling at his mother and her cries of fear and pleas for him to stop hitting her. Jamie had heard it all but he'd been too frightened to go down and try to stop his father hurting her. He knew

132

his father would just beat him as well as his mother and so he'd stayed in bed and hidden beneath the covers, then in the morning he'd run away and stayed out all day until Sister Norton came and he'd told her his ma was battered.

But if he'd gone downstairs, he might have stopped his father killing his mother. If he'd fetched help after the house went quiet his mother might have got better.

The guilt and misery were building and building as Jamie sought a place to curl up and hide. His steps had brought him towards the junior school he attended every day and he ran through the playground until he reached the door, which was locked. The school was locked and there was no one here – nowhere to crawl in and hide. He sat on the steps and buried his head in his arms, resting them on his knees as he sobbed. No one would want him near them if they knew how wicked he was . . .

Jamie sat crying for a long time until, in the end, he was worn out by emotion. He sat looking about him, reluctant to go home and yet not knowing where to go or what to do. He was so miserable and he wished he could just go to sleep and never wake up again.

'Are yer lost?'

Jamie's head came up and he found he was looking at a girl of about his own age, but she was dirty, her hair matted and tangled, her clothes badly stained, her feet bare. She looked very thin and something about her made him put his hand in his pocket and pull out the paper twist of sweets Arch had given him two days earlier.

'Want a sweet?' he asked.

'Yes, please,' she said and sat down beside him on the step. Jamie handed her the packet and she took one and put it in her mouth. Her face lit up with pleasure. 'Thank you . . . it's lovely.'

'It's a sherbet lemon,' Jamie said. 'They're my favourite. My brother gave them to me but now he's angry with me – he doesn't like me anymore.'

'Why?'

'Because his friend is hurt bad and it's my fault.'

'Why is it your fault?'

'Because there's a gang that hates me and I stood up to them and my brother helped, so they came after us with knives. Rich was a boxing champion and now he won't be able to do it anymore . . .'

'That's bad,' she said nodding her head in understanding. 'I run away when I see the gang coming. I hide because they hurt people; they frighten me.'

'Yes, I know. I should have done the same,' Jamie said and looked at her curiously. 'What's yer name?'

'I'm Cassie,' she said. 'My mummy died and they were going to put me in a bad place so I ran away.' She sighed. 'I'm so hungry. Will you give me another sweet, please?'

'Yer can 'ave 'em all,' Jamie said and gave her the bag after extracting one to suck himself. 'You speak real proper – so why are yer dirty and why 'ave yer got holes in yer clothes and no shoes?'

'Mummy always made me speak properly. She said just because we were poor and lived in a dump, we didn't have to let down our standards.'

Jamie stared at her. 'How long is it since yer ma died?'

'I don't know . . .' A tear dripped down Cassie's cheek. 'I've lost count of the days. It must be months because it was Christmas and we had no money for presents or nice food – and then Mummy got ill, fell down the stairs and died and they took her away and made me stay in a strange place with a horrid woman who said I would be sent to Australia because I was bad – so I ran away and hid and I heard people calling me, looking for me, but I wouldn't come out until they'd all gone away. It was cold and I was hungry but it's better than going to Australia!' She screwed up her forehead. 'I don't know where that is, do you?'

Jamie shook his head. 'Not really. It's a long way, over the sea somewhere. Have yer been livin' on yer own all this time?' She nodded and Jamie was amazed, because she must have been living rough for over four months and he couldn't imagine how she had managed it.

'Yes, I found places to hide, where it's dry. It was cold at first but then I found a house where no one goes and there are all sorts of things there.' Her face lit up. 'Dressing-up things and things you can sell. I sold some things and bought food, but then they asked where I got the things and wouldn't give me any money!'

'Did you steal the stuff?' Jamie asked frowning.

'No, because it doesn't belong to anyone,' Cassie said. 'Do you want to come and see?'

Jamie looked at her uncertainly. He ought to go back to Marth's before she started to worry and yet Arch was angry with him and he didn't even know it was all Jamie's fault. Once he found out – and he would, because it was sure to come out when the police arrested

Leo – he would hate him. Leo would blame everything on Jamie, because boys like him always did, and he'd tell about the robbery, which meant Jamie would go to prison and Arch would abandon him.

'All right,' he said. 'Show me. If it doesn't belong to anyone, I'll take somethin' and sell it. I know where to go. Ma used ter send me wiv little bits so I know what he'll buy.'

'Where has that brother of yours got to?' Marth asked crossly as she looked at the portion of shepherd's pie she'd put in the oven for him. 'I can't give him this now, so it's wasted.'

'I don't know where he is,' Arch said, annoyed. 'I suppose I shall have to go and look for him.'

'You don't think that gang has got him, do you?' Marth was suddenly anxious.

'I know the devil that knifed Rich has done a bunk,' Arch told her. 'Constable Jones told me earlier that he'd been to arrest him and his grandmother was abusive but eventually she calmed down and told him he'd gone. He lives with his grandmother and she said he had taken every penny of her housekeeping – and according to her that was six shillings.'

'How far can he go on six shillings?' Marth asked.

'It depends if he buys a ticket or just a station ticket,' Arch said and explained when she looked mystified. 'Some of the kids get a penny platform ticket and then ride the trains back and forth. If they get caught, they're in trouble, but they hide in the toilets when the ticket collector comes and then leave the station with the platform ticket when they've done.'

136

'You think that rogue might have got on a train with no ticket?'

'He might, but he might have got a lift on a lorry or jumped on and off of buses. There are a lot of ways lads like that can travel without spending much.'

'Well, I never,' Marth said and shook her head. 'You don't think our Jamie has gone off like that?'

'No, he wouldn't be that daft,' Arch said. 'He's sulking because I was sharp with him. I didn't mean to be but I was that worried about Rich.'

'Of course, you were,' Marth said, 'but it's odd he hasn't come back for his tea. He must be hungry by now.'

'It's weird,' Jamie said, looking around him in amazement. The house was bigger than anything he'd ever been in before and it wasn't falling down or damp and the windows hadn't been broken, perhaps because it was set back in a garden and hidden by trees; it was, in fact, a beautiful house that must belong to someone with lots of money. The river ran along the back of the house and although there were other houses, none of them were near enough for anyone to notice a child going in and out of this one. 'Everything's just been left as if someone was going to eat their tea and then they didn't and just went off.'

'Yes, it is funny,' Cassie said and smiled. 'There was even bread that was nearly fresh and butter and honey on the table when I came. There was lots of tinned stuff in the cupboards too. I ate all that when I discovered no one lived here anymore.'

'Have you been all over the house?' Jamie asked.

'Yes, in every room,' Cassie said. 'There are clothes in one of the big cupboards upstairs – and a fur coat and lots of shoes. None of the other rooms have any clothes, just the one – and that's where I found the pearl necklace the shop wouldn't buy.'

'Yer didn't try to sell a pearl necklace? That's daft – they'd know it wasn't yours.' Jamie frowned. 'These things have to belong to someone, Cassie. It's stealing to take things, specially a pearl necklace. If it was a real one . . .'

'I'm sure it was real,' Cassie said thoughtfully. 'Mummy had a fake one and the layers of shiny stuff peeled off.'

Jamie nodded, because looking at the pictures on the walls, the books in the bookcase and the little tables, chairs, cabinets and all the rest of the furniture, he knew that whoever lived here would have a real pearl necklace.

'What did you do with the necklace?'

'I put it back in the box with the other stuff,' Cassie said. 'Come on, I'll show you.'

She led the way up the stairs, which had a rich red carpet covering them and along the landing covered in the same deep red, into a bedroom. It was such a pretty room, very feminine with frills on the curtains and bed covers and white and gilt furniture. Women's clothes lay on the bed; others were discarded on the pale cream carpet, and more hung in a large wardrobe, which had been left open. On the dressing table was a casket made of something black, painted with flowers picked out in bright colours. Jamie didn't know what that would be called, but it looked delicate and expensive – as did everything else.

138

'Did you pull all these clothes out?' Jamie asked the girl who had run to the dressing table and brought back the box. She opened it and it played a tune. He looked and saw that there was all kinds of jewellery inside. Jamie didn't know what the sparkly stuff was exactly, though he thought there might be diamonds, rubies and sapphires, but he knew instinctively it all cost a lot of money.

'You mustn't sell any of these,' he said. 'They must belong to someone, Cassie.'

'Well, no one has been here since I came,' Cassie told him and frowned. 'I only sold a shiny brown hand mirror and a brass jug but the man wouldn't buy the pearls.'

'He knew you must have stolen those,' Jamie said. 'You can't take things like this, Cassie. There must be small things that will buy you some food.'

'Oh, there's lots of stuff in the kitchen,' Cassie said. 'I just thought that money from the necklace would last for a long time.'

Jamie nodded, frowning. 'Did you make all this mess?'

'Not all of it; it was like this when I came. I tried some of the clothes on and the shoes but I put them back where I found them. I like dressing up.' She stroked her hand over a pretty pink silk dress. 'Do you think this belonged to a princess?'

'I don't know,' Jamie said. 'It's someone rich anyway. I wonder why she doesn't come here now?'

'I think she's a princess and she just ran away with a prince . . .' Cassie started twirling round with the dress held against her, singing to herself.

Jamie watched her as she collapsed back on the bed, laughing. 'How did you get in?' he asked.

'The back door was open and I just walked in,' Cassie said and smiled at him. 'I called out but no one answered so I walked through the rooms. It was cold outside and I liked it here – and I found the food in the kitchen. I didn't need to buy food for weeks, because of the tins in the pantry.' She sighed. 'Now I really need some lemonade and biscuits.'

'All this must belong to someone,' Jamie said, but Cassie was singing to herself now and it was obvious that she didn't seem to realise that she was doing wrong. 'It isn't your house and the things don't belong to you.'

'Why not? No one else wants them?' Cassie looked at him truculently. Her mood had changed. She was clearly happy to show him her treasures but she didn't want to be scolded or criticised. 'I brought you here to show you. You can't tell me what to do, Jamie! I found this place abandoned and so it belongs to *me*.'

Jamie shook his head and left her singing to herself. He went back down the stairs and found the big kitchen. Cassie had used plates and knives and forks and spoons and left them all dirty on the table. She'd scattered empty packets of biscuits and sweets on the table, as well as empty cans that had contained rice pudding or fruit.

It struck Jamie that if Cassie was using the place – and if he wanted to stay here – it should be kept right. He looked round and saw an empty log bin near the range. Picking it up, he swept the mess into it and carried it outside. There was a metal dustbin near the gate, so he carried the rubbish down and emptied it into the bin. When he returned to the kitchen, Cassie had come down and was looking round.

'Why did you do that?' she asked.

'You don't want rats in here, do you?'

She gave a little scream and looked scared. 'I hate rats! We had them in the house Mummy rented . . .' She looked at him oddly, her eyes remote as if she was looking into the past. 'She was ill and she fell all the way down . . .' For a moment her eyes seemed to glaze over. 'I didn't do anything . . .'

'Of course, you didn't,' Jamie said. 'Why would you?'

'*She* said so, the horrible woman said I pushed her!' Cassie blinked as if seeing the kitchen again. 'What did you do with all my stuff?'

'I threw it out. If you leave food bits and rubbish about the rats will come,' he warned. He thought it wrong to leave a lovely home in a mess but she clearly didn't seem to understand that, so he appealed to her fear. 'We should keep the kitchen clean and tidy if we want to live here.'

'You do it, then.' She sat down and he could hear her singing behind him.

He carried the things she'd used to the sink and put them in. The water in the tap was cold but Jamie could see a little geyser on the wall. It was gas and Marth had a similar one in her kitchen. The water at hers heated in no time for the sink. His gaze fell on a candle-stick Cassie had been using and the matches beside it.

'I wonder if the gas is turned off yet?' he said and picked up the matches. Having lit one, he moved the tap on the wall as he'd seen Marth do so many times and, to his delight, the geyser lit immediately.

'That will warm the water so we can clean these things,' Jamie said. 'You could have a wash as well, if you want.'

'Why should I?' She scowled at him. 'Who told you to start acting as if this is yours? Who said you could stay here?'

'I'll leave in the morning if you want,' Jamie said. 'But I'm going to clean this place before I do – because when the person who owns it comes back, she'll be angry to see it like this.'

Cassie stared at him. 'I'm hungry. And there isn't any food left . . .'

Jamie's fingers curled round the shilling in his pocket. Rich had given it to him before they were attacked. He hadn't spent it because of his guilt.

'I can buy us some chips,' he said. 'We'll wash these things up when I get back.'

'I'll stay here.' She looked about to cry. 'You won't come back. You'll tell on me and spoil it all!'

'No, I won't. I promise I won't,' he said. 'I'm not cross with you, Cassie, and I don't want ter go 'ome yet, but we don't want rats 'ere.'

Cassie shuddered. 'All right, I'll come too. We'll eat the chips and then tidy up when we get back.'

'We can wash yer 'air too when the water is warm.' Jamie smiled at her. 'You found a good place here, Cassie, but you need to keep it nice or you'll spoil it for yourself.'

She nodded and he thought perhaps he'd made her think things through. If someone came and found her here it would be better if she hadn't done a lot of harm. Jamie felt there was something a bit strange about

Cassie, but he liked her and wanted to help her and he wasn't ready to go home just yet. He held his hand out to her.

'Come on,' he said. 'We'll get some chips and we might get some lemonade too.'

Cassie smiled and took his hand, her mood sunny once more. She was the little girl he'd offered his sweets to again, but he knew now that her mood could change in an instant. There really was something not quite right about her, but he liked her and this was a good place to stay until he made up his mind what to do.

# CHAPTER 12

'Jamie has run off?' Jean stared at Marth in surprise and dismay. 'What on earth made him do that?'

'He was upset over what happened to Rich,' Marth said. 'I think Arch was a bit short with 'im and he went off like a bat out of 'ell, ran off without his supper and we ain't seen 'im since.'

'Have you told the police?'

'Not yet,' Marth said and frowned. 'Arch went out and searched for 'im. We thought 'e might have been attacked but 'e couldn't find anyone who had seen him.'

'So, when was this?' Jean asked.

'Friday night and it's Sunday now – that's two nights he's been missing. Arch says if Jamie doesn't come back by this evening, 'e will tell Constable Jones.'

'I should hate to think anything bad had happened to him,' Jean said and saw the look of alarm in the older woman's eyes. 'I know his brother is responsible for him – but I feel I should have done more to help.'

'Nothing much you could do,' Marth said. 'The money you nurses collected for Rich's family was a lovely idea. I hope they'll appreciate it and not let pride stand in the way.'

'It was one of the nurses who thought of it,' Jean admitted. 'I volunteered to bring it round and I thought you might like to give it to the family – coming from you they may be happier about accepting it.'

'Well, I'll offer it,' Marth said. 'If they refuse, you can give it back to the nurses.'

Jean nodded. Some people had such prickly pride and the girls at the infirmary had all given with such a good will that it would be sad if the gift was refused because of pride.

'Well, I must get off,' she said. 'Please tell Rich's mother that we all want to help in any way we can.'

Jean was thoughtful as she walked home. Why would young Jamie run away from his home because of what had happened to his brother's friend? It didn't make sense and Jean liked things to add up. She suspected a mystery but knew too few details to work it out. All she could hope was that the boy would come to his senses and return home soon.

Jean spent the rest of her Sunday preparing for work the next day. Her little cottage was already as neat as she could make it and so she pressed her uniform and cleaned the heavy lace-up shoes she wore for work. In the morning, she swept her heavy hair back into the severe style she adopted for her job as a nursing sister, glancing briefly at her appearance in the mirror. She would do. Picking up her bag, she shrugged on her jacket and went out to catch her bus, arriving at the infirmary fifteen minutes before the night nurses were

146

due to leave. It was good to get in early, because it gave her time to catch up on new developments and to ask the night sister if any of the patients had been worse during the night.

'It was a quiet night,' Sister Ruth Linton told her. 'No one new was admitted to your ward, Sister Norton – but we had a busier time on the chronically sick ward.'

'I'm sorry to hear that – did you lose a patient?'

'No, but the young boy Dr Mitchell is interested in was very sick and in a lot of pain. I'm afraid the new diet is not helping and it has been decided that he will have an operation later today.'

'Oh, how unfortunate for the poor child,' Jean said. 'I know Nurse Sarah will be most concerned over that. I'll tell her as soon as she comes in, because she may wish to visit him before he is sedated.'

'Yes, he looks forward to her visits,' Sister Ruth Linton said and smiled in her serene way. 'You may tell her that both Matron and I are praying for him.'

Jean nodded her understanding. Nurse Sarah had become more emotionally involved with the young boy than was sensible, but since Dr Mitchell had expressly asked her to take an interest, Jean could scarcely prohibit the visits. She saw that Sarah had come in early and went to greet her, noting the surprise in her eyes. Normally, she would leave the nurse to approach her.

'You should visit Ned before you start work,' Jean told her. 'He is having an operation today and will be having his pre-meds soon.'

'May I go now?' Sarah looked hesitant. 'I'll make up the time later.'

'I don't think we need to bother too much about that

today,' Jean said in a gentle voice. 'What is about to happen is still very new, Sarah. It may fail and the boy could die. You should spend a little time with him, just in case . . .'

'Thank you – thank you so much,' Sarah said and hurried away.

Jean shook her head. It didn't hurt to help someone else now and then. For a long time she'd been sealed up inside her own wall of pain but now she was living again – and she wasn't entirely sure why things had changed. It might have been that Dr Mitchell called to speak to her most days and that she'd been to the pub for a drink and a snack twice with him, or it might have been young Jamie's distress over his mother. She wasn't quite sure when the ice had begun to crack, but it had started, slowly at first, seeming to gather pace as each day passed. Jean found herself thinking about Jamie and his reasons for running away whenever she was idle. For the moment, however, she was busy with a ward filled with children to care for. It hadn't even occurred to her that she had not given any thought to what would happen once George had his divorce . . .

'It was a bit of twisted gut that was causing all the infection,' Dr Mitchell told Sarah later that evening, when she went to visit their patient, who was still sleepy but well enough to smile at her. 'I managed to remove it without too much damage and now we have to see if he improves. I can't tell you he will be fine from now on, because I don't know – his condition may have other causes, but I've removed the worst.'

'Thank you!' Sarah looked at him in relief. 'I am so pleased to hear it. I know most of the doctors were baffled by his case.'

'It was just luck that I happened to have read everything known on the condition and to be interested in it,' he said seriously. 'Had I not been aware of the possible cause I think we might have lost him.'

'I'm so glad he now has a chance of a better life.'

'What do we do with him next, that's the thing,' Dr Mitchell said, arching his eyebrows at her.

'We would willingly have him until he is really well,' Sarah suggested. 'He needs someone who understands his illness and can regulate his diet until he is able to eat normally.'

'He may never be able to eat anything and everything he likes,' Dr Mitchell said, looking sad. 'However, he should have a life that is not as fraught with problems as before – and he does need someone who understands him until he is fully fit.' Sarah's heart was in her eyes and he smiled. 'Yes, I think Matron would be happy to release him into your mother's care in a few days, nurse. I understand that Lady Rosalie has already given her approval. You will have to report on his wellbeing and you may be visited by the authorities to be certain he is in a proper place. It must I think be temporary – but if you're prepared for that . . .'

'Yes, we are,' Sarah assured him. 'Mum is keen to look after Ned – and he likes me and the idea of living with us.'

'Good. As his doctor I shall recommend you as his carer until such time as his family wishes to claim him – or it is decided to place him in care permanently.'

'Thank you, thank you so much – when can we have him home?'

Dr Mitchell laughed at the eagerness in her voice. 'Ned is a lucky boy, Nurse Sarah. I want to keep an eye on him for another week, but if he is still doing well then, I shall ask Matron to release him to your care.'

'Thank you so much, sir – for everything.'

'You're welcome, nurse.'

When she returned to the ward to finish her duties for the day, Sarah was glowing and Jean nodded her satisfaction. It had all worked out very nicely in her opinion.

When Jean met Dr Mitchell that evening for a drink, he told her all about Nurse Sarah's reaction and Jean gave her approval. 'I hope it won't mean she's late for work every day, but I'm sure it is the right decision.'

'Yes, I think so. She was pleased to be told that they could care for the lad until he is functioning more normally.'

'What happens when he is able to go back to school?'

'His family may want him back – or the children's department may make an order for him to be adopted or placed in a home.'

'So, he won't be able to stay with Mrs Cartwright forever, Dr Mitchell?'

'That isn't my decision,' Matthew Mitchell said and smiled at her. 'But look, why don't you call me Matthew? I've been calling *you* Jean for a while.'

Jean blushed and then smiled as she met his teasing gaze. 'Because I'm a nurse and you're an important doctor.'

'And what has that to do with liking someone – or falling in love with them?'

Jean caught her breath. 'Nothing! But I didn't think . . . I mean, we hardly know each other, D-Matthew.'

'Not for want of trying on my part, Jean,' he replied and gave her a deep look. 'If you don't already know, I was married but she died some years ago. Since then I've had two affairs although neither of them was ever serious. I know you're not the sort to have an affair – so would you like to be courted, Jean Norton?'

Jean felt the last of the ice falling away and her eyes pricked. Perhaps she was an idiot to let a man's smile get to her, but she realised now that it had been happening little by little since that night when he'd noticed her for the first time.

'You don't know the first thing about me,' she said, feeling the need to be honest. 'I – I have loved before and had my heart broken. Since then I've had a friend but he was married and we were not intimate . . .'

'Wow!' Matthew Mitchell took a deep breath. 'You've just told me more about your life than I had any idea of – though I guessed there were secrets. Look, why don't I take you out next weekend? We can drive somewhere and have lunch and just talk – see if you like me enough to consider making me more than just a friend.'

'Yes,' she said and smiled at him. 'I should like that very much . . .'


'Why don't you talk to that policeman friend of yours?' Marth suggested as Arch finished telling her that Jamie hadn't been to school and none of his friends had seen him about.

'He likes school and he never plays truant,' Arch said. 'I didn't want ter go to the cops but I suppose I'll have to.'

'Just talk to Constable Jones at the club tonight,' Marth said. 'It's the best way, Arch.'

'Yes, I know.' He looked at her in concern. 'I'm really worried, Marth. Jamie must think I blame him for what happened to Rich, but it wasn't his fault. He may have upset the gang in some way but it still doesn't make it his fault.'

'Well, you know what young boys are,' Marth said. 'You'd best get to work, lad. You don't want to miss out on your jobs.'

Arch nodded and left the house. His brother's disappearance was puzzling. Normally, Jamie wouldn't stray far from the streets in which he'd grown up, but Arch knew the area as well as his brother and he'd made a thorough search, asking everyone who might have seen Jamie. He'd drawn a complete blank and that was worrying, because either Jamie had gone further afield than he'd ever been in his life – or he'd been murdered, his body disposed of . . .

Please God, don't let it be that! Arch thought desperately. He was fond of his brother and Jamie was all he'd got. Rich was like another brother and he was fighting for his life but, thank God, he *was* a fighter and the doctors said he was surviving better than they'd imagined he would. All Arch wanted was to get his brother and his best mate home again. He promised himself he wouldn't get mad at Jamie if he came waltzing in, even though there were times when he wanted to wring his neck for putting him through this hell!

Where on earth had Jamie got to? How was he managing to live on the streets with no money in his pocket? He must be nearly starving by now. Archie felt the worry gnaw at his insides. If anything happened to his brother, he would blame himself.

'Ma wants four shillings fer 'em,' Jamie said, offering the owner of the junk yard a pair of broken brass fire tongs he'd found in one of the sheds. He'd chosen the item because he knew the metal was worth a couple of bob and the real owner had thrown the fire tongs out. Stealing was stealing, but Cassie had wanted to sell something from the house to buy their food and he'd told her no one would buy the music box. 'They're real heavy.'

The junk yard boss looked at him and weighed the set of fire tongs in his hand. 'I'll give yer one shilling,' he offered craftily.

'Ma would skin me alive if I sold 'em fer that,' Jamie said and made to walk away.

'All right, I'll give yer two bob,' the man said. 'It's me final offer . . .'

Jamie's hand shot out and his fingers curled over the shiny coins. He was grinning to himself as he went to meet Cassie outside the yard. For a moment he stood and watched her. She seemed to be in a world of her own as she stood on one leg, her eyes closed, wobbling as her balance gave and she had to put her foot down. Opening her eyes, she looked at him and for a moment didn't seem to recognise him, but then her gaze cleared and she smiled.

'What did you get?'

'Two bob,' Jamie said. 'We can get a big loaf and a jar of chicken paste – and some broken biscuits fer that.'

'Can we buy the sort with icing on?' Cassie skipped happily at his side.

Jamie nodded. She'd told him she really liked the little biscuits with a dab of sugar icing on, which she said, she nibbled off first before eating the biscuit. Cassie never ate anything she didn't like. He'd tried sharing some squashy peas with her but she spat the first mouthful out and said they were horrid. Biscuits, tinned fruit, chicken paste on top of bread and butter were the main items of her diet. She'd eaten a few chips out of the packet and left the rest that first night. Jamie had warmed them up over the fire he'd lit in a frying pan, put them in bread and butter and eaten them the next day, while she gobbled up biscuit crumbs. He thought that Marth would have been horrified if she could see what they were eating. She cooked mounds of mashed potato, cabbage and carrots with gravy and served them up with pies made from minced beef or leftover roast joints minced fine with onions, or sometimes omelettes made with cheese and eggs. It was a healthier diet than Cassie ate every day.

Jamie wasn't quite sure what to make of the girl he'd befriended. Sometimes he liked her and wanted to look after her, but at other times, when she looked at him in that strange way that came over her, she gave him the shudders. Ma had told him to avoid a lad in the lane who had fits of strangeness; he'd been a bit like Cassie, Jamie thought, one minute laughing and friendly and the next cold and strange, staring fixedly at something no one else could see – and prone to violence. In the end the lad had hit someone in the face with a coal shovel and blinded them in one eye so the authorities had come and taken him away. Jamie had watched him struggle and scream, begging to be allowed to stay, the spittle running down his chin. He'd felt sorry for the lad and afterwards Ma said it wasn't the poor lad's fault he was touched in the head, but he had to be put away for his own good and everyone else's.

Cassie wasn't violent. At least, Jamie didn't think she was, though sometimes when she didn't seem to know him, she became hostile and the look in her eyes chilled him. He knew he wouldn't stay in her house for long, even though he didn't like the idea of deserting her. He suspected she would try to sell more things from the house; beautiful, expensive things that a child like her couldn't possibly have come by legally. One of these days someone was going to call the police and she'd be caught. They would probably put her in an institution, because they would say she wasn't right in the head, even though most of the time she was fine.

It was wrong to use the house the way they did, Jamie knew that. The gas they consumed by using the geyser wasn't theirs. Someone had to pay for it and someone paid for this house. He knew bills had to be paid if a house was involved, even though he didn't know what or where. Someone would come in time if they were not paid. He still couldn't understand why Cassie had been able to walk straight in at the back door of the kitchen. Why would anyone walk out of a home like this and leave food on the kitchen table and the door open?

The woman who owned the things upstairs was posh and she was fairly young too, because of the styles and colours. A fashionable young woman just walks out of her house and doesn't go back? No, it wasn't right. But Cassie wasn't bothered. She'd adopted the house as hers and believed it belonged to her now, but Jamie knew that even if one person had abandoned, it someone else would come. They would come and they would blame the children living there for any damage, so Jamie kept it as clean and tidy as he could, though Cassie wouldn't help. She just turned her back and went up to her treasure cave to play, leaving Jamie to straighten up the mess she made.

The weather had been fine recently and Jamie suggested eating a picnic on the lawn in the back garden. Cassie enjoyed that and made no trouble. As long as he did what she wanted and there was something for her to nibble at, she was content, but the minute he tried to tell her she shouldn't do something she ignored him or told him it was *her* house and she would do as she liked.

That Tuesday morning he bought the biggest loaf he could find and a large jar of chicken paste, some of the biscuits Cassie wanted and one banana. Jamie had rarely had a banana his whole life. It was a treat for anyone in the lanes where he lived, but the shops near Cassie's adopted house often had things like that. Cassie turned her nose up at it when he broke the soft fruit in half and gave her the best bit. She took one bite and made a face, then she spat it out on the pavement and threw the rest down, causing a passing woman to look at her in disapproval.

'Why did you do that?' Jamie asked, regretting the loss of the treat. 'That was a waste, that was.'

'Nasty, horrid, don't like it,' she said and poked her tongue out at him. She snatched the bag of iced biscuits from him and ran on ahead, cramming them into her mouth as fast as she could.

Jamie walked slowly behind her. He was frowning. He knew now for certain that something was wrong with Cassie and he was torn between going home and confessing to Arch and staying to look after the girl. She couldn't look after herself because she had no sense of right and wrong. She genuinely believed that the house and its contents were hers because she'd found it empty, apparently abandoned.

Reluctantly, Jamie followed her into the kitchen. He placed the bread on the table and cut two thick slices, spreading them with the chicken paste, because the butter they'd had was all gone. Cassie picked hers up and ran into the back garden.

Jamie had just taken a bite of his slice when he heard a sound that made his blood run cold. Someone had unlocked the front door! Then he heard the sounds of voices in the hall.

'We haven't been here since your sister disappeared, sir,' a voice said. 'We thought it best to wait for you – though I understand the police walked round the grounds after she was found, but the doors were locked and I had asked them not to break in so they did not enter.'

Jamie's mind was whirling. Cassie had told him the kitchen door was open when she found it, but she lied so easily. Was it true or had she got in through a window? The footsteps were coming towards the kitchen. He fled out the back door to search for Cassie. He had to warn her, because they mustn't be caught. She had stolen things from the house – and he'd sold those fire tongs! Guilt struck him, because *he* did know right from wrong.

Cassie was sitting high up in the apple tree. It was her favourite place in the gardens. He looked up at her.

'You've got to come down!' he hissed. 'People are here in the house – they're searching it. If they see us, we'll be in trouble.'

Cassie just stared at him. He knew she wasn't seeing him, wouldn't listen to him. She was singing one of her peculiar little songs. Desperate to escape more trouble, Jamie dashed into the shrubbery and hid, trembling with fear. He knew the people who had come must own the house and they would be angry at the way Cassie had left the bedroom upstairs, all the expensive clothes pulled from the wardrobes and left on the bed or the floor for Cassie to dress up in – and that expensive jewellery was all over the room, where she scattered it when she was playing her games.

Hidden in the bushes, Jamie heard the voices as two men came out into the garden. He heard a shout as they spotted Cassie in the tree, and then the voices were so close he was afraid they could see him, but they were looking up into the tree at Cassie and he was hidden in the dense shrubbery.

'What are you doing?' one asked in a voice Jamie knew to belong to a gentleman. He would be the brother of the rich lady who had just left her house open when she went out. 'I think you'd better come down, young lady. I want to know what you've been doing in my sister's house.'

Cassie didn't answer immediately, but her song stopped. Jamie couldn't see her, but he heard her say, 'Go away. This is *my* house. I found it and it's mine.'

'Oh, is it?' the gentleman said. He sounded more amused than angry. 'I think the law might have something to say to that, young lady. Does your mother know you're here?'

'Go away!' Cassie screamed at him in sudden anger. 'I hate you! Leave me alone!'

Jamie wasn't sure what happened next, but he thought the gentleman must have moved towards the tree, as if to fetch her down. Cassie screamed and then there was a thud and a startled cry from the men.

'The silly little fool! I wasn't going to hurt her!'

'Of course, you weren't, sir. She fell, that's all.'

Cautiously, Jamie peered out from behind the bush. The men didn't see him, because they were bending over Cassie. Her face looked pale and she was very still, but as he watched her eyelids flickered and she gave a whimper of pain.

'She's hurt,' the gentleman's voice said. 'I'd better get her to a doctor. The house can wait, Sturgeon. I'll take her in my car. You can lock up – and make sure it *is* locked this time. We'll come back later and sort Gillian's things out.'

'Yes, Mr Gillows. I'm really sorry the security wasn't better – but we didn't realise your sister had disappeared for weeks and when the police checked they couldn't get in, without breaking down doors and I'd told them not to do that. After all, when Miss Gillows was found . . .'

'Her death was a terrible accident,' the gentleman said in a sad voice. 'It was even worse that the police failed to find her body for so long.'

Jamie waited until the voices had gone. He'd heard enough to realise that the lady with the beautiful clothes had gone off one day, leaving her house open, and something bad had happened to her. Perhaps she'd fallen in the river and her body had not been discovered for a long time . . . Jamie could only guess. He knew why the house was locked when the police came – Cassie must have locked herself in and hidden. She'd been protecting her house from intruders.

He was still shaking from the fright he'd had and worried about the girl he'd befriended. Why had she fallen from the tree and was she badly hurt? Would she die? At least she was in safe hands now, because the gentleman would see she was looked after and he'd returned to take charge of his sister's house.

Jamie's mind returned to his own problems and he knew that he'd only made them worse by running away. He had to go back home to Marth, who had been kind enough to take him in, and to Arch – and he had to tell his brother everything, including where he'd been these past few days.

# CHAPTER 13

Arch was so relieved to find his brother sitting in Marth's kitchen when he got home that afternoon that he listened to Jamie's story right to the end without interrupting. When Jamie finished speaking, he stared at him in silence as he tried to make sense of the whole thing.

'Ma would have skinned you alive,' he said at last. 'I thought you would have learned right from wrong, Jamie. You know all the trouble Ma had with Pa – and you know what she thought of thieves.'

'I know it was wrong,' Jamie said. 'I'm going to earn money when I can and pay Mr Forrest back – and the tongs had been thrown out in the shed. Cassie wanted to sell something from the house so I took the tongs instead.'

'They were still pinched,' Arch said, 'but I understand you were trying to help her.' He frowned. 'From all you've said, it sounds as if she's a bit touched in the head?'

'She *is* strange,' Jamie agreed. 'I don't think she's mad or violent, Arch, but she doesn't know right from wrong.

She really thought it all belonged to her because she'd found it.'

'Perhaps it's because of all she's been through, with her mother dying,' his brother said. 'I'm glad you came home, Jamie. You should have brought her here.'

'She wouldn't have left the house, because she liked playing with all the pretty things.'

'She obviously isn't well,' Arch said and shook his head. 'Maybe it's for the best those men turned up when they did, because she needs someone to look after her proper.'

'I'm worried about her, Arch,' Jamie said and scrubbed his eyes to stop himself crying. 'It's my fault Rich is in the hospital and it is my fault if he dies – and I should've looked after Cassie better.'

'Stop blaming yerself, kid,' Arch said in his best elder brother manner. 'Leo and his gang made yer do that robbery and then they thought you would snitch so that's why they attacked us – we gave them a hiding so they came back for more with knives. They are the rogues, not you, Jamie. As for that girl – well, I don't think there was much you could do for her.' He paused, then, making up his mind, 'I'm going to tell Steve all this, because he needs to know.'

Jamie's bottom lip trembled as he looked at his brother. 'Will they send me to prison?'

'No, I don't think so,' Arch said. 'I'll talk to Mr Forrest and tell him we'll pay him back. We can pay back the two bob for the tongs, too – and that will help. I think Steve will be glad of the evidence. They've arrested a couple of the gang for various thefts and this will help convict them of several other petty crimes.

162

Overall, I think Steve will ask his boss to go easy on you – but you may be punished in some way. You must be prepared for them to give you a warning at the very least.'

Jamie hung his head. 'Yes, I know. I'm sorry, Arch. If I'd let the gang beat me up, Rich wouldn't have been attacked.'

'You can't be sure of that. We'd both won money that night. My cup was stolen – and if Rich had brought his belt home with him rather than leaving it for the club to display, that might have been stolen too.' Arch frowned. 'They are rogues, Jamie, and the less you have to do with them the better. I'm glad you had the sense to see that.'

'I hate them, especially that Leo,' Jamie said. 'I promise I'll never do anythin' like that again, Rich.'

'I believe you,' his brother said. 'Now, you're coming with me tomorrow to explain to Mr Forrest before you go to school. I'm off to work at the club when I've had my tea and I want you here in the morning, do you understand me?'

Jamie promised faithfully and Arch ate his meal and departed. Marth made a fuss of Jamie and told him not to upset himself.

'We all make mistakes, love,' she said kindly. 'Them bullies frighten a lot of the kids and you're not the first to be misled.'

Jamie ate his supper in silence. It was fried bubble and squeak with a slice of streaky bacon and a bit of Marth's bread and nothing had ever tasted so good in his life.

She made him a nice warm bath in front of the

kitchen fire and then sent him to bed with a mug of cocoa. Jamie settled into his bed and cried himself to sleep, thinking of Rich and Cassie but then he just slept, the misery of the weeks sloughing off him as the relief of confessing to his brother eased his mind at last.

Mr Forrest looked at him sorrowfully when Jamie confessed what he'd done but didn't speak until he said, 'I'm so sorry, sir. I wish I hadn't done what they said – and I'm sorry you were ill.'

'Well, lad, it gave me a nasty shock, because I thought we might be murdered in our beds,' Mr Forrest said and winked at Arch. 'But I feel better now I know it was you and I shall stop worrying it might happen again.'

'I *will* pay you back,' Jamie said earnestly.

Mr Forrest nodded, looking at him thoughtfully for a minute and making Jamie feel even worse. What was he going to demand from him as payment?

'Well, how about you come and work for me?' Mr Forrest said. 'I need a Saturday boy to take groceries out to my customers who can't get in to fetch them. I've got a bike in the back of the shop with a basket on the front handlebars and you can use that – and you'll work for nothing until you've paid me every penny back, is that a deal?'

'Yes please! I'll do whatever you say, sir.'

'Well, I think that's fair enough – what do you say, Arch?'

'I think you've been very fair, sir.'

'Well, I believe Jamie has learned his lesson,' Mr Forrest said, 'and you're a good lad, Arch. I know your brother will behave himself in future.'

'I'll thrash him if he doesn't,' Arch said, but he grinned so Jamie knew he wasn't angry.

'Well, that's the first hurdle,' Arch said after they left the shop. 'We'll talk to Steve this evening – and now I've got to explain to your schoolmaster why you're late and he might not be so forgiving!'

Jamie got five strokes of the ruler on his hands and he was made to write out that playing truant was wrong fifty times on the blackboard. His hands felt sore, but once again, Jamie felt he'd got away lightly. Mr Mackness had told him his former good conduct had stood in his favour but he'd looked very disappointed in him and perhaps that was the worst punishment of all.

Constable Steve Jones looked serious that evening as Jamie recounted how he'd been bullied into taking the sweets and cigarettes but he nodded to himself as if he'd suspected it all along.

'That's why you decided to learn self-defence, isn't it?'

'Yes, sir . . .' Jamie hung his head. 'I was ashamed of what I'd done, sir.'

'You say you gave everything to the gang and then they just ran leaving you to get out alone – and they gave you nothing?'

'Yes, sir.' Jamie raised his gaze to meet the police officer's. 'I didn't want anything, sir. If I'd 'ad it, I would've took it back.'

'And Mr Forrest has accepted your offer to work for no pay to compensate him for his loss?'

'Yes, sir, I'm sorry, sir.'

'Then I think all we need to do is to warn you not to offend again . . .' His gaze became sterner. 'Now, as to this business of the girl and the abandoned house; I'd like to hear more about that, please.'

Jamie told him everything, about how he'd first met Cassie, how he'd gone to the house she claimed was hers, how he'd tidied up the kitchen and stopped her taking the expensive jewellery to sell. However, because he liked Cassie, he made excuses for her behaviour.

'She didn't think it was stealing, sir. Cassie really thought it was hers because no one came near for months.'

'Some officers went to the property and walked round it after you left.' Steve frowned and looked at Arch. 'Did you happen to read the newspaper article about Miss Gillian Gillows?'

Arch shook his head, puzzled. He didn't often read a newspaper and Jamie had never picked one up in his life, even though Marth saved all the pictures of the King and his family for her scrapbook.

'It's a fine house unlike the others in the area and was built for a rich merchant when all of this was just fields. The young lady who owned it was a rich heiress. At first, she was reported as missing by her friend. She was supposed to meet him for tea but she didn't turn up – and then, several weeks later, her body was found caught in a reed bed in the river. Her brother was abroad at the time and he was the only one with a spare set of keys. The police went to the house and searched the grounds; they knocked but they didn't go inside, because the lawyers didn't want any damage. I think that was a mistake. The officer in charge should have broken a small window, gained access and then had it repaired.'

'If they had, they would've found Cassie,' Jamie said. He took a deep breath. 'I'm worried about her, sir. She fell out of the tree when the man shouted at her and – and she was a little bit odd sometimes anyway. I don't know what happened to her after the man took her away.'

'Well, I can tell you she is being cared for in a children's hospital,' Steve said, looking sad. 'Apparently, after her mother died in a fall, she was taken to a centre for orphaned children the council intended to send off to Australia.' He paused thoughtfully. 'Cassie ran away and although the police made a search for her she wasn't found – as for what happened to her when she fell from the tree, she suffered a broken arm – but the doctors were more concerned because her mind was wandering. They thought it might be from the fall but from what you've told me it sounds more like a long-term problem. Your information may be useful to the hospital and staff treating her and I shall make sure they get it.'

'As long as she's all right . . .' Jamie looked at him. 'I'll pay back the two bob for the tongs as soon as I earn some money.' He took a deep breath and his knees felt weak. 'Will I go to prison, sir?'

For a moment the police officer looked stern and not a bit like his friend Steve from the boxing club, but then he shook his head. 'Not this time, Jamie – but my superiors will expect some kind of penance,' Steve said at last. 'I shall recommend that you continue to attend the club and learn to defend yourself from rogues – and I shall suggest that you enrol in the police cadets and give your time to the good works they do. You will have to do well at school to be accepted, so that means you're going to be busy. You won't have time to get into more trouble!'

'But that isn't a punishment, sir,' Jamie said and Steve winked.

'My superiors won't know that, will they? And I'll be watching you, Jamie Martin. I've got high hopes you'll be another champion and I shall be most disappointed if you let me down.'

Jamie looked at him. 'I promise I'll never do that, sir.'

'In that case, you can go to your class and forget this incident. I shall be informing Mr Gillows of everything you've told me – and no doubt he'll be asking for his two bob for those tongs!'

Arch grinned at Steve over Jamie's head as he ran off to join his friends and start training. 'I think he has learned his lesson, sir. Thank you for letting him off like that.'

'He has the makings of a good fighter, Arch, and we need youngsters like him in the police cadets,' Steve said. 'He was led astray out of fear and that's why our club is so important. I think my superiors will accept what I say – and from what I hear Mr Gillows is too concerned about the little girl to worry about a few items that went astray. He may come to speak with Jamie, because he is looking for clues as to what went on there, but he may not bother. After all, Jamie only spent a few days in the house and, by the sound of it, he saved them from finding a worse mess there.'

'My brother is lucky that people have been so under-standing,' Arch said. 'He still feels guilty over Rich's injuries but I've been told he's through the worst.'

'Yes, I believe his life is no longer in danger,' Steve said. 'However, I doubt he'll be able to go on with his boxing. I know his injuries have affected his lungs and that means he'll never get a professional licence, which must be a huge disappointment to him.'

'Will it make him an invalid for life?'

Steve shook his head. 'I can't answer that, Arch. I know he won't get the professional licence but it shouldn't stop him living a normal life and doing work that isn't too strenuous.' He looked thoughtful for a moment. 'I've got an idea that might work, but I need to talk to a few people first – Rich, for a start.' He nodded and smiled. 'It might mean a small sacrifice on your part, Arch.'

'Ah,' Arch smiled, 'I think I know what *you're* thinking. I believe Mr Forrest might agree but I don't know if Rich will . . .'

Steve visited the young boxing champion in the infirmary next afternoon when he came off duty. Rich was sitting up against the pillows, his eyes shut and his face tight with misery. Guessing that he'd been told of the limitations his injury might place on him, Steve sensed that it might not be the right time to suggest he become a shopkeeper.

'How are you?' he asked as Rich opened his eyes, becoming aware that he was there.

'A bit sore,' Rich replied. 'I know I'm lucky to be alive – but at the moment I don't feel lucky.'

'Doctors told you that you have some damage to

169

your lungs?' Steve nodded sympathetically. 'It is rotten luck, Rich. You were on course to turn professional in a few years I know.'

'Yeah – bloody kids!' There was bitterness in Rich's voice now. 'Still, my mother will be pleased I can't box again. She thought I'd end up with my brains curdled.'

'Quite a few boxers do if they're caught with an unlucky punch,' Steve said. 'I know you think it wouldn't happen to you and I understand you feel bitter . . .'

'I don't know what to do now,' Rich confessed. 'What kind of a job am I fit for after this?'

'I dare say you'll think of something,' Steve said. 'Have you considered working in an office or maybe a shop somewhere?'

'Bloody shopkeeper!' Rich exploded. 'Is that all I'm fit for? My father was a ship's carpenter and my uncle was a brickie. I thought I'd go for something like that if I wasn't good enough for a professional licence.'

Steve nodded, but knew that any heavy manual labour was likely to be hard for Rich to sustain, because the injury might affect his breathing if he tried to do too strenuous a job. However, it was something he had yet to accept and Steve decided to wait before trying to help him. Rich needed to come to terms with his new situation. Perhaps, when he left the hospital in a couple of weeks, they could talk again.

Arch went to see his friend, taking him a magazine that he'd bought about racing cars. He hadn't been able to think of anything else that might amuse Rich for a few hours and they both had an interest in the big races that took place in all kinds of glamorous places, none of which they were ever likely to see because it was too expensive. It didn't stop them being interested in the cars and the glamour.

'Thanks,' Rich gave him a lopsided grin. 'You're all right, then?'

'Yeah,' Arch said. 'I got a few bruises and so did the kid – he says he's sorry. Blames himself for what happened.'

'Jamie ain't ter blame,' Rich said. 'It's that rotten little blighter, Leo. I've 'ad a few run-ins wiv 'im in the past. He wanted 'is own back no doubt – and he got it all right!'

'I'm sorry too, Rich,' Arch said. 'I know how much the boxing meant ter yer. I wish it 'ad been me.'

'Nah, it ain't yer fault either,' Rich said and made a wry face. 'It's just I don't know what I'll do. I was set on a boxing career, though Ma never wanted me to turn professional. She says I could get work in a bookie's shop.' He grinned. 'I don't think she realises that's against the law!'

'It's 'cos yer dad and grandad always had a bet on the 'orses,' Arch said. 'I suppose a pub or a shop might be all right.'

'Yeah, I thought about bein' a barman if I could find someone ter take me on,' Rich said. 'Or I might . . . nah, there's no chance of anything like that . . .' Rich shook his head and wouldn't be drawn even though Arch asked if there was anything he wanted to do. 'I reckon a bar might be all right.'

'I could ask at the club if they need anyone,' Arch said. He knew his boss liked boxing and he'd been very sympathetic when he learned of Rich's tragedy. 'They might have an opening.'

'Yeah, all right, thanks mate,' Rich said. 'I'll be stuck 'ere fer another couple of weeks – the doctor said there's a bit of fluid they need to drain.' He made a wry face. 'It ain't very pleasant, but I'll get over it.'

'Sure, yer will and be as fit as a fiddle,' Arch said, though he knew it wasn't true. 'Yer will probably find yer can do more than yer think – just not boxing.'

Rich winced but said no more. The friends knew there was no use talking about the attack that had ruined Rich's plans. He couldn't change anything so he had to make the best of what he had, but at least their friendship had continued and that meant a lot to them both.

Jamie listened to Arch telling Marth about his visit with Rich. He was glad that Rich was getting better but he still felt terrible about the way things had turned out. Everyone said it wasn't his fault, but Jamie knew that if Rich hadn't helped them fight off Leo's gang, he would still have a wonderful career ahead of him.

He couldn't do anything to help. His days and evenings were so full that he didn't have much time to think about what he'd done wrong. He was working hard at school, because he needed to pass some exams to join the police cadets, and at night he trained hard, putting all his efforts into learning every trick going. Arch and the police seemed to believe Leo had gone for good, but Jamie was pretty sure he would be back one of these days and next time Jamie was going to be ready.

He still continued to think of Cassie and to wonder how she was getting on but it wasn't until three weeks after she'd fallen from the tree that someone called at Marth's home.

The first thing Jamie knew was that a posh car was sitting outside in the lane when he got home for his tea that Friday night. It was the end of the school week and Jamie was carrying things he'd made at school and also a bag of sweets he'd been given from the school fete.

His heart started to thump as he saw the car and he knew it could only be one man. Mr Gillows had come to demand his two shillings for the tongs. Arch had put the money in a vase on the mantelpiece.

'You can use it to pay him back and you'll owe it to me,' Arch had said sternly. 'I shall make you pay it, Jamie. It's the only way you'll learn.'

Jamie had accepted his brother's decision. So, the money was waiting but Jamie's knees were trembling as he entered Marth's kitchen and saw the gentleman sitting there. It was a warm day and he was wearing pale grey slacks and a blue shirt but no jacket, his straw hat on the table beside him – and Marth had made him a cup of tea.

'There's a gentleman 'ere ter see yer, Jamie,' she told him. 'I'll be in the scullery – so you can talk by yerselves – if that's all right, Mr Gillows?'

'Yes, of course, ma'am. Thank you for your hospitality.'

The gentleman sat watching Jamie as he approached. He snatched off the school cap that had been Arch's before him and held it nervously as he met the visitor's gaze.

'I've got the two bob fer the tongs, sir,' Jamie said and fetched it from the vase on the mantle. He put it down on the table near the gentleman's cup. 'I'm sorry I took what was yours, Mr Gillows.'

Jamie rubbed his left shoe on the back of his long grey right sock awkwardly, unnerved by the man's steady gaze.

'Well, Jamie Martin, I'm glad you realise the tongs were not yours to sell. They belonged to my sister – did you know that?'

'I know now, sir. We didn't know who owned the house and Cassie found it unlocked and empty. She said there was fresh bread and honey on the table so—'

'She must have arrived soon after my sister disappeared.' The gentleman nodded. 'Cassie isn't talking to us, Jamie. The doctors think she doesn't remember what happened. All she does is sing her little songs.'

'Cassie won't talk to you if she doesn't trust you,' Jamie said. 'She talked to me – but if I did something she didn't like she walked off and played on her own. When you came, I went out and told her to come down from the tree but she wouldn't.'

'So, you were hidden in the garden?'

'Yes, sir. I saw you pick Cassie up and I didn't know what to do so I came home and told my brother and Constable Jones.'

'Constable Jones told me that you were the one who put all the rubbish into the bins and cleaned the kitchen?'

'Yes, sir. I told Cassie the rubbish would bring rats so she let me do it – but I didn't touch anything upstairs. She wouldn't let me tidy her dressing-up things. She liked trying on your sister's clothes, sir – and the jewellery. I don't think she sold anything valuable, just little things she could buy food with.'

'Yes, I believe you're right – and to be honest, I don't much care if anything *was* sold. If a great many people had found the house empty, they would have taken everything of value – and my sister had valuable things I gave her.'

'I'm sorry about yer sister, sir,' Jamie said. 'We didn't know she was missing.'

'No, I'm sure you didn't.' A sad smile touched the gentleman's lips. 'My sister loved the river. She loved nature and all the things that live in the river. What happened to her was a complete accident. We think she must have been reaching for something and tumbled into the water. She could swim, so she must have hit her head as she fell and was unconscious when she drowned. She was swept down river and caught in the reeds, hidden until a fisherman found her.'

'That was terrible, sir . . .' Jamie couldn't imagine how bad that would feel.

'Yes, Jamie, it was, because I loved her.' His eyes were so sad then and Jamie felt his throat tighten. 'We were very close. I looked after her, you see. Gillian was a gentle girl . . . not quite as others. They told me she should be shut away where she could be cared for; for her own sake, they said, but she hated to be caged. I wouldn't let her go to one of those places. I arranged for her to have someone to look after her . . .' Mr Gillows eyes misted as he looked at Jamie. 'I couldn't know that her nurse would leave her alone. I couldn't have known that, could I? She was well-paid and she swore she would look after Gillian for me while I was away.'

'Why did she do that, sir? Go off and leave her alone?'

'Her mother was ill so she just upped and left my sweet sister alone. Gillian told her she would be all right and I'm sure she was. She was capable, you see – but impetuous, and sometimes thoughtless. She wasn't insane or even retarded, no matter what people think. Some of the newspapers have said such cruel things, Jamie. I would never have gone off abroad for six months if I'd thought she would be alone or neglected.'

Jamie saw the pain in the gentleman's eyes. 'I reckon you wouldn't sir, 'cos you loved her. I caused harm to someone I like but I never meant to – and it hurts . . .'

'What could you possibly have done?' A faint smile flickered in the gentleman's eyes so Jamie told him what he'd done and Mr Gillows nodded his understanding.

'So that's why you ran away and how you met Cassie?'

'Yes,' Jamie said. 'I didn't know what to do and she came and sat next to me on the school steps. I shared my sweets with her and she took me to her house. She really thought it was her house, sir.'

'Yes, I understand that,' Mr Gillows said. 'I think my sister would have liked it that someone continued to enjoy her things after she died. I've left them all there – I couldn't bear to get rid of them, because it is so final . . .'

Jamie nodded. He was respectful because the gentleman was talking to clear his thoughts. It was obvious that he was sad and upset because of what had happened to the sister he loved and perhaps he had no one to tell – no one he wanted to tell. Jamie knew it was good to tell someone when you felt guilty and sad.

'You want to remember her there,' Jamie said.

Mr Gillows stared at him, blinked and then smiled. 'I think I was very lucky that the house had two such custodians,' he said. Jamie wasn't sure what the long word meant, but he sensed what the gentleman was saying. 'Perhaps I could prevail on you to do something for me?'

'If I can 'elp yer, sir . . .'

'Will you visit Cassie in hospital, please?' Mr Gillows asked. 'I should like you to come tomorrow morning. I will send a car – and Marth can accompany you. I shall be at the hospital and I want to see what happens when you talk to Cassie.'

'Yes, I'll do that, sir,' Jamie promised. 'I'll 'ave ter let Mr Forrest know I'll do his errands later, but I'll come and talk to her. I don't know if she'll answer me . . .' He thought for a moment. 'Can yer get some sherbet lemons for us, please? Cassie likes those – and them little biscuits with icing on the top.'

Mr Gillows picked up the two shilling coin and handed it to Jamie. 'Take this and buy what you need for her. I appreciate all you've told me and I want to thank you for helping me.'

He got up and took his leave. When Marth came back to the kitchen, Jamie told her all his visitor had said, but she'd heard every word and she looked at him thoughtfully.

'You'd best go and tell Mr Forrest the news and buy what the gentleman told yer – and I'll be coming to the hospital in the morning, just ter make sure there's no funny business. Not that Mr Gillows seemed anything but a real gentleman – but yer never know!'

Jamie nodded. He had no clear idea of what Marth

was hinting at, but grown-ups were funny that way. He'd listened to his visitor telling his story and he'd felt sorry for him. It was sad to lose a sister the way Mr Gillows had, even if she was a little bit soft in the head. Most people would say Cassie was too, but Jamie liked her and he thought Mr Gillows did too.

# CHAPTER 14

'I just had to come and tell you,' Lady Rosalie said as she entered Matron's office that morning, 'the young girl we spoke of – the one we thought might have died in the cold weather – has been found. Apparently, she'd been living in the house of that missing heiress, eating food she found there and she's physically well, apart from her arm, which she broke falling from a tree.'

'That is a little miracle,' Mary replied and smiled at her. 'Isn't it marvellous the way God works? He must have been looking out for the child – do you not think so?'

'Yes, perhaps that was it,' Lady Rosalie said. 'She is certainly a lucky little girl, because someone wants to adopt her – well, foster her first, because we like to make sure our children are happy before we allow permanent adoption.'

'Why do you say she is lucky?' Mary inquired. 'If she is a nice little thing, I daresay a few couples would be glad to take her.'

'The doctors were thinking she might have to go into an institution, because she isn't quite normal – a little hazy in her mind. It may just be the shock of losing her mother and having to live on her own – but it could be something more. A lot of foster carers wouldn't want to take a child like that on – nor could they give her all the time she needs. This person is wealthy and can afford the nurse and carers required to look after her.'

Mary nodded and smiled. 'Then I agree, she *is* a lucky little girl. Tell me, have you many children waiting for foster care now?'

'I have ten waiting for placements and only three available foster homes,' Lady Rosalie said. 'I had to turn down the last two applicants, because the husbands had tempers – and we've made that mistake before. However, I do have five couples to interview this afternoon and at least three of them sound as if they will make good foster parents.'

'Good,' Mary said. 'Ned is looking forward to staying with Mrs Cartwright and Nurse Sarah. Mrs Cartwright might help you out with another of your children if you're stuck for a place for one of them.'

'Yes, Gwen Cartwright is very capable but I think she'll have her hands full with Ned. No, I'll see how I get on in the next week with my interviews. If I don't find enough homes, I'll revisit some of my existing carers and ask if they can take another child.' She smiled. 'One of my carers already has three children.'

'Some women are so good at childcare,' Mary said. 'Now, there's another small problem that I wanted to talk to you about . . .'

'You mean the roof in the kitchen here?' Lady Rosalie said instinctively knowing what was worrying her friend.

'It is all in hand, Mary. I've raised the funds and the builder will come next week!'

Cassie opened her eyes. For a moment the light was so bright that she cried out. Someone was sitting by her bed but she couldn't see him properly because of the light in her eyes.

'Daddy?' she whispered. 'Is it you – have you come back to me?'

The man bent over her and smiled. He smelled of cigars and brandy, a familiar smell. 'Would you like me to be your daddy?' he asked softly.

Cassie looked up at him in wonder. He looked a bit different but he must be her daddy. No one else had ever spoken in a soft, kind voice to her since he went away and he smelled just the same. She couldn't remember anything properly but she knew she'd been happy when Daddy was there.

'Yes, please,' she said faintly. 'I love you, Daddy. Please, can we go home?'

'Yes, yes, of course we can,' the man said and bent to kiss her forehead lightly. 'My own dear little Cassie. I'll look after you now; everything will be all right now I'm here.'

Cassie smiled and her eyes closed as she drifted back to sleep. She had her daddy back and now she would be warm and comfortable and safe again . . .

Gerald Gillows smiled as he left the hospital. That enchanting little girl was just like the sister he'd lost. He'd loved his half-sister so much, even though she'd always been a little forgetful, a little careless. Their

181

parents had died when Gerald was seventeen and Gillian was eight and he'd looked after her even when he only had the few pounds, he'd earned from his market stall.

Gradually, he'd earned a fortune, saving and scheming, investing wisely in property – and then Gillian's maternal grandfather had died and left her thirty thousand pounds. With that money he'd bought her the house by the river and paid a woman to live in and look after her. A scowl touched his face – that woman had let him down and because of that his beloved sister had gone off alone and fallen in the river and drowned, lying there for weeks before her decomposed body was finally found.

For a moment Gerald was close to despair. He should have been here, but his business exporting to and from America provided the money for Gillian's luxuries . . . Still, he could never forgive himself for her death.

Perhaps he could atone a little for what he'd let happen? Gerald's brow lightened as he thought of the strange little girl with the enchanting smile. The hospital nurses had told him she would be sent to an institution for retarded children when she was well enough but he could do so much better. All he needed was to find the right person – someone who would agree that he could give Cassie the proper care she needed and look after her.

He'd been told of the lady who chaired the fostering service and understood she was a reasonable woman. Perhaps she would allow him to become Cassie's foster parent for the moment, with nurses and a housekeeper to look after her – and one day he might adopt her.

A smile touched his lips. Nothing would bring his dearest sister back but now perhaps he could bring some happiness to another girl – a girl who reminded him so much of Gillian as a little girl . . .

# CHAPTER 15

Sarah saw that Steve was waiting for her bus when it drew up outside the infirmary. She got off and went to meet him, smiling as he put his arm about her and hugged her. Lifting her face for his kiss, she blushed and laughed as a passing youth wolf whistled at them.

'Take no notice,' Steve said and grinned. 'He's just jealous – you look beautiful and very happy.'

'You make me happy,' Sarah said and hugged his arm. 'But you know what day it is today?'

'It's the day they're finally letting you take Ned home,' Steve said. 'I hadn't forgotten. I've got the morning off and I've borrowed a car to take you both home in style.'

'Oh, Steve, bless you,' Sarah said looking at him with love. 'That's so thoughtful of you. I was going to order a taxi but now I shan't need to.'

'I wanted to make it easy for you, love,' Steve said. 'I know how much you and your mum have been looking forward to this and I want it to be special for all of you.'

Sarah held on to his arm as they went into the infirmary together. She was so lucky to have such a thoughtful man and it gave her a little thrill of pleasure to think about their wedding, which they'd finally settled for later that year. She'd decided there was no point in waiting any longer. Her mother was quite happy to see Sarah settled with Steve and to live on her own, except that she was seldom alone. If Charlie wasn't staying with her, her friends were popping in to chat and it was clear that she'd recovered from her grief over losing Sarah's father and was now ready to make her own life. For the immediate future she would have young Ned to care for and Sarah knew how much she was looking forward to having him stay.

Dr Mitchell was waiting to release his patient into Sarah's care. She had his diet sheet and his medicines and he knew that she was well-prepared for any signs that his illness had returned and would recognise the symptoms, though for the moment he seemed far better than anyone had expected.

'Well, young Ned,' the doctor said. 'I don't have to tell you that you must stick to the diet Sarah and her mother will prepare for you. I will see you again in a month's time and hopefully we'll then gradually introduce other foods. You'll come and see me every month at first and then every three months until I can discharge you.'

'Thank you, sir,' Ned said and grinned at him. His personality was beginning to shine through now that his crippling illness was becoming just a bad memory. 'I know you, Nurse Sarah and the others have done so much for me.'

'We were glad we could help,' Dr Mitchell said. He held out his hand solemnly and Ned shook it. 'I expect to hear good things of you from Nurse Sarah, Ned.'

'Yes, sir, thank you again.' Ned then looked shyly at Sarah. 'It's kind of your mum to have me, Nurse Sarah.'

'She's looking forward to it,' Sarah said. 'Mum likes to spoil me and I'm getting too grown-up to be spoiled so she will be pleased to have you – and I told you about Charlie, didn't I?' Ned nodded, looking interested. 'He's a bit older than you but he comes to stay with us in his school holidays and he's going to be a carpenter on the docks. So, he works during the day and comes home to sleep.'

'I've got school work to catch up on,' Ned said. 'My teacher visited me yesterday and gave me some books to study. I don't mind because I like to learn and I've missed a lot this term.'

'And what do you want to do when you leave school?' Sarah asked as she picked up his little case – one she'd loaned him – and led the way out to the corridor where Steve was waiting.

'I'd like to be a doctor,' Ned said and his eyes lit up. 'Either a doctor or a nurse like you.'

Sarah laughed softly. It wasn't surprising that he should want to be like the man who had saved his life. 'I think that's a wonderful idea,' she said. 'You study hard, Ned, and perhaps you will.'

Steve came to meet them and took the case from Sarah. 'Hello, Ned,' he said. 'I'm Sarah's fiancé, Steve and I've got a car to take you home . . .'

'It seems hard that he has to stick to this diet,' Mrs Cartwright said as she looked through the list Sarah had given her. 'When I think of the way Charlie tucks in to my cooking!'

'Ned hasn't long come off an all liquid diet,' Sarah told her. 'He is used to it, Mum, and we have to be careful for him for a while yet. In a few months he may be able to tuck into treacle pudding and a bag of toffees, but for the moment it's boring things like steamed fish, mashed potatoes, rice pudding, ice cream and jelly – stuff like that.'

'Well, it's rather bland, but if it makes him better that's all that matters,' Mrs Cartwright said. 'You can see how poorly the little lad has been. I'll make sure he's looked after, don't you worry.'

'I know that,' Sarah said and kissed her. 'He's a bit quiet at the moment but he'll come out of it, Mum. He was chatting to Steve on the way home. I think he really means it when he says he wants to be a doctor – but he likes football and sports like any normal lad. He just hasn't been well enough to play them.'

'It was marvellous what your Dr Mitchell did for him.'

'He is a clever doctor, Mum. I'm just glad they sorted it all out for Ned – and he's so much better than he was, believe me. Only a few weeks ago he couldn't eat anything without having chronic pain and diarrhoea.'

'Yes, and we have to make sure he improves while he stays with us,' Mrs Cartwright said. 'Is Steve coming round this evening?'

'No, he is at the club he runs tonight, but he might call on his way home.' Sarah smiled. 'I shall wash my hair and sit up for a while by the fire.'

Steve watched the boys matching up for their first bouts of the evening. He saw Jamie arrive a little later than the others and went up to him.

188

'Everything all right, Jamie?'

'Yes, sir,' Jamie said and looked pleased with himself. 'I went ter the 'ospital ter see Cassie this mornin' and I've been there all day. She wouldn't eat nothin' and she wouldn't talk to anyone but I took her some biscuits and sweets and she ate all the biscuits and some of the sherbet lemons. I told the doctors she would 'ave tinned fruit and ice cream fer her tea and a paste sandwich fer dinner or some chips, and Mr Gillows said she could 'ave whatever she wants. He's been worried about her – but she talked ter me – and because he told her she could 'ave whatever she wants, she talked ter him too.'

'So, it was just stubbornness then.'

'It ain't quite like that, sir,' Jamie said. 'I know she ain't normal like you and me, sir, but she's all right – she talks ter yer if she trusts yer. Anyways, I stopped fer a long time and it made me late doin' me errands fer Mr Forrest.'

'So that is why you were late this evening,' Steve said and nodded. 'You haven't seen anything of Leo or the gang, I hope?'

'No, sir. An' I don't want to. I 'ope he's gone fer good – but I think he'll be back when he reckons it's safe.'

'I think you may be right, Jamie,' Steve said and looked stern. 'If you see him, please try to ignore him – and let me know as soon as you can. Will you do that?'

'Yes, sir,' Jamie said. 'I'll let yer know right away.'

Steve nodded and left him to join his partner. Jamie was already being paired with older and stronger boys, because none of the others in his age group had a chance against him. He would be ready soon to be entered in a regional competition and Steve thought he might do well.

His thoughts turned to the young man who would be sleeping in Sarah's mother's house that night. He was almost the same age as Jamie but there was a huge difference. Ned's health had made it impossible for him to do the things other lads of his age did, but he had a good mind and he'd determined to do something worthwhile with his life. Steve hoped that Rich, too, would discover something he wanted to do with his life, something that would not overtax his strength but be an occupation to be proud of . . .

'Rich, are you awake?' Nurse Jenny approached his bed. He opened his eyes and looked at her, pulling a wry face. She laughed. 'No, I haven't come to give you an enema or to take your temperature – you have a visitor.'

Rich nodded and worked his way up against the pillows. 'Is it that police officer or Arch?'

'Neither,' Nurse Jenny said and smiled at him. 'If you're feeling up to it, I'll show him in.'

Rich watched her leave, feeling puzzled. His mother and sister had been to visit earlier and he knew his father was working, so who could it be? As a gentleman walked in, Rich felt puzzled. He was pretty certain he'd never seen the man in his life.

'Hello,' the man said and offered his hand. 'I hope I'm not intruding, Mr Austin. I'm Gerald Gillows and I'd heard about what happened to you. Someone did me a favour today and I thought I might be able to do you a good turn.'

'I don't understand you, sir . . .' Rich looked at him, feeling puzzled. 'I don't think we've met?'

'No, we haven't. I've been in America until just recently, but I've heard a lot about you from a friend – a mutual friend.' He smiled. 'I believe you know a rather enterprising young lad named Jamie Martin?'

'Yes, I know Jamie,' Rich said still puzzled. 'But I don't see—'

'Perhaps I could tell you a little story,' Gerald Gillows said. 'And then you might feel able to do me a favour . . .'

'And where do you think you're off to?' Arch asked his brother on Sunday morning. 'I thought we might go and watch the cricket together this afternoon?'

It was a match between workers from a local factory and the men who worked on the docks and was to be held in the park. Arch liked all sports, though he preferred football, and he played for a local team in the winter.

'It depends if I get back in time,' Jamie said. 'Mr Gillows wants me ter go to his sister's house wiv 'im. He says he wants ter ask my advice about somethin'.'

Arch looked at him hard. 'He ain't one of them queer blokes is 'e?'

'Nah, don't think so,' Jamie said, though he wasn't perfectly sure what his brother meant. 'He feels sad about his sister dyin' and I think he wants ter keep the 'ouse in 'er memory.' Jamie thought for a moment. 'I ain't sure what he meant, but I think he might be goin' ter adopt Cassie. He ain't got anyone else yer see – and I think she reminds 'im of his sister what died. I ain't certain, but that's what I reckon.'

'Sounds a bit odd ter me,' Arch said. 'I think I'd better come with yer, Jamie. If he's all right, I don't mind yer helpin' 'im – but I'll come just ter be sure yer all right.'

'Suits me,' Jamie said. ''Sides, I'd like yer ter see the 'ouse, Arch. It's a real picture and yer won't believe all them things in it – paintings on the walls and silver and all sorts.'

'Well, it belonged to an heiress,' Arch said and shrugged. 'It all sounds a bit strange ter me – but I'll tag along and see what's what.'

When the car arrived to fetch Jamie, Arch slid into the back seat beside him. The seat smelled of polished leather and it was comfortable as they were driven through the streets and across the river. He stared in surprise as they went straight up a gravel drive to an imposing front door.

'Is this it?'

'Must be. We never used the front door,' Jamie said. 'We always went in the kitchen door or through a window. Cassie sometimes put the bolt on the door and we'd climb out through the pantry window.'

'Didn't you feel wrong using a 'ouse like this?'

Jamie nodded, feeling a return of his guilt. 'Yeah, I did – that's why I cleared up all the rubbish. I knew it belonged to someone and that they would come to claim it one day. And I was right, wasn't I?'

'Yeah . . .' Arch got out of the car and Jamie scrambled out after him. Gerald Gillows was coming towards them, a smile on his face.

'This must be your brother Archie,' he said offering his hand. 'Thank you for letting Jamie come, Mr Martin.'

'Call me Arch, everyone does,' Jamie's brother said

and shook hands. 'I don't quite understand what you want Jamie ter do.'

'I'm preparing a room for Cassie,' their host said, 'and I wanted Jamie's advice.'

'What would Jamie know about things like that?' Arch frowned. 'He's just a kid.'

'Cassie responded to him and he knows what she likes,' Gerald Gillows said and looked at Arch. 'I've lost the only person in the world I loved and because of me Cassie was hurt in the fall. She has no one – and unless I adopt her, the authorities will lock her away in an institution where she will be treated worse than I would treat my dog. I propose to employ a housekeeper and a nurse to look after Cassie. She will live here in this house and play with my sister's things as she likes. I intend to employ a gardener who will keep an eye on her outside – and follow if she wanders off.' A deep sadness was in his eyes now. 'I shall do all I can to see that Cassie doesn't suffer an accident in the way my beloved sister did.'

'I can tell yer the kind of things Cassie likes,' Jamie said. 'I'll show yer her favourite things in the house and she'll be happy if yer put them in 'er room fer 'er.'

'That's what I'd hoped, Jamie,' Gerald said and smiled at him. 'If you would like to visit Cassie on a Sunday sometimes, a car can be sent for you – my gardener will also drive a car to take her where she needs to go.'

Arch was listening but not quite believing what he heard. It all sounded a bit too good to be true, but he kept his mouth shut and followed Jamie and Gerald Gillows into the house. First, they visited a big room at the front of the house. It was painted in a bright blue and Jamie shook his head as soon as he saw it.

'Cassie won't like this, sir,' he said. 'She likes pink and yellow and silver, bright colours but not like this.'

Gerald made a note in his little book. 'I'll have it painted pink then,' he said and smiled. 'Would she like a big bed or a small one?'

'Cassie likes to feel safe, so I think a small one – and a big armchair. She likes curling up in a chair to sleep. She likes the dressing table in your sister's room. Something like that – white and gilt – is what she thinks is pretty, sir.'

'I shall give her a white dressing table and stool, a matching wardrobe and a desk for her drawing things. Does she like dolls or other toys?'

'I don't know,' Jamie confessed. 'Most of all she likes to dress up and play with sparkly things. She loves the apple tree and I think she would like a swing.'

'She can have a swing in the garden and one in here too,' Gerald said. 'Anything to make her happy . . .'

'I think she might like a music box,' Jamie suggested. 'I saw one in a shop window once. It had a little lady that twirled to the music. Cassie likes to sing so she might like that.'

'I knew it was a good idea to ask you,' Gerald said and smiled. He put his hand into his pocket and pulled out a wallet, extracting a large white note, which he gave to Jamie. 'This is for you, to thank you for what you've done . . .'

Arch looked at the money and shook his head. 'Five pounds is far too much, sir. Jamie doesn't want anything for helping you.'

'No, sir, I don't want anything.'

'Please take it,' Gerald said. 'I want you to promise that you will visit Cassie sometimes. She likes you and I want her to be happy – and the money will make it right for you.'

Jamie looked at his brother. Arch shrugged, as if he wanted nothing to do with the decision.

'If I take it, I shall give it to Mr Forrest for the things I took,' Jamie said. He lifted his head and reached out to take the money. 'If you're sure it's what you want, sir. I don't need it – but I'll take it for Mr Forrest if you want me to have it.'

'I shall be disappointed if you don't.'

'All right then, I'll take it – and I promise I'll visit Cassie sometimes on Sundays. I can't come other days because I have school and running errands for Mr Forrest, but I'll visit when I can.'

'Thank you.' Gerald smiled at them. 'I shall prepare Cassie's room – and thank you for your time. My driver will take you home now.'

In the back of the car Jamie looked at his brother.

'I can pay Mr Forrest back for what I took now,' he said. 'He told me he lost just over that amount so if I keep workin' fer nothin' I shall make up fer what I did to upset him.'

'It's a lot of money,' Arch said and shook his head. 'I reckon Mr Gillows must be a bit soft in the head 'imself, givin' yer all that – and havin' all that done fer a girl he don't know.'

'He's lonely and unhappy 'cos his sister died and he blames 'imself,' Jamie said. 'I took the money 'cos he needed me to, Arch. I reckon he knows he should never 'ave gone orf and left his sister with just a nurse to look after 'er and this is 'is way of makin' it right.'

Arch stared at him and then nodded. 'Yer a bright kid,' he said and smiled. 'I reckon what yer said is about right. I read somethin' in the papers recently – they say a lot of family money was hers through a will and he inherits it now she's dead. They was hinting that he left her like that, because he wanted her money – but I reckon that's a rotten thing to say. Yer can see how sad he is, over what 'appened, can't yer?'

'Yeah, I reckon,' Jamie said. 'How come she had the money and not 'im then?'

'She was his half-sister,' Arch said and frowned. 'Her grandfather left it in his will to her and she made a will leaving it to her brother.' He nodded to himself. 'That's why the paper said them awful things. I thought he might be one o' them queer devils but he ain't – and he ain't a murderer either. I feel sorry fer him . . .'

'Yeah, I do too,' Jamie said. 'We're all right 'cos we've got each other, Arch, but some folk ain't got anyone. Mr Gerald is right about Cassie. They would lock her up in an institution or send her off somewhere like they tried to when her mum died. She needs someone to look after her – and Mr Gerald, he needs someone to look after.'

'It sounds simple when you say it like that,' Arch said and smiled. 'Trouble is, things don't usually work out as you want. If the papers get ter hear of this they'll write terrible things and the authorities might not let him adopt Cassie.'

'You mean they'd rather shut her away than let her be happy in her house?' Jamie looked at him in disbelief. 'Mr Gerald only wants to 'elp 'er.'

'Well, let's hope it works out fer them both,' Arch said, 'but I reckon them papers will have somethin' ter say and if they do . . .' He shook his head.

'I hope they don't spoil Cassie's chance ter be 'appy,' Jamie said and shook his head.

Arch could see that his brother didn't understand what people would think of a single man wanting to adopt a little girl who was a bit strange in the head. He'd wondered himself until he'd spoken to Mr Gerald Gillows but the papers would write their story and not care if it was true, because their righteous attitude would sell lots of copies and that was all newspapers ever cared about. It didn't matter that lives might be ruined or people made miserable as long as they sold their papers . . .

# CHAPTER 16

*June*

'Look at that then,' Kathy Saunders showed Sarah the story in the newspaper. 'I reckon that's romantic – he gave up a kingdom to marry her because he loved her.'

Sarah glanced at the picture of the Duke of Windsor and Wallis Simpson who was now his wife and apparently very happy. She nodded as she read the article. 'They're going for a honeymoon in Austria. Do you think it's right what the papers say – that she sympathises with Hitler and his fascists?'

'Perhaps it's him,' Kathy said. 'If he is a fascist, I'm glad he's not our king anymore. I think our new king is lovely, don't you?'

'Yes, I do,' Sarah agreed. The coronation the previous month had been exciting for the whole country and things had seemed a little dull when the flags started to be taken down. 'Anyway, how are the plans going for *your* wedding, Kathy?'

'Oh, Mum has charge of that,' Kathy said and didn't seem particularly interested. 'We went shopping for a dress last Saturday. I liked three of them and couldn't pick so Mum said it would be best to spend less and buy a nice costume for going away. She says a wedding dress is only worn once, unless you cut it up to make a christening gown for your babies.'

'Yes, I suppose that's right,' Sarah said. 'But I think it is best to have the dress you like – after all, you only look to get married once, don't you?'

'Yes, that's true,' Kathy said and smiled serenely. She waved as Nurse Jenny Brown passed by on her way home. 'Good morning, nurse.'

'Good morning, Kathy.' Jenny nodded and smiled. 'Have a good day. I'm off home to sleep. We had a long night on the chronically sick ward last night.'

Sarah gave her a sympathetic look. She knew only too well how that could feel. It was bad enough when the ward was busy during the day but things always seemed worse if there was a crisis at night.

'Have a good rest,' she advised and Jenny blew her a kiss.

Sarah looked at Kathy. 'I'd better get to my ward. Sister Norton is back on today and she will be watching the clock, as always.'

Sister Norton had had a few days off at the end of May but she was back now and Sarah would need to be on time in the mornings.

Jenny was yawning as she queued for the bus to take her home. The streets were busy, people everywhere, rushing here and there, making her feel isolated, as if she were not a part of the world. It was because she was so tired, she knew, this odd feeling of being cut off from what was happening, and yet it was also because her life seemed hemmed in and frustrating.

When Chris was in town it was fine. He took her out and they enjoyed themselves at nice restaurants and the pictures or even the occasional dance. Jenny loved dancing but Chris wasn't very interested and she had to ask before he would take her. Sometimes when the other nurses spoke of going dancing with their boyfriends or husbands, Jenny felt envious, as if her life was passing her by. She was only in her early twenties and she wanted some fun, yet most of the time all she did was work and go home to bed and it wasn't enough.

Sighing, Jenny boarded her bus and paid the ticket collector her fare. She'd thought she might be in love with Chris and when he'd told her that he was really a spy for the Government and not a Blackshirt, she'd felt proud of him and what he was prepared to do for the country, but now she felt restless. She wanted to go out with a crowd of friends on a Saturday night, flirt with handsome young men, and have fun rather than sit in and read a book or knit. Yet if she did that, she would have to finish her relationship with Chris, as he might not like her having a good time without him; she just didn't know what to do. Why did life have to be so difficult? She shook her head and scolded herself. Why couldn't she be sure of what she wanted like Sarah or a dedicated nurse like Sister Jean Norton? Jenny was certain neither of them got themselves into a mess like she had.

Jean sighed as she straightened her cap in front of the mirror. She'd enjoyed a few days at the sea, visiting her aunt and cousins. She didn't often see them but they sent cards every Christmas and they'd asked her down because Aunt Rosemary's granddaughter Anne was getting married. It had been a pleasant break and Jean had enjoyed being part of a family again. Sometimes she forgot that her mother's sister was still living and had a big family. The wedding hadn't been a lavish affair but it had been a happy one.

'We keep thinking that you'll get married one of these days,' Aunt Rosemary had told her. 'I know you're a dedicated nurse, Jean – but don't you ever think about finding a husband and having children before it's too late?'

'I shall only marry if I find someone I can love,' Jean had replied and smiled, because she didn't want to spoil a happy day. However, her aunt's remark had set her thinking about what she *did* want out of life.

For a long time after Rodney had let her down, Jean had decided that she never wanted to care about a man again. Rodney Southerby was now a successful architect and wealthy in his own right, though at the time he'd merely been an apprentice. Looking back now, Jean realised that she ought to have known he was never going to settle for a nurse from a working-class background. She should have known that giving into his flattery and his seductive smiles would lead to unhappiness and shame for her. As soon as she'd told him she believed she was pregnant, Rodney had shown his true colours. He'd accepted a big job up in the north somewhere and she'd never heard from him again. The fact that she'd miscarried his child had left her feeling empty and bitter, knowing that Rodney hadn't cared whether she lived or died, he'd just wanted to get away and deny all knowledge of any child – in fact, he'd had the cheek to ask her if she was sure he was the father. As if she'd gone from one lover to the next!

She'd felt so bitter it had taken her ages to even speak civilly to a man again. Tears had turned to anger and her heart to stone. She'd grown a hard crust that hadn't been touched by her relationship with George or anyone else. Perhaps that was why she hadn't wanted to visit with her aunt and cousins, all of whom were happily married. It was only now that she'd found Dr Matthew Mitchell that she felt able to allow herself to feel emotions again.

She would be seeing Matthew that evening for dinner. A smile touched Jean's mouth as she remembered their drive into the country and the wonderful lunch they'd had that day a few weeks ago. It had been a treat to remember, all her favourite foods but eaten with a man she felt she could trust and perhaps love. Perhaps she already did love him . . .

Jean wasn't quite sure how she felt, though she knew she wanted their relationship to progress. She'd deliberately taken this little holiday to give herself time away to think about the future. Was she ready to give up nursing in favour of marriage and a family? She would certainly go on until she had a child, but then she would need to stay at home and care for her family. Jean thought she might be ready, though she knew Matron would not ask her to resign even if she married. Many hospitals still didn't permit their nurses to marry, but Mary Thurston, the Rosie's matron, had always said that she didn't want to lose her dedicated nurses just because they wished to marry. So, Jean could carry on – at least until she had a child . . . and she might go back one day, if she had leisure and felt the desire to continue her nursing.

Was there still time for her to have children? Jean hoped there might be. She'd put such things out of her mind after Rodney left her in the lurch and she'd lost her baby. Would she be able to carry a child full term now?

Jean's thoughts went round and round and when Nurse Sarah spoke to her, she jumped. 'Ah, Nurse Sarah,' she said. 'I didn't notice you come in – will you give little Jeanie a bed bath please? I think she has had an accident and I imagine the sheets will need to be changed.'

'Yes, Sister,' Sarah said and smiled. 'I just wanted to tell you that Ned is settling in well with us and he seems very happy.'

'I'm glad to hear it,' Jean said. 'Not that I doubted your mother would cope. After all, she has you to help her if anything bothers her.'

'Yes, we're very lucky,' Sarah said. 'Did you enjoy your family wedding, Sister?'

'Yes, as a matter of fact I did, very much,' Jean said and nodded. 'Now, get on with your work, nurse. Doctors' round will be at ten o'clock this morning and we want everything spick and span, don't we?'

'Yes, Sister.' Nurse Sarah went off to begin her work and Jean continued her round of the ward, her quick eyes noting a sheet that needed changing, a vase of dead flowers at the end of the ward that must be taken away, toys on beds and uneaten food left on bedside tables which must be removed so that everything was perfect when the doctors made their rounds.

'Good morning, Sister Norton,' Dr Mitchell said and nodded to Sarah. 'Nurse – how is your visitor?'

'Very well, sir.'

'Good, good.' He smiled and looked at the patient in the first bed. 'And how are you, young Jimmy?' he asked, checking the board he carried. 'I see you're over the sickness and your temperature is down – have you any pain at all now?'

'No, sir,' the patient said and folded the sheet between nervous fingers. 'Is my mum coming to see me today?'

'She is – and I should think she can take you home,' Dr Mitchell said, turning to the senior nurse. 'Is that your opinion, too, Sister?'

'Yes, sir,' Jean said resisting the urge to smile into those melting brown eyes. 'Jimmy seems very much better. He's restless and wants to be up and about.'

'Yes, then we'll let him go home when his mother comes,' Dr Mitchell said and nodded to the patient. 'We'll send you home with some medicine and your mother can look after you – you should be back at school in a few days.'

Jimmy's face lit up as the doctor and Sister Norton walked on. He looked at Nurse Sarah, who was slightly behind the other two.

'Did he mean I'm better, nurse?'

'Yes, your tummy upset has cleared up,' Sarah told him with a smile. 'You feel well now, don't you?' He nodded at her. 'When doctor has finished his round, I'll get you washed and dressed, ready for your mum to take you home.'

Dr Mitchell worked steadily through the ward. Most of the patients had minor illnesses, festering cuts and boils, or tummy upsets that had been impossible to cure in homes that had no proper sanitation and were laden with germs despite all the women did to clean them; but a broken arm, a fractured ankle and a nasty chest infection were the worst at the moment and the round was soon done.

Sarah could see Dr Mitchell was talking to Sister Norton before he left and, to her surprise, the senior nurse was smiling and blushing. She hadn't noticed anything before, but now she wondered – was there more than a professional relationship between them? Sarah thought it would be lovely if it was true, a real hospital romance, unlike the fairy-tale romances some of the patients read when they started to recover.

At most hospitals such relationships were frowned on. Doctors and nurses were not supposed to fall in love, become engaged or marry, though that had always seemed nonsense to Sarah, because surely only a nurse could understand the hours a doctor needed to work. It was the reason why many marriages between doctors and women of their own social class did not work as they should. Ladies who expected to hold lots of parties and be escorted to the theatre did not take kindly to having their husbands on call evening after evening.

However, she decided to put all thoughts of the possible romance to one side. It wasn't Sarah's business to pry, though in the infirmary news about marriages and engagements was usually quick to pass from mouth to mouth. She smiled as she thought that perhaps Jean Norton wasn't so different to the other nurses after all!

Sarah's thoughts turned to her own love life. Steve was going to meet her after work that evening and they were going to the pictures. She would grab a sandwich from the canteen to keep her going at teatime and then they would buy some fish and chips on their way home later.

Jean had brought a nice dress to work that morning and she changed out of her uniform when she came off duty, putting on a little dab of lipstick and powder and combing her hair free of the grips and pins that kept it tidy on the ward. She applied a little of her expensive Elizabeth Arden cologne behind her ears – a treat to herself for her birthday – and smiled at her reflection in the mirror. As she waited just outside the Lady Rosalie Infirmary, she saw Jenny Brown arrive for duty and nodded to her. Sister Alice Burton followed her in, stopping to exchange greetings. She was still chattering when Matthew Mitchell arrived and came up to Jean with a smile. He'd been home and changed and she could smell the fresh scent of soap on his skin.

He nodded to Sister Burton. 'Good evening, Sister – I hope you have a quieter night on the ward this evening.' His smile warmed as he looked at Jean. 'I hope I didn't keep you waiting?'

'No, of course not, Matthew. It's a lovely night anyway.' She smiled inwardly, knowing that by morning it would be all over the infirmary that she was going out with Dr Mitchell. Sister Alice Burton liked to gossip and she would pass the news on to anyone who would listen.

Deciding that she didn't care, Jean took Matthew's arm and allowed him to lead her to the comfortable Morris car he had waiting. He opened the door for her to slide into the passenger seat, where she was greeted by the smell of cherished old leather, and his smile made her feel special. Jean knew she was happy – happier than she'd been for a long, long time . . .

It was only as she was driven away that she happened to glance out of the window and caught sight of George standing on the pavement. He was staring after them, a look of shock mingled with anger on his face. Oh dear, that was unfortunate! Jean bit her lip. She'd been putting off thinking about George but she knew that, after this evening, she would have to tell him the truth. Even if Matthew did not ask her to marry him, she could no longer consider having an intimate relationship with George and it was only fair to let him know.

As it happened, Matthew did ask her to be his wife that evening. He ordered some of the sweet white wine she liked to have with their pudding and then reached for her hand across the table.

'You don't have to answer yet,' he said. 'But I wanted you to know that I'm in love with you, Jean – and I'm hoping we can marry. I want to be with you, make love to you, and I wouldn't dream of anything less than marriage. I'm not like that so-and-so who seduced you and left you as soon as he knew you were with child.'

Jean had told him about Rodney the day they'd driven into the country. Matthew had sworn softly and called him a swine, but he'd been thoughtful and quiet afterwards and she'd wondered if he found it difficult to accept that she'd had an intimate relationship when she was younger, though he'd thanked her for telling him. It was a risk to tell her secret but she wasn't the sort of woman who would marry and then let him find out that she wasn't the perfect virgin he might have thought her.

'I know I was married and some women don't want to marry a man who has been married before – but I'm hoping you won't feel that way . . .'

'I don't see why that should make a difference,' Jean said. 'I know it is possible to love more than once. I told you that I'd had a relationship, too – and I do care for you very much, Matthew. I think perhaps – no, I'm *sure* that I should like to marry you, if you're quite sure that you want—'

'Of course, I'm sure!' he exclaimed and smiled. 'I'm not a young boy in the throes of infatuation, Jean. I don't expect you to be an immaculate virgin. I've admired you for a long time, but you seemed to be so remote. When you told me your story, I was so angry that he'd hurt you so badly, too upset to ask you to marry me then – but it just makes me want to look after you more. I don't want you ever to be hurt like that again, my darling. I want you to be mine so that I can always love and protect you . . .'

'Matthew . . .' Jean's eyes were wet with tears but she blinked them away. It was stupid to cry when she was being offered something wonderful. 'Yes, please. I should like that very much!'

'When shall we do it?' he asked. 'Shall we make it a

big thing or slip away quietly, marry, have a lovely honeymoon and then tell our friends when we get back?'

'I don't have many friends,' Jean said, 'and my family live a long way off – I think if I just tell them we'll go down and visit once we're married it would be enough. But we could invite a few of our colleagues for drinks before the wedding, if that suited you?'

'Whatever makes you happy,' he said. 'It's my birthday in August and it happens to be a Saturday – the fourteenth. Shall I set it up for that day?'

'Yes, please.' Jean smiled contentedly. 'I think I'll ask Nurse Sarah to be my witness – I don't have anyone close in London.'

'I've got a few friends I'll ask for drinks and one in particular to be my witness,' Matthew said. 'How would you like to go to France for a honeymoon? I can't take much more than ten days but I'm due some leave.'

Jean laughed; it was all happening so fast and she felt reckless, swept along on a tide of relief as something let go inside her. 'Where shall we live? My cottage is small but it's not bad . . .'

'Well, I've got a nice house with a garden by the river,' Matthew said. 'I'll take you to see it at the weekend. If you like it, we'll make it home – if not I'll look for something else.'

'I'm sure I'll like it . . .'

Matthew squeezed her hand. 'I bought it after my first wife died, so it will be *your* home, Jean. You can bring your things there and we'll throw out whatever you don't like.'

'You're mad!' she said and he kissed her hand. 'But I do love you . . .'

'We'll go shopping for your ring together,' Matthew said. 'I don't know whether you like diamonds or coloured stones so you must choose . . . but we'll do it soon and then invite our colleagues for a drink and tell them.'

Jean nodded. 'I think they will already have some idea. Sister Alice saw us meet this evening and you know she likes to talk.'

'Yes,' Matthew chuckled. 'I dare say they will be laying bets in the rest room so we'll keep them waiting until we get the ring.'

Jean lifted her wine glass to toast him. 'To future happiness,' she said and he touched his glass to hers.

'To us,' Matthew said. 'I love you, Jean, never forget it . . .'

'I shan't,' she said, then felt an icy chill at her nape. She hadn't told Matthew about George's divorce, but there wasn't really any reason to bring it up. After all, it had never been more than a convenient friendship. Because she was lonely, at times Jean had wished it was more and she knew George had certainly wanted it to be more after his divorce but she'd been sensible and it wasn't fair she should be blamed for the break-up of a marriage that had been all but over before she even met him.

Jean's blood ran cold at the memory of their last meeting. George's wife was convinced that he was having an affair with her and she might try to name Jean as correspondent in her divorce. If she did that it could damage Jean's reputation and it might sour her happiness with Matthew. Suddenly, she wished that she'd mentioned the problem to Matthew before this, but couldn't bring herself to speak now and spoil their evening. Perhaps George's wife would accept that he'd been with a woman he'd paid to help him get a divorce and Jean's name would never be mentioned.

One thing was certain, she would need to make it plain to George that she was never going to marry him and he might even make it up with his wife . . .

# CHAPTER 17

It was almost the end of the school term. Jamie had been busy working for Mr Forrest and training at the club each night and he'd heard nothing from Mr Gillows since the day he and Arch had visited the house by the river. Mr Forrest hadn't wanted to take the five whole pounds but Jamie had refused to let him give him any of it back.

'I took them Woodbines and the chocolate,' he told the elderly man. 'I want ter pay yer back, sir. It's only right – and I only took the money Mr Gillows give me, 'cos I wanted to give it ter you. Don't tell me it don't matter, 'cos it does.'

'In that case I'm going to pay you a shilling for your Saturday work,' Mr Forrest said and smiled. 'I'd like you to continue working for me, Jamie, if you'd like to.'

'Yes, I should,' Jamie said and his face lit up with a huge smile. 'Thank you for trusting me, sir.'

Mr Forrest nodded. 'Your brother is a good lad and I was wondering if both of you would like to live over the shop with me? I've got plenty of rooms for you and I'd feel safer with someone here at nights. My grandson is unable to come most of the time – and I still feel a bit uneasy at nights.'

'I'll ask Arch – and Marth,' Jamie said. 'Marth was good when me ma died, sir. She's me foster mum, though we didn't ask the council; she just done it herself. I think Arch gives her a few shillings for us so she might miss it, but I'll see what they say.' Jamie thought he might prefer to live here, because it was a better area than his home and closer to his school and the club.

'That would suit me,' Mr Forrest said. 'But I don't want to put either of you out, lad.'

Jamie promised to speak to his brother and Marth and did so at teatime that evening. Marth stared at him for a moment and then nodded.

'I don't mind either way, lads. To tell the truth, my sister has been after me to move in with her for a while now. I said no because my sons were wed and their wives needed a bit of help with the children, but they're growing now and I sometimes get the feeling I'm in the way – whereas Jilly needs me.'

Jamie nodded, because he knew Marth's elder sister was an invalid since she'd been ill in the winter. 'What do you think, Arch?'

'I wouldn't mind fer a while,' Arch said thoughtfully. 'When I've got a bit saved, I'd like a house of my own – but fer the time bein' it would suit me – as long as Marth don't mind?' He looked at the woman who had been so kind to them. 'You've been good to us and I shouldn't like to put you out or make yer feel we ain't grateful for what you did – we are very grateful, Marth. Jamie would have been in an orphanage if it hadn't been for you.'

'I wouldn't see that 'appen,' Marth smiled warmly. 'The council ain't got no 'eart and that's the truth of it. You're good lads and you've been no trouble but it's time I gave up this place – it's more than I need now my family are settled.'

'Then we'll tell Mr Forrest we'll help 'im out fer a while,' Arch said. He frowned as he thought of something. 'Where should we take our clothes to be washed, Marth? Should we send them to the laundry?'

'Nay, lad, they'll charge yer through the nose,' Marth warned. 'I know someone as lives down Fetters Lane – she will do the lot for a couple of shillings, sheets and all once a fortnight.'

'Right,' Arch looked relieved. 'I can cook us a bit of tea – though it won't be like yours, Marth – I ain't never had such good grub as yours!'

'Bless you,' she said and smiled. 'I'll miss the pair of yer but I'm glad yer asked because I might 'ave 'ad to ask yer ter leave and I didn't want ter do that.'

Mr Forrest was delighted when Arch told him the news. His daughter came over and gave the spare bedrooms a good turning out, as she said, declaring them to be fit for a lord when she was done. Arch and Jamie moved their stuff in that Sunday. It didn't take them long and the look of contentment on the old man's face was something to behold.

'We're doin' 'im a good turn,' Arch said to Jamie when they were alone. 'I know his grandson has signed up for another year or more in the army but he'll probably come to live here then and we'll get our own place – it will suit everyone that way.'

215

Jamie nodded, looking about him thoughtfully. His bedroom was larger than the one at Marth's and the bed had a feather mattress, which was so comfortable he fell asleep as soon as his head touched the pillow. He felt pleased that he'd repaid his debt to Mr Forrest and settled into the life of helping about the shop, visiting the club and enjoying the last days of school before the end of the summer term.

Because his life was filled with work and play, Jamie hadn't thought much about Cassie or Mr Gillows. He hadn't been back to the hospital, because they wouldn't let him visit Cassie unless he was with an adult, and Mr Gillows hadn't sent a car for him. Jamie supposed that the adoption would go ahead and that Cassie would be looked after by the servants her new father would employ to care for her.

So, when Rich came to the shop one evening just before closing time, the brothers were both pleased to see him and surprised by his news.

'I wanted ter tell yer first, Arch,' he said and grinned. 'And you, Jamie – it's because of you that I've got me new job.'

'What job is that then?' Arch asked.

'I'm goin' ter work fer Mr Gillows,' Rich said and laughed as he saw their faces. 'I've got a couple of rooms over the garage at that house by the river and I'm ter look after the garden and drive the car when I get my driving licence – and it pays fifteen shillings a week.'

'Blimey!' Jamie said feeling pleased for him. 'I reckon that's a real good job, Rich.' It was a lot more than most young men of his age earned round here.

'When did this happen?' Arch asked.

'Mr Gillows put the idea to me a couple of weeks back,' Rich confessed. 'I wasn't sure whether it would suit me but the doctors said it would be good fer me – not too strenuous and plenty of fresh air. I couldn't work in a factory or a place where there was a lot of dust, because of the damage to me lungs.'

'You look better,' Arch said and smiled. 'Why didn't you tell us sooner?'

'I wasn't sure what ter do,' Rich said. 'Mr Gillows was busy with getting the house ready for the little girl.' He hesitated, then, 'That was the only bit I didn't like, you see. I've got to watch over her when she's in the garden and if she wanders off, he wants me to follow and make sure she's all right.'

'It's because he doesn't want Cassie to have an accident like his sister did,' Jamie said, frowning. 'She won't know you're there most of the time, Rich – but if she likes yer, she'll probably talk ter yer sometimes.'

'Well, I've met her now,' Rich said, 'and I can see why he's worried – she *is* a little bit strange. He told me they wanted to lock her away in an institution but he's applied to adopt her and I 'ope it works out fer 'im. It would be a shame to shut her away somewhere, even though she needs watchin' all the time.'

'I ain't heard anythin' from 'im fer a while,' Jamie said.

'He's been away on business again,' Rich replied. 'But he was there yesterday when the doctors released me and he had the little girl with 'im. She calls 'im Daddy, so I suppose they've let 'im adopt her or at least foster her.'

217

'That's good,' Jamie said nodding, because it was surely the best thing for Cassie. 'When do yer start work then?'

'I've already started. I came to fetch a few things today. Ma told me I was ter bring me washing back to her once a week so she sees me – and so she can see I'm eating properly. I told her the housekeeper starts today and she's a good cook or so Mr Gillows says.'

'We shan't see much of yer about then,' Arch said frowning at his friend. 'They miss yer at the club, Rich. Steve was sayin' yer could 'elp ter train some of the youngsters if yer felt like it.'

'Nah, not for the time being,' Rich told him and the smile died from his eyes. 'It would be too much to accept just yet, Arch. It hurts too much that me career is gone. I'll get used to the idea in time, but fer now . . .' He shook his head. 'I'll be busy where I am – but my day off is Sunday, because Mr Gillows hopes to visit every Sunday. So, we could meet sometimes, watch the cricket or football – and I can get away fer a drink after nine in the evenings. The house will be locked then and the little girl in bed. I'll come ter the club you work at and we can talk there.'

Arch nodded but Jamie thought he looked disappointed. He'd hoped Rich would return home to live and they would meet most days, even if just for a brief chat. Now their lives were diverging and already there was a change in Rich. He had found a good job and a different life from the one he'd known in the grimy streets that ran alongside the docks, and Arch sensed the rift widening. He wasn't jealous of his friend's good luck, but he did feel a bit left out.

'I know you've been invited ter visit the child,' Rich said to Jamie, 'and I don't see why Arch shouldn't come too – maybe on a Saturday. I've been told I can have a friend to tea in the garden room once a week if I like. Mrs Benson – the housekeeper – told me to invite me ma, but you two could come sometimes.'

'Yeah, maybe we will,' Arch said but didn't smile. 'We're pretty busy too. Since Jamie started doin' deliveries for Mr Forrest his trade has picked up a lot. I do most of the heavy work mornings, lifting and stacking the shelves, and that's when the customers are in and out; it's fairly quiet afternoons, but then busy again from five to seven when the workers come home. We go to the club in the evenings – and Saturdays is always busy, and I've got me work as a bouncer in the night-club.' He reminded Rich that some of them still had to work hard for their living rather than having a cushy little job driving and a bit of gardening.

'Well, see yer around,' Rich said and there was a hint of sadness in his voice, as though he sensed that the close friendship they'd had since childhood had begun to crack.

'I hope he's done the right thing,' Arch said after his friend had gone.

'He's gettin' well paid,' Jamie said. 'And his room and board on top.'

'Yeah, that's what worries me,' Arch said. 'Why is he being paid so much? I don't quite trust that man . . .'

'You mean Mr Gillows?' Jamie said and wrinkled his nose. 'Why don't yer like 'im, Arch? He seems a generous man to me.'

'Yeah, he's generous wiv money,' Arch said and shook

his head. 'Sorry, kid. I know yer like 'im and maybe I'm bein' daft but there's somethin' . . .' He shook his head. 'No, I can't explain what I mean. It's just a gut feelin' that's all.' Perhaps there was resentment too, because Mr Gillows had lured his friend away with money.

'Well, Rich is big enough ter look after 'imself.'

'Yeah, I know.' Arch ruffled his hair. 'Yer a good kid, Jamie. It's a good thing yer too innocent ter know what the world is like – save that until yer older, kid.' He grinned at him. 'How would yer like to go to the flicks this week? There's what looks like an exciting sea thing called *Adventure's End* on at the Odeon.'

Jamie's eyes lit up. A trip to the cinema was a rare treat, normally reserved for birthdays. 'Yeah, I've seen the poster,' he said. 'That John Wayne is in it and I like the look of 'im.'

'We'll go on Friday night,' Arch said. 'Right, we'd better get back ter work. We've got a load of boxes ter unpack and then we're goin' ter Marth's fer dinner for one last time before she moves to her sister's.'


'I shall miss seeing you,' Jean Norton told Marth as she called in on Sunday morning. 'However, I shan't be living in my cottage much longer either. I wanted to tell you that I'm getting married on August the fourteenth.'

Marth's face lit up with pleasure. 'That's wonderful news, Jean. I'm so happy for yer. I've often wondered why yer weren't married and now yer will be.'

'Yes, I shall, and I couldn't be happier,' Jean said smiling. 'Well, I wish you future happiness too. I think you'll find it quieter living out at Hampstead with your sister.'

'Yes, I expect it will seem strange at first,' Marth agreed. 'Jilly was in service as a housekeeper for many years, never married – though I suspect she had a lover or two. Her last employer left her the house when he died. He had no one of his own, you see, and he said she'd looked after him so well that she deserved to have all he had. It's not a big place, but it's a lot better than anything round 'ere. She's been after me to go and help her now she's not so well and I thought perhaps it was time – my sons and their wives are settled and I'm not needed anymore.'

'I'm sure you are,' Jean said, 'but perhaps your sister needs you more?'

'I think she does,' Marth agreed. 'The Martin lads have gone to stay with Mr Forrest, which suits him – so everything is all settled and I move next week.'

'Then I'm glad I called before you leave,' Jean said. 'If you send me your address I'll keep in touch – just a card now and then.'

'Yes, that's right,' Marth said. 'I'll wish you good luck and happiness for the future then, Sister Jean.'

'And the same for you,' Jean said and they clasped hands before she left.

Jean was lost in thought as she walked home. She wouldn't be sorry to see the back of this lane. It was the shortest route home but now there was no one she knew well enough to call and see – and soon she would be moving to Matthew's lovely home near the river, a beautiful light house she would love to call home. It would mean a longer journey into work each day, but most days she would travel in with her husband – she smiled as the word came into her mind. The thought of being Matthew's wife filled her with joy. She'd thought that kind of happiness long behind her but now it looked as if she might have all she could ever want.

As she approached her cottage the smile died from her lips when she saw the man standing outside. Jean had hoped when he got the letter she'd sent him George would just accept that she'd ended their relationship. After all, it had been little more than a casual friendship, even if there had been times when it might have been more.

'George,' she said as she came up to him. 'Do you think it is wise to come here? After all, if your wife is divorcing you . . .'

'No thanks to you!' he snapped and she saw that he was angry. 'I really cared for you, Jean. I thought I meant something to you – but it seems I was wrong!'

'You were a friend, George,' Jean said flatly. 'Never anything more. I'm sorry if anything I said or did led you to think otherwise.'

'I certainly thought it was more,' he muttered furiously. 'My wife thinks we're lovers – and she is going to name you in her divorce suit.'

Jean felt as if he'd punched her in the stomach. 'I thought you said she would agree to you providing evidence with someone paid to do it?'

'She says she has all the evidence she needs and won't listen,' he said, his eyes cold. 'And why the hell should I bother to protect you or your reputation when you just throw me over the minute something better comes along?'

'Because I'm innocent!' Jean told him. 'We did nothing but keep each other company, George. I was a shoulder for you to cry on – and you were someone to talk to now and then. I considered it might become something more once, but it didn't, you know that! Why should I be branded as a marriage wrecker when I've done nothing?'

'You let me fall in love with you,' he said bitterly. 'My wife knew I wanted someone else so she had me followed. She thinks her evidence is enough to gain her freedom – and I wouldn't have contested it because I wanted to be free for you!' His eyes darted accusation at her and Jean nodded.

'I'm sorry if that's what happened,' she said. 'But no one can help their feelings, George. I've never been in love with you, even if I did fancy you – but I am in love now. I never meant to hurt you – or your wife.'

'Well, I wanted to warn you,' he said. 'You'll get a writ from her lawyer. I couldn't stop her anyway. She threw me out of the house – at least, she made it impossible for me to stay. I'm living in a hotel until I find a flat, I can afford.'

Jean saw his misery and her heart twisted with sympathy. She'd liked him well enough and didn't enjoy being the cause of his despair.

'I told you it was over,' she said gently, 'but I'm giving this cottage up in August. If you wanted to move in, I think it could be arranged.'

'Thank you, but a small flat will do for me.' He glared at her. 'So, it really is finished. Well, I've warned you; it's out of my hands now.'

Jean watched him walk away. She hadn't invited him

in, because it was better to be brief and she didn't want gossip amongst her neighbours.

When the door was closed and locked behind her, Jean leaned against it and closed her eyes, the tears stinging. She was going to be named and shamed in a divorce court and it wouldn't matter that she hadn't done anything wrong, her reputation would be gone. Whether George contested the divorce or not, there would be a scandal and Jean would have to tell Matthew.

How on earth was she going to explain? Even as her frantic mind sought a way of telling her fiancé about it, she knew it would sound sordid. The saying, "there's no smoke without fire," was widely believed. It would be reported in the newspapers and everyone would laugh and gossip behind her back. The stiff and starchy Sister Norton caught red-handed – and engaged to the most popular doctor in the infirmary! How the gossips would love that!

Jean didn't sleep much that night and she felt washed out when she got up the next morning to make a pot of tea and some toast. She might see Matthew at work but she might not. They hadn't arranged to meet that evening because he was on call until eleven and she would have left work long before that time and she couldn't just drop this bombshell on the man she'd promised to marry in a rushed moment. It would have to wait until they could meet and talk properly.

The realisation that George's wife could ruin her life hung over Jean as she caught the bus to work. However, she managed to get through her morning without snapping the nurse's head off but she was in no mood to smile or chat and Nurse Jenny Brown looked at her oddly a few times. She didn't often work in the children's ward, but Sarah had a day off and Jenny was her replacement for the day. Jean took her lunch break and saw Matthew enter the hospital as she was on her way back to the ward.

'Jean!' he called, smiling as she halted and let him catch up to her. 'I know you're busy and I shan't keep you – but I wondered if we could take the day on Saturday? You're not on duty, are you?'

'No, I'm not,' Jean agreed. 'Did you have something in mind?'

'I want to buy the ring,' he said, 'and there's a friend I would like you to meet . . .'

'I-I shall look forward to it,' she replied and tried to smile but her heart felt heavy. 'Actually, there's something I need to talk about, Matthew . . .'

'Guilty secrets?' he teased but the smile in his eyes died when he saw her face. 'Just teasing, darling. You know you can tell me anything.'

'You may not be quite as forgiving when I do,' she said. 'I know there's no time at the moment so on Saturday we'll meet early and talk before we do anything else.'

He nodded, but looked anxious. 'You haven't changed your mind?'

'No, of course not. I love you . . .'

He nodded gravely. 'In that case nothing else matters,' he said and reached for her hand, giving it a squeeze. 'I can see you're worried, Jean, so I'll try to make time tomorrow. Perhaps we can manage a few minutes in your lunch hour . . .?'

'Yes, all right, thank you,' she said. 'I have to go and so do you.'

Matthew nodded, touched her hand again and walked off. Jean returned to work. She would be on thorns until she told him about the divorce and she was afraid of the look in his eyes when he heard that she was about to be the object of a disgraceful scandal . . .

After another restless night, Jean went downstairs to put her kettle on. As she passed through the hall, she saw a white envelope lying on the floor and bent to pick it up. It had been delivered by hand and had no postmark and she could smell the faint perfume of lavender.

Opening it, she read the few lines with shock. In large red letters the words – Harlot! Whore! Tart! – were scrawled all over the page. It was, of course, unsigned and Jean wondered which of her neighbours had pushed it through her door. Was she already the subject of gossip because of George's visits to her home?

She screwed it into a ball and thrust it into the fire, not wanting to look at the hateful thing. Her stomach was already tying itself in knots and she could hardly force down her buttered toast and marmalade. She knew she must eat, especially as she wouldn't feel like eating in her lunch break.

Once again, Jean was numbed with anxiety as she rode the bus to work, but managed to put on her professional face as she tended her patients. Sarah was back at work and she smiled at her, looking happy. Jean recalled that the nurse had been to see the house she would live in after her wedding in early September.

'How did you get on yesterday?' she asked when they had a free moment.

'It's a nice house, two bedrooms, a parlour and kitchen, and a lovely back garden,' Sarah said. 'We measured up and I'm going to buy some material for the curtains on the market and make them myself.'

Jean nodded, forcing a smile. She glanced at her watch. Only half an hour to get through and then she would meet Matthew. He had sent word that he had managed to squeeze half an hour from his busy day.

Her heart was beating as she went down the main stairs and found him waiting for her. They went to the pub across the road and Matthew ordered coffee and a sandwich for them both. He looked at her as the waitress departed.

'I think I should tell you that I received a letter today,' he said.

'A letter?' Jean was startled. 'What do you mean?'

'A rather nasty letter . . .' Matthew passed it across to her. 'Is that what you needed to tell me?'

Jean scanned the letter. It accused her of being a harlot and a marriage wrecker and was so horrible that it made her feel sick. She folded it and returned it to him.

'It isn't the truth,' she said quietly, 'but people will believe it . . .'

'Tell me,' Matthew said and looked deep into her eyes. 'I want your version, not that filth, Jean.'

'George was a friend, nothing more. Ever,' she said simply. 'His marriage was already falling apart when we met and he was unhappy. I had no one and so we met for coffee or the occasional concert. We were not

227

lovers. We kissed a couple of times and because we were both lonely it might have been more but it wasn't – and he knows it is over.'

Matthew looked at her in silence and then nodded. 'I take it this lady is planning to name you as the cause of her marriage break-up?'

'Yes. She seems to think we had an affair. George came to my cottage twice, to tell me about his wife's plans for a divorce, but he *never* came to my bed. I didn't tell you about him, because it wasn't important. I told you of Rodney, because that mattered.'

'Yes, I understand, but did George – did he think you meant it to be more?'

'He says he wanted more now but never once did he mention a divorce or remarriage when we were meeting. I thought it was against his principles – or his wife's . . .' Jean sighed. 'If I *had* gone to bed with him it would've been wrong, because I didn't love him. It's such a mess and I know what everyone will say and my reputation will be gone.'

'We can fight it,' Matthew said. 'If she tries to name you, we'll get a lawyer to defend you – and we'll counter-sue for defamation of character.' His eyes met hers. 'We can do that – if you're sure that there is nothing she can prove . . .'

'George has only ever been in my cottage for perhaps fifteen minutes; last time I didn't even ask him in – but people talk. I had a horrible letter too but I burned it.'

He nodded, a determined look in his eyes. 'I believe you, Jean, and my lawyer will stop this if he can, I promise you.'

'What if we can't stop it?' she said. 'How will you feel if everyone is naming your wife a harlot?'

'*I* will know the truth,' he said and looked grim. 'Anyone who says it to my face will wish they hadn't – but we'll stop it if we can, Jean.' He reached across and took her hands, holding them firmly. 'I'm sorry you've been put through this, my love. You've had enough sorrow in your life without someone throwing malicious spite at you at a time when you should be happy.'

He was so understanding and thoughtful. Jean felt the tears on her cheeks. 'I thought you might wish you'd never asked me to marry you!'

'No, I could never wish that,' Matthew assured her and the look in his eyes warmed and lifted her. 'Don't cry, Jean. We'll get through this together. I'll contact my lawyer straight away. It's a pity you burned your letter. If you receive more give them to me. We'll fight this every step of the way.'

Jean brushed the tears from her cheeks, relief driving out the despair. She felt as if she'd stood on the brink of hell and been pulled back from the fires. The love in Matthew's eyes was undiminished, even though it had been joined by anger – anger on her behalf. He was there to sustain her through the difficult times ahead and she felt gratitude flow through her. She wished that she could stop the scandal that was bound to happen once the case was brought to court, but at least it hadn't lost her the man she loved.

# CHAPTER 18

'There's a letter waiting for you, Jamie,' Mr Forrest said when he came in after his last day at school before the summer holiday. He smiled broadly. 'In fact, there are two – what do you think of that, lad?'

'Two letters for me?' Jamie was stunned. The only letters he'd ever been given were end-of-term reports addressed to his parents. The latest was for Arch and was in his back pocket. He looked at the envelopes. One was a thick creamy paper and the other was brown and official. His stomach clenched as he opened the brown one, because he wondered if he was in trouble but a smile lit his face as he looked at Mr Forrest. 'I've been accepted for the police cadets!'

'Well, now, that's something,' Mr Forrest said. 'Quite the feather in your cap, Jamie. You'll enjoy that, won't you?'

'It's just one evening a week,' Jamie said. 'So I shan't have to give up the club or running errands – though I might have to go sometimes on a Saturday or Sunday when there's a parade or a sporting event we have to attend, that's what Steve said. The cadets do stuff for charity and that.'

'Well, I never,' his kind host said. 'So, who is the other letter from – the posh envelope?'

'I think I know . . .' Jamie turned it over doubtfully in his hand before tearing it open. He read the message inside and frowned as he handed it to the elderly man. 'I've been invited to tea at Cassie's house.'

'You mean Mr Gillows has invited you?'

'No.' Jamie shook his head. 'It's from Cassie, at least it says it is – and she has invited me for tea in her house on Sunday.'

'He wouldn't have given her the house,' Mr Forrest looked puzzled. 'Would he?'

'I don't know. She *thinks* of it as her house – but it's a bit odd. I think he's trying to put Cassie in place of the sister he lost although Arch is suspicious.'

Mr Forrest nodded wisely. 'Arch is a sensible lad, but if the child is living with this Mr Gillows it must be all right – the authorities wouldn't have let him adopt her otherwise, would they?'

'I don't think so,' Jamie said doubtfully. 'He seems all right to me, sir – but he might be a little bit . . . you know . . .?' Jamie made a screwing gesture at the side of his head. 'His sister wasn't all there so perhaps he isn't either.'

'Jamie! That isn't a nice thing to say about a gentleman who was kind to you.'

'I didn't mean it wrong, sir,' Jamie said, 'but he does seem a bit . . . I think *obsessed* with Cassie. Is that the right word?'

'Yes, I know what you mean,' Mr Forrest agreed.

'He's not mad or queer or anything like that – but just single-minded and overcome with grief.'

'Yes, that's what I mean,' Jamie said and smiled in relief. 'I didn't know how to put it – but I don't think he means her any harm. I'm sure he just wants to look after her, because he wasn't there to look after his sister.' It was his guilt, just the way Jamie felt guilt over leaving his ma lying on the floor all day and breaking into Mr Forrest's shop.

'Out of the mouth of babes,' Mr Forrest said and shook his head in wonder. 'I think you've put your finger on it. I've read some of the stuff that was in the papers – and if I were that Mr Gillows, I'd have sued them reporters. Wicked cruel they were, some of them the things they wrote about him, hinting he left his sister alone because he wanted her inheritance.'

'They shouldn't be allowed to write lies,' Jamie said. 'It isn't fair!'

'No, it isn't,' Mr Forrest replied and smiled at him. 'So, shall you go then, on Sunday?'

'Yes. Mr Gillows is sending Rich with the car. Fancy him being allowed to drive a posh car.'

'I expect the regular driver will be with him until he passes his driving test,' Mr Forrest said. 'But it is a wonderful thing for Rich to learn. Once he has the skill it will stand him in good stead for lots of jobs – especially now the lad can't do what he'd hoped.'

'It was rotten luck, him being knifed like that,' Jamie said and remorse struck him again. 'If that Leo ever shows his face round 'ere again I'll tell Steve the minute I see him. He deserves to be in prison for what he did.'

'Yes, I agree,' Mr Forrest wholeheartedly agreed. 'Let's

233

hope he stays away, Jamie. Now, what shall we have for tea tonight – would you like a paste sandwich or a bit of scrambled egg on toast? It's what I'm havin'.'

Rich was driving the big black car when it drew up outside Mr Forrest's shop. He tooted the horn and Jamie came running out to find the car already surrounded by all the kids in the lane and they were pointing and looking at Rich as he got out, opening the door for Jamie to sit in the back.

'Cor blimey, ain't we posh?' a lad mocked and Jamie recognised him as one of the boys who had been with Leo's gang; the one who'd hung back when the others attacked. Jamie fixed him with a hard look and he backed away, then turned and ran off down the lane. The other boys just craned to get a look inside, envy in their eyes as Jamie was driven away. He knew he would be mocked about being posh every time he walked down the street, now, but it was just something he had to put up with; he would get enough mockery once it was known he was a police cadet anyway.

'Are yer all right back there?' Rich asked, glancing in his driving mirror. 'Ain't like you to be quiet, Jamie.'

'I was just thinking it was nice seein' you drivin',' Jamie said and grinned back at him. 'I'd like to learn when I'm old enough.'

'Yeah, it's not somethin' I expected ter do just yet, if ever.' Rich glanced at Mr Gillows' regular chauffeur. 'Sam has been teaching me in the evenings – he's been driving for thirty years. It's a skill I'd never have had if he hadn't taught me.'

'I'm glad yer gettin' on all right,' Jamie said. He

looked about him, noticing the changes as they left the mean streets he knew so well and headed across the river where the houses were immediately better. Rich drew into the drive of the house which had belonged to the tragic heiress and Jamie could see that the garden looked tidier than it had when he last visited, when it was a bit wild and overgrown. Rich was clearly making a difference.

He drove round to the back and Jamie got out of the car, waving at Rich and the chauffer as he walked through to the kitchen. It smelled of baking and the woman at the sink turned to smile at him.

'You must be Jamie,' she said in a friendly manner. 'I'm Cassie's friend – she doesn't like me to say I'm her nurse – and I cook for her as well. My name is Meggie and she's waiting for you in the front parlour.'

'In the parlour?' Jamie knew where it was, but they'd never used the front parlour and he felt uncertain, a little awkward, as he walked across the highly polished hall floor, which was all kinds of wood arranged in a herringbone pattern and a bit slippery now. The house smelled different than it had when he lasted visited, of polish and flowers he decided, and he saw a woman in a black dress and a white apron arranging a vase of tall roses and lilies on a table. She nodded at him but didn't smile; her neat black dress and scraped-back hair gave her a stern look.

Jamie went into the parlour and saw that the wood floor had been polished in here too, but a large washed-pink and green patterned rug covered most of it, which made it more comfortable. On the mantelpiece were photographs in silver frames, some of people Jamie had never seen, but a few of Cassie and Mr Gillows together. A big round table near the window had a white lace cloth on it and was covered with plates and dishes. Cassie was sitting at the grand piano and Mr Gillows was standing by her side, showing her how to play the notes. With his guidance she was managing to play a few notes in tune and it was a moment or two before they knew he was there.

Cassie turned first, her attention wandering. She looked at him, blinked and then laughed and clapped her hands. 'Daddy, Jamie is here!' she said and jumped down to run to him. 'You've come to tea! Oh, I've lots to show you . . .' Cassie took hold of his hand. 'Come on, I'll let you see my room.'

Jamie glanced at Gerald Gillows who inclined his head and Jamie allowed Cassie to lead him up the stairs to the big front bedroom. It had been painted pink since he'd last seen it and the curtains at the windows were frothy cream lace. The bedcover was pink with a cream lace overlay and it was strewn with pretty dresses. Jamie guessed that Cassie had taken out most of the dresses she'd been given and tried them all on before deciding which one to wear. Meggie must have a lot of tidying up to do when her charge had finished playing at dressing-up.

The room was filled with pretty things; everything a young girl could want was crammed into the available space and Jamie smiled as Cassie flitted from one object to another, showing him her toys and beautiful possessions. To his surprise, she had the jewellery box that had once belonged to Gillian Gillows and all the pretty beads and brooches were still there. He thought some of the more expensive diamond rings might have gone, but the string of pearls and some of the gold rings were still in the box. She also had another lacquer box which played music, dolls with painted china faces and pretty dresses, several expensive-looking stuffed toys with tags bearing the word Steiff pinned to their ears, a rocking horse and a swing fixed from a bar on the ceiling. It was like a toy shop and a giant dressing-up box and Jamie thought Mr Gillows must have spent a lot of money to make Cassie happy.

Her hair was clean and curled about her face in soft wisps. It looked much lighter now that it wasn't so greasy and he realised that she was a very pretty girl. She was happy and seemed to take everything in her stride, as though she had always lived in such luxury.

'Are you coming to live with us?' she asked suddenly.

Jamie stopped looking around the crowded room and met her gaze. 'No, I've just come for tea,' he replied. 'Besides, yer wouldn't want me here all the time.'

'No, I *do* want you to come,' Cassie said and pouted at him. 'I've got no one to play with when Daddy is working. You're my friend, you should be here!'

'I can't live 'ere,' Jamie said and saw the stubborn look he knew so well on her face. 'I can come sometimes ter play, though. Yer should ask Rich ter play wiv yer if yer lonely.'

'He doesn't like me.' Cassie dismissed the gardener with a toss of her head. 'Meggie likes me, but the other one doesn't. I hate her. She wants everything tidy – and she touches my things.'

'Do yer mean the housekeeper?' Jamie asked and she nodded, the sullen look still in her eyes. 'I told him to send her away but he won't. He says she looks after the house for us but I *hate* her!' Something in Cassie's gaze then sent a chill down Jamie's spine.

'She doesn't matter,' Jamie said. He narrowed his gaze. 'She doesn't hit yer, does she?'

Cassie shook her head. 'I hit her once and she said I was a spoiled brat and didn't deserve to have all these lovely things. She said Daddy was a fool to make so much fuss of me.'

So far, the housekeeper had kept her spite to the verbal variety, probably because she knew to hit Cassie would gain her nothing but instant dismissal. Jamie knew instinctively that Mr Gillows had made a mistake in hiring the woman; he needed someone more like Meggie, who would understand the girl.

'That's because she's jealous,' Jamie said. He waved his hand to encompass the room. 'This is all fer you, Cassie, and she thinks it's too much fer a little girl – but she's just a servant. You can ignore her. She won't dare hit yer 'cos Mr Gillows would send her away without a reference.'

Cassie laughed and the gleam in her eyes told Jamie that she was aware of the power she held. 'He gives me lots of nice things,' she said. 'But I wish he would send the old dragon away. Meggie can stay. I like *her*.'

'Yes, she told me she was yer friend,' Jamie said and grinned. 'Meggie will play wiv yer if yer ask her.'

Cassie shook her head. 'The other one makes her work all the time. Meggie says the dragon is in charge and she has to do what she says and I just wish Daddy would send her away.' Cassie's mouth set stubbornly. 'I might make him send her away. If I stare at him and don't answer he gives me my own way to make me smile again . . .'

'Do you think that's fair?' Jamie asked. 'He's done such a lot fer yer, Cassie.'

Cassie turned her back on him and he thought she was going to sulk, but then she ran to her swing and sat on it. 'Come and push me,' she said. 'I'll let you have a turn after.'

Jamie went to oblige her. He pushed her so that she swung high and shrieked with delight, but then the door opened and the housekeeper walked in, looking on with disapproval.

'The tea is all ready, miss,' she said. 'Bring your friend down to have his tea now, there's a good girl.' Her tone would have set anyone's back up and Jamie disliked her at once. He could see what she thought of him, with his patched trousers and scuffed shoes in the glance of disdain she sent his way.

Jamie saw the flash of anger in Cassie's eyes and for a moment he thought she would refuse, but then she jumped off the swing and turned to him.

'Come on, Jamie,' she said. 'You must be hungry.'

She ran from the room and Jamie followed. He saw the expression on the housekeeper's face as passed her. She looked disgusted as her eyes swept the untidy room and shook her head, as if it pained her to see the lovely things strewn everywhere. She wasn't a bit interested in the child she was supposed to care for, just the lovely house she lived in.

Jamie was tempted to tell her that she should leave Cassie's things alone, because he sensed that as soon as they'd gone, she would start putting the dresses back

239

into the deep wardrobes. Her actions would anger Cassie and increase the tension which was already simmering under the surface. Jamie knew how volatile Cassie could be and he suspected that one of these days the situation would boil over. Mr Gillows would be wiser to send the woman away. Cassie didn't need to live in a house where there wasn't a speck of dust; she preferred to do as she liked and leave her things wherever she wanted. Perhaps it didn't suit the housekeeper, but she was here to care for Cassie and there was no sense in expecting the beautiful, careless girl to act like other people. She wasn't normal or ordinary and yet, when she was happy, she could be lovely.

Cassie had made up her mind to be on her best behaviour during tea. She nibbled the paste sandwiches, which had been cut into tiny triangles and had no crusts, and Meggie had made coconut pyramids, which were sweet and crispy on top, strawberry jelly and tinned pears, and a sponge cake filled with jam and cream, which Jamie thought delicious. He just wished he could take a piece home for Arch and Mr Forrest.

Mr Gillows had tea poured from a silver pot, but Jamie and Cassie had lovely fresh orange juice that had been cooled to make it even nicer. Jamie tucked into all of it and had seconds of the jam and cream sponge. Cassie nibbled a sandwich, ate half a coconut pyramid and a tiny piece of sponge, but she drank all her orange juice and asked for more. When she went to the kitchen to fetch another glass of orange, Jamie looked at Mr Gillows.

'Cassie looks better,' he said. 'You've been kind to her, sir.'

'She is a sweet child – most of the time.' He frowned slightly. 'She may have told you that she doesn't like Mrs Benson?'

'The housekeeper?' Jamie nodded. 'I don't think that lady understands Cassie, sir. She wants her to be good and keep her things tidy but Cassie . . . Cassie's attention wanders. She can't do things the way other people do and she likes her things to be where she leaves them. The only time we fell out was when I tried to tell her not to do something.'

'I thought she would learn to be sensible,' Gerald Gillows said frowning. 'People think she doesn't understand, but they're wrong. Cassie has a mind of her own and once she decides she doesn't like something . . .' He sighed deeply. 'There's no changing her.'

Jamie nodded, because Mr Gillows seemed to be learning to understand Cassie. The girl was lovely, the picture of an angel, but there was a streak of pure devil in her and you had to know how to handle her or she could turn in an instant.

'She likes Meggie, though. And, you know, the house doesn't need to smell of polish all the time, sir . . .' He was willing Mr Gillows to understand, because he didn't seem to realise the danger.

'It's for Cassie's sake I hired Mrs Benson – to watch over her. One person isn't enough, because I don't want her left alone . . .' Gerald Gillows looked anxious. Jamie understood that he was thinking of another lovely but fey girl, a girl who had ended her life in the river because there was no one to look after her and stop her being reckless. 'I'm not sure what to do, Jamie. I thought living in her own house with all the things she likes would be enough . . .' Shadows were in his eyes. Was he thinking of Cassie or his sister at that moment?

'I expect it is enough for most, sir, but Cassie is different,' Jamie said. It was a big problem and he didn't feel able to solve it. If Mr Gillows sent the housekeeper away it might mean that Meggie had too much to do to watch over the girl – but if she stayed, Cassie might run off to spite her. However, Cassie's return with the fresh glass of orange juice curtailed the discussion.

'I ought ter be goin', sir,' Jamie said soon afterwards. 'I've got things ter do at 'ome.'

'Yes, you're a working lad,' Mr Gillows said and smiled at him. 'I'll go and tell Rich to bring the car round.' He looked at Cassie, who seemed to have forgotten her guest for the moment. 'Thank Jamie for coming, Cassie, and ask him to come again.'

Cassie finished drinking her orange and wiped her mouth on the back of her hand. 'I wish you would live here,' she said and for a moment he saw the girl he'd first made friends with and liked. 'Will you come next week?'

Jamie hesitated but saw the look of appeal in her eyes. Lots of presents couldn't make up for what Cassie lacked, and that was the lack of a mother to care for her and love her. In that moment he understood that Mr Gillows was kind – but he didn't love Cassie; he was using her to ease his conscience. 'Yeah, I'll come,' he said. 'Let's go and thank Meggie fer a lovely tea.'

Cassie's face lit up and, taking his hand, they ran into the kitchen together. 'That was a smashing tea,' Jamie told Meggie. 'I'm comin' again next week and I wanted ter say thank yer for what yer did today.'

'Bless yer, lad,' Meggie said. 'It was a pleasure. Miss Cassie is always a pleasure ter look after.'

Jamie looked her in the eyes. He saw that she was the nearest thing to a mother that Cassie had and he liked her. 'Look after her for us, Meggie.' He jerked his head towards the hall. 'Yer the one she likes not that other lady.'

Meggie nodded but didn't answer. She took a freshly baked jam tart from the table and handed it to him. 'This will keep yer goin' on the way 'ome, lad.' She winked at him. 'Yer a good boy, Jamie, and I know what yer mean . . .'

Jamie was thoughtful as he sat in the car on the way home. Cassie hadn't changed at all; she was still the wilful waif he'd met on the streets, though she seemed happy most of the time. Mr Gillows probably hadn't realised how difficult she could be, because when Jamie was around, she talked and laughed. Left to herself she was perfectly happy, but if Mrs Benson tried to discipline her, Cassie would sulk and stare at the wall – and Jamie knew she was capable of doing something violent if she became angry. He recalled the look in her eyes when she'd told him she hadn't pushed her mother down the stairs – a look that had chilled him . . .

He wished he'd told Mr Gillows that he should send Mrs Benson away. Meggie and Rich would surely have been enough to look after one small girl and the house-keeper disliked Cassie and her careless ways. Yet it wasn't Jamie's place to tell an adult what to do; he would be fourteen in a few days, nearly old enough to start work if he hadn't wanted to stay on at school and pass his exams, and the problem was too much for him to solve, though he was perhaps the only one who truly understood Cassie's moods. Mr Gillows thought it was enough to spoil her and expected affection in return, but Cassie didn't think logically. He wasn't sure she knew how to love, but he hadn't seen her with her mother; perhaps she'd been different then – and yet there was a nagging suspicion at the back of his mind that Cassie had caused her mother to fall even if she hadn't meant to. He wondered if her mother had been ill, perhaps shouting or complaining and Cassie had clutched at her and sent her tumbling to her death. There was no way he could ever know and yet he suspected it must have happened that way, was perhaps the reason Cassie wasn't quite as she ought to be from hints she'd dropped . . .

'You're quiet in the back there,' Rich said suddenly. 'Didn't you enjoy your tea?'

'It was great,' Jamie said. 'I liked Meggie – she's lovely.'

'Yes, she is,' Rich agreed. 'I don't much like that Mrs Benson, though.'

'Cassie doesn't either,' Jamie told him. 'You should try to talk to Cassie, Rich. She thinks yer don't like her.'

'She's strange,' Rich said and shook his head. 'I feel sorry fer her in a way – but she's got Meggie and Mr Gillows running after her all the time. I was brought up different, Jamie, and so were you. I don't believe in givin' her all her own way; it just makes her a spoiled brat.'

'Yes, I know – but she can't 'elp bein' the way she

is, Rich. I'm a bit worried about her – I'd appreciate it if yer tried to make friends wiv her – just so she trusts you.'

'I'll give it a go fer yer sake,' Rich said and grinned at him in the driving mirror. 'It's a good job fer me, Jamie. I don't want ter mess things up.'

'I'm worried what Cassie might do if that woman upsets her too much,' Jamie said. 'I know she seems selfish and spoiled, Rich – but she isn't, not really. It's just that she doesn't think about right and wrong like we do.'

'Yeah, I know.' Rich smiled at him as he stopped the car outside Mr Forrest's shop. 'I know this much – yer a thoughtful lad, Jamie. I'll do what I can fer the little girl, just fer you.'

Jamie thanked him, grinned at Mr Gillows' chauffeur and stood waving on the pavement as they drove off. Feeling that he was being watched, he turned around and looked down the street but couldn't see anyone. No doubt some of the other kids in the lane had been watching, giggling and making rude remarks. He couldn't expect anything else when he was driven about in a posh car. It set him apart from kids who should have been his mates, but it didn't matter that much. After his experience with Leo and his gang, Jamie had made his mind up that he was going to be different. He didn't want to hang about on street corners or get involved with thieves and crooks.

The invitation to join the police cadets was a step in the right direction. Jamie wasn't sure yet what he intended to do when he left school, but being in the cadets was sure to stand him in good stead. He might even join the force if he liked it – and one thing he wasn't going to do was stand about begging for work like his father had and then, in the end, took to stealing because he despaired of earning an honest living.

Jamie seldom thought of his father. He'd gone off after hitting Jamie's mother and killing her, and while Jamie knew it had more than likely been an accident, the result of his violent temper, his father hadn't hung around to explain. If the police had found him, he would be in prison – and would probably have been hung for his crime – but they'd given up looking for him after a few weeks. Jamie knew his father would have left London, perhaps gone to a port elsewhere and found work on the ships. He would have given a false name and might never return, perhaps leaving the ship in a foreign port. Because if he came back to London his life was over and Jamie didn't want to be told that his father had been hung; it was better if he never returned. Jamie and Arch had each other and it was all they needed for the moment. One day Arch would get married, but that was a long way off – and even further in the future for Jamie.

He shrugged as he went into Mr Forrest's shop. They were lucky to have a comfortable home and jobs to keep them going. Jamie wouldn't want to change anything, except have his mum back, but he knew that couldn't happen. He blinked the sudden tears back, because he didn't want to think of her lying there on the floor. Life didn't get better for a few tears. You had to make things happen the way you wanted. He certainly didn't want to live the way Cassie did and he'd only promised to go back for tea the next week because he felt sorry for her. She was a lonely little girl and all the money Mr Gillows had spent on her hadn't changed that, because Cassie had lost her mother and Jamie now believed it was the trauma of whatever had happened then that had turned her mind. She was hiding something, but he knew there was no point in asking. Cassie only told him what she wanted to tell him and if she had a secret, she wasn't ready to share it.

Cassie stamped her foot when she saw that the horrible woman Daddy had employed had put all her things away. How dare she touch them! Cassie hated her. She was just like that spiteful woman who had threatened that Cassie would be sent to Australia.

In a surge of temper, Cassie flung open the door of her wardrobe and started to pull everything out. She threw the pretty dresses, coats, nightclothes, shoes and bits and pieces on the bed or the floor and then she opened her box and took every sparkling bauble out, scattering them all over the dressing table top as she liked them.

Satisfied with her work, Cassie picked up her teddy bear and curled up in the big armchair, surveying her room in content. Now her room was how she wanted it to be. She started to sing to herself, the song she remembered Mummy singing when she was happy.

The door opened then and the horrid woman came in. Her face blackened with anger as she surveyed the room and saw what Cassie had done.

'You wicked, wicked girl!' she cried. 'You deserve a good slapping for what you've done – after all my work!'

'I hate you!' Cassie cried. 'Go away and leave me alone – or I'll push you down the stairs and you'll break your neck!'

'You're an evil brat and Mr Gillows is a saint to put up with you,' the nasty woman said and her mouth stretched into a tight line. 'One of these days he'll find out what a viper he's harbouring and then he'll send you back where you came from. I wouldn't be a bit surprised if you *did* push your mother down those stairs!'

'Go away!' Cassie screamed and threw her teddy bear at her. 'If you don't leave me alone, I'll tell my daddy and he'll hit you and send you away!'

'If I didn't need the job . . .' the woman said furiously. 'You wait, young madam, you'll get your comeuppance one of these days . . .'

Tears rolled down Cassie's cheeks as the housekeeper went out and closed the door behind her. She was happy with Daddy but that horrid woman would spoil things for her if she could . . .

# CHAPTER 19

Nurse Jenny met Nurse Sarah as they passed on the stairs and stopped to have a word with her. They seldom met these days as their shifts didn't often cross but Jenny had stood in for her sister Lily the previous evening and so she decided to have a chat rather than rushing straight off.

'Is everything going well for the wedding?' Jenny asked, smiling at the other girl. 'Thank you for the invitation. I'm definitely going to come to the church, even if I can't stay for the reception. Lily can't come to the church, because she is on duty that afternoon, but she'll come to the reception later when she's off duty – so we'll share the day between us, if that's all right with you?'

'Yes, of course it is,' Sarah said and laughed. 'We're all such busy people, aren't we? – and Matron couldn't possibly let us all have the whole day off. As you know, Kathy is getting married the week before us so she will be away and I think they're looking for help in the kitchens to cover that period.'

'I know someone who would like a job for a few

days. A girl I know, Laura, is going to college in September and she's been looking for little jobs during her holidays to earn some money to take with her. She lives down the road from us and I could ask her to come in and see Matron.'

'You should tell Matron and ask Laura to make an appointment,' Sarah said and arched an eyebrow. 'What about you, Jenny? Are you courting? I thought there was someone last year?'

'Well, there was – still is, really,' Jenny said and made a wry face. 'It's just that I seldom see Chris these days. He works all over the place and makes brief visits to London. While he *is* here, he takes me out a few times, but it's mostly letters.'

'It's not much fun like that, is it?' Sarah shook her head. 'It happened to me once and it broke up what I thought was a true relationship – but then I met Steve and I couldn't imagine being with anyone else now.'

Jenny nodded her head thoughtfully. 'At first, Lily was against Chris. She thought he wasn't to be trusted but now she likes him. She keeps pushing me into his arms and I'm not truly sure it's what I want, Sarah. I thought I loved him and he says he loves me but . . .' She shook her head and sighed. 'I suppose it will work out one day, but for the moment . . .'

'I'm sorry about that,' Sarah said. 'But you must do whatever makes you happy, Jenny. Don't let anyone rush you into marriage unless you're sure.'

'I shan't,' Jenny said and suddenly hugged her. 'Thanks for that, Sarah. I was feeling a bit down. You'd better get to the ward or you'll be in trouble. I'll see you at the wedding, if not before.'

'Oh,' Sarah said. 'We're having some of our colleagues who can't come to the wedding for a drink at the pub the week before so you must come then.'

Jenny promised she would and the two parted company, Sarah glancing at her watch and increasing her pace as she hurried to the ward where Sister Norton would be watching the clock.

Hurrying to catch her bus, Jenny made up her mind that she would go out with some friends that weekend. They'd asked her to a party they were having in their garden and she wanted to go. Sister Rose was having the party for her brother, who had just come out of the army and was going to join a firm of builders. She'd asked a lot of people to the party and Jenny thought it would be fun and it was time she had a little more fun in her life.

Sarah saw that Sister Norton was busy looking after a patient at the far end of the ward. She read through the notes on the desk and noted that a boy named Keith Wright had been rushed in that night with stomach pains and vomiting and by the looks of it he had been sick again. Collecting a trolley with towels and warm water in an enamel bowl, Sarah went to join the senior nurse.

'Shall I give Keith a nice little wash, Sister?'

Sister Norton looked at her and she saw the relief in her eyes. 'Yes, thank you, nurse. I should get on with my round and give out the medicines. Doctor will be here before we're ready for him.'

'Hello,' Sarah said to the young lad lying in the bed. 'I'm going to wash all that nasty smelly stuff away and make you feel more comfortable. Does your tummy still ache, Keith?'

'No, not now, nurse,' he said. 'I just feel sick.' To suit his actions to the words, he jerked over and vomited on the floor at her feet.

'Poor you,' Sarah said sympathetically. 'I wonder what has made you so sick, then.'

'It was them jellied eels,' Keith said and looked at her pathetically. 'Pa made me eat them even though I told 'im they smelled bad. He said it was all I was goin' ter get so I ate them and they was *'orrible.*'

'I don't like them either,' Sarah said. 'I've always wondered how anyone could keep them down.'

'They're all right if they're fresh,' Keith told her, 'but they'd been in the pantry two days.'

Sarah nodded. Keith had all the symptoms of mild food poisoning, a common enough occurrence in homes where every scrap of food was used, even if it was going off a bit. Some of the parents didn't seem to learn that leftover food they hadn't eaten couldn't be fed to their children days later, especially things like jellied eels that were dubious at the best of times, unless the supplier was scrupulous.

She stripped the stained sheets and blanket from the boy's bed, washed him and dressed him in clean pyjamas, and cleared up the mess from the floor. Keith was lying back against the pillows, his pale face wan, but for the moment his urgent need to vomit seemed to have calmed down.

When Sarah returned to her duties, she noticed that the boy was fast asleep and she was able to get on with washing other children and changing beds through the ward until all of them were settled and tidy. The smell of the breakfast trolley made her turn round and she went to greet Kathy as she wheeled it on to the ward.

'Don't give the child in bed six anything at all,' she warned. 'He can't have anything by mouth at the moment. Perhaps when the doctor has been, we can give him liquids but not just yet. He has a drip in his arm.'

Kathy looked at the boy who was lying with his eyes shut. 'Poor little lad,' she said. 'What's wrong with him?'

'Jellied eels his father left in the pantry two days.'

'In this hot weather?' Kathy looked horrified. 'It's a wonder they didn't kill 'im. I wouldn't eat those nasty things even if I was starvin'.'

Sarah nodded her agreement. 'How are things with you?' she asked. 'The wedding all as planned?'

'Yes,' Kathy nodded and smiled. 'I'm sorry we shan't be back in time for yours, Sarah, but we don't get home until that evening.'

'As long as you're happy yourself,' Sarah said. 'We'll have a cup of coffee and some cake somewhere – just you and me, Kathy. Fit it in during our lunchbreak – or after work if you like.'

'Yes, please.' Kathy beamed. 'I've bought you a little wedding present, Sarah. I can give it to you then. I know Matron is arranging something from us all, but I wanted to give you something myself.'

'I felt the same about you,' Sarah said and smiled. 'We'll meet up before your wedding and swap and talk about things.'

Kathy looked pleased as she started her round of the

ward, dispensing the children's breakfasts. Sarah followed her, stopping to help a little girl who was having difficulty in cutting the bacon on her plate. Sarah cut it into small pieces and watched her pop a piece into her mouth. Her little face showed surprise and then pleasure as she chewed. It was possibly the first time she'd tasted a piece of crispy bacon.

Keith was just stirring as Sarah reached him. He moaned a little, opened his eyes and then made a face as he retched. However, nothing came up and he flopped back against the pillow, his face strained and reflecting his discomfort.

'I feel awful,' he told Sarah, 'but nothin' came up.'

'I expect it is all out by now,' she said. 'Doctor will be here soon and he will tell us what to give you to settle your tummy.'

Keith rubbed his eyes. 'Is that bacon? Oh, I love bacon. I ain't 'ad it fer ages.'

'Well, I'm sure we can get you some when you're well enough to eat it,' Sarah said and stroked his hair back from his forehead. It was clean now, because she'd washed it for him, but she doubted his mother had done it for a while. 'How many brothers and sisters do you have, Keith?'

'Four brothers and three sisters at home.' He made a face. 'Me eldest brother ran orf ter sea when he was fifteen. We ain't seen 'im since.'

'Do you miss him?'

'Nah, he never bothered about me.' Keith sniffed. 'Ma ain't got time ter do much either. She goes scrubbin' every mornin' and leaves us to look after ourselves.'

'And what does your father do?'

254

'Nothin'! He can't keep a job and when he gets one, he spends all he earns in the pub!'

Sarah nodded but made no comment. She'd heard the same tale many times before and knew that in the hard times that had gripped the country these past few years many working men had no regular jobs. It led to misery and abuse in the poorest homes, the men often drinking heavily to forget their feelings of failure. Keith's mother was clearly doing her best to keep the family afloat, but with seven children at home, her wage as a cleaner wouldn't go far and luxuries like bacon for breakfast would be out of the question.

Sarah wanted to give the boy a hearty breakfast but she knew his stomach wouldn't take it. Once the doctor had prescribed medicines to settle it, soft foods or toast would be the next step but it would be a while before he could tuck into scrambled eggs and bacon.

Her thoughts turned to Ned. He was used to his plain diet now, and she'd seen signs that he wanted to eat more of her mother's good food of late. She could hardly believe the change in him since he'd been living with them, and he'd immediately taken to Charlie when he arrived to stay with the family. Charlie had taken him under his wing and Ned's health seemed to improve with leaps and bounds. Sarah hoped that Dr Mitchell would relax his strict regime after Ned's next check-up at the infirmary. Compared to Ned's illness, Keith's was nothing and he would soon be up and eating normally – however, the quality of the food his mother could give him was not likely to compare with the food Sarah's mother cooked for them all. She sighed, because it would never be possible to help all the children in need.

'I'll make sure you get some bacon as soon as you're well enough,' she promised. 'I should close your eyes and sleep for a while if you can.'

Keith gave her a wavering smile and lay down, closing his eyes. Sarah passed on to the next patient, making sure that each child was eating or had finished their meal.

Sister Norton approached her as the last of the used dishes was whisked away. 'Open the window, Nurse Sarah. I don't want the smell of breakfast in here for doctor's rounds.'

Sarah went to open the windows at the end of the ward. The sun was shining and she allowed herself a moment to think of her wedding in September. Kathy's was at the end of August and Sarah had heard rumours that Sister Norton was also planning a wedding in August but as yet she had been told nothing official.

Returning to Sister's desk, she saw that Dr Simpson had arrived. He was an elderly man and Sarah always felt sorry when he was on duty. A doctor of the old school, he seemed to have little sympathy for the children and rarely spoke to them. His round was brief. He barked orders for treatment at Sister Norton and nodded when she made a suggestion, but the children were merely numbers in a bed to him.

After he'd left, Sarah looked through the notes he'd scribbled on a pad. 'I wish it had been Dr Mitchell,' she remarked. 'Do you think that is the right treatment for food poisoning, Sister?'

Sister Norton glanced at the sheet. 'He hasn't given any instructions for Keith at all.'

'He must think it was just a tummy upset,' Sarah

said. 'I think it was more serious. Dr Mitchell would listen.'

'Yes, unfortunately, he isn't here today,' Sister Norton said. 'He was asked to give his opinion on a case at the London Hospital.' She nodded thoughtfully. 'I think we'll continue the drip for now, Nurse Sarah, and I shall speak to Dr Mitchell this evening.' She paused and then said, 'I don't know what you have heard – but I am to marry Dr Mitchell on the fourteenth of August. I know you're not on duty and I wondered if you would be my witness, Sarah. It is a small civil wedding – but if you're too busy . . .'

Sarah looked at her in surprise. 'That's lovely, Sister Norton. I should like that very much indeed. Thank you for asking me.'

'I know you're planning a family wedding in September but I have no family – or none that could come up to town just for my wedding. It's why we decided on a quiet affair – but we intend to invite colleagues for a drink one evening before.'

'Good. I know a lot of the nurses will want to wish you well,' Sarah said, genuinely pleased.

Sister Norton looked a little odd, then cleared her throat. 'It is possible that you may hear unpleasant rumours about me and a married man, rumours that I enticed him to leave his wife . . . They are untrue, Sarah, and I may have to fight them in court, which means there will be stuff in the papers, but I wanted you to know it is all lies. I was friendly with the man in question but not intimate.'

Sarah nodded. 'I wouldn't have believed them anyway, Sister. I'm sorry if someone is trying to blacken your name, but I think we all know you too well to believe such lies.'

Sister Norton moved her head, visibly upset. 'Well, that's settled then. I shall tell you when we're having our little party – but the wedding is the fourteenth. And I shall speak to Dr Mitchell as soon as possible about Keith's treatment . . .'

Jean spoke to him later that afternoon. He was back from his consultation at the London and he made a quick visit to check on Keith at her request.

'Are you still feeling sick, lad?' Dr Mitchell asked as he saw the boy's wan face. 'Any more pain in your tummy?'

'No, it just aches,' Keith said. 'I retched a few times but nothing came up.'

'I think we'll continue the nil by mouth until tomorrow,' Dr Mitchell said. 'However, the drip will replace the fluid he's lost and I don't think we need to bother about dehydration. I think otherwise it's best just to keep an eye on him and let his body rest and recuperate. Dr Simpson was right; we don't need to do much at this stage.'

Jean nodded and smiled. 'We thought it might have been food poisoning rather than just an upset tummy.'

'Yes, it may well have been,' Dr Mitchell replied. 'But it was mild and I think if we did a stomach pump it would upset him more than he already is – so rest is the best medicine for the moment, poor chap.'

Jean nodded her agreement. Sometimes the remedy could be worse than the symptoms and if there was no need for further treatment, rest would often do all that was needed.

'Thank you for coming. My nurse and I were anxious for him, because he was so poorly earlier.'

'Stomach upsets can be violent and distressing, but unless there was a quantity of blood in the vomit, I feel he is progressing well enough.' He smiled at her. 'I know Simpson is a bit abrasive but there's nothing wrong with his treatment as far as I'm aware.'

Jean nodded. She would never have dared to question a doctor's decision with any other doctor but Matthew and even he had given her a mild reprimand, because no doctor ever liked being questioned by a nurse!

Jenny yawned as she got up at four that afternoon. She'd slept through from about eleven, when she'd finally crawled into bed after seeing her sister off to work. Lily was on from eleven until nine that evening and Jenny didn't start until eight. She washed, dressed in her uniform and went down to the hall. A letter lay on the mat and she bent to retrieve it, sighing as she saw it was from Chris. He seldom wrote unless he was coming to London on a short break and she knew before she opened it that it would contain precise details of his arrival and departure, suggestions for their time together and very little else.

Lily said she expected too much. 'Men are not good at writing letters,' she'd told her sister. 'You should be happy that he writes when he can – he does have an important and dangerous job, you know.'

'Yes, I know,' Jenny agreed, because she knew Lily spoke the truth. When he was home Chris made a great fuss of her, taking her to expensive restaurants and the theatre. He'd taken her to the ballet once, because she'd expressed a wish to see it, and the dancing had brought tears to her eyes. It was something she would never have visited alone, and she was grateful for the things Chris did and the gifts he brought her, but something wasn't right inside her. It was all very well for Lily to praise his sensible ways, Jenny needed more, but she couldn't quite put into words what was lacking – perhaps a sense of romance?

Laughing at herself for being foolish, Jenny opened Chris's letter and read it. As always, it was brief and told her that he would be arriving at the weekend, would stay in London for ten days and would like to take her to theatre or to dinner on each night she was available. Checking her diary, Jenny saw that she didn't start her round of night duties until two days before Chris left again. She might arrange to swap with someone if she wanted, but otherwise she would be quite content to have had six or seven nights out with Chris.

Unfortunately, it meant she couldn't go to Sister Rose's party and she felt a bit annoyed over that, because Chris thought she could just drop everything whenever he chose to visit. Bother! She scolded herself for being a misery, because after all, Chris's visits were always marked with gifts for her and treats to the best places. She ought to think herself lucky!

Smiling, she made herself a pot of tea and some toast. If Lily had been home, they would have eaten a proper meal, but since Gran's death from a nasty flu earlier that year, Jenny didn't bother when she was alone. Lily enjoyed cooking for the sake of it and she was good at it – but Jenny only cooked when she had to and her efforts could be best described as adequate, not delicious.

However, Jenny knew that Lily would want a meal when she got home so she scraped a few new potatoes, popped some fresh peas and washed some baby carrots, putting them in water in saucepans. It was the least she could do for her sister – the days of them being at loggerheads was long gone and Jenny was very fond of her elder sister. Lily was always there for her and Jenny couldn't help wising that Lily would find a man she could love. It would be a lonely life for Lily if Jenny did marry, which she would one day, she hoped, even if it wasn't to Chris.

Washing up her own used dishes, Jenny glanced at herself in the mirror. She was silly to doubt Chris. When he was here, she believed that he loved her and she was attracted to him, but when she didn't see him for ages . . . a sigh escaped her. She didn't know her own mind, that was her trouble. Lily said she was lucky to have a generous lover and perhaps she was – except that they were not lovers and she sometimes felt they never would be. Sometimes, she wondered why Lily seemed to be so much on Chris's side . . .

Lily met Sarah as she was leaving the ward that evening. They smiled and stopped to have a word. Lily was seldom on the children's ward but she always enjoyed the duty and wanted to know all about the various children.

'Keith is still feeling sorry for himself, but he should be able to start eating normally tomorrow,' Sarah told her. 'And, if he is able to keep food down he really wants a bit of bacon!'

'Yes, well, we'll have to see what Sister says about

that,' Lily said and smiled. 'I might be able to get him a bacon sandwich – but only if Matron says it is all right, of course.'

Matron made her round of all the wards at night. If she had a terminally ill patient in her particular ward, she sometimes sat with the unfortunate person all night, caring for them and comforting them until the end. Otherwise, it was her habit to tour the wards and even the doctors generally allowed that Matron's word was law. She seemed to have a feeling for a patient's condition and often proved she knew as much as any doctor.

'Well, I'll leave them all to your care now, Lily,' Sarah said and smothered a yawn. 'I'm glad Steve is at the club tonight; all I want is to get to bed.'

'Busy day?' Lily smiled in sympathy. 'I'm really looking forward to your wedding, Sarah. Jenny and I have been discussing what we should buy you – and I wanted to ask if there's anything you really don't need. Some brides have drawers filled with linens or boxes of china.'

'Oh, we don't mind anything,' Sarah said. 'Mum is giving me her silver teapot. She says she doesn't use it now – and I've got a nice porcelain tea service put by and some linen, but we need most things. We've started to buy furniture. Steve asked if I wanted new, but apart from the beds I'd rather have something that has been loved. I like oak so we've bought an old Welsh dresser for our kitchen. It's staying in the shop until we get the keys to our house but the owner has put a sold notice on it.'

'How lovely,' Lily said and looked wistful. 'Jenny and I inherited our parents' things. We've added things as we go along, of course – but it would be lovely to plan a home with someone.'

'Yes, it is rather nice,' Sarah said. 'I'm very lucky.'

Lily nodded and glanced down at the notes Sister Norton had left. 'I'd better make my first round, see how things are before Matron comes.'

Sarah walked off and Lily began her tour of the patients. Most of the children were recuperating from minor illnesses and none of them seemed to need particular watching. It was likely to be a quiet night, unless a new case was rushed in.

Sometimes, Lily wished that her life was a little more exciting. For years she'd harboured a grudge that had soured her life, but that was behind her now. Whatever she'd suffered in the past was gone and she knew she was ready for something more – a new adventure. She wasn't old and yet she felt as if life had passed her by; sometimes she found herself envying Jenny and her chance of love and marriage.

It was strange how she'd disliked Chris so much at the beginning, warning her sister to have nothing to do with the man who appeared to be a member of Mosley's Blackshirts. Her disgust had turned to admiration when she discovered his bravery in penetrating that organisation in order to inform on their activities. His present work was secret and dangerous and Lily lived in fear that he might be killed and they would never know. She lived for the letters he sent Jenny, which her sister generously shared with her.

Lily shook her head, refusing to let herself admit that she had become far too interested in her sister's boyfriend. It was Jenny who Chris loved and would eventually wed and Lily knew that was the way it should be. She would not allow her thoughts to dwell on what it might be like to be kissed by Chris or held in his arms. No! That was disloyal to her sister and wicked. If it caused her pain sometimes when Jenny was out with Chris and she was sitting at home alone, then it was deserved. What kind of a sister lusted after her younger sister's man?

It was disgusting and disloyal and Lily was ashamed of the feelings that crept up on her as she lay in bed and thought about Chris, his dark eyes that seemed to hold his soul, his soft mouth that would feel so firm against hers, and the strength of his body . . . No, no, no! It was wicked of her to let herself dream of being his lover and she hated herself for it.

Lily thrust the wayward thoughts from her mind. In bed she could not always control them, but here, at work, she would not allow them to distract her. She was a nurse – and if her life consisted of nothing else, it was a job she could be proud of. Glancing at her watch, she thought that Matron should be here by now. Perhaps something had delayed her . . .

'Well, my dear, how are things with you?' Lady Rosalie asked as she sipped her sherry in Matron's office. 'I wanted to pop in, even though it is a bit late – my son is coming home this weekend and I shan't have time to visit for the next week or so . . .'

'You must enjoy his visits so much,' Mary said, smiling.

'Oh, I do – but I'm even happier because I've settled all but two of the children on my waiting list and that is a weight off my mind.'

264

'That's marvellous,' Mary agreed. 'So, you found some good people?'

'Yes – and two of my long-standing carers took an extra child each.' She sighed. 'The two I can't find homes for are a brother and sister, nine and seven – and they're inseparable, so I'm waiting until I find the right place for them. I know they hate it at the orphanage, but until the right family comes along, they will need to stay there.'

'What about young Cassie?' Mary asked.

Lady Rosalie frowned, pausing before she replied. 'I visited her last week. She is a strange little thing – but Mr Gillows has given her everything she could possibly want. I approve of the nurse. Meggie has years of experience with children and couldn't be better – she had to give up nursing full time because of her back.'

Mary nodded; it was a common complaint amongst nurses. 'What didn't you like? I can see there was something . . .'

'The housekeeper was a bit – well, uncaring is the word I would use. Keeps the house spotless but I'm not sure that is necessary. Cassie doesn't like her, I know that.'

'Ah, I see.' Mary nodded, understanding the look in her friend's eyes. 'You're thinking whether you should have a word with Mr Gillows.'

'Yes, I am. I don't want to seem interfering and he has so obviously done all her can for the child but . . .'

'You should warn him about the housekeeper, Rosalie. You have a good instinct and if *you* disliked her, she isn't right for the job. A child like that needs a great deal of love and understanding, not great housekeeping.'

'As usual, you've given me good advice. He is away on business at the moment but I shall telephone when I get the chance.'

With her son home for the long summer holiday, Lady Rosalie was going to be busy and so she had, for the next few weeks, handed over most of her responsibilities as chairwoman of the fostering service, but she would make time to ring Mr Gillows and warn him that the woman he'd employed as housekeeper was not quite suitable for the care of a delicate girl . . .

'I hate you!' Cassie yelled at the housekeeper when the woman summoned her for her lunch. 'I told you not to touch my things – and you've stolen my brooch. It has gone and I know you took it!'

'Please do not be ridiculous,' Mrs Benson said primly. 'I haven't touched your brooch or even seen it – besides, it is ridiculous that a child like you should have a sapphire and diamond brooch. It must be worth a lot of money . . .'

'It's mine and you've taken it!' Cassie accused and saw the guilt in the woman's eyes. 'I'll tell Daddy when he gets back.'

'You, spiteful girl!' the horrid woman snapped back at her. 'What difference does one brooch mean to you? He gives you all you want!' She raised her hand and slapped Cassie's cheek. 'I'll show you what they'll do to you when they shut you up in the institution! You're a filthy little deranged brat and I know you killed your poor mother—'

'I'll push you down the stairs too and kill you!' Cassie cried wildly, though she didn't really know what she was saying. The horrid woman slapped her again and she screamed. In a furious temper, Cassie picked up the silver hairbrush she used and threw it at Mrs Benson. It struck the woman hard on the face, cutting the skin and bringing blood to the surface; she stumbled away, screaming in shock and anger.

'You're dangerous and mad! I'll have you put away if it's the last thing I do!'

Cassie stamped her foot and threw everything she could at the housekeeper's back as she retreated from the room.

'Cassie! That's not very nice is it? I thought I taught you better manners.'

'Mummy?' Cassie whirled round looking for her mother and saw her standing near the window. It was her mummy the way she used to be, pretty and smiling and smelling of perfume. 'Mummy, you've come back to me!'

'Come outside, Cassie. We'll go down to the river and play – you know it's for the best, don't you? You should have come with me that day, like a good little girl . . .'

'Yes, Mummy . . .' Tears were streaming down Cassie's cheeks now. 'Mummy, I love you and I'm so lonely . . .'

'We're both lost and lonely,' Mummy said, smiling at her. 'I will come again soon, my lovely girl and we'll go down to the river and play, darling, and then you'll never be alone again . . .'

# CHAPTER 20

Jamie loved his first evening in the police cadets. His tutor was an older man and he welcomed Jamie to the class with a fatherly pat on the shoulder, nodding as his eyes went over him in approval.

'I've heard good things of you, lad,' he said. 'Constable Jones told me you had the makings of a good officer – and it's my job to see that you become one of us. If I give you reason to enjoy being with us, Jamie, I hope to see you go on to join the force when you're older. You're still a bit on the small side, but I've been told you're growing.'

'I've grown two inches this summer so far.'

'That's good, because we need our officers to be big lads.'

'I might join the police,' Jamie agreed and grinned at him. 'Or I might go in the army – it depends on what I'm good at, sir.'

'I'm Sergeant Carter but the lads call me Sarge,' the officer said. 'Right – come and join the others, Jamie. We'll show you the ropes this evening. It's mostly drilling, marching, first aid, finding out about the various badges you can earn, like learning all the street names and traffic signs so you can direct folk, and how to defend yourself for a start. We shan't bother with a uniform for the first couple of weeks – so nothing wasted if you get fed up with us.'

'I don't think I'll do that, sir,' Jamie said. He liked the sergeant and the description of how he would be spending his time had caught his interest. 'What other badges can we earn, sir?'

'Well, we'll teach you to cycle safely – and if you stick with us, you'll learn to drive one day.' He smiled at Jamie. 'Sometimes we take the cadets to big sporting events and they help us to direct the crowds and – well, we're wasting time. Come and join the others, lad. You'll find out as you go along.'

Jamie thanked him and followed into the big hall. It looked as if the boys were all training for sport. Dressed in dark shorts and white vests, they were doing physical exercise, arms up and out and then down to sides, feet apart and then together. It looked fun and Jamie hurried to take his place in the line. He was wearing his normal trousers and shirt so he looked a bit out of place but as Sergeant Carter had told him, they wanted to be sure he was going to keep coming before they kitted him out with his bits and pieces.

It was nine o'clock before Jamie left the hall where the cadets held their meetings. He'd made several friends and walked with them for part of his way home. As he got to the end of his street, he was alone and for the past five minutes or so he'd felt as if he were being followed. He glanced over his shoulder a few times but there was never anyone to see. However, the feeling continued until he saw Arch leave Mr Forrest's shop and walk towards him.

'I'm off to get some chips,' he said. 'Mr Forrest said he fancied some chips from the shop so I said I'd get them. Want ter come?'

'Yeah, please,' Jamie said. 'I'm hungry. It was great at the cadets' club, Arch, but all that exercise makes me hungry.'

'Me too,' Arch said. 'I was at the boxing club earlier. Steve wants me to enter the regional championships again – and I think he means to put you in the under fourteen class too.'

'That would be great,' Jamie said. 'I'm glad you've been chosen again, Arch – but I can't help feelin' sorry fer Rich. It must be rotten bein' left out of it when he was so good.'

'I know.' Arch frowned. 'It makes me sick when I think of that rotten little bugger gettin' away with it,' he said. 'I don't suppose the police will ever pick him up. He'll have the sense not to come back 'ere.'

'I'm not so sure,' Jamie said. 'I think he might just be cocky enough to defy everyone. I've had the feeling someone was behind me a couple of times, Arch, though I might be wrong.'

His brother glanced behind them but the street was empty. 'Just be careful, Jamie. If he approaches you, or you see him coming, try to avoid confrontation – and tell Steve if you think you've seen him.'

'Yeah, I know what yer mean,' Jamie said. 'But I'm a lot stronger now.'

Jamie didn't tell his brother that he had no intention

of running away from a clash with Leo. Bullies would keep coming back unless you stood up to them and taught them a lesson. Jamie had been afraid of Leo and his gang once, but not anymore. He knew that he had to look out for knives, but he'd been working on a trick to disarm a man with a knife and he intended to try it out the next time Leo or one of his cronies attacked him. Rich had fought fair. He hadn't expected a knife in the side when he wasn't looking – and that was what you had to look for, a sneak attack from behind, but there were dirty tricks and clever tricks and Jamie knew a few of each of those now. He would be ready next time Leo came at him, and he knew it would happen; it was just a case of when.

On Sunday afternoon, the car came to fetch Jamie to Cassie's home. Rich talked to him and told him that he'd been making friends with Cassie that week.

'I talked to her when she came into the garden,' he said. 'I offered to push her on the swing and she liked that – I think she trusts me a bit now.'

'That's good,' Jamie said and threw him a grateful look. 'She's a bit contrary but she can't help it.'

'Where did *that* word come from?' Rich asked and laughed.

'Someone used it the other night when I was at the police cadets,' Jamie said. 'It's not as good as the boxing club, but I like it, and it's a good thing fer the future. I want a job fer life, not standing on street corners looking fer work.'

'Yeah, I know what yer mean,' Rich said and there was regret in his voice. 'I wouldn't have minded the army.'

Jamie nodded and felt dreadful. 'Are yer gettin' on all right where yer are?' he asked.

'It's all right,' Rich said. 'I like the driving and I don't mind the gardening. At least I'll have a skill when I leave Mr Gillows' employ.'

'You're not thinkin' of leavin'?'

'Not yet,' Rich said and glanced at the chauffeur. 'Not while Mr Gillows needs me.'

Jamie nodded. He supposed it wasn't much of a job for a young man who had wanted to be in the army or become a boxing champion. It made him feel rotten for talking about the fun he was having when Rich was denied so much that had been important to him. It was so unfair and it made him want to punch something, but getting angry wouldn't change anything.

'It's a good start fer me,' Rich told him and smiled. 'Don't feel bad, Jamie. I'm gettin' used to things the way they are.'

Jamie nodded, but knew he would always feel guilty about Rich. It was a part of the reason he'd made up his mind he wouldn't run away when Leo came after him. The gang leader had to pay for what he'd done and Jamie would do whatever he could to bring him to justice.

Cassie was waiting for him to arrive. She didn't take him to her room this time, but they played card games in the sitting room under the watchful eye of Mr Gillows, and then had tea. When it was time for Jamie to leave, Cassie said goodbye but she didn't come to the kitchen with him nor did she ask him to return the next week, although Mr Gillows did, and he gave his word he would return.

Meggie was in the kitchen. She looked worried and Jamie sensed she wanted to tell him something. Because she cared about Cassie, she knew something was wrong too.

'Is it that Mrs Benson?' he asked.

'Yes, Jamie,' Meggie said and glanced anxiously towards the door. 'I heard her getting on to Cassie yesterday and Cassie threw something at her – a shoe or something. She carried on something dreadful, threatened to leave – and to go to the authorities. She complained to Mr Gillows that the child was dangerous and ought to be locked up in an asylum and I'm sure Cassie heard her.'

Jamie nodded. 'I knew something was wrong. She was all right wiv me but she's brooding. Look out fer her, Meggie; that woman will make her do something bad and then they might take her away and lock her up like they threatened before.'

Meggie promised she would and Jamie left the house. He felt anxious about his friend, because Cassie had definitely been brooding, even though he'd made her laugh a few times. He wished Mr Gillows would send the unpleasant housekeeper away before it was too late . . .

Jamie told Steve of his suspicions concerning Leo at the club that evening. Steve looked at him steadily for a moment and then nodded.

'Instinct is part of what makes a good officer,' he said. 'If you think you're being watched, Jamie, you probably are – and we know who will be out to make trouble for you if he can.'

'I'm a lot stronger than I was,' Jamie said confidently. 'I've grown, too. Arch bought me two new pairs of trousers, because my old ones were too short. He said it looked as if my pants had quarrelled with my socks.'

Steve laughed and nodded. 'I thought you'd shot up an inch or more and you're broader too, Jamie; it's all the exercise you're doing these days. I don't think you'd fit through that window now.'

'I wouldn't try,' Jamie said. 'They can't make me do wrong now, sir.'

'There's more than one way for a bully to force his will on you.' Steve frowned. 'Expect threats and blackmail, but tell me rather than give into them.'

'Yes, I shall,' Jamie said. 'I'm not afraid of them now.'

'That's good but don't be too reckless. I don't want to lose a friend – or a potential officer of the law.' His eyes teased and Jamie knew he was a mate, someone he could trust.

Jamie laughed. It was nice being the friend of a man like Steve and he knew the warning was sensible. He had no intention of seeking a confrontation with Leo, but he also knew it would happen.

It was after his second night with the police cadets that Leo's gang showed itself. He was walking home, alone now that the other cadets had peeled off to their homes, his sense of being followed so strong that he turned and challenged whoever was in the shadows.

'I know you're there,' he said strongly, his voice carrying. 'I'm not afraid of you – you're all cowards. You think you're clever when it's one against four but none of yer dare fight me alone.'

He saw three faces he knew slink out of the shadows and prepared to defend himself. Steve had taught him a couple of moves he couldn't use in a competition but which might save his life.

'Leo wants ter see yer,' one of them said in a threatening tone. 'He says he's goin' ter finish the job he started.'

'Yeah?' Jamie took a step forward his fists up in front of him in a fighting stance. 'Well, you tell him from me I think he's a stinkin' coward. He uses knives and daren't fight on his own. If he's got the guts to fight me alone, I'll show 'im whether or not I'm scared of 'im – or you lot!'

One of the gang made a sudden move towards Jamie, a knife glinting in his hand. Jamie's arm shot out, his hand grasping the boy's wrist and twisting it sharply. The knife went spinning away in the darkness just as Jamie's leg went behind the other boy's and brought him crashing down to the hard pavement. The shock on the bully's face made him want to laugh and he hardly noticed the other two gang members scuttle off into the shadows once more.

'How did yer do that?' the boy on the ground asked, looking stunned.

'I learned,' Jamie said and extended his hand. The other lad took it warily and Jamie hauled him to his feet. 'What's yer name then?'

'Vic,' the boy said. 'Me dad's Victor Broughton – he's a foreman down the docks.'

'Then why are yer wastin' yer time wiv Leo's gang?' Jamie asked. 'There's other ways of being tough than hanging about wiv a load of cowards and fools.'

'Yeah, that's what my dad says.' Vic looked at him with a glimmer of respect. 'Leo said yer were a weaklin' but yer ain't.'

'Not anymore – and I ain't afraid of Leo. Yer can tell him that from me.'

'I might,' Vic said and backed away. 'But yer want ter watch yer back, Jamie Martin. He'll kill yer if he can.'

'He'll hang if he does,' Jamie countered. 'That stuff is fer mugs, Vic – you should try standin' up ter him and make somethin' of yer life.'

Vic disappeared into the darkness without answering and Jamie shook his head. He'd shown Leo's gang that he was a match for them one by one, but he knew that if they rushed him, he would still be in danger of dying with a knife in his back.

He would tell Steve that the gang leader was back. Without Leo the others wouldn't bother him again. Perhaps Steve could find him and arrest him before it went any further . . .

Jamie's thoughts about Leo were pushed to the background by the news he received when he came home from his errands for Mr Forrest that Thursday evening. A car was waiting to take him straight to Cassie's house and the chauffeur told him it was urgent.

'You need to come at once,' he said, looking upset. 'It's a terrible thing – and the young lady is asking for you.'

Jamie jumped into the car without arguing. He'd been on edge ever since he'd last seen Cassie and it wasn't just because of Leo. Steve had told him his colleagues would be on the lookout for the gang leader and warned him not to walk home alone if he could help it. Yet it was Cassie who lingered at the back of Jamie's mind and he'd known immediately he saw the car that something was wrong.

'Where is Rich?' he asked, but the driver just shook his head.

'It's best you hear it from him and Mr Gillows,' he said.

Something had happened to Cassie! Jamie knew it and couldn't wait to get to the house and find out what was wrong. As soon as the car stopped, he shot out of the back and rushed round to the kitchen. Meggie was standing at the sink crying and Jamie went cold all over.

'Is she dead?' he asked and Meggie shook her head.

'The poor little mite . . .' was all she could say and shake her head over and over again.

'Jamie, I'm so glad you're here,' Mr Gillows said entering the kitchen. 'She has been asking for you – I'm not sure how long . . .' He choked on the words. 'It's all my fault. You told me to get rid of that woman and I wish I had listened.' He shook his head. 'I don't know what she did to Cassie but she upset her badly and – and Cassie tried to push her down the stairs. Mrs Benson caught herself before any damage was done, but the fuss she made before she went off! Screaming and carrying on blue murder– it's no wonder Cassie made a bolt for it.'

Jamie looked at his grave face and shot up the stairs, taking them two at a time and stumbling in his haste. He slowed to a stop as he reached Cassie's room, then reached out carefully and opened her door, his heart clattering in his breast as he went in.

Cassie looked so pale, like a little wax doll against the pristine sheets. A doctor was standing by the bed looking grave. He turned and frowned as Jamie entered, making his way towards the bed. He was almost afraid to reach out and touch her, but as he reached her side, Cassie's eyes flickered open and she smiled.

'Jamie,' she said and her fingers fluttered, though she looked too weak to move her hand. He sat on the edge of the bed and held her hand in his. She felt so cold, so very cold . . . and his heart jerked with pain, because he instinctively sensed that she was dying. He bent down to whisper in her ear, not wanting anyone to hear but Cassie.

'I love yer,' he said softly. 'Don't go, Cassie, don't leave me . . .'

For a moment he thought her fingers tightened on his and she smiled. She looked so beautiful, a fragile, pretty doll who had no life or mischief left in her.

'Mummy,' she whispered through white lips. 'Mummy, I'm sorry. I didn't mean to make you fall . . .' Tears dripped down her cheeks. 'Mummy, please love me . . . come back to me. I'm frightened . . .'

'I love yer . . .' Jamie said and bent to kiss her cheek. 'I'm 'ere, I'm wiv yer . . .'

'Mummy . . .' Cassie's voice was barely a whisper but she was smiling as though she could see something he couldn't. 'Wait for me . . .'

'No, Cassie!' the cry left Jamie's lips as he saw the last of her colour wash out of her cheeks and he knew, even before the doctor shook his head, that she had gone. 'Cassie . . .' Jamie's tears trickled down his face.

He didn't try to brush them away or hide the fact that he was weeping. 'Oh, Cassie, what did that woman do to yer?'

He felt a hand on his shoulder and looked up to see that Rich was standing at his back, a look of concern in his eyes. 'I tried to save her, Jamie. I give yer my word . . .'

Jamie let go of Cassie's cold hand and turned to look at him. 'What happened to her – what did that woman do to her?'

'I didn't hear the argument, only the screams and the shouting. I saw Cassie run from the house and head off towards the river and I followed her. I kept calling her to come back, telling her it would be all right but she wouldn't listen and then she just went into the river . . .' Rich shook his head. He looked so upset that Jamie put his hand on his arm. 'She ran so fast I got out of breath and couldn't keep up with her.'

'It wasn't yer fault,' Jamie offered, because he could see how upset his friend was.

'She must have thought I was chasing her to punish her,' Rich said. 'But I didn't know what else to do, I was afraid she'd hurt herself. I think she just jumped in the water – and I went in after her. I'm not much of a swimmer but I grabbed her and fetched her out. She must have swallowed a lot of water before I got her . . .' He shook his head in distress. 'She brought some of it up and I carried her home. We phoned the doctor and Mr Gillows – but she just lay there like a dead thing, staring at the wall . . .' He looked down at her. 'She opened her eyes once and said your name over and over so we sent the car for yer – hours ago.'

'I was delivering stuff,' Jamie said. 'I came as soon as I could – but it made no difference . . .'

'Your friend no longer wished to live.' The doctor's voice made them both stare at him. 'There was no reason for her to die. She was saved from drowning by Mr Austin, who acted promptly and bravely, and she ought to have recovered, but it is my opinion she did not wish to live.'

Hearing a groan from behind them, Jamie spun round to see Mr Gillows standing in the doorway. He looked terrible, his eyes red from crying and his face drawn with misery.

'It was that damned woman!' he cried. 'She'd slapped the child and told her she'd see her locked away for the rest of her life. Cassie ran after her and caught her at the top of the stairs.' He paused, then, 'Meggie told me Cassie pushed past Mrs Benson as if she didn't see her and the woman stumbled down the stairs but caught the bannisters before she fell. Only then she started screaming murder and the child ran away in terror.' He shook his head. 'I should have sent that woman away after we spoke, Jamie. I could see you thought she was the wrong person to run this house, that Cassie didn't need it to smell of polish all the time . . .' A deep tearing sob escaped him and he turned and walked abruptly from the room.

'Cassie couldn't bear to be shut away,' Jamie said with wisdom well beyond his years. 'She would rather die . . .'

'I rather think that is the truth of it,' the doctor said. 'I believe this young lady was suffering from a deep trauma connected with her mother's death.'

281

'They told her they were sending her away after her mother died,' Jamie said. 'So she ran away – and found this house.'

'There was some mystery surrounding her mother's death, I believe,' the doctor said and shook his head. 'Well, there is nothing more I can do for the poor child now. I must speak to Mr Gillows about the arrangements . . .'

Rich looked at Jamie and then gave him a little push towards the door. 'No sense in us bein' here, lad,' he said. 'You can't help her now, Jamie.'

'I wish I'd made Mr Gillows send that awful woman away,' Jamie said regretfully. 'Cassie might have been happy here then.'

'Perhaps – perhaps not,' Rich said frowning. 'I know you thought a lot of her, Jamie, but she was more than just a bit strange – something wasn't right, and I'm sure you know that deep down. Perhaps if she'd been left to the doctors in the hospital they might have found out what her problem was and helped her, but here she had no chance between a man who spoiled her but did nothing to teach her and a woman who went out of her way to upset her.'

Jamie was silent. Rich was only saying what was true, even though he wanted to deny it. Mr Gillows had meant right by her but perhaps he wasn't the best person to care for a troubled child, like Cassie. The housekeeper had been entirely the wrong person to look after Cassie, who needed a loving environment. Meggie had loved her and he was sure, in his own mind, she would have been all right if they'd just sent the self-righteous Mrs Benson away. However, there was no sense in getting angry and saying anything now; it was

282

too late for Cassie. Her tragic little life was ended and perhaps she would be reunited with her mother in Heaven. Jamie wasn't sure what happened after someone was dead. The parson who came to the school talked about resurrection and peace in God's love, but could a tortured soul like Cassie's ever be at peace?

Downstairs in the kitchen Meggie was still crying. The doctor had gone and Mr Gillows sat at the kitchen table with his head in his hands. He looked devastated and Jamie felt sorry for him. He'd wanted to replace his dead sister with Cassie and he'd done his best to make her happy, but now she was dead too. He must feel double the pain Jamie did and there was nothing much to say.

'I'm off now, sir,' he said. 'I'm sorry . . . you did yer best fer her . . .'

Mr Gillows didn't answer or look up. Meggie came to him and embraced him and then slipped a warm cake in his hand.

'You're a good lad,' she sniffed. 'I know yer cared for the little lass.'

Jamie nodded and scuffed his eyes as he felt the sting of more tears.

'Come on,' Rich said. 'We'll get yer 'ome, Jamie.'

No one spoke on the drive back to Mr Forrest's shop. There was just nothing to say, because everyone felt the same. They'd all known Cassie wasn't quite right, but only a heart of stone could have remained untouched by her beauty and her sweet innocence.

Jamie waved to his friend as he went inside Mr Forrest's shop where the elderly man looked at him and seemed to understand he wanted to be left alone.

'I'll come through in an hour or so, Jamie. Get yourself some tea or whatever you want.'

Jamie nodded. The last thing he needed was food or tea. He was filled up with sorrow and he didn't know how to get it out; crying didn't help and he was beginning to feel the anger build inside. He knew that woman must have deliberately set out to upset Cassie, provoking her to the limit and Jamie knew that his friend needed understanding, not scolding or discipline. She was a wild thing, a free spirit, and even if her mind didn't work the way other people thought it should, she'd been sweet and loving in her own way. Jamie had loved her. He hadn't realised how much until he saw her lying there with the life slipping away from her eyes.

'Damn her! The bitch wants locking up,' he said fiercely, but he wanted to hit out at something or someone and his anger was hard to control.

Hearing a cry from the shop, Jamie realised something was wrong and rushed back as he heard a cry of pain from Mr Forrest. As he entered the shop, he saw two lads trying to snatch goods from the shelves. Mr Forrest had tried to bar their way and one of them had struck him. Jamie didn't think. His pain over Cassie was such that he just struck out blindly, bringing down first one of the boys and then the other with a couple of well-aimed blows. The stolen biscuits and chocolate were dropped as the lads scrambled to their feet and ran like scalded rats.

Mr Forrest sat down on his chair and looked at Jamie. He didn't speak, just stared and stared, as if he couldn't believe what he'd seen.

'Are you all right, sir?' Jamie asked. 'Should I get the doctor fer yer?'

'No, I'm just gettin' my breath,' the elderly man said and then he smiled. 'Arch told me yer were handy with yer self-defence, but I never thought to see yer chuck them around like that, lad. It was a bit of luck for me yer were here, lad.' He shook his head. 'Yer only look a bit of a lad, but yer clever with it.'

Jamie looked at him and found that tears were slipping down his cheeks. 'I was just so mad at them and everythin',' he said. 'My friend Cassie died and it was all so wrong . . .'

'Aye, I know how yer feel,' Mr Forrest said and got up. He put an arm about Jamie's shoulders. 'Let's shut up shop and go and have somethin' ter eat and drink, me and you together, lad. I reckon you've got a story to tell and I've got all the time in the world to listen . . .'

Jamie went to the club that evening, because Arch made him. 'Steve is puttin' yer fer the regional championships, which means yer need ter practise – besides, what good will it do ter sit 'ere and brood?'

'I know – it can't bring her back, can it?'

'No,' his brother said. 'You've lost yer ma and now you've lost a friend yer cared for, Jamie. I know how that hurts. I ain't said anythin' much about Ma but I felt it too. I've missed Rich as well, but it don't help, blamin' yerself.'

Jamie nodded, because his brother was right. He'd cried for his mother and he'd cried for Rich and for Cassie, but he couldn't make things better for them so the only thing to do was to go on with his own life and try to do right.

Steve was pairing the boys for their first fights of the evening when they arrived. He told Arch where to go but asked Jamie to wait for a moment. When he'd got everyone training, he turned to Jamie.

'I heard what you did at Mr Forrest's shop this afternoon,' he said. 'One of the boy's mothers came to the station and made a complaint. However, when my sergeant told her she should discipline her sons better, she went off in a huff. I was asked to have a cautionary word but I'm only going to say, Be Careful!' He smiled at Jamie. 'You've been given a wonderful skill. You must use it wisely. One of those lads had a fractured elbow, where he landed badly, and it might have been worse. The stronger you get the more you need to think before you act.'

'I didn't mean to hurt him like that,' Jamie said and flushed. 'I'm sorry, sir. I know you told me never to use my skill in anger – but I was upset as well as angry . . .' He hesitated and then explained what had happened to Cassie.

Steve nodded, looking concerned as the story unfolded and then understanding. 'Yes, I see why you wanted to hit out at someone – and those lads should not have been trying to rob Mr Forrest. However, when we're stronger or cleverer than others we have to control ourselves. We all feel anger when something unfair happens, Jamie – and it was very unfair that Cassie should have been treated like that – but we have to manage our anger. To hit out in temper is to lose control.'

'Yes, I know.' Jamie hung his head. 'I'm sorry. Do

you want me to go round and apologise to the boy whose elbow I broke?'

'I think his mother might break your neck,' Steve said grimly. 'In this case the best thing would be just to learn your lesson. Life is very unfair at times and it makes us want to hit back – but we can only do so in the right way. Your skill is to defend yourself, not to attack boys even if they are in the wrong.'

'Yes, I know,' Jamie agreed, biting his lip. 'Am I in trouble with the law, sir?'

'I've been told to give you a warning and I have – however, I personally think you did a good job. I very much doubt Mr Forrest will have any more trouble with the local lads.' He smiled at Jamie and then winked. 'But officially I can't approve of attacking those lads – do you understand?'

'Yes, sir!' Jamie grinned back. He felt better than he had all day, some of the blackness that had fallen over him melting away as he realised that Steve had only been doing his duty. He thought Jamie had done right scaring the thieves off, but was giving him a warning in accordance with the law. Breaking the other boy's elbow was a bit hard on him and Jamie hadn't meant to do it, but he'd let his anger over Cassie rule his head. It was a lesson for the future and he had taken Steve's words to heart. Anger was something everyone felt when they were thwarted or hurt, but you couldn't let it rule you, even though you might want to hurt someone for what they'd done. If everyone went around using their strength to gain their own way there would be no law.

'I shan't forget what you've told me, sir,' Jamie said. 'Those boys were wrong but I should've warned them off first – and I shouldn't have used so much force. It wasn't necessary. If I'd given them a clip on the ear, they would probably have scarpered.'

Steve nodded. 'I'll make an officer of the law of you yet,' he said and laughed. 'Go on and find yourself a partner, Jamie. I intend you to win next month's regional championships in your group!'

## CHAPTER 21

Jenny smiled and kissed Chris on the lips. She'd enjoyed his visit and the outings he'd taken her on, but she was almost certain now that her feelings for him were not those of a woman who wanted to be his wife.

'Thank you for everything,' she said as he released her, looking at her in a puzzled manner. 'It has been a lovely few days and I do thank you for the present you bought me. Lily loved the French perfume you gave her too.'

'Is there something you are trying to say?' Chris asked but he knew – she could see it in his eyes. 'You do know how fond of you I am, don't you?'

'I am fond of you too,' Jenny said reluctantly. She'd known this must come but hadn't looked forward to it. 'I'm sorry, Chris, but I've realised that I'm not in love with you.' She saw his frown and rushed in before he could speak. 'It is nothing to do with how we met – or you being in the Blackshirts – or even that you're away so much . . .'

'Then what is it?' he asked, looking puzzled. 'I don't understand what I've done, Jenny.'

'You haven't done anything wrong,' she replied sadly. 'I hate to say it, Chris – but I just don't want to kiss you or – or anything else.' She'd come to the conclusion that she could never make love with him and that meant she could never be his wife.

The look of shock in his eyes tore at Jenny and for a moment she wished the words unsaid, but knew that she was right to have spoken out. Lily would think she was a fool to break it off, but Jenny knew she couldn't continue like this any longer; it wasn't fair to either of them.

'Is there someone else?' Chris asked, trying to make sense of it.

'No, there's no one else I promise – and I do like you as a friend,' Jenny said. 'I'm just not in love with you, and I won't marry for anything else.'

'I see . . . In that case, I'd better go!' Chris turned and walked away and Jenny felt the tears start. She felt awful for breaking it to him so harshly but how else could you tell someone that you didn't love them? Once, she'd thought she might love him, but that was months ago and whatever she'd felt then had cooled. Did that make her fickle? Jenny wasn't sure. She didn't think she was a bad person but perhaps she was . . . She felt all mixed up inside and when she went into the house and saw the eager look in Lily's eyes, she was struck with guilt. Lily so looked forward to seeing Chris.

'Is Chris not coming in?' Lily asked.

Jenny took a deep breath. 'No – and I shan't be seeing him again, Lily. I know you will tell me I'm a fool – but I don't love him. I've told him I don't want to go out with him.'

Lily stared at her, the colour draining from her face. 'I don't understand,' she said in a low voice, 'what has happened?'

'I just don't want to see him again – I don't fancy him, Lily. I'm sorry but that's the truth of it.'

'You stupid little girl!' Lily said angrily and rushed out of the room.

'Lily – don't be angry, please!' Jenny went after her, but her sister's bedroom door slammed in her face and she heard the key turn in the lock. Jenny knocked at the door. 'Please talk to me, Lily. I'm sorry. I know you liked him . . .'

Lily's door flew open. Her face was streaked with tears and passion. 'I didn't *like* him – I *loved* him,' she said and then slammed the door in Jenny's face again.

Jenny stared at the door in stunned surprise. How could she not have known that her sister was in love with Chris? Lily had never ceased to praise him and to speak out for him since she'd learned what he truly did, working as a government agent. Jenny *was* a stupid little girl, as her sister had called her; because she could have thrown them together, let Chris go gradually, and perhaps then he and Lily would have got together. Now, she knew, Chris would never come near them again. Regret swept through her as she realised that she'd ruined Lily's chance of being happy again . . .

Lily still wasn't speaking to her in the morning when she went down for breakfast. She'd made a pot of tea, a plate of buttered toast and some scrambled eggs, but she never looked at or spoke to Jenny once.

Jenny thought about apologising to her, but then felt

annoyed. If Lily was in love with Chris, why hadn't she ever mentioned it to her?

The answer was so obvious that Jenny didn't even ask the question. Her sister had sacrificed her own feelings because she believed that Jenny was in love with Chris and she would not come between them. Jenny felt the emotion rise in her throat and she wanted to weep and beg her sister's pardon, but that wouldn't change anything. At the moment Lily was bitter, wrestling with her feelings of loss and sadness – and perhaps her folly in sacrificing her own desires in order that her sister should have a chance of love and marriage.

'I wish I'd known,' was all Jenny felt able to say. 'Please don't let it come between us, Lily. You're all I have and I do love you. I can't help it if I didn't feel the same as him.'

Picking up her nurse's bag and her cloak, Jenny left the kitchen. She'd eaten one piece of toast but it had stuck in her throat and she needed to walk off this feeling of misery that had settled over her. She was on from ten in the morning until seven that night and was glad that she would be too busy to think about the rift that had sprung up between her and Lily. For years they'd lived with a barrier between them, but it had come tumbling down when Lily told her younger sister of her painful experiences in the past, but now it looked as if Lily was ready to erect it again.

Jenny had plenty of time to walk into work so she did. It was a pleasantly warm morning and she enjoyed the physical exercise that helped to drive her feelings of despair away. Once she was on the ward, she would have no time to think about the quarrel with Lily – which was of her sister's making, after all.

Why couldn't Lily have been honest with her? If she'd told Jenny how she felt, she could have stood back, left them together – given Lily her chance to win his regard. She knew that Chris thought highly of Lily. She was a good nurse, a loyal citizen and perhaps more understanding than her younger sister – in fact, the perfect match for a man in his position. He'd fallen for Jenny because she was pretty and had sparkled at him, arousing his protective instincts and making him feel he wanted her for his wife. Yet Lily would have made him a better wife.

'Hi, Jenny,' Kathy's voice called to her. 'I just wanted to check you're coming to my wedding?'

'Yes, of course – I wouldn't miss it for the world . . .' She smiled and waved as Kathy disappeared in the direction of the kitchen.

Jenny dashed the tears from her eyes. It was going to be a beautiful day. She was glad that she'd had the courage to break it off with Chris. For the moment she wasn't bothered about courting, her work and her friends were enough, even Sarah and Kathy's marriage plans hadn't made her feel she wanted to be Chris's wife. For the moment she would concentrate on her work and hope that the barrier between her and Lily would crumble once her sister had had time to think things over.

Lily stared at herself in the mirror. Her face was pale and she could see the dark misery lurking behind her eyes, part of which was caused by the rift with Jenny – which was her fault. She'd just felt so distressed for

Chris and angry at her sister for hurting him. He'd lavished time and money on her this visit and Jenny had just casually dismissed him. Lily knew that Chris adored Jenny. He'd sat with her in the kitchen and told Lily how devastated he'd been when he'd believed that the revelation that he was with Mosley's Blackshirts had lost him the girl he loved.

'I owe it to you that she gave me another chance,' he'd told her. 'Dear Lily, how can I ever thank you? I know how much you hate the fascists and how you must have despised me when you thought I was one of them.'

'Yes, I did,' Lily said, and laughed as she saw the look in his eyes. 'But then I knew your heart was good, Chris, and I thought there must be another reason – and I was right. I think Jenny is very lucky to have you.'

Had she given herself away then? Lily had feared it, had got to her feet on the pretence of needing to take a sponge cake from the oven. She'd seen doubt flicker in his eyes – the eyes that made her feel weak at the knees and want to drown her whole self in him. If she'd stayed where she was, let him see the love in her eyes, would it have been different?

Lily shook her head. She was being foolish! Chris was in love with Jenny, so why would he look at her older sister? Lily knew she was attractive in her way, but she couldn't compete with Jenny's beauty – her lovely hair that curled about her face even when it was drawn back tightly for work and her bright eyes that sparkled when she was amused or happy. Lily's smile was slow to appear and she looked older than her years, more serious. Life had taught her that she could not expect happiness and she had not, but just being able to see Chris when he called for Jenny, to spend a few minutes with him in quiet conversation had given her something to look forward to. His letters, which Jenny always shared, and the gifts he brought – he was so generous, always bringing Lily a gift when he came – had been enough, even though in her bed at night she had longed for more.

How could Jenny not want such a man? Lily had called her a silly child because in that moment of despair it was how she felt, but she knew that it was not fair. Jenny had been doubtful for a while but Lily had pushed her into continuing her relationship.

Perhaps she was the fool after all? Lily smothered the desire to rage or cry. She would not try to persuade Jenny to make it up with Chris, because his pride would never allow it – but perhaps she could keep a small spark of friendship alive?

Going up to her sister's room, Lily opened the leather writing case that lay on Jenny's dressing table with her perfume and hair brushes. She took out the last letter from Chris and wrote his address on a piece of paper from her sister's stationary. She would write to him and tell him how sorry she was that Jenny had hurt him, say that she remained his friend and would be pleased to see him if he was ever this way.

She doubted that he would visit or even reply, but it was all she could do. Jenny would hate it that she'd done it – and in a way, Lily felt it disloyal – but she had to do something. If Chris had gone from her life it left very little but her work . . .

Jean looked at the official letter lying on her mat when she returned home that evening and felt sick. She knew

295

before opening it what it must be and was reluctant to do so, because then there would be no getting out of it. She was being named in a divorce case and she would have to make an appointment with Matron and explain to her that it was likely she would be named in the papers, especially as Matthew was insisting on contesting it. He had already briefed his solicitors and they'd told Jean she must give the letter to them immediately it arrived.

She picked the envelope up and slit the seal, reading it briefly. The stark words made her feel sick. It was worse than the hate letter, which she'd put on the fire. *That* had not been repeated but this was upsetting enough and Jean put it away in her bag. She would give it to Matthew the next day and then she would tell Matron what was going to happen. Thankfully, the date of the court hearing was not until October, which meant Jean would be Matthew's wife, so at least she wouldn't have to face it before her wedding.

Sighing, Jean made a mug of cocoa and took it up to bed. She wished that she had a telephone so that she could talk to Matthew about the letter but it was not something she wished to discuss in the public telephone box, especially as others might stand waiting to use it.

Sipping her hot drink in bed, Jean remembered that it was Kathy's wedding on Saturday. She must remember to take the gift and card she'd bought for the popular pair in tomorrow, because she would not see them on the wedding day. Jean had been invited but had volunteered to work so that some of the other nurses could attend.

'Well, this is rather unpleasant, Sister Norton,' Matron said, peering over the little glasses that perched on the end of her nose. 'I am sorry that you have been involved in such a sordid affair.'

'I admit to having a friendship with George but it was no more,' Jean said defensively. 'It is very unfair that I should be named as an adulteress when I'm not guilty.'

'Oh quite,' Matron said, making a steeple of her hands. She had narrow, soft white hands with well-kept nails. Her pride in her hands was a guilty secret but something she had not been able to subdue despite her feeling that it was vanity. 'I do not doubt your word, Jean, but I fear others will . . .'

'Do you wish me to resign?' Jean asked, steeling herself for the request.

'Certainly not!' Matron said and smiled at her. 'I hope we have more backbone than that, Sister. It is not something I would choose to have associated with one of my staff but I shall not desert you in your time of need. No, indeed, it is unjust and I shall speak up for your reputation if given an opportunity.'

Jean felt the sting of tears. She had thought it very possible that she would have to resign, because many employers would not have been so understanding. Divorce was still seen as slightly shameful, which was the reason why King Edward had abdicated the throne of Britain for a woman who had been divorced twice. Jean knew that, even though Matron had accepted her word, many others would not. Those who liked to gossip would enjoy speculating on the truth and making ribald hints. Jean felt she didn't mind so much for herself as for Matthew and for Matron who ran the infirmary, for she might be criticised by Lady Rosalie and the

Board for employing a woman of low morals since some were bound to believe the lies if they were written in a newspaper.

'Well, I shall write to this solicitor,' Matron said and nodded. 'I shall tell him that you are an outstanding nurse with an impeccable reputation and that he is making a mistake in trying to blacken your name.'

'Thank you so much,' Jean said and blew her nose. Her emotions were running high and she flicked her head back as she struggled to recover. It was unprofessional to give way to tears.

'I shall not keep you from your duties any longer,' Matron said. 'And I do hope you will attend the little tea we are giving for Kathy this afternoon – just some cake and a few presents, you know.' She beamed at Jean as if it was all forgotten.

Jean said that she would pop down for five minutes because she had something for the young girl who was getting married and left Matron's office. She made her way back up to the ward, recovering her composure enough to speak with the various members of staff as they passed on the stairs.

In the ward, Nurse Sarah was talking to a woman standing by one of the children's beds and Jean remembered that Keith's grandmother had promised to fetch him that morning. She was taking him home with her for a while.

'Ah, good morning, Mrs Smith, is it?' Jean said and smiled.

The woman turned to her and nodded. She was a tall woman, full-breasted, with big arms that were revealed by the cotton dress she was wearing and she

298

smelled slightly of sweat. However, the expression in her eyes as she watched her grandson tie his shoelaces was benign and her look was kind.

'Are yer ready then, lad?' Mrs Smith asked. 'I persuaded yer Ma that I need yer to live wiv me ter look after me – is that all right then?' She winked at him in a way that showed they understood each other.

'Yeah, please, Gran,' Keith said and a huge grin lit his face. He looked at Nurse Sarah. 'My gran makes the best treacle tart yer've ever tasted. If yer visit us, she might give yer a taste – if I've left any!'

Nurse Sarah laughed. 'I'm glad to see you happy, Keith – and thank you for coming to fetch him, Mrs Smith.'

'I'm Hazel ter you, love,' the big woman said. 'I shouldn't 'ave known how they was treatin' my lad if yer hadn't come and told me – and now I've got 'im fer as long as I'm alive. I threatened his pa with what I'd do to 'im if he stopped Keith living wiv me and he caved in – he always was a bit of a coward.'

Jean watched as the woman picked up his belongings in a bundle tied in a shawl and ushered him out of the ward, before turning to Sarah.

'So, you went to see Mrs Smith then, nurse?'

'Yes, Sister,' Sarah said and smiled. 'He told me she made wonderful food and said he was happy with her, so I paid her a visit the other night and she promised to sort things out. As you know, he could have gone home ten days ago if we'd been satisfied, he would be looked after.'

Jean nodded her approval. 'You are a very caring person, Nurse Sarah. I've always believed you to be an excellent nurse – and you've proved that you will go that bit further to help the children we care for. I'm only sorry that I didn't know about his grandmother.'

'Keith talked to me a lot as he got better,' Sarah said. 'As soon as I realised what kind of a woman she was, I decided to take a risk. She could have thrown me out, but apparently Keith is her favourite and she has wanted him to live with her for a while. Now she has her way.'

'Thanks to you,' Jean said. 'Now, let us get on with our work, nurse. This afternoon we both want to pop down to Matron's tea party for a few minutes so there is no time to waste gossiping now!'

Sarah was smiling as she paid her visit to Kathy's party. A table filled with cakes, sausage rolls and tiny sandwiches had been prepared together with urns of tea and coffee. Kathy was liked by all the staff and many of them had brought her small gifts as well as contributing to the main present, which was a silver teapot and stand. It was the gift every bride longed for and Sarah smiled, because she could just imagine Kathy's excitement when she opened the special gift from them all. A silver teapot meant you were somebody, or that someone cared for you a great deal.

Sarah had bought Kathy a pretty lace tablecloth and Sarah's mother had bought some linen napkins edged with similar lace. They'd signed a card from all of them, including Ned and Charlie, who had added a couple of kisses at the bottom. He was working hard at the wood yard on the docks during his holiday from school and he'd told Sarah he couldn't wait for next Christmas, when he would leave school for good and come to live in London with Mum.

Kathy had hugged and thanked Sarah for her gifts. She'd already given Sarah something for her own wedding, which she hadn't opened, because she was waiting for Steve to come that evening so they could open several wedding presents together.

Sarah stayed long enough to toast Kathy and Bert in lemonade and then returned to the ward. Sister Norton wanted to take her gift and they'd agreed to split the time between them.

She was just in time to see that a new patient had arrived while she'd been absent, a young girl of perhaps thirteen or fourteen. She looked as if she'd had a nasty fall, because her arm was in plaster.

'This is Milly Foster,' Sister Norton said as Sarah went up to her. 'She has been given a milky drink, which will help her to sleep. Milly has been in a little pain since she fell down the stairs.'

Sarah saw the flicker of pain – and something else – in the child's eyes and knew instantly that something wasn't right. However, she was clearly sleepy and still a little tearful, her mother having departed, it seemed.

'Well, shall we just settle down then?' Sarah said gently and nodded to Sister Norton. 'She will be all right now, Sister. I'm sure I can manage.'

'I shall only be gone a few minutes,' Sister Norton said and walked to her desk, taking a small parcel from one of the drawers.

Milly Foster was lying back against the pile of pillows supporting her and her arm, her eyes just closing as

301

Sarah heard the tearful words, 'No, Daddy, don't hit me! Please don't hit me again!'

Sarah looked down at the child, who was not aware of what she'd said and her expression hardened. It was yet another case of abuse that whoever had brought Milly in had disguised as an accident. They were used to it at the infirmary and could only help or expose cruelty in a very few cases. Sarah had manged to help Keith, but here was yet another child in danger. She must be watchful and look for signs, because only if she had proof could she report her fears to the police. However, she would tell Steve what she suspected that evening and let him make a few inquiries. If the father had a history of violence it was sometimes possible to have him warned or even removed from the home, although many women would lie to protect their husband, if only because they relied on them for the very food on the table.

Kathy looked at all the lovely things she'd been given and brushed her eyes. It was so foolish, but everyone had been so kind to her. She'd never thought of herself as being popular, but all the good wishes, cards and small presents she'd been given told a different story.

Lying back against her pillows, Kathy smiled at the beautiful white dress her mother had bought for her wedding. After tomorrow she would never sleep here alone again; Bert would be here beside her. She felt a flutter of nerves, because somehow it hadn't seemed real until now.

She liked Bert a lot. He was good fun, nice-looking, though not like the film stars she admired when he took her to the flicks, and he always smelled nice. Some men stank of beer or cigarettes or sweat, but Bert smelled of soap and peppermints and Kathy liked that – she liked it when he kissed her too.

They hadn't gone beyond kissing, because Bert thought too much of her. He was always thoughtful, always concerned for her, looking after her and finding small ways to please her. He didn't have a great deal of money, because his job was regular but not well paid. It would be easier for them living here with Kathy's mother, and she wouldn't want to leave her alone anyway.

A smile touched Kathy's face. She was glad she was going to marry Bert. She understood that some folk thought he was too old for her – and yes, he *was* older, but because of that he was also more caring and thoughtful. Kathy wasn't sure she was madly in love but what was love? Her mother said it wore off after a few months of marriage and that respect and caring was far more important and Kathy believed her.

She hoped it would be a nice day for her wedding and she thought about Bert preparing to leave his home and live with her. It would be a bit strange for him, too, she thought. Closing her eyes, Kathy gave a contented sigh and went to sleep. She was a lucky girl!

# CHAPTER 22

'Come outside and look,' Rich said that Sunday morning in early September. 'When Mr Gillows gave me the five hundred pounds, I knew exactly what I was going to do wiv my life.'

Arch and Jamie trooped out to look at the shiny black taxicab that had been parked outside Mr Forrest's shop. Although not new, it had been polished to within an inch of its life and Jamie whistled admiringly.

'Is it really yours, Rich?' he asked, almost disbelieving that anyone he knew could own such a thing.

'Yes, it is.' Rich ruffled his hair affectionately. 'And it's all down to you, young'un. Mr Gillows gave me the money to thank me for saving the little girl from drowning, even though the doctors couldn't save her life – and he'd already enabled me to learn to drive, so now I'm going to be a taxi driver. I'm working on the knowledge and once I get that I'll apply fer me licence and the money will last me until I get going.'

'The knowledge?' Jamie questioned and Arch grinned.

'Taxi drivers have to know where every street and lane is in London,' he said. 'They call it the knowledge

305

amongst themselves.' He clapped his friend on the shoulder. 'That's wonderful, mate. Really good news! Where is Mr Gillows now?'

'He's put the house up for sale and returned to America; I don't think he'll ever come back to London. Meggie and me are staying on until it is sold and by then I'll have me taxi licence and I can work as an independent cabbie.' He looked at Arch earnestly. 'I'll have more spare time then and I'll teach yer ter drive, mate, and then yer can get yer own cab.'

Arch hesitated, then, 'I'd love ter learn ter drive, but it will be years afore I could afford somethin' like that.'

'Mebbe – mebbe not,' Rich said. 'I've been asked to tell Jamie he can have anything he wants that belonged to Cassie and to give him this . . .' He handed Jamie a large brown envelope. Jamie opened it and peeped inside. It was stuffed full of what he knew to be white five-pound notes. 'I reckon you've got a thousand at least in there.'

Jamie shook his head in wonder. 'Why? I didn't do anythin' – I cared about Cassie but I never done anythin'.' It was far too much money for Jamie to comprehend and he didn't know what to do or say.

'In Mr Gillows' opinion you're a hero. He says if he'd listened to you Cassie would still be alive,' Rich said. 'He's a sad man and he's already gone away, Jamie. There's no one for him to give his money to now so my advice is to keep what he gave yer and do somethin' wiv yer life.'

'I'll do that anyway,' Jamie said staunchly and then offered the envelope to Arch. 'Use it for us, Arch – fer a motor or a house or a business. It's ours, not mine.

I'd like Cassie's music box, Rich, just as a keepsake – but the rest should be sold with the house or given away to kids that ain't got much.'

'Well, it's all yours so if you want, we'll put her stuff in the cab and take it ter an orphanage,' Rich said looking at him as if he liked him a lot. 'And yer can tell Steve that I've decided ter take him up on his offer to help train the kids. I love the sport and it don't make sense ter waste what I've learned.'

'That's the best news of all,' Arch said and nodded to his friend. His gaze moved to Jamie. 'Are yer sure yer want me to take care of the money, Jamie?'

'Yer me brother,' Jamie said and grinned. 'Mr Forrest gives me enough fer me pocket money fer runnin' errands and I'd rather you did somethin' sensible wiv the money from Mr Gillows. Somethin' ter benefit us both.'

Arch nodded, looking thoughtful. 'We'll have to talk about what we want ter do,' he said as Rich drove off after promising to come back later with Cassie's things and to start Arch's driving lessons. 'It's not a decision to be made lightly. I'm glad Rich has his cab – it's the right life for him, but I'm not sure I'd want it. I'd love to drive and the money will help us in lots of ways – but there are so many things we could do. We'll put the money away safe first thing tomorrow. A Post Office account in both our names – and then we'll decide together. Not many get such a huge windfall, Jamie, and we need to make the most of it.' He put an arm on Jamie's shoulder. 'I should like ter thank Mr Gillows and I will. I misjudged him and I want ter make up fer that – his solicitors will know where to send a letter.'

'I think he couldn't wait ter get away from that house,' Jamie said wisely. 'It must seem cursed to him now – and I reckon the newspapers 'ave been cruel sayin' wicked things about 'im when all he did was to try and make folk happy. He did his best, Arch.'

'I read one article and put the filthy rag straight in the bin,' Arch replied grimly. 'We know the truth and they just want ter make sensation so they can sell papers.'

Jamie nodded. He hadn't bothered to read the paper, even though he'd seen Mr Forrest shaking his head over it. Mr Gillows had done his utmost to make Cassie happy but there was something in her past – something that made it impossible for her to be as other children were. He could never know for certain whether Cassie had somehow caused her mother's fall, either in a temper or as the result of an accident, but it had played on her mind and made her ill. He felt certain that must be the cause.

Sarah looked beautiful in her wedding dress that lovely sunny September morning. Not just because she was a bride but because the happiness shone from her eyes and she glowed from inside. There was a radiance about her that made her friends and relatives smile just to look at her. Her mother kissed her and hugged her and then cried.

'Don't take notice of me, I'm an idiot,' Mrs Cartwright said, 'but I'm so proud of you, my darling girl. You're as lovely inside as you are out and I'm so very happy that you found Steve. He is exactly the right man for you.'

Sarah kissed her and then rubbed off the pink lipstick that had transferred itself to her cheek. 'I know, Mum. I thought Jim was the one for a long time but I was disappointed in him. I know I'll never be disappointed in Steve. We have the same ideals and the same hopes, and I know we'll have a good life together.'

'Yes, you will,' her mother said and gave her a blue lace garter. 'Put this on for luck, my love – but you won't need it with a man like that.'

Charlie's aunt had brought him and Maisie up to town for a few days so that they could attend Sarah's wedding and Steve had several friends and an aunt and uncle, as well as half a dozen cousins that he'd invited to the wedding. His own parents had died some years earlier but his uncle had always been close and so he still had a big family. Sarah had her mother, Ned and the other children and a host of friends from the lanes.

On the day of her wedding a card arrived from Ruby and Sam, with a pound note tucked inside. Now how had Ruby known Sarah was getting married? Sarah's mother had shaken her head and smiled.

'I might have known Ruby would keep her tabs on her old haunts,' she said. 'I wish she'd sent an address then I would've sent her an invitation.'

'Ruby and Sam went off in a hurry,' Sarah said. 'If she doesn't tell you where she is there's a good reason, Mum – but it was nice of her to send us a card and that money.'

'Ruby thought a lot of you,' her mother said. 'One of these days she'll turn up and surprise us, you'll see.'

Sarah nodded happily. She'd had more than a hundred cards and small gifts, some from neighbours and colleagues but most from former patients or their grateful parents. It had made her wedding a very special occasion and her mother had kept open house for a day, offering tea and cake to anyone who wanted to call. She told Sarah that she'd almost run out of tea!

When they left for the church in the special cars Steve had ordered for their big day, Sarah's stomach was fluttering nervously like all brides on their wedding day. Would Steve be there, would everything go as it should – would the cake be all right?

Sarah and her mother had made and iced the two-tier cake themselves. The reception for fifty guests was in the local church hall and was a sit-down meal of grapefruit cocktail, cold boiled ham, new potatoes and salad, followed by fruit, meringues and cream, coffee or tea and the wedding cake. There would be sherry before the meal and sparkling wine to toast the bride and groom and a selection of biscuits and fruit for the children who preferred to pick at bits rather than eat a meal.

Steve was waiting for her with his best man. He turned his head to watch Sarah walk up the aisle in her flowing white gown of lace and the smile in his eyes calmed all her nerves, making her flood with happiness. This was the most special day of her life and she intended to enjoy every moment so that, when she was old, she would be able to close her eyes and remember.

Handing her bouquet of red roses and white lilies to her bridesmaids, Julie, one of Steve's cousin's daughters, and Nurse Jenny, she looked into Steve's eyes as the vicar began the marriage rites. Sun was shining through a beautiful stained-glass window and showering them all with sparkling colour. Then they were following the vicar into the registry to sign their names, before leaving arm in arm and emerging into beautiful sunshine.

'Happy the bride that the sun shines on,' Jenny said and smiled at her brightly. 'Thank you for letting me share your day like this, Sarah . . .'

Sarah nodded and returned the smile, too full to speak as she felt Steve's hand on her waist and knew that they were both feeling the wonder and joy of sharing their day with the people who meant most to them. From the pews on her side she saw many of her mother's friends, Ned, Charlie, his sister Maisie and their aunt, and as many nurses as Matron could spare from the infirmary.

Cars took everyone to the reception and the meal that was waiting. It wasn't the most expensive reception ever, because Sarah's mother had boiled the hams herself and her friends had prepared the salads and new potatoes fresh that morning, but it was tasty and everyone seemed ready to be pleased, tucking into the food and toasting the bride and groom in the wine – which Steve had bought plenty of and was rather scrumptious. It flowed right from the start and consequently it was a merry party who gathered for photographs afterwards, one or two smart hats not quite straight as the camera flashed.

When it was time for Sarah and Steve to leave, they discovered their hired car had been suitably decorated with slogans, balloons, tin cans and an old boot. Steve groaned and made a laughing face at some of his friends from the force and club members who had gathered outside to shower them with confetti.

'We'll stop down the road and untie it all,' he told Sarah, 'but we'll let them have their bit of fun for now.'

'Why not?' Sarah said and laughed up at him.

Glancing out of the window as he drove away, she caught sight of a man staring at her. The intensity of his gaze made her heart catch, because once Jim had been so important to her and the look in his eyes made her feel slightly guilty.

He was the one who had spoiled it! Sarah thrust any guilt from her mind. Jim had chosen another life above Sarah and she'd been hurt – if he was hurt now, she was sorry, but Steve was her life from this day on.

'Well, that went off as it should,' Sarah's mother said to Charlie after the bride and groom had gone. She smiled at Charlie's aunt, who had his sister Maisie perched on her lap. The little girl had become very attached to her aunt since she'd been living with her and had probably substituted her for her mother in her mind. Ned had devoted most of his time to talking to the child and amusing her during the reception. 'Shall we go back to mine for a sit down and a cup of tea? It's been a long day.'

'Yes, very long – and I'm glad we're staying with you and going back in the morning,' Charlie's aunt said with a nod. 'The children start school again next week so they will have tomorrow to get ready.'

'Yes.' Sarah's mother smiled at them. 'Before you know it, you'll be back with me and working for a living, Charlie – are you looking forward to it?'

'Yeah,' Charlie said. 'It's great livin' with my aunt and Maisie, but I can't wait ter get back ter London and start me job proper.'

Sarah's mother nodded. Her daughter might have left

home, but Sarah would visit as often as her busy life allowed and Charlie would be living with her after Christmas. She knew she was lucky to have a full life, which could be as busy as she chose. With so many friends, she could be on several local committees and join a dozen clubs if she wished, but gossiping with a few friends now and then, cooking, knitting, cleaning and sewing were enough for now – and when she had the chance she loved to read, romances mostly. Books by Annie S. Swan and Ethel M. Dell, though she also enjoyed a good Agatha Christie mystery when she was in the mood.

At home in her small cottage, Sarah's mother soon had the kettle on and brought out her seed cake and some jam tarts she'd made for the children, who loved them. Here she was comfortable and had no fears about the approach of her later years, even though she had no partner to share those years.

There were times when she regretted the accident that had caused her husband's poor health, giving him a painful back and eventually seeping his energy and his will to live. Yet she knew that hers had never been the ideal marriage; she'd cared for him, but she'd never known the kind of all-consuming love that Sarah had for Steve.

She supposed that, in her forties, she was too old to think of that now. No, she must make up her mind to becoming a grandmother and look forward to the foster children who would visit her and fill her declining years.

Sarah turned in her husband's arms and kissed him passionately. They had just made love again and she'd discovered that being close to a special man was more than she could ever have dreamed. Her body had responded to his gentle but passionate loving and she'd found herself crying his name as he carried her with him to a sweet and fulfilling climax. His hands were stroking the length of her naked back, making her press against him urgently as she felt the need to be one with him again.

'Sarah, Sarah, my love,' Steve whispered against her throat. 'I adore you, my darling. I never knew love – being with someone like you could be so wonderful . . .'

'I love you,' she said and looked up at him. 'I'm so happy, Steve. I knew you would never let me down, but I never expected to feel anything like this . . .' Her mouth parted as her breath came faster and she surrendered once more to his kiss and the urgency of his body as he possessed her, making her his so thoroughly that she was left feeling sleepy and relaxed into him, safe and warm and utterly loved.

Later they woke, kissed, laughed, washed and dressed, hungry now for the food that awaited them downstairs. Afterwards, they sought the warmth of the September sunshine, walking along the promenade in the peaceful Devonshire resort and then down to the sandy dunes, where you could lie sheltered from any breeze if you wished. Foam-crested waves drove restlessly against the seaweed-strewn shore and the breeze lifted Sarah's hair, blowing it back from her face and bringing colour to her cheeks.

'You're so beautiful,' Steve said and touched her face with reverent fingers. 'How did I get so lucky?'

'I'm the lucky one,' Sarah said and her fingers curled

about his as they held hands. 'I don't know what I'd do if I ever lost you . . .' Why had she said that? She didn't know but a little chill slid down her spine and for a moment it was if a cloud had obscured the sun.

'You won't lose me,' Steve said and turned her to look at him. 'I know you see a lot of pain and death in your job – I do, too, but I'm a big strapping lad and I shan't ever leave you . . . at least until I'm ninety-nine and can't remember my own name any more!'

Sarah giggled as he'd intended. She laughed up at him and then set off at a run towards the sea edge. Flinging off her leather sandals, she ran into the water and started splashing. Steve followed moments later and splashed her by kicking water at her. Sarah gave him a wicked look, bent down cupping her hands and splashing water all over him. He shook his head and advanced on her purposefully. She gave a shriek and tried to run but he caught her and swept her up in his arms, lowering her down to the surface of the sea as if he would drop her in. Sarah looked up at him trustingly and he gave a groan, brought her back up, set her on her feet and kissed her.

The dark moment had gone as if it had never been and Sarah smiled as she caught the smell of warm doughnuts. 'Let's go and investigate those doughnuts,' she said. 'I don't know about you, but I'm hungry already . . .'

'After that breakfast?' Steve teased. 'You'll get fat – but they do smell good. Come on, let's go and find them.'

# CHAPTER 23

'So, what do yer think?' Arch said when Jamie had eaten his slice of toast and dripping that Sunday morning towards the end of September. Outside the sun was shining, highlighting the dingy street and the stray dog hunting in the gutters. 'Mr Forrest says he would sell us the shop and the stock for six hundred and fifty pounds, which would leave us a good bit in the bank. He'll go on livin' wiv us and doing a bit in the shop until he's had enough and decides to live wiv his daughter – and then I'll take over. That won't be fer a few years, and in the meantime, I'll keep working. My boss at the club is pleased I'm learnin' ter drive and he's given me a rise – wants me ter drive him about. This shop would always be somethin' fer us to fall back on, Jamie. It's a home and a business – and one day we'll make it better, more modern, but not while Mr Forrest wants ter stay on.'

'Yer wouldn't rather be a taxicab driver like Rich?' Jamie asked and his brother shook his head.

'Nah, I don't think it would suit me,' Arch said. 'I might do private chauffeuring fer someone like my boss at the club, but fer the moment I like where I am splitting my time between the shop and the club.'

Jamie nodded. He enjoyed his life here and hadn't wanted to leave Mr Forrest in the lurch. Jamie had adopted him as his grandfather and felt warm affection for the generous old man. Now they could stay on and know their money was safely invested while their friend still had an interest in his life without the worry or the responsibility.

'I think it's a great idea, Arch,' Jamie said. 'Mr Forrest wants ter watch the competition fer the boxing and judo tomorrow night; we're goin' ter lock up a bit early so we can all travel together – Rich is comin' ter fetch us.'

'Yeah, I know, kid,' Arch ruffled his hair affectionately. 'It's yer big night. I'll be there rootin' fer yer – and I expect yer ter win. Don't yer let me down, now.'

Jamie nodded and smiled. He was feeling confident he would win his bout and go through to the next round, but he didn't want to say that because it would sound as if he had a big head.

'Yeah, that's great, Arch,' he said now. 'I'm glad I told yer ter look after the money. Are yer gonna change the name or keep it as Forrest's?'

'I shan't change anythin' fer a while,' Rich said. 'While Mr Forrest stays on, we'll keep the purchase private. His family know and they don't mind, because none of them want to run the shop. His grandson loves the army and wants to stay on when his present term of service ends – and Mr Forrest's son and daughter all have good jobs.'

'Then nothin' changes,' Jamie said. 'That suits me, Arch.'

He went off, whistling, to buy some of his favourite Tom Thumb drops. It was good having a few shillings in his pocket, especially because he'd earned them. Jamie had handed the money over to his brother because he hadn't wanted to use it or spend it. The money was tainted for him, because of Cassie's death. He was glad to help his brother and he knew the purchase of the business would give him a bit of security in the future, but he didn't intend to be a shopkeeper. Jamie loved being in the police cadets and he now knew it was what he wanted to do when he left school. The officers who ran the cadet classes were pleased with him and he'd already earned two merit badges, so he knew his hopes for the future had a good chance of coming true.

On Monday night, the hall was packed with parents and friends of the contestants. Jamie was proud that he had his brother, Rich and Mr Forrest out there in the audience to cheer him on, and Steve was on his side. Back from his honeymoon, Steve looked fit and tanned, and he seemed as happy as a lark on a summer's morning.

Several contests took place before Jamie's and three of the club's members won through to the next round. When it was Jamie's turn, he went out to enthusiastic cheers and realised that the other club members were in the audience cheering him on.

It made him grin confidently, even when he saw his opponent was bigger and older than he. Once they closed with each other, Jamie found the other lad's weakness straight away. He was slower and slightly unbalanced on his legs and although he had a strong back and powerful arms, he was vulnerable to a tackle from below. Jamie brought him down within a few seconds and, although the second fall was a little harder to achieve, that came to Jamie after what he considered an easy tussle. He was declared the winner and awarded a silver medal, and he was through to the next round, which would be the national championships held in late October.

'That looked easy,' Rich said when they were on their way home, after Jamie had received the congratulations of all his friends from the club and even some from the police cadets. He hadn't expected them to come and he was thrilled to see so many faces he knew clapping him as he received his medal.

'It was easy,' Jamie admitted. 'I don't think he was up to the standard of some of the other competitors. I was lucky.'

'Don't be modest,' Arch said. 'You were quick and clever and you deserved it. Next time it may not be so easy but Steve knows the opposition and he reckons you'll win the nationals – though I wasn't supposed ter tell yer!'

'Shall we get some fish and chips ter celebrate?' Mr Forrest asked. 'I'll buy them, lads, but one of you can go in and get them.'

They all agreed with enthusiasm, because nothing beats a fish and chip supper to celebrate a good night out. Rich drew the cab to a stop near the shop and Arch went to fetch them. He brought them back to the cab and the smell made them all hungry.

Jamie was glad to see that the shop was locked up safely when they got back, because he'd wondered if

Leo's gang might take the opportunity to try and break in while they were all out, but the new locks and the lights over the back door would make it less inviting than in the old days.

Fish and chips and pickled onions with a cup of tea for Mr Forrest, a glass of pale ale for Arch and Rich, and a fizzy Vimto for Jamie went down a treat. It had been a good evening with nothing to spoil it.

As he went to bed that night, Jamie wondered what would happen to spoil things. Everything was too perfect, which meant that Sod's Law would have a hand in the game soon, because that was how life went.

# CHAPTER 24

Lily's hands trembled as she picked up the letter from the mat. She recognised the handwriting instantly and it was addressed to her! Tearing it open, her heart racing wildly, Lily saw that Chris had addressed her as, *My very dear friend Lily . . .*

Her eyes were wet with tears as she read. Chris told her how much her letter had meant to him and said how sorry he was that their friendship could not continue in person, because he could not embarrass Jenny by coming to her home.

*I do enjoy receiving letters and writing them. If now and then in your busy life you felt able to pen a few lines, I should be grateful. My work makes it difficult for me to form a lasting relationship and I do completely understand that Jenny wants a different kind of life than I could give her. Now I have had time to think about it, I can see that it wouldn't have worked, I was in love with the idea and maybe it was more wishful thinking on my part. Jenny was right, a marriage that made her unhappy would have*

*been a disaster, and better for us both to find the*
*right person. I have important work to keep me*
*occupied – work that is necessary for our country.*
*One day I may be able to tell you more, my friend,*
*but for now you must trust me. I do wish Jenny well*
*and hope she finds the right person . . .*

Tears stung Lily's eyes because his letter betrayed his
sadness, but to her it was precious and she would keep
it, treasure it and any others that he chose to write. Lily
knew that she did not have his love, but in a way that
didn't matter so much now that he was not Jenny's. She
could think of him, dream of him, long for the day when
they might meet. It would not be soon, she knew that,
but at least Chris was hers now. He was her secret, her
dearest friend, and that was enough for the moment . . .

Smiling, Lily tucked her letter away in her writing
case. She would sleep first and then she would write
back to him – tell him about her life at the infirmary,
about the patients she tended and the other nurses. She
would even tell him what Jenny was doing, sometimes.
They would be the letters of a friend, not a lover, but
in her heart, Lily would keep that hope alive. She was
a patient woman and perhaps in time what she wanted
most in the world would be hers . . .

Jenny met Sarah on the stairs at the infirmary as they
so often did, stopping for a moment to chat. 'You've
got such a lovely colour, Sarah,' Jenny said. 'I do envy
you your trip to Devon. It was lovely weather while
you were there, wasn't it?'

'We got on the beach every day,' Sarah agreed. 'The

morning we were leaving for home the sky was grey for the first time so we were very lucky.' She looked at Jenny. 'Have you had a holiday this year?'

'I had some days out when Chris was home earlier in the year,' she said. 'I like the sea but I've only ever been to Southend. I know Torquay is lovely, because Lily went once with some nurses she trained with – but I haven't been.'

'You should go,' Sarah told her. 'I loved it down there and Steve says we'll go again next year – but we might take a cottage next time. We could afford two weeks then instead of just six days in a hotel.'

'I know; they are so expensive,' Jenny said, 'but I'm glad you had a lovely time.' She hesitated, then, 'Have you heard about Sister Norton – well, she's Sister Mitchell now, of course.'

'No – and if it is gossip, I'm not sure I want to.'

'Well, I didn't either but Sister Harwell told me she'd heard she was to be named in a divorce case as the other woman.'

'No, I don't believe it!' Sarah said. 'It is ridiculous. She just wouldn't – well, you know her. It is malicious gossip and I shall not listen to it.'

'That's what I said but then I wondered . . .'

'Well, don't,' Sarah said. 'It's unkind and I'm sure it is a lie. We really shouldn't listen to nasty tales, Jenny.'

'No, I won't – and if anyone else repeats it I'll tell them it can't possibly be true.'

Sarah smiled at her. 'Sister Mitchell seems happy since she married last month and I should hate it if some nasty gossip upset her.'

'Sarah, you're right – and now I have to dash. Lily

325

and I are going shopping for some new clothes this afternoon, and I want a couple of hours in bed first.'

Sarah nodded and went on up the stairs. She frowned as she thought of what Jenny had said, but then dismissed it as nonsense. Sister Rose must have been mistaken. Jean Norton wasn't the sort of woman who got involved with a married man!

Jean saw the odd looks one or two of the staff gave her when she passed them on the stairs or in the room where they had coffee if they had time to sit down for a while and she knew that somehow they'd got hold of the story of the divorce.

Sighing, she lifted her head high and set her face in a look of determination. She'd known it would happen and she couldn't change that, but she wouldn't let it affect her. Matthew loved her and believed her so what else mattered?

Although their wedding had been quiet and their honeymoon brief, Jean knew her marriage was a success. She'd responded to Matthew in bed instinctively and he'd shown her how much he loved her. They were happy and life would have been perfect had not the shadow of George's pending divorce hung over them.

It was so unfair, when Jean had been resolute in not letting George into her bed, but perhaps he had loved her and, in its way, that was a betrayal of his wedding vows. However, Matthew was determined to defend the case and restore his wife's good name, even though Jean feared it might only make the case more notorious . . .

The lawyer stood as the woman entered his office, which was situated in a narrow lane just off Oxford Street and showed the prosperity of his practice in the soft carpets and shining glass and wood interior. She was not wearing her uniform but he knew her as the Matron of the Lady Rosalie Infirmary, more usually called the Rosie by the folk who used it. A tall thin man wearing a pinstriped suit, white shirt and subtle blue tie, his eyes had a piercing quality that only the brave or the innocent could meet without flinching. Matron met his gaze and held it and he nodded, smiling as he indicated the comfortable chair that had been set for her.

'You wrote that you wished to see me, Miss Thurston – or should I address you as Matron?' he said. 'May I know what troubles you?'

'I have come here on behalf of one of my nursing staff,' Matron told him with a stern glance. 'Sir, I must warn you that you are in danger of despoiling the reputation of a good and respectable woman – and I have come here to ask you not to do it.'

'I think you should tell me everything,' he said gently. 'I know quite a bit about you, Matron – and I know the person in question. I have the greatest respect for you and what you do, and not only as Matron of the infirmary. I know of your kindness to others, especially some of my own people – and we may speak of that more later – but I must act for my client in her best interests, unless you can convince me otherwise?'

'I think you a man who fears God,' Matron said, 'though your God may not be mine – or at least we know him by different names. Your people have suffered great acts of violence against them, sir – and you are called the killers of Christ. Yet the Jewish community believes in one God, as do we, the followers of Christ.

I believe that we should understand one another – and I think that once you have listened to me, you will convince your client that to press her case would not be in her best interests.'

Nurse Anne entered the children's ward. She had taken her preliminary nursing exams at the London and had now rejoined the staff at the Rosie to finish her training. Always a favourite with the children when a probationer, Nurse Anne did not often have time to visit them now, because she'd been assigned to the chronically sick ward, under the strict eye of Sister Ruth Linton. She smiled at Sarah as she came up to her.

'Sister Linton asked me to come and help, because Matron needs to see Sister Mitchell.'

Sarah nodded and handed her a sick pot. 'Can you take that to bed number five, please, and look after the child? Milly is feeling queasy this morning – and I have some injections to give. I'll tell Sister Mitchell she is wanted in Matron's office . . .' Anne was still a junior nurse and Sarah preferred to give the injections of certain drugs herself.

Leaving the nurse to care for the little girl who was now vomiting noisily, Sarah went off to deliver her message to Sister Mitchell.

'Sister Mitchell!' Sarah caught up with her as she was checking the medicine trolley. 'You are needed in Matron's office.'

Jean nodded and Sarah noticed an odd look in her eyes before she went into the little cloakroom to check her hair and uniform were in place, as if she were nervous for some reason. Sarah carried on handing out medicines and giving the three injections the doctors had ordered. Children usually shrank from the needle and one little girl shed a few tears, complaining that it stung, but the boys took it with a grimace and a glare.

Tea was served on the ward just after and Kathy appeared with the trolley. Egg and cress sandwiches, sausage rolls and jam tarts were on offer for the children, with one or two exceptions who were offered rice pudding with jam or strawberry blancmange instead. They were the tonsillectomy cases, who were still sore after their operations and couldn't swallow hard food yet. It was only for the first or second meal that such food was offered, after that they would be given sandwiches and then toast, because when your throat was able to tolerate toast you were deemed ready to go home. Having your tonsils removed was a very unpleasant experience for children, but tonsillitis made them dizzy and often sick with sometimes nasty headaches too, so an operation was performed when necessary but that, too, was unpleasant to say the least and sometimes invited more infections, but in extreme cases the child was so ill that it became the only way.

'How are you, Kathy?' Sarah asked the girl who had brought up the children's tea. 'Do you like being Mrs Rush?'

Kathy didn't answer at once and then she shrugged. 'Yes, it's fine, not much different, really. Mum doesn't try to stop us goin' anywhere – so Bert takes me dancing and to the flicks. We're goin' to see a Charlie Chaplin film this evening . . . Oh, and I think there's a cowboy on as well. Bert likes those.'

Sarah nodded. Kathy wasn't glowing with happiness

the way she felt herself – and suspected Sister Mitchell did, too. She'd seen content in the senior nurse's face when she returned to work after her short honeymoon, even though she thought Sister Mitchell might have something on her mind. Perhaps it was why Matron had asked her to visit her office . . .

'Ah, thank you for coming so promptly,' Matron said and smiled from behind her large and very untidy desk. 'Please sit down, Sister Mitchell. I wanted to talk to you about that unfortunate divorce business.'

'Yes, I think some rumours have reached other members of staff.' Jean felt guilty and avoided looking directly at her employer.

'That can be dealt with quite easily. I shall make it known that I do not believe the stories and that should quell most of it – but you will be anxious.' Matron made a steeple of her hands and smiled serenely. 'I visited the lawyer who sent you that obnoxious letter this morning and I am glad to say Mr Symons saw my point of view. He will be advising his client that she may incur financial penalties if she makes accusations in court which are later proved false because you could, of course, sue her.'

'The lawyer will advise George's wife not to go ahead?' Jean stared at her in disbelief. 'But his letter was so forceful!'

'Ah yes, but you see – Mr Symons discovered that we have mutual friends and interests and he understands that if he besmirches the good name of my nurse, he will deeply offend me. Without being boastful, I am a woman of some standing, with influential friends. He

330

decided that if I was willing to go on the stand and swear, on oath, that you were a woman of impeccable behaviour and that I had certain knowledge that you were innocent, his case was unlikely to prevail. He will advise the lady to sue for a separation on grounds of incompatibility – and various other legal terms.'

'Would you really do that for me, Matron?' Jean was stunned. 'You cannot know what I have done outside working hours.' She had never expected Matron to take up her cause so forcefully.

'I have always believed that one's soul is reflected in the eyes if one knows how to look,' Matron said. 'I have looked into yours and seen pain and grief over many years and now I see love and happiness. I should not wish to see that destroyed or even tainted. Your behaviour has always been immaculate as a nurse, an example to others. As I believe myself to be a good judge of character, I think myself justified in taking the oath.' She smiled. 'I think my experience of life makes me a good judge of character in others.'

Jean didn't know whether to laugh or cry. There was no certainty that George's wife would withdraw the accusations, for she could find another lawyer to take her case, but it was doubtful she could win if Matron took the stand for them. Very few would doubt the oath of a woman who had dedicated her life to caring for the sick for so many years. She blinked hard and then smiled, the tears very close.

'Thank you so much, Matron. I did not expect you to do anything like this . . .'

'It was quite enjoyable,' Matron said and her eyes sparkled with mischief. 'I expected a battle but once we discovered that we had so many causes and friends in common it was not necessary. Mr Symons quite saw my point of view!' She stood up and offered her hand, clasping Jean's and patting it sympathetically. 'I do not guarantee that this foolish lady will see sense, but I think her case weakened . . .'

'I cannot tell you how grateful I am,' Jean said. 'It has lifted the shadow of impending doom and shame . . .'

'Had you been a shameless harlot you would not have cared a jot,' Matron said. 'I think your honesty shines through, my dear – now go and look after your patients. I need Nurse Anne back on the chronic ward, for she is good with elderly patients, of whom we have many who near the end of their lives.'

'I don't know what Matron said to her,' Sarah told her husband when he came home that evening. 'It lifted the shadows from her eyes, though – so it was good news.'

'I've got good news for *you*,' Steve said. 'I've been put forward for a sergeant's exam. If I pass, I'll earn more money and I'll be behind a desk most of the time rather than at the sharp end of things on the streets.'

'Is it what you want, though?' Sarah asked, looking at him in surprise, because she knew he enjoyed the life he had, despite the cuts and bruises after a tussle with rogues that were the lot of any policeman on the beat. 'Don't do it just for me, love. I know you love your work.'

'Yes, I do,' Steve said, 'but I've had several years at it and the younger men are faster on their feet – and I shall still keep on my other duties at the club. I might be asked to help with the cadets as well, so it doesn't mean I'll be home at six every night.'

'Well, I go on nights next week for a month,' Sarah said. 'We're busy folk and just have to make the most of the time we have together. I thought we might take Mum and Ned out this Sunday, for a meal and a ride around, if you can hire a car?'

'I'll borrow one from Jackson,' Steve said. 'He's on duty so he won't mind – I'll give him a bottle of whisky and he'll be happy.'

Sarah nodded and smiled. Steve had good friends at the station and they'd come to her wedding, showering her with confetti and giving her a lovely china tea service as a gift. She was happy for Steve to go to the boxing club some evenings, because it gave her time to catch up on her housework or pop round to see her mother. Not that her mother was always at home these days. She and Ned had taken to going to a club three nights a week; it was a social club that had activities for the young ones as well as their parents, and while Sarah's mum played cards or gossiped or watched a film slide show, Ned joined in other activities like the Scouts and learning how to make models of planes and cars.

Sarah fried chops and served up the mash with cabbage and onions, which made a tasty supper. It was quick and easy and then Steve was off to the club for a few hours. Sarah had decided that she would go to the social club her mother and Ned had joined and see what it was all about.

Sarah saw her mother seated at a table with three others. Two of the three were women and the third was a rather distinguished-looking man. He had silver-grey hair and a moustache and looked a little like Ronald Coleman, the film star. He was obviously partnering one of the other women and he called hearts as trumps and laid a small heart, taking the first trick. Sarah smiled as she saw her mother glance up and give him a rueful smile. She lifted a hand and walked to the table.

'What are you doing here, love?' her mother asked.

'I just thought I'd see what you and Ned get up to,' Sarah replied. She glanced at the man seated opposite curiously, because he didn't look like someone who worked on the docks.

'Sarah, I'd like you to meet my friends – Jane, Merry, and Mr Thompson, who is a fairly new addition to our little group.'

'Oh, Gwen, I told you to call me Theo,' the man said in a warm pleasant voice, that of a well-educated man. He stood up and offered his hand to Sarah. 'I know you must be Gwen's daughter. I'm very pleased to meet you – and may I call you Sarah?'

'Yes, of course,' Sarah said and smiled. 'I'm pleased to meet you – all of you.' She shook hands with Theo and liked his firm grip. 'I shan't disturb your game. Mum, carry on with your evening. I'll have a word with Ned and then have a look round. Don't think you have to stop for me.'

'I wasn't thinking of it,' her mother said and laughed. 'You can't walk out on your partner in a game like this, Sarah. Find someone to talk to – it will do you good to have a bit of relaxation.'

Sarah nodded and wandered off. She saw that Ned

was doing gentle exercises with the Scout group and watched for a few minutes then wandered over to where a few women were seated, making baskets and other handicrafts. One of her mother's older friends recognised her and invited her to join them. Sarah sat down and looked at the various crafts on offer.

'I like making these baskets,' Maud Hastings told her. 'You can use them for so many things, Sarah – and they make lovely gifts for birthdays and Christmas if you fill them with treats. This one is going to be filled with homemade sweets and biscuits for my grandmother. It is her ninetieth birthday next week and I was going to ask you and Gwen if you wanted to come.'

'I'd love to, Maud,' Sarah said. 'What does your gran like that I could bring for her –sweets or fruit?'

'She loves plum jam,' Maud said. 'If your mum has any of hers left that would be as good a gift as any for Granny.'

'I'm sure she has, she made loads just recently,' Sarah said. 'We'll bring the jam and some nice buns of some kind.'

She took up a piece of felt and looked at the patterns on offer. She could cut out and bind a purse or a case for scissors as a gift; it was always useful to have a few things you'd made yourself to form part of a present, and at Christmas the infirmary would be needing lots of little presents for the patients.

'Do you mind if I have a go?' she asked. 'What do we pay for materials?'

'You just put a contribution in that box, a shilling or two,' Maud said, pointing out a collection box at the end of the table. 'Fancy you joining our little group!'

Maud said. 'I persuaded Gwen to come and bring Ned with her – and it looks as if she is enjoying herself.'

Sarah glanced over and saw that her mother was laughing at something Theo was saying. He was teasing her and, if Sarah was not mistaken, showing a definite interest in being her friend, if not more.

'Yes, well she needs to get out a little, have some fun. I'm not much of a card player, but I like making things . . .'

'I'll budge up a bit and give yer room,' Maud said and smiled at her. 'Your mum is never lonely, Sarah. Yer don't need ter worry, she's always got a visitor and if any of us needs anythin' we know where ter go.'

Sarah nodded and smiled. She had worried that her mother might feel a bit lonely when she married, but it was obvious that she had a life of her own and that made Sarah feel even more content, because she wanted her mother to be happy. Marriage had given her a permanent glow but she'd worried about her mum and now she saw that there was no need, because the woman playing cards with her friends looked perfectly happy.

Jean looked at her husband as he brought their drinks that evening. They had decided to have a meal in a pub before going onto the theatre. Sipping her glass of white wine, she smiled.

'I feel more hopeful that it will all fizzle out,' she said as he sat down and took a bite of the cheese and pickle sandwich he'd chosen. 'Matron was wonderful, Matthew. I was afraid she might ask me to leave when I warned her of the scandal but instead of that she went into battle on my behalf.'

He nodded and swallowed the last bit of sandwich,

then took a swig of pale ale. 'I would never write Matron off in any fight,' he said after swallowing. 'She might look mild as milk – unless she is angry, of course, which I've hardly ever seen her, because that woman is an oasis of calm – but there is a rod of steel in her back.'

'That sounds so painful,' Jean said and laughed, though she knew exactly what he meant. 'I couldn't believe it when she told me what she'd done; I knew some of the staff had somehow got hold of a bit of gossip but if it doesn't come to court it will all be forgotten in no time.'

'Good,' Matthew replied and smiled at her. 'We can put it behind us and enjoy life as we ought.' He eyed her remaining ham sandwich hungrily. 'If you aren't going to eat that, I'll help you out – and then we'll get going.'

'You're welcome,' Jean said and pushed the plate towards him. Matthew looked lean but he was always starving by evening and, if they were at home, she would have cooked a large meal; as it was, he would probably be ready to eat again when they got home after the concert. 'I ate a piece of wedding cake earlier. Sarah brought it in for the patients and it looked so good I had a slice for myself.'

'She's a good nurse,' Matthew said. 'Do you think she would be willing to push on and become a sister like you?'

'I think she could quite easily,' Jean said. 'I've thought about it myself so I'll have a word. Though Sarah may be more interested in becoming a mother rather than taking on more responsibility at work!'

'I do blame myself,' Lady Rosalie said as she sat sipping her sherry in Matron's office. 'Had I phoned or visited him when I felt that woman was unsuitable that poor little girl might still be alive . . .'

'You should not blame yourself,' Mary said and touched her hand in sympathy. 'He was responsible for Cassie's welfare and should have seen for himself that the woman was all wrong for the post. A disturbed child like Cassie needed nursing care and love – not a house that shone like a new pin. In my opinion the woman is guilty of manslaughter at the least and I'd put her in prison if I had my way!'

'Unfortunately, she did nothing wrong in law. We have been blamed for placing her in Mr Gillows' care, as he is now believed unsuitable – and yet he did all he was capable of.'

'Perhaps the one thing he didn't give her was what she needed?' Mary said. 'Money and gifts are not the same as love, Rosalie. That child needed love – and from what Constable Jones told one of the nurses, the only one to show her any love was a young boy who helped her when he found her wandering on the street.'

'Yes, that is so sad,' Lady Rosalie said. 'How the police managed to miss the fact that she was living in that house I have no idea – and yet perhaps it was as well they did, because she would have probably died of cold on the streets long before.'

'It makes me so angry that a child can slip through the net and something so tragic results,' Mary said. 'Thank goodness for the foster carers, Rosalie – and you do far more good than harm, so you can't blame yourself for one failure.'

'Yes, I know,' Lady Rosalie agreed and then brightened. 'We've found a home for that young sister and brother I told you of – and now we have six more youngsters on our list.'

'It never ends,' Mary agreed and then frowned. 'And have you heard anything about the girl we thought was being abused by her father and you informed the police about?'

'Not yet – I must check up on that. There's only so long you can keep her safe here though it's hardly a lie that she is poorly – and no wonder if that's what she is going through at home! Well, I have a meeting . . .' Lady Rosalie rose to her feet, smiling as she pulled on her gloves. 'It always makes me feel so much better talking to you, my dear Mary. You have such calm surety and that helps so much.'

# CHAPTER 25

'Only three weeks to the national championships,' Steve told the youngsters who had gathered in the hall that night. 'I've almost completed my list of those who are going forward to the contest. As you've all come through the regional heats it isn't an easy choice because in some groups there is more than one of you worthy of the honour of representing us. So, work hard, show me your best efforts and next week I shall announce the final four.'

The boys gave a little cheer and separated to start training. Seven of them had won regional contests, but the nationals were stricter and there were fewer groups. It was a more prestigious championship but the regionals had many more chances for lads to win prizes and medals. Now the contests were honed and the boys knew that three of them would not be picked, but because they were all friends there wasn't as much resentment as might have been expected.

'You will be picked for our age group, Jamie,' a boy named Terry said. 'I know yer better than me.'

Jamie looked at him seriously. 'Yer might get it, Terry.

Yer bigger than me and I think yer could've beaten the one I beat in the regionals, easy.'

'Yer faster and yer work it out quick,' Terry said and grinned at him. 'If we had pairs, I'd like to fight wiv you, Jamie.'

'Yeah, that would be good,' Jamie agreed. 'Come on, let's practise the falls and 'ave our own contest.'

Terry nodded and moved towards him. Much to his delight, he gained the first fall easily, though Jamie took the next two. Afterwards, as they were sipping orange squash, he asked if Jamie had let him win the first one.

'Nah, you won it because yer strong and yer grabbed me first,' Jamie said. 'But I knew what yer would do then and so I went in first and took yer off balance. If yer want ter win against someone as good as you are, yer need to think harder, mate. Take 'im by surprise. Yer 'ave ter vary what yer do.'

Terry looked at him thoughtfully and then grinned. 'Thanks, that's helpful. Maybe I'll beat yer next time.'

'Yeah,' Jamie grinned at him. 'I'm orf now – I want ter get back afore it's too dark. I don't like Mr Forrest bein' alone too much at night, even though he has a good lock on the door.'

'Yer like 'im don't yer?'

'Yeah, he's like a grandfather to me,' Jamie said. 'A lot of blokes would've knocked me 'ead orf after what I done but he were real good to me – and it makes me mad when someone tries to take advantage of 'im 'cos he's old.'

'Where's Arch this evenin'?' Terry asked, looking round.

'He went to his job at the nightclub early. They had a load of drinks delivered and they were a man short so Arch went in to help set up early. He does a lot of extras and they pay him more now.'

Terry nodded. 'I'll walk part of the way home wiv yer if yer like.'

'All right, yeah I'd like that,' Jamie said. 'It was a good fight this evenin', I enjoyed it.'

The boys walked home together, talking about their lives and what they were going to do when they left school. Terry was destined for his father's yard on the docks, where they loaded and unloaded goods bound for coastal regions in Britain.

'Dad says I can take over from him when I'm old enough,' Terry said. 'It sounds grand when I tell folk Pa buys and sells goods, but it ain't much fun. Pa buys coal and wood, sometimes steel or even loads of corn and barley – anythin' that will turn a penny, as he says. Some of the stuff stinks and it's hard work. I'd rather be in the army and if I 'ad my way that's where I'd be orf to as soon as I'm eighteen – sooner if they'd take me.'

'They don't take yer no younger unless there's a war,' Jamie said. 'My pa said in the last war they had lads of as young as fifteen marching wiv 'em.'

'Yeah, I heard tell of one of 'em what run when the guns came too close – and my pa says they shot 'im fer desertion.'

'That's wicked!' Jamie looked at him in horror. 'They wouldn't, would they?'

'It's what Pa said, but I think he says it to frighten me, 'cos he's afraid I'll join up afore I'm eighteen.'

'Well, they wouldn't take yer in peace time – someone down our lane tried to join and they wouldn't have him 'cos he'd got flat feet.'

'There might be another war, though, leastways, Pa thinks it could 'appen. It's one of the reasons he don't want me ter join up.'

'Surely not?' Jamie said shaking his head. 'They said the last war was, "The War to end all wars" didn't they?'

'Yeah, that's what they said, but there's a bloke called Hitler in Germany now and Pa reckons he's out fer revenge because we beat 'em last time.' Terry was thoughtful. 'They reckon he's a nasty bit of work and he'll turn the world upside down if we let him.'

Engrossed in their talk, the boys had walked further than either of them realised. They had reached the end of Jamie's lane and he stopped and looked at his friend in dismay.

'We've come past our turnin', mate. So, yer want me to—'

Whatever Jamie intended to say was lost as four lads came slinking out of the gloom and stood in front of them. They were looking at Jamie in a way that boded ill and he saw immediately that Leo was one of them. All of them were carrying knives or coshes and it was obvious that they'd come determined to give Jamie a beating.

'Go on, Terry, run,' Jamie said. 'Yer don't need to be caught up in this.'

'I ain't a coward,' Terry said and his face set in determination. 'I shan't desert yer, mate – and we can beat these dopes easy.'

'Yeah, we can.' Jamie grinned at him. 'But watch out fer the knives, 'cos they'll stab yer in the back soon as look at yer.'

'Let's stand back ter back,' Terry suggested. 'Then we can look out fer each other.'

Jamie nodded and swung round so that his back was against Terry's. The gang was calling out insults, jeering them as they stood and waited for them to attack. Clearly, Leo had expected one or the other to run but, because they'd stayed together, he was hesitating. He'd obviously heard that Jamie was tougher than the last time they met.

'Did yer think I'd forgot yer, yer little runt?' Leo sneered as he advanced slowly, two of his three companions at his sides. The fourth lingered at the back of the group and Jamie knew it was Vic, the lad he'd warned to stay away from the gang. 'I lost money and face 'cos of yer, but when I've finished wiv yer, you'll wish yer 'ad crawled into a hole and died.'

'Big words, Leo,' Jamie challenged. 'How big are yer without that knife? I know who the coward is – too frightened to fight me on yer own yer brought all yer mates to 'elp!'

'Damn yer!' Incensed, Leo sprang at Jamie and he felt the knife score his cheek, but in an instant his hand was up and he had hold of Leo's wrist. His grip was like iron and he saw the surprise in Leo's face as Jamie exerted pressure and suddenly twisted the other's wrist in such a way that he heard something crack and then the yell of pain and anger from Leo as he jerked back, nursing his wrist. 'Get the bugger!' he ordered his gang.

Another lad came for Jamie but Terry moved swiftly and grabbed him by the arm, twisting it up his back so that he too cried out in pain and dropped his weapon, sinking to his knees. The third looked at Jamie and moved towards him purposefully but a cry from the fourth made him pause and look round.

'Coppers! Run fer it!' cried the lad Jamie had warned to get a better life. The third lad looked into the distance and then they all heard the sound of a police whistle. Two of the lads ran off, each heading in a different direction, and Leo tried to do the same but Jamie moved like lightning and grabbed his jacket, hampering him so that when he did tear free it was too late to escape the charge of the three officers who were coming down the lane at full pelt.

Terry's strength meant that his victim was going nowhere until he was handed over to one of the officers. Jamie grinned as he recognised one of the instructors from Cadet's class.

'Yer broke my wrist!' Leo said bitterly, looking at Jamie in disbelief. 'Arrest him, he attacked me.'

'Did you?'

'I defended myself,' Jamie said. 'There were four of them and they came at me. Terry tackled one, I disarmed Leo and—'

'Yer broke my wrist,' Leo accused wildly, his eyes darting back and forth as the police hemmed him in. 'Yer should be locked up!'

'I think I may have accidentally damaged Leo's wrist, sir,' Jamie said. 'I disarmed him – the knife is over there – but perhaps I used too much force.'

'I'd say he got what he deserved!' the officer said and

glared at the thug. 'Earlier today Leo and two members of his gang robbed an old lady of her bag after she'd been to the Post Office to draw some money, and when a passing workman went for him, he stabbed him in the chest. He's in hospital, fighting for his life. You lads were lucky we got a tip off he'd be here tonight'

'You got a tip off?' Jamie nodded as he realised who it must have been. Vic, the lad he'd warned, would have been bullied by Leo to join them – but, sick of the violence and frightened for his own life, Vic must have let the police know. It was why he'd hung back and taken no part in the attack. Jamie was sure of it in his own mind, but he kept the information to himself.

'We had information about a planned murder – you were to be the victim – and that means we've got a nasty little specimen heading for our cells this night.' He glanced at Terry. 'Well done, lad, that was a good arrest, couldn't have done it better myself. If you want a job when you leave school you know where to come.'

'I'm goin' in the army,' Terry said grinning with pride, 'but thanks fer the offer.'

As the police led a scowling Leo and his accomplice away to a van that had just drawn up, he said, 'That was a bit of luck, the cops comin' – though we 'ad 'em beat, didn't we?'

'Thanks, Terry,' Jamie said. 'I couldn't 'ave done it on me own – there were too many of 'em.'

'Told yer we'd make a good team.'

'Yeah, we would,' Jamie said and grinned. 'Mebbe there's somethin' we can join as a team. I'll ask Steve if he knows.'

'Whatever, we're mates now fer life,' Terry said and Jamie gripped his arm, feeling a surge of emotion, because something like this made a bond that took a lot to break . . .

'Steve told me they'd renewed their search for 'im,' Arch said when Jamie related his tale the next morning. 'I wish I'd known, I'd 'ave come to the club ter fetch yer.'

'It was best the way it happened,' Jamie said. 'I hurt Leo and Terry 'ad the bravest of the others in an arm lock, but it was good that the cops turned up when they did.'

'I suppose in a way it may teach the gang a lesson. Leo thought he could beat yer because yer ain't a big lad. I know yer've grown, Jamie, but yer still small compared ter 'im and he's a bully. He picks on those he thinks are weaker but he's found out yer strong despite yer size and that will teach him somethin'.'

Jamie nodded thoughtfully. Before his training he'd been weak, but now he had more strength than he really knew. 'If that man he stabbed dies, he'll never come out of prison.'

'They should hang 'im but they won't 'cos he's young – and he won't be in prison forever, but by the time he gets out . . . well, who knows.' Arch smiled at him. 'It's a good thing yer mate was wiv yer.'

'Terry is bigger and stronger,' Jamie agreed, 'but I can beat him in a fight, Arch. I know a lot of tricks that would put even you over. I ain't afraid of Leo and if he ever comes after me again, I'll be ready.'

'Good fer you,' Arch said and smiled. 'You'd best get off to school if yer feel up to it?'

'Why shouldn't I?' Jamie said. 'He didn't get the chance to stab me, Arch. It's the best thing ever, self-defence. Leo got the shock of his life when I broke his wrist – not that I meant ter do it.'

'I doubt it is broken, just badly twisted,' Arch said. 'The fact that he screamed and made such a fuss just shows what he's really made of.'

Jamie nodded but he'd heard something snap and felt that he'd done his enemy some serious damage because he thought he'd seen blood on his hand. Leo had been in a lot of pain when he was hustled away by the police. Jamie would have to remember not to use that trick in quite the same way when he was fighting the competition, because he would be in trouble if he harmed another competitor, but it was useful to know if he was ever in a fight for his life.

He pondered Terry's words as he walked to school. His friend's father thought Hitler was looking for a war – was that just talk or was it a possibility? Jamie hadn't been born when the last war ended and nor had Arch, but their father had fought in the trenches and the brothers wondered if it was the war that had made him a brutal bully who had killed his own wife.

Jamie was reflective as he thought about his own character. He'd been pleased when he beat Leo with a simple trick that disarmed him of his knife, but he shouldn't have been pleased to break his wrist. He'd used too much force when those lads robbed and upset Mr Forrest, too. Did he have his father's anger inside him? It wasn't something Jamie wanted to inherit and he wondered if he should talk to Steve about it. He'd learned to defend himself out of necessity but he didn't want to turn into a bully just because he could.

Steve listened intently when Jamie confided his fears the next time they met. He looked at Jamie for a few moments before nodding. 'Yes, I see why you're worried, Jamie, and I understand it's a concern. We both know you do have anger inside you, but I think you're in control of it – and we'll work on that together. However, you didn't break Leo's wrist, you snapped an ivory bangle he had on his wrist. It was old and thin, as dry as a bone, and it snapped, digging into his flesh. It caused him pain, which made him scream, but it served him right, because he stole that bangle from one of his victims and the sharp point went right into a vein, causing it to bleed. That's why it looked as if you'd done serious damage. You're clever and quick, Jamie, but I don't think you have the strength to break a wrist bone just like that – at least, not yet, and by the time you do, I hope we'll have that anger inside you under control.'

Jamie breathed a sigh of relief. 'Thank you, sir. I felt pleased I'd beaten Leo but I don't want to feel good about inflicting pain. I don't want to be a bully like my father.'

'I know.' Steve smiled at him. 'You're a special person, Jamie, emotional and young to have been through so much – and I know you're going to make a good officer of the law. You have all the right instincts and we can train them to cut out the reckless side if we work at it.'

'I knew you would understand,' Jamie said and

hesitated, then, 'I want you to put Terry in for the regionals this time, sir, and not me – if you were thinkin' of me that is.'

'Why is that?'

'Because I owe it to him,' Jamie said. 'I might be fighting fer me life in hospital if it hadn't been fer 'im.'

'Well, now that's a turn up,' Steve said with a smile, 'because he just said the same thing to me – he wants you to have the honour.'

Jamie smiled at that and said, 'He's me mate, but he deserves it most.'

'Well, you'll both just have to wait and see what I decide,' Steve said and went off, leaving Jamie to wonder.

The announcement was made later that evening and the first name read out was Terry's, but he'd been picked for the next group, a year ahead of Jamie, so it wasn't much surprise when his name was also called out.

'Steve told me he thought I should move up a group,' Terry told him as they left the club later together. 'He says because I'm bigger and stronger it would be a more even match, even though it might mean I don't win.'

'Do you mind?'

'Nah,' Terry replied and grinned. 'It means we'll both be there – together, as mates, cheerin' each other on.'

'Yeah, that's great,' Jamie said, 'and I've thought of somethin' else we could do together. One of the cadets told me about a junior rowing club. They're lookin' fer new members and I reckon we'd be good – it would build up our strength and I'm small enough to be a cox fer a start.'

Terry wanted to know all about it and so they talked until they reached Terry's street and stopped by the fish shop, the tantalising smell of hot food making them both hungry. 'Do yer want me ter come wiv yer?' he asked and Jamie shook his head.

'Nah, Leo's safely locked up. Get orf home, mate, I'll be all right – so I'll sign us both up for the rowin' on Sunday then?'

'Yeah, do that,' Terry said and grinned. 'See yer around.'

Smiling, they parted, making their way home alone. It was just as Jamie reached his home that the dark shadow came forward. Jamie tensed, ready for an attack but then he saw the lad's face and knew him.

'Thanks fer what yer did the other night,' Jamie said.

'How did yer know it was me?' Vic asked

'I guessed.' Jamie gave him a steady look. 'It was a good thing, so don't feel guilty.'

'I don't,' Vic said. 'We're off down south soon. Me dad's got a new job and he says he wants to move the family, so I shan't see yer again.'

'Well, good luck!' Jamie offered his hand but Vic held back.

'I saw what yer did to Leo . . .'

'Yeah, well it was 'im or me so I had to,' Jamie said, 'but I wouldn't do it to you.'

'Right . . .' Vic started to edge away, still refusing to shake hands. 'I don't reckon yer will 'ave any more trouble at the shop now – the kids all look up to yer. They say yer a hero standing up to that bully.'

Jamie laughed and shook his head. 'I had help,' he

said. 'It's just guts – remember that and yer can't go wrong. Bullies are all cowards at heart.'

Vic nodded and walked off into the dark. Jamie was smiling as he went into the house. It looked as if life was taking a turn for the better . . .

As he entered the kitchen, Jamie's blood suddenly ran cold, because there, standing by the table, was someone he'd never expected to see again in his life . . .

'Ain't yer goin' ter say hello to yer pa then, boy?' the man asked, his eyes glittering. 'I've come 'ome ter be wiv me family.'

'What are you doin' 'ere?' Jamie asked him, his nails digging into the palms of his hands. He was nervous, because his father was a big man, but nowhere near as frightened as he had been before he learned to protect himself. 'You must know the police are lookin' fer yer? After what yer did to Ma.'

'It was an accident, Jamie,' his father said. 'Yer wouldn't split on yer old man, would yer? I 'eard yer had a bit of luck . . .' He looked around the kitchen. 'Nice cosy place this. I reckon it would just suit me to stay 'ere.'

'You killed my mother in a drunken temper,' Jamie said, the anger throbbing inside him. 'I saw her lying on the floor, blood all over her face – you'd battered her to a pulp!'

'Shut yer mouth, runt,' his father said, 'or I'll shut it fer yer!'

'You can try,' Jamie said meeting his eyes 'but even if yer kill me it won't 'elp yer. Arch wouldn't have yer 'ere and nor would Mr Forrest.'

'What are them pair goin' ter do,' his father muttered.

'I could knock the old man over with one finger and Arch wouldn't fight me – he went off rather than stand up to me.'

'If you've touched Mr Forrest, I'll see yer swing fer it,' Jamie said fiercely. 'Yer a bully and a coward, Pa, and it's only 'cos yer me pa that I'm tellin' yer to go while yer can. If yer don't, I'll be reportin' yer to the cops and they'll lock yer up fer life if they don't 'ang yer.'

'I told yer, it were an accident!' Jamie's father moved towards him menacingly. 'I'll teach yer to threaten me, yer runt . . .'

'Stand away from him, Ted Martin, or it will be the last thing you do in this life!'

Mr Forrest's voice from behind them made both Jamie and his father swing round to look. The elderly man was holding a pistol in his hand and it was pointed at Ted Martin's chest.

'Yer old bugger!' Jamie's father muttered in a rage, his face red with fury. 'I'll do fer yer both!'

'I'm warning yer, I'll shoot ter protect that boy,' Mr Forrest said and there was a determined gleam in his eyes. 'You were always a fool, Ted Martin, drinking yer money away with not a care fer yer wife and family – but that lad is worth a hundred of you, and I'll shoot afore I let yer touch 'im.'

'Bloody old fool,' Ted muttered and raised his arm as he moved forward to strike Mr Forrest. The sound of the pistol shot was loud in the small kitchen as it fired and the bullet struck its mark in Ted's right shoulder, causing him to cry out in pain and clutch himself. He looked at the blood trickling through his fingers in bewilderment, clearly shocked that the elderly man had had the guts to fire at him. 'Damn you!'

For a moment Ted Martin stood still, undecided whether to attack again and risk another shot, but then the back door opened and two young men walked in. He looked at his eldest son and his companion and glared at them.

'So, yer 'ere an' all then,' he muttered. 'That old devil has just shot yer pa in the shoulder – what are yer goin' ter do about it?'

'Hand you over to the police,' Arch said immediately. 'You're not wanted 'ere, Pa, and yer shouldn't 'ave come back. After what yer did ter my mother, I'd kill yer and dance on yer grave – but even better I'll let the law hang yer!'

'Fine sons I've got,' Ted said resentfully.

'Jamie, go down the corner and ring the police,' Arch said, but before Jamie could obey, his father shouldered him out of the way and was through the still-open back door and into the night.

'Should I ring the station?' Jamie asked, looking hesitantly at his brother.

'Nah, let 'im make a run fer it,' Arch said. 'I don't think he'll try that one again, unless he wants ter die.' His glance went to Mr Forrest, who was now sitting down at the kitchen table, his hand shaking. 'That was a brave thing you did, sir – where did yer get the gun?'

'My grandson got it for me because I was nervous after the break-in and he left it loaded, showed me how to take the safety catch off and fire. I didn't think I would ever use it, but when Ted threatened Jamie, I couldn't let him do it.'

'It was brave,' Jamie said, 'but what would yer 'ave done if he came at yer again?'

Mr Forrest met his eyes steadily. 'Next time I might have had to shoot to kill . . .'

'I'm glad yer didn't,' Jamie said. 'The police would've arrested you then and I don't think yer would like even a short stay in prison.'

'I was willing to do it to save you, lad,' Mr Forrest said and sighed. 'My hands are shakin' like a leaf – pop the kettle on, would yer? I need a cuppa.'

'And a drop of somethin' stronger,' Arch said. He looked at his friend. 'You can never tell anyone what 'appened 'ere, Rich. Mr Forrest might be in serious trouble fer keepin' a firearm without a licence.'

'I'll never tell,' Rich said and moved forward to touch Mr Forrest on the shoulder. 'It was a brave thing ter do, sir, but why don't yet put that thing away now – just in case someone reports a shot and the cops come to investigate?'

'Put the safety catch on and pop it in the dresser drawer,' Mr Forrest said and accepted the small glass of whisky that Arch handed him. 'Thank you, lad. I can do with that!'

Jamie put the kettle on and fetched plates for the chips Arch had brought back for their supper. He was numbed, unsure of his feelings. Confronted with his father and the threat of violence, Jamie had been prepared to defend himself and yet there was a tiny voice inside his head that felt a bit sorry for the man who was now searching for a place to hide with a bullet in his shoulder. The pain was probably less than he'd inflicted on their mother but he'd be alone and frightened

– and he *was* Jamie's father even though he'd forfeited the right to concern or love. It would be best if the law got him, but neither he nor Arch would feel right reporting him.

He thought then that if Mr Forrest hadn't had a gun, he would probably have promised him money to go away and leave them in peace. He deserved to be in prison and perhaps he deserved to hang, but for himself Jamie was glad that his father had chosen to run. Even after all the brutal things he'd done, Jamie didn't want to condemn him to death at the end of the rope . . .

Later that night, Arch came to Jamie when he was in bed and sat on the edge, looking at him seriously. 'Are yer all right?' he asked. 'It's hard knowing he's out there, isn't it?'

'Yes,' Jamie sighed. 'He's bad, Arch, I know that, and I know what he did to Ma – and to both of us but . . .'

'Yeah, I know, kid, that's why I let 'im run. I could've stopped him, but I don't want ter be the one who hands 'im in – and nor do you.'

'I hope he never comes back,' Jamie said. 'If he does, we'll 'ave no choice next time.'

'I know.' Arch yawned. 'I'm orf ter work then, Jamie. We'll talk again tomorrow, but I'll make sure we're locked up – and I doubt he'll try again tonight.'

'If he has any sense, he'll be on the next ship he can get,' Jamie said. 'I don't want ter be like 'im, Arch. He's a mindless bully.'

'Ma said it was the war turned 'im – she always made excuses fer 'im. It was why I went orf, 'cos I knew I could take him with the same tricks as you use, Jamie, but if I started, I'd batter 'im for what he did, so it's best if he runs and keeps on running.'

'Yeah.' Jamie smiled. 'I'm glad yer me brother, Arch . . .'

'Me too,' Arch said, and leaned down and ruffled his hair. 'Sleep tight – it's a new day tomorrow and we've got lots ter look forward to.'

# CHAPTER 26

Sarah woke suddenly and jumped out of bed, making a dash for the bathroom. She leaned over the toilet and the vomit came rushing up her throat, its bitter taste making her pull a face of disgust. Now, what had she eaten the previous night to make her feel sick?

She washed her face and went downstairs to the kitchen, where she filled the kettle and put it on the hob to boil. She thought about Steve's breakfast, because he would be in shortly after his shift. It was the first spell of night duty he'd had since they were married and, since Sarah was also on nights it had suited them, but the previous evening had been her night off and so she'd gone to visit her mother and Ned, eating supper with them before returning home. She'd gone to bed early and read for a while, but the romance she'd borrowed from the library hadn't held her for long. It had a nurse who ended up marrying her wealthy patient as its heroine and the story just hadn't rung true to Sarah.

She decided she would cook a couple of rashers of bacon and some bubble and squeak for breakfast. Steve would appreciate that after being out in the cold all night – even though it was only late October it was very chilly at night. However, even as she started to prepare the meal Sarah felt the vomit rise in her throat and made another dash for the toilet. This time very little came up, other than thin bile and she frowned. Her mother's food the previous evening had been delicious and she was sure it couldn't have upset her; it never had before.

She'd just returned to the kitchen when the door opened and Steve entered. He took off his helmet and overcoat, hanging the coat on a hook inside the door and then came to Sarah to kiss her. She looked up at him and smiled.

'Was it a busy night?' she asked as he yawned and moved away to wash his hands at the sink.

'Not too bad. We had a few incidents with drunks but nothing serious – one burglary reported at a warehouse on the docks but when we got there it was just a tramp sleeping rough. He ran off before we got to him but it looks as if he's been sleeping there for a while – we found some bloodstained rags, but they weren't fresh. Must have been a while ago, whatever the cause.'

'I'm just getting breakfast ready,' Sarah said and then gave a little yelp of distress. 'Sorry!' She made a dash for the sink and vomited, because there was no time to get upstairs. Hardly anything came up this time.

Steve looked worried as she turned towards him, wiping her mouth on a handkerchief. 'What's wrong? Have you caught a bug?'

'I'm not sure . . . that's the third time this morning,'

Sarah said and washed her hands with cold water from the tap. 'I don't think it's anything I've eaten . . .' She looked at him and then something clicked in her mind, something she hadn't taken too much notice of the previous night when she'd undressed. 'I think – but I might be wrong . . .' Her eyes met his anxious ones. 'I think I could be pregnant, Steve!'

'Sarah!' He stared at her, stunned for a moment, and then a smile of delight broke over his face. 'Really? You think there is a chance this soon?'

'Yes, I do – the more I think of it, the more I think it may be the reason. I've noticed a little change in my breasts and I've put on a little weight . . .'

'Oh, darling . . .' Steve moved towards her, reaching out to embrace her. 'That is wonderful news.'

'Yes,' she smiled up at him, 'it is – but we mustn't get too excited yet in case it *is* just a sickness thing.' But even as she advised caution, Sarah was sure that she was carrying her husband's child. She didn't have a temperature and she didn't feel ill, just sick whenever she thought of food. 'I'm sorry – but do you think you could get your own breakfast for once?'

'Of course, I can,' Steve said. 'Sit down and I'll make you a cuppa and then get the breakfast, but what about you?'

'Tea is all I want for now,' Sarah assured him.

'Is it natural to be ill like this?' He looked at her anxiously.

'It will ease off soon, I'm sure,' Sarah said. 'It's called morning sickness for a reason but if I'm lucky it won't last too long.'

Lily couldn't believe it when she opened the letter from Chris. It was the third she'd had from him and he wanted to meet her. His letter said:

*I'm on a brief visit to London. I'll be there on Monday and we could meet for lunch, perhaps at the Golden Horn, which is near the infirmary. I'll arrive at twelve thirty and I'll wait until one thirty. I know it's short notice and if you don't arrive, I'll understand that you couldn't get away.*

Lily's heart soared. She was going to see Chris again. She'd thought it might be years before they met, if ever, but now he was making a brief stop in London and he wanted to see her. It was even her day off and she felt as if the heavens were shining for her. Running upstairs, she pulled her best dress from the wardrobe and changed into it. She could just catch the bus if she hurried!

Jenny arrived home to an empty house. There was no smell of food and no sign of her sister, nor yet a note to say where she'd gone or when she would be back. It was so unlike her sister that she frowned. Surely, if Lily was ill, she would have left a note to let her know?

'Lily?' Jenny called up the stairs again, then went to the back door and looked out, still no sign of her sister. She walked upstairs and went into her own bedroom, taking off her uniform and putting on a dressing gown before going to her sister's room. A skirt and blouse had been thrown on the bed, shoes kicked off at random, and the wardrobe door was still open. 'Lily? Where have you gone?' Jenny said wonderingly, because it was

362

so unlike her tidy sister to leave things all over the place.

As she turned away, Jenny saw the letter on the dressing table. She hesitated, because whatever had caused Lily to leave in such a hurry had probably been something to do with the letter. Knowing it was wrong to pry, Jenny found herself driven to pick it up and scan the few lines written there. The shock of seeing Chris's signature made her gasp – Lily had gone off in a hurry to meet him. She must have been writing to him ever since Jenny broke it off with him.

Replacing the letter, Jenny walked into her own room and sat down on the bed. Her first reaction was one of pain, because her sister had gone behind her back, but following on swiftly was the realisation that she had no right to feel anything of the kind. She'd given Chris up willingly and Lily liked him – perhaps even loved him.

But why hadn't she told Jenny that she was writing to Chris? It hurt a little that Lily had shut her out but did she really mind if they were together?

Jenny sighed and went into the bathroom, turning on the taps. She was tired and a good soak in hot water would ease both her mind and body. It truly wasn't her business what Lily chose to do, though she did feel a little shut out and that hurt.

Closing her eyes, she lay back and a part of her wondered if she'd thrown away something precious. Had she been too blind to see what she had? No, it had been her choice to break up with Chris – and if he'd turned to her sister, Jenny would wish them well.

She felt more peaceful after she'd reached that

decision and lay half dozing in the water until it grew cold and she got out, drying herself before heading for her bed. When Lily came home, perhaps she would tell her about her lunch with Chris . . .

'I wanted to meet and talk before I leave,' Chris said and looked at her across the table in the busy little pub. It was a dark wood table with woven straw mats and a small vase of flowers, and they had ordered a meal of salad and ham with fresh crusty bread and white wine. 'I may not be able to write to you for a long time, Lily, and I wanted you to understand that it isn't because I don't want to.'

'Where are you going?' Lily asked, her gaze never wavering. 'Can you tell me?'

'I'm going to be a spy,' Chris said without hesitation, showing his complete trust in her. 'I have to infiltrate Hitler's followers and discover all I can about his plans for the future.' He smiled at her. 'I know I can trust you, Lily, but no one else can know, because I've just broken the Official Secrets Act! However, you deserved to know . . .'

'I'll never breathe a word,' she promised. 'I know it's your job, Chris – all I'll say is: take care for my sake. Remember that you are loved . . .' She tingled with the shock of saying the words, because he might think her forward, but she'd known she had to say them so that he understood he had something to come back for if he wished.

'Dearest Lily,' he said and reached for her hand. 'I had to see you before I left, because I've realised that I was not really in love with Jenny. We weren't right for each other. You see, I haven't been able to stop thinking about you and when you wrote me that letter… I haven't been thinking about Jenny at all. Oh, I'm not saying this right . . . I wish we could go back to the beginning and start again . . .' His smile tore at her heart. 'I was such a fool . . .'

'No, of course you weren't,' Lily said. 'Jenny is lovely and she did think she loved you – whereas I thought you despicable at the start.' She laughed as his hand tightened on hers. 'I was the fool, Chris. Had I known my own heart at the beginning . . .'

'Perhaps . . .' He sighed. 'I only know that I wasted so much time. Now I only have a few hours before I leave and it isn't enough, because it might be all we have.'

'Then we should make the most of what we do have,' Lily said and he smiled at her.

'What would you like to do? Walk – visit a gallery together?'

'I should like you to take me to bed,' Lily said, looking deep into his eyes. 'Let's make a memory that will give us both something to think about in the days and months to come . . .'

'Oh, Lily,' he said and caught his breath. 'Now I truly know how much of a fool I've been!' He stood up and offered her his hand. 'I have a room in a hotel, my love. I just didn't know if I dare ask you . . . I don't deserve this . . .'

Lily moved towards him, putting a finger to his lips. 'No talk of right or wrong or regrets,' she said. 'This is what I want, Chris, and whatever happens I shall be happy that we had these brief hours.' She radiated her happiness and saw it reflected in his eyes. She could give him these few precious hours even if they had nothing more.

Jenny was dressed and ready for work, in the kitchen cooking cheese and tomatoes on toast, when Lily came in after a lunch that must have lasted nearly four hours. The younger girl had decided that she wouldn't ask questions nor would she let Lily know that she'd guessed her secret. When her sister was ready, she would tell her.

'I thought you might have left for work,' Lily remarked when she entered the kitchen. 'That smells good . . .'

'Want some?' Jenny offered without turning around.

'No, thank you, I had something to eat while I was out shopping . . .'

'Did you buy anything nice?'

'No, I couldn't find what I wanted,' Lily replied, but Jenny knew she was lying about going shopping. Even if she hadn't seen the letter, she would've known her sister was hiding something from her the moment she turned and looked at her. Lily was glowing in a way that Jenny had never seen her. Her eyes were shining and her lips looked sort of swollen, as if she had been kissed passionately again and again.

Jenny felt her stomach tighten. Lily had been to bed with Chris! It had never happened between her and Chris, even though she'd gone out with him so many times. She hadn't even thought of it and he'd never suggested anything but a few kisses. Despite her determination not to feel resentment over Lily's deceit, she was shocked. Lily had only been writing to him for a few weeks and she'd gone to bed with him in a hotel somewhere in the middle of the afternoon! It seemed decadent and not quite decent to Jenny and she wasn't sure how she felt.

'I'm going up to have a bath,' Lily said as the silence lengthened between them. 'Leave the washing-up for me, Jenny. I don't start work until nine tomorrow evening.'

'Yes, all right,' Jenny replied and carried her meal to the table. Of course, it wasn't Lily's first affair. She'd trusted a man once before and been badly hurt. Jenny hoped she knew what she was doing this time. Would Chris marry her if she became pregnant? Had he fallen in love with Lily now – or was he just using her to get back at Jenny?

Jenny pushed the unkind thoughts from her mind. Lily was old enough to do as she chose and it wasn't for Jenny to tell her to be careful.

She wasn't jealous, she decided, but she was still a little shocked. Was it so easy to fall out of love with one sister and into love with the next?

Lily slipped into bed after taking her bath. She closed her eyes and relived the hours of passion she'd spent in Chris's arms, letting herself thrill to the intense pleasure she'd discovered. Nothing in her life had prepared her for the wonder of his loving; all the dreams and imagining had come nowhere close. He was such a wonderful lover!

Lily smiled as she remembered his touch and the feel of him inside her as he possessed her utterly. She knew that, whatever happened she would always be glad that she'd given herself to him that afternoon. Even the knowing leer of the hotel receptionist hadn't bothered Lily. She'd been serenely happy to have her lover for the brief interlude that might be all they ever had.

Chris had told her that it would be too risky for him to contact her while he was involved in the dangerous work he did for the British Government. Because of his German background, he was to get close to Hitler and discover, if he could, what his plans were for the future. It might take months or even years to gain the ruler's confidence and Chris could do nothing that might jeopardise his mission.

'It means I can't write to you and you can't write to me,' Chris had told her as he looked down at her and stroked her cheek. 'I shouldn't even have told you, but I wanted you to understand, my love. There will be no contact, perhaps for years. If my letters were opened, and they might well be, it would lead to my arrest and execution. I know it isn't fair to ask you to wait . . .'

Lily put a finger against his lips. 'You don't need to ask. There will never be anyone else, Chris, and I never expected to have so much. I thought you were Jenny's and I could never have come between you – this afternoon is a gift and I shall treasure the memory forever.'

'I love you,' he murmured as they came together once more in unspoken need. 'My way was chosen when I was born, Lily. I don't think I ever had a choice, but if I had I should choose to live in peace with you . . .'

'I know,' she whispered against his chest, tasting the salt of his sweat. 'But we have this and it will be enough until you come back to me – because it has to be.'

It wasn't enough for either of them. She knew it, even as she said it, but it was something to hold on to and there was always the hope that one day they would have more – and in her heart Lily had known it wasn't goodbye when they parted. They would be together again one day, even though it might be years into the future . . .

Jean opened the letter with shaking fingers. She knew it had come from the solicitor George's wife had engaged and she feared it would be a summons to appear in court. As she read the brief message, a shudder of relief went through her and silent tears slipped down her cheeks.

'What is it?' her husband asked, entering their kitchen at that moment. He was dressed in slacks and an open-necked shirt, because it was a rare day off for him. 'Is it bad news?'

'No, no it's good news,' Jean said and smiled at him. 'The case has been dropped. George's wife has decided that she will attempt reconciliation with her husband.'

'Poor George,' Matthew said and came over to put his arms around her, smiling down into her eyes. 'I told you it would be all right, didn't I?'

'Yes.' Jean wiped her eyes on the handkerchief he offered her. 'I don't know why I'm crying, it's wonderful news!'

'Yes, it is,' he said and kissed her. 'I knew that we'd win, love, because I knew you were telling me the truth – and that is all that mattered to me. Now we can put it all behind us and look forward to our future together.'

'Yes, we can.' Jean smiled up at him. 'I feel so lucky . . .'

'*I'm* the lucky one,' Matthew said. 'You don't have

to work today – shall we go for a ride out somewhere and have lunch?'

'Yes, that would be lovely,' Jean said and nodded. 'Sarah is the senior nurse on today – but I don't know for how much longer. She told me that she couldn't consider taking further exams just yet, because she is pregnant.'

'Ah . . .' Matthew looked at her. 'Well, that is good news for Sarah and her husband, but a loss to the infirmary.'

'Sarah says she will work part-time after the birth. No doubt her mother will have the baby sometimes – but I'm not sure she will wish to try working for a sister's position; babies make you tired and take all your energy.'

'They certainly do,' Matthew agreed and looked at her again. 'However, they bring their own love with them so it's worthwhile – isn't it?'

'Yes, and I hope . . .' Jean shook her head. 'No, I'm not pregnant yet, Matthew, even though I have been emotional. I hope I shall be one day.'

'So do I,' he said and kissed her again, 'but I can wait until it happens. All I really care about is that you're happy . . .'

'Of that you need never doubt,' Jean told him with a look of love. 'I never expected it to happen, Matthew. I thought love had passed me by until you looked at me and smiled . . .'

As he bent his head to kiss her, Jean gave herself up to his caress. Sarah's news had made her slightly jealous, because she longed for a child and she knew her husband also wanted a family. She wasn't a young bride – she

370

was almost seven years older than Sarah and many years older than Kathy – it might be that her body would not quicken with child as easily as the women she knew and worked with, but she could only trust in the future and hope that she would be blessed . . .

# CHAPTER 27

'You called me about Milly,' Lady Rosalie said, looking at her friend anxiously. 'How is she now?'

'In a sad condition,' Mary replied tight-lipped. 'We had to send her home as you know, because we had no proof – but her father got drunk that night and battered her again, and this time the woman next door heard it and went to investigate. She rang the police. They arrested Milly's father and she's been made a ward of court. She's with us for the moment and I'm going to keep her until I know she's better and you have a good home for her.'

Lady Rosalie smiled. 'I'm interviewing a couple this afternoon – and I have high hopes for them. The husband is a driver on the railway and his wife was in service before she married. They desperately want a family and she is unable to have a child.'

'They sound perfect,' Mary said and nodded. 'If they pass your criteria, I suggest they visit Milly here and then, if they all get on, we'll apply for them to become her foster parents.'

'I believe they want to adopt in time if possible,' Lady

Rosalie said, 'but that is for the future. We can only deal with fostering for the moment – adoption is more permanent so we'll have to see how things work out.'

'Yes, Milly has suffered enough from her abusive father and a mother too frightened to stop him,' Mary said and smiled. 'So, let me know what is happening and I'll prepare the child gradually – one thing is certain, I shall not allow her to return home and I'm willing to stand up in court and tell the judge why.'

'Good for you,' Lady Rosalie said approvingly. 'If you were not so busy, Mary, I might suggest you take the child yourself.'

'I am here for the many,' Mary replied calmly. 'One day, when I'm ready to retire, I may put my name down to take on teenagers – because they are always the most difficult to place.'

Her friend sighed and frowned. 'How right you are, Mary. I have this young lad on my books now. He's been in trouble with the law twice and they've removed him from his home, because it was his father's influence that made him steal – but I can see no hope of finding him a home.'

'Because of his trouble with the law?' Mary nodded. 'Yes, I understand. It does take a special person to take on a boy like that.'

'Quite . . .' Lady Rosalie looked speculative. 'I don't suppose . . .'

'No, not yet,' Mary said firmly. 'One day, maybe – but for the moment I think my patients and nurses need me more.'

'Yes of course,' Lady Rosalie agreed but there was a little gleam in her eye as she took her leave. Mary spent far too much time at her work, perhaps because she lived alone. If she had a young lad to care for – and Sam was a decent sort underneath all the swagger and bravado. Give him a loving, secure home and he might surprise them all. He was on probation for the moment but perhaps, in a few months, he would be allowed to live with a foster carer.

Mary would need a little talking round but by the time Sam was ready . . .? Lady Rosalie smiled as she walked away from the infirmary. Perhaps another of her unhappy youngsters would soon be settled in a good home . . .

# Read more about Cathy Sharp's orphans whose compelling stories will tug at your heartstrings.